ROME HAUL

New York Classics

Frank Bergmann, Series Editor

ROME HAUL

WALTER D. EDMONDS

Foreword by FRANK BERGMANN

SYRACUSE UNIVERSITY PRESS

Syracuse University Press Edition 1987
93 92 91 90 89 88 87   5 4 3 2 1

The paper used in this publication meets the minimum requirements of American National Standard for Information Sciences—Permanence of Paper for Printed Library Materials, ANSI Z39.48-1984. ∞™

Library of Congress Cataloging-in-Publication Data

Edmonds, Walter Dumaux, 1903–
    Rome haul.

    (New York classics)
    I. Title.
PS3509.D564R6   1987   813'.52   87-9972
    ISBN 0-8156-0213-8 (pbk. : alk. paper)

Manufactured in the United States of America

TO

CHARLES TOWNSEND COPELAND

WITH

THE WRITER'S

ADMIRATION, AFFECTION, AND GRATITUDE

THE author has made use of two songs taken from *The American Songbag:* "The E-ri-e" (page 90) and "The Erie Canal" (page 92). For permission to reproduce this material he wishes to thank Mr. Carl Sandburg and Harcourt, Brace and Company.

CONTENTS

FOREWORD

Rome Haul (1929) has been hailed as the first novel about the Erie Canal and Walter D. Edmonds as the great canal's second builder. The book not only established a literary sub-genre, it confirmed its author as a major writer of regional fiction.

Walter D. Edmonds was born on July 15, 1903, in canal country—at his parents' summer home near Boonville, in northern Oneida County. The farm, called Northlands, was not far from the Black River Canal, which joined the Erie Canal at Rome and was in active use all through the writer's youth. Although Edmonds spent winters in New York City and, after he had started school, even longer stretches in New Hampshire and Connecticut, he always looked forward to his summers at Northlands. The farm and its environs were a boy's paradise and so deeply filled him with love of the land and its animals that there is hardly a page of his writing that does not radiate with it. He learned about people, too—common folk, mostly—about their ways and the energy and determination it took to make a living where the snow comes in October and does not disappear until May.

As a grown man, Edmonds regularly summered at Northlands, until he sold the property in 1976. Northerners often prefer to retire to the South, but Edmonds now lives in Concord, Massachusetts. Concord is also an ancestral village, not far from Harvard University where he went to college in the 1920s. His father wanted him to become a chemical engineer, but Edmonds discovered that his talent and inclination lay elsewhere. By the time he finished the famed writing course English 12, taught by Professor Charles T. Copeland, he was well on his way to becoming a professional author.

Edmonds recalls that Copeland did not really *teach* writing: Copeland honed talent that was already there. He knew that writing was an individual matter, so he pushed his students to discover who they really were. To be authentic meant first of all not trying to be someone else. Although he had them read the great English authors, he did not want his fledgling writers to copy them. He wanted his students to sound a new—an individual—note, and the "sound" was as important as the "new," for Copeland believed in the oral quality of writing: something that sounded good when it was read aloud was well written. To write well meant to write simply and clearly; style was to be functional in delivering a writer's message, not ornamental in adorning it. Edmonds learned these things thoroughly and became Copeland's "last star"; the great teacher's biographer, J. Donald Adams, noted that Edmonds was one student "in whose accomplishment Copey took great pride."

That accomplishment numbered not only a good many short stories printed in the *Advocate*, Harvard's literary magazine, but also a story Copeland thought so highly of that he interested *Scribner's* magazine in it and thereby launched Edmonds' career. The best of Edmonds' stories were set in his own North Country, and when Copeland and Ellery Sedgwick of the *Atlantic Monthly* encouraged Edmonds to try his hand at a novel, he went back to his native region. This is Edmonds' own account of how he wrote his first novel:

I know that in my own case when I sat down to begin *Rome Haul* near the end of the first week of November, 1927, there was never a moment's hesitation, Title, chapter heading, and the opening sentence came out without a pause, and by lunchtime that first morning Chapter One was finished. And the book never stopped writing at that pace. By the end of February the manuscript of 100,000 words was done, and in between I had taken a week off to do a story for the *Atlantic*. But the point was that I had been stirring *Rome Haul* round and round in my mind for nearly three years, and when I finally took off the lid to see what I had cooked up, the book practically blew up in my face. I needed no notes, I had no outline: the book seemed to write itself. It was a wonderful experience. ("A Novelist Takes Stock," *Atlantic Monthly*, July 1943)

The book, carefully shortened and edited by Sedgwick's staff (and affectionately dedicated to Copeland), became an instant success. Nevertheless, someone told Edmonds "that *Rome Haul* was too formless to lay much claim to art," and so he tried to stick to an outline for his next two novels. Soon, however, he realized that his original impulse in writing *Rome Haul* had been the right one after all, for "the outline was always getting under the feet of my characters." Like his upstate predecessor, Harold Frederic, Edmonds had learned that one of the many choices a writer has to make is to give a story and its characters room to breathe and unfold.

It is true that one of *Rome Haul*'s charms is its splendid succession of scenes (my favorites are Dan Harrow's buying a team of horses at the Whitesboro fair, and Fortune Friendly's sermon in the hay), but Robert M. Gay went too far when he said of the episodes in *Rome Haul* that "they are so good, in fact, as to suggest that the author is really most at ease in the concentrated narrative of the short story." Many of the book's chapters could indeed be printed as self-contained stories, and some of the individual stories collected in Edmonds' *Mostly Canallers* could easily be worked into *Rome Haul*, but it would be doing Edmonds an injustice to overlook the novel's unity. Not only does the great canal with its feeders anchor the book topographically and historically, it also is the stage—as the peddler's handing Dan a volume of Shakespeare suggests at the very outset—on which "the whole shebang of life" moves back and forth.

And yet the canal is not the whole of it, for its dynamism, its ceaseless flow, is set against the farmland's stasis, against a man's need to find himself and, when the time has come, put down roots. Lionel Wyld overestimates the novel's conflicts (boy-girl, hero-bully, canal-railroad) when he singles them out as the book's unifying principles. Above all else, the novel tells the story of Dan Harrow's initiation into adult life. The young orphan, who has a cultivator's name and loves cows, walks out of the bleak Tug Hill country to boat it for a spell on the canal, but the conflicts Wyld identifies only serve to swing him back to his real destination, a farmer's life on better soil in the Black River valley. In between, Dan encounters many firsts, as is fitting for a novel of initiation: his first look at the world beyond the horizon, his first real job, his first piece of property, his first girl, his first fight. Dan Harrow is another exemplar—and a very likable one—in a long line that reaches from Brockden Brown's Arthur Mervyn to Cooper's Deerslayer to Frederic's Seth Fairchild all the way to Salinger's Holden Caulfield and beyond.

But a novel is more than themes and scenes. It is also texture, which means characters and language. Henry James required of a writer "solidity of specification," that is, the creation of "the air of reality"; fiction's business and secret, he said, was "catching the very note and trick, the strange irregular rhythm of life." For a writer who, like Edmonds, looked to the living past for his province, T. S. Eliot identified "the historical sense" as involving "a perception, not only of the pastness of the past, but of its presence." As we have seen, Edmonds had stirred the past "round and round" until it was to him like the present. Robert M. Gay paid him a high and well-earned compliment when he said that "it is a faculty of living in the past as if it were today that gives his fiction its air of vitality." And there is the art to conceal art; Edmonds insists that to be authentic and vital a writer must know things: "For the more you *know*, the less your atmosphere depends on listed details for its veracity. Your knowledge becomes the underpinnings of the story—it is there but does not show." The reader feels this knowledge in the spare body and taut mind of Dan Harrow, in the brutal physicality of Jotham Klore, in the seductive mixture of submission and independence of Molly Larkins. It is there in the inimitable Lucy Cashdollar and the wise Jacob Turnesa. It takes hold of us when Dan feels the length of a horse's leg, when Fortune Friendly plays cards, when we hear the people talk—not as people sometimes talk in books, but as they always talk in life.

No wonder that *Rome Haul* attracted playwrights and moviemakers. Frank Elser turned it into a play called *Low Bridge* (1932); with Marc Connelly, he rewrote it as *The Farmer Takes a Wife* (1934), which is also the title of the motion picture (1935) starring Henry Fonda as Dan Harrow. (Fonda also had leads in the movie versions of *Drums Along the Mohawk* and *Chad Hanna*.) But, as is generally the case, the book is better than its adaptations, and so Syracuse University Press takes pride and pleasure in making *Rome Haul* available once again.

For those interested in further reading, Lionel D. Wyld's *Walter D. Edmonds, Storyteller* (1982) is indispensable, despite some factual errors and misspellings. For canal lore, the first book to go to is Wyld's *Low Bridge! Folklore and the Erie Canal* (1977). Additional discussions of Edmonds and of the literature of upstate New York may be found in Frank Bergmann, ed., *Upstate Literature: Essays in Memory of Thomas F. O'Donnell* (1985). All three books were published by Syracuse University Press. Edmonds' own essay "A Novelist Takes Stock" (*Atlantic Monthly 172, 1* [July 1943]: 73–77) sheds light on his convictions and techniques; so does Robert M. Gay, "The Historical Novel: Walter D. Edmonds" (*Atlantic Monthly 165, 5* [May 1940]: 656–58).

Utica, New York   Frank Bergmann
November 1986

ROME HAUL

I

THE PEDDLER

IN 1850, the road to Boonville wound out of the Tug Hill country through long stretches of soft wood. On the steady downward slopes it curved back and forth through the balsams and scrubby pine; only on the occasional small ascents it ran straight; so that whoever traveled the road saw fellow travelers at a distance below him, or not at all — until he came upon them in the shadow of a bend.

Along the road a young man was walking. He strode easily, his feet meeting the ground as if they were used to earth. He was tall in spite of the stoop that took inches from his stature. His shoulders were broad and sloped. There was a cleanliness about his face and straight short hair suggesting inexperience of men.

The road, in his hours of walking, had laid a film of grey dust on his cowhide boots and had coated his trousers halfway to his knees. He wore a battered faded green hat with a narrow brim, a blue shirt open at the neck, and a brown homespun coat which puckered under his arms. In his right hand he carried a small carpetbag, ornamented on one side with a design of flowers, which he held turned inward against his leg.

The road brought him to the top of a long easy hill, and as he walked over the lip he heard the creak of a wagon round a bend ahead of him.

It was an odd-looking turnout. Both horse and wagon were of grey antiquity and capable only of slow and cautious movement. The horse leaned gingerly upon his breeching. It was not in him to hurry up hill or down. He footed the road slowly with a shambling sensitiveness and wove from side to side to lighten the effect of the grade. With the lines hanging loose on the dashboard, his head had free play so that he was able to combine his scientific descent of the hill with the demands of his appetite.

On the box, a man was reading a book. His eyes ran from side to side of the page as though he was hurrying to finish a chapter. After a moment he marked his place with a piece of string and closed the book smartly.

"Whoa!" he shouted, catching up the reins and throwing his weight backward.

The horse pricked his ears at a tuft of grass and made for it.

"Dammit!" exclaimed the man. "Have a lift?"

He did not appear to notice that the walker moved with twice the speed of his horse.

"Where're you goin'?"

"Boonville is my destination," replied the driver, dropping the reins. "Will you climb on?"

"Thanks."

The walker jumped over the nigh front wheel and took his seat.

"My name's Jacob Turnesa," said the driver. "Peddler, I am. Peddles clothes and dress goods and jewelry. It's a good business. What's yours?"

"Ain't got any now."

"Name."

"Dan'l Harrow."

"Pleased to know you. Shake hands."

He grasped Harrow's hand with long thin fingers. His eyes over his hooked nose had drooping underlids which showed startlingly red in the pallor of his face. They surveyed Harrow appraisingly before he shifted them to his horse.

He pulled a clay pipe from his pocket and pointed it.

"There's a horse," he said.

"Yeanh."

"There's a horse," he repeated.

"I seen him."

"Ahhh! He's a great one to go, he is."

Harrow nodded.

"He is at that, though. After you get him started where there's grass along the road, there ain't no stopping him."

He nodded, ruminatively spat, and began filling his pipe from a pouch of grey buckskin.

"Look at him now," the peddler continued. The old horse had reached the bottom of the slope, where a small brook stole under the bridge and balsams made the air sweet; and he quickened his pace on the upward grade. "Funny horse. Has notions in his head like a human. Goes slow downhill 'cause he hates to think of the updrag beyont. And when he hits the updrag he ·perks up his ears, thinking of the downhill he's going to find on the other side. If he was a man, you'd call him a philosopher."

"I would n't," said Harrow, dubiously looking at his fists.

"No," agreed the peddler, his thin mouth grinning behind his whiskers, "you'd call him a damn fool."

He struck a match on the iron brace of the dashboard and put it to the bowl of his pipe. A puff of rank sweet smoke popped out of the charred bowl like a recoil and swept into Dan's face.

"Where you come from?" Turnesa asked, flipping the dead match at the rump of the horse, who switched his grizzled tail with irritation.

"Tug Hill way."

"That's lonely country. Leave yer family?"

"They're dead."

"Ahhh."

"Pa, he died. The man that bought the place did n't want no help. I was plannin' to go anyhow. There ain't nothing to that land."

"Like horses?"

"Horses and hogs pretty good. Mostly I admire cows."

They came out on a level piece of road where the trees opened on either side into meadow and pasture, with here and there a house.

"It ain't very far to Boonville, now," remarked the peddler. "That's a nice town."

Men were working in the fields, mowing oats. As the wagon passed a yellow house under big elms, a woman came out of the door. She wore a pink sunbonnet and carried a bucket in her hand. The squeak of the wheels attracted her attention and she looked up and recognized the peddler.

"Hullo, Mr. Turnesa," she called. "Have some root beer?"

"Afternoon, Mrs. Sullivan. Thanks."

He picked up the reins and yanked them. The woman pressed close to the off front wheel and lifted her bucket, in which a dipper lay, mysterious in the brown drink. Turnesa held down his beard with his left hand and brought the dipper, brimming, sidewise to his lips. He drank noisily.

"Won't your friend?" suggested the woman, nodding out from under her bonnet. She had a plump, red, pleasant face, blue eyes, and a mouth suggesting capability. Harrow thanked her and drank eagerly. The beer was cool and very good.

"Done any peddling down the canal?" she asked.

"Only down the feeder. I don't go below Rome any more. That railroad spreads my line of goods too quick through the main line."

"Awful things, them railroads. Some say it'll kill the boating in time."

"Maybe," said the peddler. "But I don't think it will. It ain't got the traction. Mules have, and the railroads can't use mules. I say let the railroads take all the people that's fools enough to risk 'em. Packet boats was a nuisance anyhow."

"That's right," said Mrs. Sullivan. "Lord help me, though, I wouldn't ride in one of them trains. They go too fast."

"Yeanh."

"Any news Rome way?"

"They say Mary Runkle's trial 'll come up next month."

"Who's she? Oh, I remember! It was she choked her husband to death while they was in bed together. It don't seem true."

"You can't tell," said Turnesa thoughtfully. "She had the strength."

"Say," exclaimed Mrs. Sullivan, "Drake Gallup was up from Boonville last night. He says all the folks down there is turble brustled up about there being a criminal loose on the canal."

"I wonder who it is?"

"Don't know for sure, but they think he's the man's been pulling these holdups on the canal. Stopped Drake."

"Did Drake get a look at him?"

"No. The man wore a handkerchief over his face. He rode a big grey horse and was dressed like a spark, pipe hat and all. They call him Gentleman Joe Calash. He don't seem to hang in one place any length of time."

"He will one day."

Mrs. Sullivan laughed.

Young Harrow had been listening attentively with a gleam coming into his eyes.

"Excuse me, mam. What do they want him for?"

Mrs. Sullivan smiled at him.

"Plenty. The posters is made out, 'Dead or alive.'"

"Yeanh," said the peddler. "I guess he's a bad one, all right. Say, I'll have to get on. Thanks for the drink. Geddup!"

He struck the horse with the ends of the reins and leaned back on the seat. Mrs. Sullivan nodded to Harrow.

"Good-bye. Young man going to Boonville?"

"Yeanh," said Harrow, diffidently. "Aim to get work there on the canal. Thanks."

The horse walked.

"So you're going on the canal?" said the peddler.

"Yeanh."

"Who with, if I might ask?"

"Pa said once that Hector Berry might give me a job."

"That's right, he needs a driver. He's here now — Boonville, I mean. He's boating one of Uberfrau's fleet. Guess he'll take you on."

He puffed his pipe in tune to the click and creak of the wagon.

"It 'll be a new start for you."

He glanced at his companion. Harrow sat leaning forward on the seat, elbows on knees, staring at his large-jointed hands, a kind of hesitation in his blue-green eyes. He did not look stupid. He had been hatched by solitude, which nourishes men on musing, not on thought. But as he glanced up in answer to a question the peddler saw a native shrewdness lurking in the corners of his eyes.

"Well, I hope you 'll like it. The Erie is a swarming hive. Boats coming and going, passing you all the while. You can hear their horns blowing all day long. As like as not there 's a fight at every lock. There 's all kinds of people there, and they 're all going all the while. It ain't got the finish and style as when the packet boats was running, but you 'll find fancy folk in the big ports. It 's better without the packet boats; let the railroads take the passengers. It leaves the pace steady for growing. There 's freight going west and raw food east, all on the canal; there 's people going west, New Englanders, Germans, and all them furrin folk, and there 's people coming east that 've quit. But the canawlers keep a-moving."

The peddler folded his hands over his knee.

"Water-level trade route, they call it, and it is. By grab, it 's the bowels of the nation! It 's the whole shebang of life."

He glanced at his companion. Harrow was staring over the old horse's ears. The cool of evening was born in the air, and shadows began to take a longer shape. Behind them Tug Hill and the sun were sinking together.

"A man can't tell what 's coming to him," said the peddler after a while. "The Constitution of these here States says we 're all born alike, and I guess maybe that 's right. But something takes hold of us different after that. Some people goes after money, and some after women, and some just drinks. I don't know but what they 're right; but me, I 've set on a wagon all my life, so I don't rightly know. You 're a-going out after something."

"I'm wondering where the road will fetch me out," he added after a moment.

"Yeanh."

"Geddup," the peddler said to the horse, but the old beast switched his grizzled tail and snatched at a morsel.

The peddler glanced at Harrow from under his tufted brows.

"What'll you do if you don't like the canal?"

"I ain't thought."

"Thought only how he'd like it," the peddler said to himself.

"Well," he said aloud, "you're to rub around with a queer lot. If I was you I'd stick to Berry. He's all right, I guess. I hope you'll like it down there."

"Reckon I will."

"Ever do any reading?" the peddler asked, after a pause.

"Some. Pa learnt me. I went to school by Turin for a spell."

"Well, then, here's something to take with you."

The peddler felt about under his hams and presently produced the volume he had been thumbing when he greeted Harrow.

"It's a good thing to have a book if you're tied by alone for the night."

Harrow took the book hesitatingly and weighed it in his hand. Then he looked at the title.

"Say, we had a book like that to home. Said 'Shakespeare' onto the back of it. I never read out of it, though."

"Maybe you'll like it," said the peddler. "It's a funny thing. Books is all right — stories, I mean — when there's people around. But when you're so by yourself you keep thinking about it, a play is better. There's people talking all the while, and coming in and going out, and it seems right you should be sitting where you be to see 'em. But in a book you can't go around with anybody without knowing all the while you're setting by yourself."

Harrow did not understand, but later he found that it was so.

The wheels of the wagon began to spin suddenly at a fair rate of speed that seemed miraculous after the lethargic manner of their former revolutions. Both looked up to see the old horse bestirring himself.

"Durned if we ain't almost there," said the peddler.

Harrow saw a neat village street growing out of the road directly in front of him. Large trees sprang on either side, and the sunset behind sent the shadow of the horse's head before them into the town.

"Boonville," said the peddler.

The horse trotted on past an open triangular space of trees and grass and swung into an alley beside a three-story building of grey limestone with pillars running all the way up the front to support three tiers of porches.

HURLBURT HOUSE read the black-and-white sign.

They stopped in a large yard, with wagon sheds opening on two sides and the doors of a great stable on the third. A heavy man with a black beard and unpleasantly light blue eyes was sitting on a bucket in one of the open doors watching a cricket, which was persistent in its efforts to enter the barn. Whenever the insect reached the boarding, the man spat unerringly and counted. "Five!" he shouted for the benefit of someone in the stable. Then, seeing the cricket turn away, "Buttoned him up that time, too," he said. Hearing the creak of the peddler's ancient wagon, he glanced up.

"Got your usual truck of junk, ain't you?" he asked. He rose from the bucket, spat on the horse's legs, stuck his hands in his pockets, and started out to the street.

"That's Jotham Klore. He's pretty near the bully of the canal." The peddler grunted. "But some day he's going to get whipped — and it 'll be bad."

He watched Harrow put the volume of Shakespeare into his carpetbag; then they got off the wagon and faced each other.

"Reckon I 'll move on," said Harrow. "Thanks for the ride and the book."

"Nothing at all, son; see you again sometime. You 'll find

Berry's boat at Uberfrau's dock; it's the Ella-Romeyn. It's got a red stripe around the cabin roof. You go out on the street and turn left and go on till you get to the basin, and then follow that to the right, and you'll get there."

They shook hands. The peddler began to unhitch.

Harrow walked out into the street.

II

THE HAUL TO ROME

The Man on the Docks

It was growing dark. The windows of the Hurlburt House threw rectangles of light across the stone porch floor and out on the plank sidewalk. For a while Dan Harrow lingered by them, listening to the clatter of knives and forks and crockery, and drinking in the smells of roasting pork and boiled turnips. The sky was fleeced with small clouds which the moon had just begun to touch, and the streets were quiet.

A lull in the noises from the dining room of the hotel caused him to glance toward the door, and his eyes fell upon a sheet of paper tacked in a conspicuous position beside the frame. He walked over to it and began to read.

$2000.00 REWARD

FOR INFORMATION LEADING TO THE CAPTURE, DEAD OR ALIVE, OF JOSEPH P. CALASH

"Desperate criminal," remarked a high voice at Dan's shoulder.

Turning, Dan saw a stoutish man dressed entirely in brown, with a black pot hat on his head and a green tie loose round his neck, who stood with his legs wide apart and his hands thrust into his hip pockets. The man regarded him out of shiny brown eyes, almost hidden between puckered lids, and pursed his lips in a silent whistle.

"Not that they 've got a great chance of catching him," he went on, "giving such a innocuous likeness."

"Yeanh?"

"Yeanh, my boy. What does it say? Six feet, thin, dresses like a gentleman. Hell! They 'll get information about half the county."

"What 's he wanted for?" Dan asked.

"Plenty," said the man. "Dead or alive! Two thousand dollars!"

He pulled a cigar out of his waistcoat pocket.

"Have one?"

"No."

The man stuck it into his mouth and began rolling it from side to side, while Dan turned back to his inspection of the poster.

"Last seen in Utica. Riding a grey horse. Sixteen hands."

"That's what interests me," explained the stranger. "I'm a horse trader by profession — I might say by nature. I had a horse like that taken out of my string in Utica. That was a loss! I 'm looking for that animal."

"That 's hard," said Dan.

"Sour! Prettiest horse you ever see. Sixteen hands and dappled grey. White mane and tail. Gent's horse." He sighed gustily. "Well, it 's a hard business. Here to-day, there to-morrow. A man can't find an honest man outside of himself in a horse trade — and if he 's honest himself, he 's either a fool or a damn sight cleverer than the other feller."

"Yeanh," said Dan. "I guess that 's right."

"You ain't seen him?" the man asked hopefully.

"No," said Dan. "Have you got any notion who took him?"

"Stableman said he was a thin, tall man. Could n't see his face."

"You 'd ought to watch out for him," said Dan.

"That 's what I 'm doing."

"Sounds like this feller," said Dan, pointing his thumb at the notice.

"Think so myself," said the man. "Say, son, if you was to see that horse, I 'd call it an almighty favor if you 'd notify me where. You can write to the Odd Fellow's Lodge, James Street, Rome. Sam Henderson's the name, care Alva Mudge, Esquire. Here it is wrote out."

He scribbled the address on a slip of paper and handed it to Dan, who read it over, folded it, and put it in his shirt pocket.

"What's your name, son?"

"Dan'l Harrow."

"Pleased to meet you," said Mr. Henderson, holding forth his hand. Dan took it dubiously.

"It's worth fifty dollars to you, if you find that horse. Best I ever got my hands on!"

He sighed.

"Yeanh," said Dan. "I guess he was. They most generally be."

He stepped into the street. Once he glanced back to see Mr. Henderson staring after him, framing a whistle with his lips — and the cigar for a note.

Figures were running in Dan's head.

"Fifty," he said to himself; then, "Two thousand dollars."

He walked on.

"The dirty twerp!"

Following the peddler's directions, he went down a street marked SCHUYLER high up on a limestone house, where nobody in the world could be expected to see it, and where nobody was expected to. Perhaps a hundred yards, with a slight incline at the end, brought him to the basin, a long, rectangular strip of water, with the feed canal flowing in round the base of a hill opposite, the Watertown Branch flowing out on the left, and far away to the right the Rome Canal winding out of sight between low hills.

Warehouses with big stupid windowless fronts ran along the shore, and stubby quays jutted into the water from their sides. Dan went down to the waterfront and walked along a planked run wide enough for a wagon, with turnouts on the wharves. There were no boats near him, but a little down the basin he saw one of the docks outlined by a lighted window cut into an indistinguishable shape, very low upon the water.

A slight breeze tickled his forehead. The night was cool and the air thick with the odor of grain. He stopped to listen to the slap of the ripple against the piles.

He was to ask Hector Berry, whom he had never seen, for a job; but first he would eat a supper he had in his bag. So he sat down on the planks of the dock with his back to a warehouse, in the thickest of the shadow, and ate slowly two great sandwiches of salty butter and ham, and a piece of green-apple pie.

As he finished the last bit and wiped his hands along his trouser legs, he became aware of a horse walking slowly along the dock. He sat still.

Suddenly the horse stopped, and low voices broke out round the corner of the building. With slow ease Dan rose to his feet and stepped noiselessly to the corner. The moonlight fell at a slant between the high walls, upon a tall dappled grey horse with high raking withers and straight hind legs the very look of which spelled speed. He stood quietly with his head at the shoulder of a man whose back was turned to Dan, but whose pipe hat shone grey in the white light and threw a long zigzagged shadow anglewise against the clapboards. Facing him was a big man with a long-visored cap, who leaned against the wall and talked in a hoarse harsh voice. The moon fell on his face and brought his black beard into vivid contrast with the pallor of his eyes. As he talked, he punctuated his sentences with long squirts of tobacco juice. In the action Dan recognized the man he had seen in the stable yard.

It took Dan a moment to accustom his ears to their low voices. Even then he was able to hear only occasional snatches of their talk. "Two thousand dollars," from the bearded man. "Better not get me riled and helping them . . . They 've got a Department man after you . . . Half and half . . . Nothing to you . . ." And the man in the pipe hat, "Go ahead . . . Watch out if you do . . . No marshal . . . If there is, he 's scared . . . One dead . . .

Jotham Klore . . ." And Klore again, "Bitch, Calash . . .
I will . . . Marshal . . . Damn right . . ."

Suddenly Dan thought of the poster and the fat man and
the grey horse.

Then he saw the tall man's left hand stealing to the
saddle holster, saw the moon trace the revolver barrel and
Klore turn round to face the wall, while the tall man walked
up behind him and raised the barrel and brought it down.
Klore dropped to his knees and the tall man hit him again,
and Klore stretched out on his belly. It all happened without a sound for Dan to hear, only the men and their shadows in a corner of the moonlight. Then the horse dropped
his head and shook himself, jingling the stirrup irons, and
let out a long breath through blubbering lips.

After watching Klore for a second or two, the tall man
backed to his horse, mounted quickly, and galloped off up
the canal. Dan stared at Klore, lying beside the warehouse
and snoring heavily.

"Calash," he said, to himself. "Gentleman Joe. Jeepers!"

He wondered whether he should go for help; but it seemed
to him that Klore was only stunned. "Buttoned up," he
said to himself. His sympathy was all with the hunted man,
a stranger, like himself, to the canal. He felt a secret kinship between them, roused, perhaps, as much by the beauty
of the man's horse as by the man. There lay no temptation for him in the reward.

He gazed up the canal. He wished that he might have
seen the man's face. Stepping back round the corner, he
picked up his bag and walked on down the dock to the
lighted window.

The Ella-Romeyn

A few steps more, and he found himself staring through
the lighted window in the cabin of a boat which had been
tied up to the dock, stern on to the bank. The name of the
boat was cut in two by the tiller shaft, rising stubbily above

the roof of the cabin to the ponderous sweep. The name, which had once been dressed in gilt, still carried enough of its paint to be legible. Though Dan spelled out the frank capitals — ELLA-ROMEYN — he scarcely noticed them, for his eyes had been caught by the dark band above the windows. Brown in the lamplight, it would look red to the sun.

He stood back a pace and looked the boat over carefully. Freighted to the gunwales with early potatoes, the Ella-Romeyn squatted on the water with the pregnant massiveness of a farrowing sow. Now and then her timbers grunted under the new load as she shifted against the tie-ropes.

Through the window and the geranium leaves that made a fringe along the sill, Dan caught a diagonal view of the cabin. The cookstove stood against the forward wall with the dish cabinets on each side of the stovepipe and the iron ventilators up above the heating shelf. To the right, under the windows, was a small sewing table, with a shelf over it bearing a ball-dialed clock on a shaft of imitation crystal. And on either side of the clock were cast the shadows of the occupants of the room, themselves invisible from the window.

Using the shelf for a table, and oblivious of the clock, these shadows were playing a comedy at cards. There were three of them: a stoutish man, with his back to the light, who played cautiously, putting his cards on the table with deliberate motions of his invisible hands; a very small man, his right hand to the light, with an egg-shaped head drawn out ridiculously by the angle of the wall; and opposite him an enormously fat woman, gesturing her paddle-like shadow hands with irrepressible flair. The two men were solemn in their game, though the little man was nimble in putting down his cards, in motions which the light carried clean across the shelf to the end of the fat woman's nose. And she, with indefatigable good humor, leaned forward to meet the thrusts, and then leaned back, with chuckles that reached all the way to her bonnet, until the ribbons quivered in grotesque parody of her gargantuan heaving. He was infected with the fat woman's sense of humor, ridiculous in its parodied motions on the wall; he wanted to see her in the flesh, to mix with her kind, to be accepted as one of kindred joviality. As the comedy proceeded, he chuckled to himself and went aboard the boat. The unfamiliar feel of the gangway beneath his feet brought back the timidity he concealed under his slouch; yet he felt his way aft to the steersman's position, where sufficient light escaped under the cabin door to show him the steps down.

The fat woman's laughter echoed against the panels.

"Mix me another of them rum noggins," she said, "and put in lots of lemon, and don't forget the sugar like you did last time. Dealing makes me dry. What's your bid, Sol?"

"Two hundred!" exclaimed a cracked voice in high determination.

"It's by me," said the third player mournfully.

"I got two suits stopped right here," said the fat woman, "so I'll say two-twenty."

"Two twenty-five," said Sol, with returning caution.

"Thirty," bid the fat woman.

"Five," said Sol, grimly hanging on.

"Take it," said the fat woman, after the figure had reached three hundred and forty-five.

They must have looked at the "kitty."

"Oh, my God," wailed Sol's voice. "Three hearts and two of them nines, and me with one hundred and fifty in spades and diamonds, lacking only queen and jack."

"Them's the suits I got stopped with my double pinochle!" shrieked the fat woman. "Three hundred points, not counting them hundred aces. Look! Look!"

"My God, Hector, let's quit!" cried Sol.

Hector! Dan knocked.

"Come in," cried all three beyond the door.

Dan opened it and stepped into the room.

"Hello. Is Mr. Hector Berry here?"

He took off his hat in deference to the fat woman. About the table, which had not appeared in the shadow pantomime, sat the three players, and, facing the door, the medium-sized man stared at Dan over square spectacles, a look of bewilderment on his plump pink features.

"That's my name, young man," he said. "My name's Hector Berry. Now what do you want? You needn't be afraid to speak to me, young man."

"No," said Dan, slowly. "I ain't."

He glanced at the fat woman. The chuckle he had heard still lingered in her snapping grey eyes.

"The young man ain't afraid to speak to Hector Berry," she whispered to the little man.

"Not a mite," agreed Sol.

"Desperit character," said the fat woman, shaking her head seriously. And she burst into a fit of laughter, till the ribbons of her black silk bonnet appeared to topple for their balance, and the leaden yellow cherries rattled like dice. Her face became redder and redder; her cheeks bulged explosively; and the red-centred paisley shawl on her shoulders worked up the back of her neck to her high knot of red hair.

Berry rubbed his hands nervously and compared his watch with the clock.

"Now," he said irritably to Dan, "what did you say you wanted?"

Dan looked again at the fat woman.

"Set down," she suggested, pointing to a chair.

"Thank you, mam."

"Looking for a job?" asked Sol, with impetuous inspiration.

"Yeanh. I wanted to see if Mr. Berry would take me on as a driver."

"What's your name?"

"Dan Harrow."

"You ain't kin to Cap'n Henry Harrow, be you? He was captain of the packet boat Golden City. He made the smartest run, Schenectady to Buffalo, of any captain on the Erie — three days, eleven hours, and thirty-seven minutes. Three hundred and forty-six miles." Hector Berry clasped his hands over his belly and sighed. "Figger it out for yourself

— it's a danged sight better than four miles the hour. Them was the days! Speed? You've got no notion how them boats could travel! Son, you ought to have been there then."

"Well, he wasn't," said the fat woman, "so why not give him a chance to answer what you asked?"

"What was it?"

He cast a reproachful look at her.

"Be you kin to Henry Harrow?" she asked Dan.

"Pa's name was Henry Harrow. I didn't know the rest."

The little man glanced up.

"Where'd he go? I always wondered where he went to."

He nodded his head briskly and put his feet on the rungs of his chair.

"Had a farm up Tug Hill," said Dan.

"Just think of it," exclaimed the fat woman. "Way up there, and him so fancy-dandy in his ways!"

"How is he?" Sol asked.

"He's dead."

"My, my," sighed the fat woman, pushing her hand up to her heart. "We all suffer. Give the young man some rum noggin, Hector. I'll have another glass."

The canal folk looked at each other.

"My, my," they said.

"Good with horses?" asked Berry after an appropriate interval of silence.

"Yeanh," said Dan, looking into his hat.

"Well, the man that drives for me's to Rome. I'll take you on that far; I'm pulling out to-morrow. I'll pay you a dollar for driving me to Rome."

"Thanks."

Berry handed out glasses all round.

"Now, then," remarked the fat woman, when they had all sipped for the taste, "make the young man to home, Hector. Introduce us."

Hector blushed.

"I'd clean forgot. Beg pardon, folks." He cleared his throat, turned to Dan, and began, a trifle pompously, "Young Harrow, this lady, which I want you to meet, is Mrs. Lucy

Gurget — Mrs. Gurget, this here 's young Harrow. Mrs. Gurget cooks for this gentleman, Mr. Solomon Tinkle. I 'm Hector Berry — you know it; and I 'm real sorry my wife, Mrs. Penelope Berry, ain't with us now."

"She ain't dead, be she?" Dan asked commiseratingly.

"No chance —" began Berry; then hastily, "No, she 's a-visiting with some of her folks to Westernville. We 'll pick her up off the towpath when we get through the Lansing Kill."

"You don't play pinochle, do you?" Mrs. Gurget asked hopefully.

"No," said Dan. "I ain't a very good hand at cards."

"That 's a shame. Now we might have had another game if you was. But I guess Sol, here, he 's too sick of my skillful playing anyhow."

"Skill!" snorted the little man, slapping his hat on. "It 's time you went to bed, talking that way, Lucy." . . .

Left alone with Hector Berry, Dan found the time dragging. He was sleepy under his long walk; and the warmth of the fire and the rum noggin in his insides started him nodding. The kettle purred, the clock ticked, and Hector talked.

He was excusing himself for not offering Dan a longer job. But then he was a poor man, and his wife would probably object anyway. . . . This man Calash made him think of old days. Two thousand dollars reward! He 'd like to get it. Perhaps he would. He wondered where the man had come from. . . . Now in the old days such doings were n't unusual. There were a bunch of them. They used to hang out at Joshua Ricket's place in the Montezumy swamp. Dan's pa used to be a light in those days. Snabbest packet on the Erie. Great hand to race. Full of dodges as a rabbit's hind legs.

Hector looked at Dan, and Dan looked back sleepily. He had been barely listening, catching the drift but not the words. Hector suggested bed, showed him a bunk forward beside the two horse stalls. The blankets smelled a little sour from lack of washing, but the bunk had a good straw pallet. Dan glanced at the rumps of the horses as he passed — a big black team.

He blew out the lantern after Hector had left, listening to the breathing of the horses and the insistent slapping of the ripple below his ear, and breathing in the sweet smell of new timothy. One of the horses grunted; and Dan turned to the wall and slept.

Early Morning

Dan might have been sleeping in the lonely house on Tug Hill in which he and his father had lived by themselves ever since he could remember. He lay straight out upon his right side, never moving, while the first white bar of light tunneled the dusty air of the stable. A fly buzzed in along a beam, and its wings, brushing Dan's cheeks, woke him.

It was a cold morning, with a smell of frost in the air. The horses were on their feet stepping from side to side in their narrow stalls, nosing their mangers.

Mechanically, Dan heaved his feet to the floor and began pulling on his trousers and lacing his boots. Pans rattled in the kitchen aft, heralding an early breakfast. He brushed the horses down. The off one, which had white stockings on its hind legs, fidgeted; but his quiet words and the unhesitating movements of his hands seemed to reassure it; and it stood easily, leaning against the brush, skin twitching with enjoyment. Dan looked up from finishing the white stockings to see Berry in the door.

"Say, Mr. Berry, how much do you grain 'em?"

An expression of amazement lengthened Hector's usually round face.

"You are pretty good with horses. Say, that off horse, he won't let my driver touch his heels."

Dan was embarrassed.

"Why," said Hector after a moment, "give each one this measure level full."

"Them's their regular harness?"

"Yeanh. Come to breakfast when you're done."

Dan harnessed the horses and fed them. In five minutes he was walking back along the left-hand gangway. The eighty-foot boat looked older by daylight. Her timbers were scarred along the edge of the pit, and the rail was worn smooth, to the detriment of a coat of white paint, now weathered as grey as the wood. But the cabin walls, with the small square curtained window and the blue vein of smoke coiling from the hooded stovepipe, gave her a comfortable hominess.

Berry appeared in the cabin door.

"Come on, Dan. Ain't got no time for daddling. We want to be the first two down-boats into the gorge."

Dan went down the short steps into the kitchen. Sunlight streamed into the small windows and shone on the varnished maple walls. On the table, covered with yellow oilcloth, stood two plates, bearing three fried eggs, bacon rare, and a piece of chocolate cake. Beside them Berry placed two cups brimming with black boiled tea.

They ate silently, until Dan reached for the sugar bowl. It was empty.

"By Cripus!" exclaimed Hector. "Nell said she'd filled it."

He got up and went over to the sink, lifted the gingham curtain, pulled out the garbage tin, and filled the bowl.

"We plop scraps out there," he explained, pointing to a little sliding door in a corner of the wall. "Every man scrapes his own plate. It all goes down to N'York anyways; and the tin is real useful for sugar."

He sat down again.

"You see, we pick up rats every time we stop to a port. They travels into the country by our boats — five years and they'll be the only packet passengers left to the canal. You pick up lots in Albany, and if you goes to New York you'll fill your pit up with 'em enough to give your boat the itch. And they're masterful fond of sweet."

He grew melancholy.

"Every time we hit the Erie by Rome, Nell she 'll up and moan for me to drive out the rats."

"Why n't you get a cat?"

"Jeepers! A cat would n't stand no show at all. Them rats 're that savage they 'd drink the sweat off a man's back."

Footsteps suddenly banged on the deck, clattered on the stairs, and, turning, Dan beheld Mrs. Gurget.

"Morning, mam."

The fat woman was dressed in a red flannel petticoat and a yellow blouse. But on her head she wore the same bonnet. It was becomingly rakish, and under it, with her vivid eyes and sturdy carriage, Mrs. Gurget assumed a kind of unflinching handsomeness.

"Say!" she cried. "Somebody laid out Jotham Klore last night with a bang on the head. Young Uberfrau found him around back of the Butterfield warehouse, dead for all. But he come to after a while. And he claims it was this Joe Calash. Gentleman Joe done it, he says, and took twenty dollars off him. Ain't it awful!"

"I 'd say it was a good job," said Hector.

"Well, you boys 'll have to step smart. Sol, he 's harnessing his mules, and he aims to start as soon as you 're ready."

"We 'll be ready right off. I 'll show young Harrow here how to get out the towrope. He 's good with horses; brushed that off black of mine clear down to the heels. That shows he 's good with horses, sure 's my name 's Hector Berry."

"Sure," said the fat woman, giving Dan a smile that set him blushing to his hair. "I could see that right off. All animals like him."

She shooed them to the door with her hands.

"Now, then, hustle along. I 'll give the dishes a rinse while you 're getting ready."

"You get the team out, Dan," said Berry, after they had run the rope out to the towpath and hooked it to the heavy elm evener. "Lift the hatch they 're facing and leave 'em be."

Dan went into the stable and bridled the team, then swung

up the hatch, which raised half the wall of the boat with it, and watched the team pick their way off the boat and over to the whiffletrees as nonchalantly as if they were leaving a two-story barn.

"Last link of the traces!" shouted Hector, standing by the gangplank. The fat woman came down and hurried ahead to Solomon Tinkle's boat. There was amazing elasticity in her step.

"Thank the Lord!" she sighed gustily to Dan. "I declare to gracious I 'm glad we 're leaving this town."

She ran aboard the other boat and swung in the plank just as Solomon started his mules. Then, running to the sweep, she bore it to the left, and the boat nosed out into the water round the bows of the Ella-Romeyn and swung into line with the towpath. Little ripples jerked round the corners of the blunt bow, and evened into lines that grew and grew until they touched either shore. The fat woman swung the rudder away from shore to keep the nose of the boat in midstream. She sat down in a rocking-chair with an abbreviated back, to miss the low bridges. She reached down with her left hand into a box beside her chair, drew out a glass and a long-necked bottle, from which she dexterously poured a measure of whiskey.

"Bridge!" called Solomon from the towpath, his bow-legs trotting nimbly beside the mules.

"Bridge!" roared the fat woman.

As the boat passed under the Main Street Bridge of Boonville, Dan saw Mrs. Gurget tilt her head until the cherries on her bonnet hung as on their native branch, and she downed the whiskey in a single gulp.

"Here 's going down to Rome!"

The full light of the early sun followed her broad back under the timbers; the two stern windows of the boat glistened like eyes; and under them Dan read the name, NANCY HASKINS, *Utica*.

"Well, we might as well get a-going," cried Hector.

Looking over his shoulder, Dan saw him standing spraddle-legged behind the cabin, the rudder sweep grasped in both hands, a low black flat-crowned hat upon his head, a huge cigar, tip-tilted, filling his lips to capacity. His was a mouth made for nestling a cigar.

The team picked up a smart pace. They were fast walkers and would quickly overtake Tinkle's mules.

Dan felt the shadows of the Main Street Bridge over him.

"Bridge!" he shouted in imitation of Solomon Tinkle.

"Bridge!" replied Berry with an approving grin, adding, "Better hop up. Going with this flow even with a load on ain't nothing for a good team. It's a five-mile current."

He pointed, and Dan, looking ahead, saw the little man straddling his off mule. Dan looped the reins over the hames of his off horse and vaulted to his back. Evidently it was a customary thing to do, for the animal merely shook his head and grunted once. Dan hooked one knee over the hames and sat sidewise, facing the canal. The swift walk of the blacks had brought him opposite the stern of the Nancy Haskins; but there, they took their stride from the mules and kept pace so evenly that the two boats might have been hitched together.

Once it had left the town, the feeder wound away due south between raw banks, in the cuts of which grass was just getting a foothold. The canal had been opened only the year before. It was the principal feeder of the Mohawk section of the Erie Canal, but it also opened all the Black River country, as far as Watertown, to trade.

The shadows in the wooded bends still held a taint of frost, and out of them the sun drew wraiths of mist that trailed away among the trees, leaving a dank touch lingering on the passer's cheeks. A sadness came into Dan's eyes. It might have been the sight of the open cuts through the meadows, or the scars left by the diggers in the woods, neither offering promise of the future beauty of the dark water which would in a few years reflect banks green with nature's healing, but which now moved sombrely like a soul laid bare.

He started to hear the fat woman clearing her throat.

She had been studying him for some time with a sort of smile tugging at the corners of her mouth. When she caught his eye, the smile broke into a grin, like a man's, and he felt an answering grin on his lips. She was amusing in her bright clothes, with all that substantial liveliness of hers.

"Boonville," she said, "will sure grow, now this ditch's been opened up."

"Yeanh."

"Ain't you never had no ma?" she asked after a time.

"Not to recollect it."

She shivered.

"It must have been lonely up there on Tug Hill."

"Yeanh."

"Awful lonely."

"Yeanh."

"Me — I could never have stood it so long."

"No. There weren't pasture to keep good cattle there. Just little crossbred dinkeys.

"Holsteins," he went on, slowly, "is all right if you can keep big, blooded ones. Or red cattle. But them little dinkeys," — he glanced at his hands, — "a man can't hardly fetch a-holt of their teats."

"When did your pa die?"

"Two months ago."

"I used to know him, once."

"Yeanh?"

"Everybody knew him on the canal. He was a fine big man. I was just a gal then."

Before them the pasture land narrowed in the hills, and the road came in to the towpath; and way ahead the sky came down upon the level fields.

"The Lansing Kill," Mrs. Gurget said to Dan. . . .

The white beams of lock gates stood out against the autumn green, and as they came closer Dan saw a small square house beside the towpath, and, farther on below, more locks, and next to each another house. He saw that they were entering a narrow deep gorge. On his left the Lansing Kill plunged eighty feet into a foaming cauldron and then

roared downward over a long series of rapids. It had cut
away a wide amphitheatre where it came first on the soft
limestone, and the water fell in a broad curtain. An overflow from the canal shot another, more broken fall into the
whirlpool of water. Between the two falls, on a small island,
the froth feathering its roots, a white ash grew by itself,
its smooth trunk glistening and its leaves trembling with
the spray.

On the right side of the gorge, the road and canal went
down together; the road in sharp curves and a steady
descent, the canal following a straighter course, stairlike in
its series of locks, so that to go down it made the boater
feel as though he rose and fell. For at times the road ran
high over his head, and at times it would lie below him,
halfway to the valley floor, while his boat crept into the
series of locks with its reflection in the reflection of the
sky. . . .

There were no farms in the Lansing Kill Gorge; there
were the forest, the stream, the canal, the road, and the
lock-tenders living alone. Only the boats and the shadows of
clouds went up or down the long defile. A commissioner had
called it "a link in transportation." "The Lansing Kill,"
Mrs. Gurget said to Dan. But Solomon Tinkle, after a
backward glance at the upland river country with its rolling
hills from which they had just come, called to Dan, "Seventy
locks in five miles. Regular stairs, I'd call it. Jeepers! It's
the stairways to the Erie!"

"Yeanh," said Mrs. Gurget, "so it be. There's life down
there, Dan."

"Yeanh," said Hector Berry. "That's right."

In the Kill Gorge

As if he were an outpost there to hail them, they saw a
man sitting his horse in the shadow of the bridge. Both
boats stopped.

"Hey, there!" he shouted.

Far down the Kill Gorge they heard, in the instant following, another cry, faintly, "Hey, there!"

The man glanced over his shoulder suddenly, as if he were not sure it was an echo. There was a pastiness about his cheeks which might have come from a bilious constitution or nervousness, or both. While he talked to the boaters, his eyes, which were set flush with his cheeks, kept covering the road and the towpath ahead of him; and he held his right hand inside the flap of his coat resting near his left hip.

Mrs. Gurget had brought the Nancy in close to the towpath, and now she leaned forward toward Dan and said in a low voice, "It's Nick Spinning — he's sheriff to Rome."

Solomon Tinkle engaged the sheriff in conversation. The little man had climbed down off the back of his mule and now stood leaning against it, his head resting on the animal's flank. They had finished exchanging views on the weather.

"What 're you doing up this way, Spinning?"

Spinning glanced round him again.

"You 've heard of this feller, Calash? Well," — he opened a small saddle bag and pulled out a sheaf of bills, — "I 'm going up to Boonville to set these up."

Dan went over to him. "Two thousand dollars reward," he read, "for information leading to the capture, dead or alive, of Joseph P. Calash."

"Sheriff Jones told me to set these up here. I don't see as there 's any point in it. They say there 's a special marshal, Department of Justice man, working on the job — regular hound for trailing. But he ain't reported to us yet. Those marshals are rated too damned high. But there ain't any point in hanging up these papers in Boonville."

"No," said Dan. "That 's right. There 's some posted there already."

"Who done that?" exclaimed the sheriff, open-mouthed with astonishment.

"The marshal, maybe," said Dan.

Spinning swore.

"I'll bet that's right. Jeepers Cripus! How can they expect us to help a marshal if he don't let us know who he is? It ain't right in the first place, their sending him in here to pick up the money."

"Well, there's your chance, Spinning," said Solomon. "Calash is up there now. He laid out Klore last night on Uberfrau's dock. You'd ought to catch him coming out."

"I'd like to see him," said the sheriff. "Just once."

"Damned if I would," said Hector Berry.

"I mean the marshal. I want to know who he is. You don't know who he is?" he asked Dan.

"No," said Dan slowly, "I guess not."

He was thinking of the fat man, Henderson, who claimed he had lost a horse.

"Sol!" cried Mrs. Gurget. "Move them mules along. You'll have the towline tangled!"

The boats had crept on with the current until they were opposite the teams. Now the mules took the weight of the boat upon the towline again and forged ahead until they came abreast of the gate beams of the lock.

"The Five Combines," said Mrs. Gurget.

As if he liked their company, Spinning let his horse follow the boats. Mrs. Gurget glanced at him and said in a low voice to Dan, "Spinning's scared. There's no doubt of it."

After feeling under her chair, she straightened up, a long brass horn at her lips. Her bonnet rose as she drew in her breath, and then it sank behind a long-drawn braying that moaned in echoes on the wooded hills.

"My God!" chattered Hector. "Don't do it again! It chips my teeth to hear it. Wait, I'll ring my bell."

"Shucks!" she mocked Hector. "Ben can't hear your bell. The Angel Gabriel will have to punch him on the nose come Judgment Day to make him hear."

Again she blew an unearthly blast, until the vein stood out between her eyes.

Solomon ducked his head and screamed.

"Cripus, Lucy! Stop it! Here he comes."
Up from below the level of the lock they heard in the fallen quietness a hoarse voice singing out of key: —

> "Oh God! that I Jerusalem
>   With speed may go behold!
> For why? the pleasures there abound
>   Which cannot here be told.
> Thy turrets and thy pinnacles
>   With carbuncles do shine,
> With jasper, pearls, and chrysolite,
>   Surpassing pure and fine.

> "There be the prudent prophets all,
>   Th' apostles, six and six,
> The glorious martyrs in a row,
>   Confessors in betwixt.
> There doth the crew of righteous men
>   And nations all consist;
> Young men and maids that here on earth
>   Their pleasures did resist!"

The singer was an old man with a white beard falling to his waist, hiding his red flannels (for he wore no shirt), and white hair hanging on his shoulders. He came forward with a swinging, rugged stride, head back and shoulders squared, a six-foot knotty staff in his hand, and his blue eyes peered at Mrs. Gurget like those of a hermit, who has seen no woman since his youth.

Mrs. Gurget cupped her hands to her mouth and shouted, "Two boats going down to Rome!"

"Happy New Year," said the old man.

"Merry Christmas yourself," said Solomon Tinkle. "We've got to get through this lock."

"Course it ain't really a happy new year," observed the old man mildly. "That was just season's greetin's."

He moved over to the sluice levers.

"First boat in," he ordered.

The Nancy Haskins was already nosing in under the

skillful direction of Mrs. Gurget. On one side Solomon and
on the other Ben leaned on the balance beams and trod them
round to close the gates. Then Ben pushed on the sluice
lever at the lower end of the lock, a rush of water hissed
through the sluice, and rapidly Mrs. Gurget's bonnet sank
from view between the limestone walls. Solomon had un-
hooked the team, so they poled the boat into the second of
the five locks, which went down one after the other like a
set of steps.

As soon as the gates had shut behind the Nancy, Ben
came back and opened the sluice of the first lock to fill it, and
then he and Dan opened the upper gates and closed them
behind the Ella-Romeyn. So the boats went down a lock
apart, each taking two minutes to a lock, while old Ben ran
from sluice to sluice, bending his back as he ran and swinging his staff, with the sweat springing out on his cheeks and
a gleam in his eyes like the gleam in the eyes of Elisha the
prophet.

As the Nancy came out of the lowest of the five locks,
they all heard a horn braying round the bend before them.
By the time the last gates opened in front of the Ella, they
heard another horn sounding. Then a boat came in view,
hauled by three mules, almost on their knees under the heavy
load they had to move against the current. Behind them
walked a man who was very tall. He appeared to be making
knots and patterns with his bull-snake whip over the backs
of his mules. They cowered at each report and lunged in
their collars, as if generally the patterns were marked upon
their backs. And when they came closer Dan saw signs of it.

But the driver knew that a mule works best when he is
afraid of being hurt, not when he is hurt.

"They're beasts of extraordinary imaginations," Solomon
explained to Dan.

The man who steered the upstream boat kept throwing
glances back over his shoulder.

"Hurry up, George," he shouted. "Jason's just cleared
the last lock."

"By grab," exclaimed Hector Berry, as Dan passed him

to fetch down the two teams to the foot of the five combines, "by Grab, they must be line boats! If the second boat gets up afore the other commences to lock through they 'll fight for it."

The shadow of the sheriff's head moved onto the deck. "Danged if I 'll let 'em," he said.

Beyond the bend, volleys of profanity burst at them and a team of mules came round on a trot, followed by a great bear of a man who heaved upon the towline at their heels and goaded them with a spike in the end of the whip handle. He made no articulate comment, but rumbled to himself, until he saw the leading boat still waiting at the lock.

"Put her in, put her in!" he shouted to the steersman, and as the boat came into the bank he ran back, caught the rope flung to him, snubbed it round a post, and before the steersman could jump ashore, had started for the lock at a lumbering run.

"By Jeepers, George," cried the steersman on the first boat, "there ain't no ways out of it now! You 've got to stand up to him."

"That 's the first honest-to-God thing you ever said." The driver of the second boat stood facing them on thick bow-legs, his arms half raised, his flat heavy hands half clenched, his pig's eyes jumping from one to the other.

"You cheated me out of place down below, George, but you 'll have to hold it now or let me through."

The tall man looked a bit scared, but he wanted the place. The first boat through would lead into Boonville.

"Go wipe yourself," he said.

The sheriff rode down to them.

"I 'm sheriff of Rome," he announced. "Quit it!"

"Horse to you!"

The steersman of the first boat heaved on the sheriff's right leg, and as he came down over the other side of his horse the steersman of the second boat caught him by the neck and thumped him on his back, and then they both sat on his belly, side by side, and threw pebbles at his horse until it trotted off.

Spinning swore furiously, so the one nearest his head dropped sand into his mouth.

"No sense in you and me arguing," said the second steersman.

"No," said the other, reaching into his hip pocket, "have a chaw."

"Surely."

He helped himself from the bag, chewed, and waited politely for the other to spit.

"Go ahead," they said to the drivers.

The drivers walked up to the level space beside the upper lock. There they faced off, the man George head and shoulders taller than the other, with four inches more of reach. But there was a solidity about the second driver, that grew upon the onlookers.

"He can't be hurt," said the second steersman.

The crews of the down boats stopped where they were. "I guess we can spare the time," said Hector.

"I wouldn't miss it for a keg of real Jamaicy," said Mrs. Gurget. She wiggled her shoulders and settled herself comfortably in her chair.

Solomon Tinkle squatted down beside his mules, and Dan drew in his breath and waited.

Between the drivers and beyond them they could see old Ben leaning on his staff with the sun shining over his shoulder. Below the locks the roar of the Kill falls came upon their ears and filled their heads and took their hearing from them, so that they saw Jason lower his head and rush upon the tall man and take two hard right smashes on his face and turn with his mouth wide open; and there was no sound at all. But they could see his cry.

"All he has to do," explained his steersman, "is to hit him once; then he'll mow him down and set him up in shocks."

"I guess that's right," the other agreed affably. "George isn't no hand for punishment."

They spat together.

Up above them Jason rushed again and again on his

deceptively clumsy legs, but each time the other's longer reach helped him to dodge and get in a blow. At first he smiled confidently; but after a time his wind shortened and his hands grew sore, and the other's rushes missed him more narrowly.

Dan had never watched a prolonged fight between two men. He stepped over to Solomon Tinkle and sat down beside him. The sun caught the face of the man Jason as he rushed, and the cheeks showed red and puffed like overripe tomatoes, ready to burst at the pat of a small stick. The two piglike eyes gleamed from the close lids in a controlled frenzy. Then the head sank again and the man bored in.

The sudden glimpse of color flopped something inside of Dan, and he swallowed convulsively.

The tall man landed again, left and right, and the blood came out upon his hands and touched the cuffs of his shirt.

Dan cried aloud. And the tall man grinned.

"Now look!" cried Solomon, hunching forward.

For the grin on the tall man had suddenly become frozen, and it hardened and set and became a leer, and all at once his mouth sprang open; but they heard no scream.

"No doubt it was low," said Solomon. "We might as well pull out."

He spoke to his mules and they took up the slack in the rope. Dan kept on staring.

The bearlike Jason was standing close in on the tall man, his legs spraddly and his back arched, and his hands drove straight in from the waist. The tall man looked over his head, and it seemed to Dan that he was looking straight at him. His fist jumped out at the other's face, but fell aside, as though there were weights hung from his elbows. He gave no sign of moving any more; but he grinned.

"Come on, Dan," cried Hector. "We've got to get along."

Dan started the team, and as they went round the bend he looked back once more. The bearlike man stood in the same position, but old Ben's arms were stretched above his head and he stared at the tall man on the ground at his feet.

Mrs. Gurget glanced at Dan and saw that he was still a bit queasy from the fight. "Pore old man," she said, as the trees shut off their view of the lock-tender. "I reckon he's got religion bad."

"Yeanh?"

"Yes, I guess he has. He used to take tolls at the weigh-lock to Utica; but one day he bumped his head and went twirly."

"All lock-tenders is twirly," Hector said sententiously from the rear. "I reckon that's why they're lock-tenders."

A few hundred yards farther on, they came upon another lock, with a tender's house standing close beside it, and again Mrs. Gurget woke the echoes with her horn. A small black-haired man with a twisted shoulder stepped out of the door.

"That's Ethan Allen McCarthy," Mrs. Gurget said to Dan. "He's got ideas against God, and him and Ben don't speak any more."

"Hullo, Ethan," she called. "How be you?"

"Morning, morning," he said.

And then, as he walked over to the gate beams, "George Marble just went through with Jason Brown pushing him close."

"They just had it out at the Five Combines. George got a beating."

"Glad to hear it. I'll bet old Ben took a frenzy watching them."

"No, nothing to notice."

"He will, he will. He'll have to think out the sin of it first. He don't mean harm, but he's crazy as a hot bitch with his religion."

He locked them through.

"Do you believe in God?" he asked Dan.

"Well, I ain't thought."

"Don't, young man. Don't do it. You can't get anywhere doing it. Eat your vittles and thank God you ain't got religion to raise a gas on a good meal."

A wind had begun to pick its way down the pass; by

eleven o'clock it was blowing strong from the northwest, and tumbled cold grey clouds showed over the northern hills.

Still they wound on with the tops of the trees close to their feet; and again and again they sank between the limestone walls. The canal had come to life; behind them now they heard, in eddies of the wind, the horns of other boats, long-drawn and broken by echoes. And they met boats coming up, hauled by sweating teams, the drivers cracking their bull whips as they walked with long slow strides, and the steersmen stiff beside their rudders at the stern. When they passed, Dan learned to trip his rope by holding back the horses while Hector steered the boat to the far side of the canal, so that the slack of the towline sank into the water as the boat came abreast, and the upstream craft, horse and boat, passed over it.

They locked through number thirty-nine and hauled out onto a stretch a mile and a half long, and for a way the hills were high above them and the roar of the Lansing Kill close at hand. The road stayed up on the hillsides, appearing here and there between the trees.

In a cove where the canal set back, they saw a shanty boat, a hovel on a platform with a porch facing the stern. Tethered by the towpath, an old mule cropped up grass with short, tobacco-brown teeth. He did not look up at them, but one long white ear followed the sound of their passing. On the porch of the boat, a man with a white beard sat smoking a corncob pipe. Dan could see the smoke pop from his lips and hover under the roof before the wind snatched it away. A line between two posts on the roof held a snapping string of clean clothes to the wind. Inside, a woman was singing softly.

"Queer place for a shanty boater," said Mrs. Gurget.

"They come and go," said Hector Berry.

The singing ceased, and the woman came out to stand beside the old man and watch the boats passing. She looked very young and slender and dark. Mrs. Gurget waved to her, but her eyes followed Dan and she did not reply. The old man turned his head to speak to her, and she went in.

"Queer folk," Mrs. Gurget said to herself.

The old man took another puff on his pipe, and the wind carried the smoke away; and a moment after, the boats turned a bend.

Mrs. Gurget's glance fell upon Dan. She did not wonder the girl had looked at him. There was a light in his eyes as he walked. He kept his gaze far ahead to the outlet of the gorge. He was handsome, she decided. He had good features, and the wind had brought a color into his lean high cheeks.

"Seeing things," said Mrs. Gurget. "Young."

She heaved a sigh and caught the tiller in against her side with her right elbow that she might pat smooth her hair and settle her bonnet.

She smiled at him.

"Dan!" she called softly. He did not hear her.

She sighed again, and put her hand to her heart. Presently she felt for the bottle under her chair.

Dan had seen the young woman on the shanty boat. Over the water she had seemed very pretty. He had flushed. . . .

"It must be lonesome living on a shanty boat," he said to Mrs. Gurget.

The fat woman smacked her lips against the rim of her tumbler.

"I guess so — but they're queer folk."

"It must be hard on a girl."

"I don't know," said Mrs. Gurget, "perhaps it is."

"It must get lonesome for her, alone with her father."

"Good land!" exclaimed the fat woman. "I guess it would be lonesome."

"Jeepers!" said Dan. "He's too old for her to marry." He looked at her accusingly; but Mrs. Gurget, with considerable delicacy, was taking another drink.

At noon they tied up to the bank. After they had grained the teams, Hector and Solomon and Dan sat on the deck of the Nancy, while Mrs. Gurget cooked dinner. They leaned their backs against the low wall of the cabin to be out of the wind, and the iron ventilators, just over their heads, exhaled the smell of coffee and of frying chops. The clouds had swept full across the sky, and there was a keenness in the wind suggesting snow. Far up the valley a small shower was crossing the hills. A hawk circled dizzily back and forth, his wings on an almost vertical plane when he crossed the force of the wind. Now and then his piercing whistle reached their ears.

All at once Solomon tilted his head.

"What's that?"

They turned their faces to the wind. The road ran along the hillside on their left, and through an opening in the trees almost opposite the Nancy a section of it which had been freshly planked shone white.

In a gust of the wind, from up the valley, they heard clearly a thunder on the wood, and all at once, in the opening, they had a clear view of a tall man riding a grey horse hard.

A spatter of rain struck their faces.

"Jeepers, he was traveling," said Solomon.

Dan had recognized the horse. There was no doubt in his mind that he had seen Calash for the second time.

"Dinner's ready," called Mrs. Gurget as they went into the cabin. "What's the matter with you?"

Solomon told her about the horse they had just seen.

She served them with a platter of pork chops and a round pan of fried potatoes. The smell of her coffee was forewarning of heaven.

"Them chops," she remarked, "is A-1. I guarantee 'em. They raise first-rate hogs to Boonville. Now set down and eat."

She gave them a good example.

"I wonder what that man's hurry was?" said Hector, swishing his coffee round and round in his cup.

"Grey horse?" asked Mrs. Gurget.

"Yeanh."

"Tall man riding him?"

"Pretty tall."

"Well, my gracious! Didn't you read a poster this morning, Sol?"

"By grab! I'll bet it is!"

"What?" asked Hector.

"Gentleman Joe."

"Gol," said Hector.

Hector's Sad Case

There was a pause while Mrs. Gurget brought on an apple pie.

"We ought to pick up Nell by four o'clock," said Solomon.

"Yeanh," said Hector. He turned to Dan. "That's Penelope Berry, my wife."

"We ought to get going pretty quick," said Mrs. Gurget. "She don't like to be kept waiting."

"That's true," said Hector. "She's a remarkable woman, Dan. You'll be pleased to know her. But if you ever get married, make sure she's got no moral sense — either way."

They pulled out shortly afterwards. The wind had died down, but the clouds still hung in the sky.

The locks they came to were spaced farther apart, and at last they reached the lowest three combines, from the top of which they looked down on the village of Northwestern. Before them the hills sloped away and the canal ran again through level farming country.

Three boats were tied up to the Northwestern dock in front of Han Yerry's Saloon, and laughing voices reached out to them from the windows under the long porch. An old man sat with his back against a cleat and fished for sunfish and bass.

"Pushing on?" he asked.

"Yes, sir. We aim to reach Delta to-night."

"That ain't far."

He pulled a paper bag from his pocket, licked his forefinger, thrust it in, and rubbed the snuff that stuck to it back and forth along his gums.

The two teams plodded ahead steadily. The sun came out from under the clouds to the west and shone upon the meadows with brown and yellow tints.

"We ought to pick up Nell Berry pretty soon now. She's staying at a farm behind those trees over there. Some of her kin."

The fat woman pointed out a grove of trees to Dan.

"Poor Hector," she sighed. "If he'd up and lace her once or twice, he'd work some of the cat poison out of her liver. She's a good enough body, too, but he's let her boss him until she's got unhealthy notions.

"Now you wouldn't think it," she went on, smiling, "but Sol, he won't take any nonsense. No, sir. But Hector, he was like one of them Bible men and courted her five years before she said she'd take him. And then on the day of the wedding, when the minister came early, she said there'd be no marrying, but he might as well stay to the wedding dinner that had been cooked anyhow. She told Hector the same thing — he'd ought to 've dragged and kicked her to the marrying state, but she was like an old mare that hadn't been harness-broke, and she balked. He asked when; and she made it one year. They ate the dinner and married the next year without it, her pa saying that a woman hadn't ought to have more than one dinner to a wedding. And on the night of the wedding she told him she'd be damned if she'd sleep with him — and I guess she hasn't yet. But that ain't so bad — it wouldn't be no privilege."

The fat woman tossed her head.

"Hector! Hector!"

The cry was shrilly imperative. A little woman with a grizzled knot of hair pushing her straw-colored bonnet over her eyes, and a big carpet bag in her left hand, ran down to the towpath.

"That you, Nell?" said Hector mildly.

"That me? I should guess it was, waiting here for you with this bag in my hand for all of half an hour. What made you so late?"

"I had 'em all into the Nancy for dinner," explained

Mrs. Gurget. "I made 'em come, and we killed a little time."

"Who gave you leave to boss my husband?" shrilled the little woman. "If Hector was n't so mild-mannered, people would n't impose on him and keep me waiting like this. Now put that boat against the bank, Hector. Think I 'm going to jump eight foot of water?"

Hector swung the Ella in obediently and put out a plank to the towpath. The little woman started up, then stopped and backed off, raising her wizened face to glare at Dan.

"Who 's that man, Hector? I never seen him. I won't sleep on board that boat if that strange man is going to be on it."

"Well, this is just Dan Harrow who 's driving to Rome for me. That 's all."

"I don't care who he is. A good woman can't afford to take risks. Either that strange young man will stay ashore, Hector, or I will. Do you hear?"

"Not you," Hector answered ingratiatingly, and winking at Dan until the tip of his cigar was almost screwed into his eye.

"That 's all right," said the fat woman. "He can come aboard with us. I 'll give him a good piece of pie for supper."

"No better than what he 'd get here if he was n't a strange man, Lucy Gurget!"

"Bigger, though," said Mrs. Gurget with a broad grin.

"Lucy, you shut up!" said Solomon, coming back from his team. "If you two get arguing, we won't never get to Delta House. Now then, Mrs. Berry," he soothed the little woman, "better get on."

Mrs. Berry put one foot on the plank, and then drew it off as if it had scorched her.

"Hector, you throw that nasty-smelling cigar overboard, you hear me?"

Her husband complied with one last wistful and tremendous puff that left the smoke trailing from his nostrils for a good minute.

This point gained, Mrs. Berry trotted up to the gang-rail, where she stopped stock-still.

"Hector, them rats? Are there any left? Either there are rats, and I won't go, or there ain't — which?"

But Solomon, with a triumphant chuckle, had seized the shore end of the plank and with a strong heave yanked it from under her. She pitched forward with an angry scream and disappeared from sight. Then he ran to the blacks and switched their rumps with his hat. They jumped ahead, and Hector swung the boat away from the bank.

"Gid-ap! Gid-ap! Lift a hoof, by Cripus, or I'll stomp on your innards!" yelled Solomon at his mules.

Both boats gathered way.

"Mercy, Sol," gasped Mrs. Gurget after a volcanic eruption of laughter. "You ought n't to have done that. You might have hurt the poor woman. Hector!"

"Eh?"

"Nell ain't hurt, is she?"

"I guess not. She lit on some potatoes that was kind of soft."

Black shadows lowered over the canal. The setting sun had left a twilight of pale green; and the wind had begun to rise again, with a piercing note among the trees. Dan walked on the off side of the team, for there was only an occasional white gleam on the water to mark the edge of the towpath. The outlines of the woodlands blurred, and farm buildings merged with their shadows. Here and there they saw a light across the fields. It was quite dark when they came to the Delta House and tied by for the night.

Rome

There was still a star or two way down in the west when they started ahead in the morning. The dark hulk of the Delta House, in which they had heard men laughing and singing the night before, loomed silent beside the dock. The ghost of the night's fires rose in a thin line from the centre chimney. The thump of the horses' hoofs on wood echoed against the walls. But when they had cleared the dock the boats moved into stillness, except for an occasional whimpering of water round the bows.

The hush of morning was all about them; in it small sounds grew suddenly. As they passed a herd of cows, standing at ease in their night pasture, they became aware of their deep rhythmical breathing; and they heard the thin suck of mud about their feet. They could see united clouds hovering above their horses, and the flat green gleam of their eyes; but the cows stood so quiet there was no voice of bells.

With a loud rustling a muskrat ran out of the grass on the side of the towpath and slipped into the canal so smoothly that they barely saw the ring he made; but the slop of his belly against the water came to their ears like a report.

On the stern of the Nancy Mrs. Gurget sat, a mountain of wraps and shawls, with only her face visible. Now and then she would raise a hand to her lips and blow a cloud of steam over it.

"Early morning travel when it's warm is the best there is," she said to Dan; "but this late in the year it's so cold it gives a body the flesh-creep."

It was cold. Both Dan and Solomon stamped their feet as they walked, and, by the rudder of the Ella-Romeyn, Hector Berry was whipping his arms round his middle and puffing and blowing from the exercise. The lights in the cabin windows, where Mrs. Berry was moving about in comfort, shone behind misted glass.

The low hills to the east began to assume clearer outlines; far behind them a white light was growing; but before the sun rose wraiths of mist began to play upon the water, and gradually merged and thickened, until without warning the boats were traveling in a dense white that glistened like hoarfrost on the decks and turned the worn leather on the teams into handsome harnesses. A rich earth smell of potatoes issued from the pits of the boats and followed them along; and though they could not see, and though sound had dimmed and lost its frosty music, the boaters became aware of the smell of barns when they passed them, and the stinging scent of barnyards.

For an hour and a half they pushed on through the mist, feeling their way blindly, as if they were approaching birth. Dan walked behind the black team, his eyes following eagerly the line of the towpath. The grey shapes of Solomon Tinkle and the mules were barely visible a hundred feet ahead. With each stride into the dim whiteness, progress seemed more futile; and distance became an immeasurable quantity. And yet after a time the wetness on Dan's face felt less chilling, and he became aware of something stirring ahead of him.

At first it sounded no louder than the breathing of the herd they had passed earlier in the morning; then it turned into a steady drone, thin, like the awakening of bees; and it gained volume as they approached it, and the mist wavered now and then, so that at moments he saw Solomon quite clearly, and there were articulate sounds in it, and a long *trahn-ahn-ahn-ahn,* repeated over and over like a melody in music. Suddenly Mrs. Gurget sat forward in her chair.

"Listen. There's the horns. Hear 'em, Dan? Them's horns! They're blowing on the Erie Canal."

All at once they heard a cart rattling along a wooden street, the sound of a bell; and the mist lifted without noticeable motion, and they saw upon their right the outline of a town.

And then they felt the sun warm upon them, and a burst of color came upon the buildings; rising smokes, shot with gold, were pulling away to the westward; windowpanes gleamed reflected light; carts and wagons and the voices of men moving rose about them with increasing vigor; and the two boats came round a bend into a long line of docks and warehouses, reflected in the water of a long basin. And everywhere Dan looked upon the water there were boats, of all colors and of many shapes, with men and women moving on their decks. Boats coming in and hauling out, both east and west, the drawn-out wailing of their horns a sound behind the stirring sound of the town.

Solomon stopped the mules upon the dock, and the Nancy swung in close with the Ella-Romeyn at her rudder, and Mrs. Gurget and Hector tossed tie-ropes ashore and came down the gangs.

The fat woman was laughing.

"By Nahum, Dan! What do you think of Rome?"

III

ERIE CANAL

Port of Rome

Mrs. Gurget walked over to Dan, who was hitching the Ella's tie-rope round a post.

"Dan, Sol and me are going to push on for Syracuse right off. It 'll have to be good-bye for now."

"Yeanh," said Solomon, trotting up behind her. "Hullo, good-bye; that 's the way it is on the Erie."

"We like you a lot, Dan," Mrs. Gurget went on. "Sol and I, we talked about you last night after we went to bed. We 'd like to give you a job, but we figger we could n't pay you as much as you 'd get somewhere's else."

"That 's right, Dan, we 're kind of slow folk."

"No, we ain't. How can you look at me, Sol, and say that?"

"Well, we take our hauling slow. We don't get into no competition for speed. He would n't see so much going along with us."

"No, he would n't. So we 're going to say good-bye. Ain't we, Sol?"

"Yeanh. We 'd better." He took hold of her fat hand. "You give it to him," he said in a low voice.

"Well, good-bye, Dan. Good luck."

He shook hands energetically.

"Keep your eye open for that rapscallion, Calash. You can't tell when you might n't see him and make a penny. It 's always a good idee to keep your eye open, Dan; though it 's handy not to tell everything you see."

He shook hands once more and trotted off to his mules. "Hurry, now, Lucy," he called.

Dan noticed him busy unhitching the tie-ropes, but keeping an eye on them over his shoulder.

"What do you aim to do, Dan?" Mrs. Gurget asked.

"I guess I 'll get a job."

"Well, it ought n't to be hard nowadays."

She hesitated a moment and poked at a wisp of her dyed red hair.

"Me and Sol was thinking maybe you ought to have a little extry in your pocket, Dan. Maybe you won't need it. If you don't, you 'll want to give it to some gal maybe when you 're lonely. Good-bye, Dan. If you get bad off, come and find us. We 're apt to be somewhere anywhere."

She caught him suddenly to her with her right hand, and he had the feeling of being smothered against her breast. She kissed him loudly close to his ear and turned away. He watched her hustle over to the Nancy, settling her bonnet as she went. He put his hand in his coat pocket and drew out some bills she had put there. A couple of men, coming along the dock, jostled against him. When he recovered his balance, the Nancy was under way, Solomon cracking his whip over the mules and keeping his face to the path, and Mrs. Gurget steering on the stern. He felt a sudden weakness in his legs, and his eyes blurred. Then a boat cut in behind the Nancy and he had one view of Mrs. Gurget waving a pudgy arm before she disappeared up the canal to the west.

Dan counted the money in his hand—five dollars and twenty-five cents; it was a handsome gift.

As he returned it to his pocket, someone took hold of his other arm.

"I 'm real sorry," Hector Berry was saying. "Real sorry. This here 's my regular driver. Mr. George Williams, meet Dan Harrow. A man can't have but one driver to his boat, can he — if he ain't working for one of the line companies?"

"That's right," said Dan in an embarrassed voice. "A man can't."

He wondered what the fuss was about.

"Well," said Hector, "here's your pay."

He took a dollar out of his pigskin wallet. Dan mechanically pocketed it.

"Well, good-bye," said Hector, making a motion to go.

"Luck," grunted Mr. George Williams. "Pleased to meet yer any time." And he went aboard the Ella.

Immediately Hector took Dan by the arm again and began to speak hurriedly in an undertone.

"I'd keep you with me, Dan. Honest to hunkus I would, I like you, for a fact, and he's no good" — he pointed a thumb over his shoulder in the direction of Mr. George Williams. "Men that drinks like him is no good, Dan, and mind I said so. Oh, I don't mean a swaller on a cold day is going to rumple your innards for the rest of your life — not me. But when a man drinks so long the likker commences running over at his eyes, there ain't no chance left for connection of thought. By dang, I'd fire him tomorrow."

He raised his fist.

"By dang, I would, by holy dang. When I say a thing, by dang, I mean it. But he's Nell's nephey, and she's took a notion against you. Regular snarl she gets into when I say, 'I guess I'll hire Dan Harrow — he's good with horses.' I mean what I say, 'Good with horses.' You're a good boy, Dan; I like you."

He wrung Dan's hand.

"Your pa done me a turn once. Any time you need anything you come and see me."

"Hec-tor! Hec-tor!"

"Coming!" bawled Hector. "Luck to you, Dan."

He turned round and went hurriedly aboard. Dan saw Penelope Berry's wizened face thrust from the cabin door under a mammoth pink night bonnet, her grey hair full of skewers over her forehead, and curl-papers dangling to her shoulders. He grunted.

"The danged old coot."

But his eyes watched her until the turning of the boat cut off his view of the door, and then he stared after Hector's plump, spraddle-legged figure on the poop of the Ella-Romeyn, until the glare of the sun on the canal brought the water to his eyes. At least they were familiar. . . .

It was all strange to him. The boats, more than he could count, coming in and going out, many passing through without a stop, each with a man steering and a man walking behind the towing team, moving at a slow pace, but giving an impression of an intense, suppressed desire for speed. The line boats, recognizable for the hard faces of their captains, largely Irishers, brought in gangs when the great work of the canal was coming to a close; they had an air about them of men aware of physical well-being. Boats bearing emigrants out to the West, Germans, an old man on one with a mug in his hand and a long china pipe to his mouth and a nightcap on his head, stiffly promenading the deck in his stocking feet; and tow-haired children on another. A New Englander going by, driving a boat, a cold-faced bearded man who spoke in a nasal tight voice ordinary words to his horses more impressive than oaths; a boy steering, his young face grimly serious. Two boats of tall, light-haired folk, — "Hunkers" said a man at Dan's back, and his companion answered, "Damn fool Swedes," — but they had a light in their blue eyes.

Boats of all colors — greys, greens, blues, reds, muddy magentas, and many white, floating on their reflections, many bearing strange folk, entering a strange country, the look of whom made Dan uneasy, so that he found comfort in the figures of the boaters, who rolled their *r's* in swearing, and who walked as if they knew what their hands were doing. They wore no uniform to tell them by; they were careless in their dress, but their clothes suited them individually—small high felt hats, and broad-brimmed hats with flat crowns, and caps with ear flaps turned up; and some wore coats, and some suits of homespun, and some heavy woolen shirts of dark blue or brown; and one old captain went by wearing a peajacket, and he had a conch at his lips, and his face was red with blowing, and the sound of it swallowed the sounds of the people round him so that he could not hear their laughter, but stood with his pegleg braced in an augur hole; and perhaps he felt the ocean.

The words of the old peddler Turnesa, on his wagon, occurred to Dan: "The bowels of the nation . . . the whole shebang of life." He could see it in the hurry and a certain breathlessness above the easy noise; he could smell it in the boats coming from the West, the raw foods, the suffocating odor of grain, the scent of meat, of pork, the homely smell of potatoes, to be digested in the East and produce growth. It mystified him, though he seemed to understand it, and it stirred a great affection in him for living, for the people round him, and the clean light of the sun.

His hand went to his face and lingered there. A missionary, who had been observing him for several moments, came up behind him and laid a kindly hand upon his shoulder. "What is it, my boy?" he asked, perceiving an opportunity to assist in the regeneration of a soul. "It's a hard life you've had to live, but there's help for every man here." He opened a small bag he carried in his left hand and selected a tract, which he held out to Dan. It was titled, *Esau; or the Ruinous Bargain*.

Dan stared at him vacantly, and the missioner smiled reassuringly.

"Come with me," he said. "Perhaps I can help you."

He was dressed in black clothes, and wore a rather soiled white tie.

"Thanks," Dan mumbled.

The missioner's long face brightened.

"You see the way ahead of you," he said encouragingly. "You're puzzled now; but I'll help you find it if you'll come with me."

Dan's face cleared, as if he understood.

"Yeanh," he said. "That's right. I was wondering where there was a barber."

Perhaps it had been a bad morning for the missioner, or perhaps the work was new to him, for he sighed and told Dan he did n't know and went on down the dock.

Dan picked up his bag and faced the row of warehouses. A couple of teams pulling heavy lumber wagons thumped past him.

"Looking for something?"

A middle-aged man, well dressed in a black coat and black satin waistcoat, grey trousers, and a pipe hat, regarded Dan out of cool grey eyes. He had lean, fine features, a thin mouth sufficiently curving not to be cruel, and his head was set handsomely on his neck. He was of a type new to Dan's experience; there was the clever fit of his clothes, for one thing.

"Yeanh," said Dan. "I was looking for a barber."

"Well, you go up that right-hand street, two blocks, and turn left down the second street, about five houses down. What's your name, if I may ask?"

"Dan'l Harrow."

"Was your father Henry Harrow? He was? I thought I recognized something in your face. I knew him well. Where's he been all these years?"

"Tug Hill way. He's dead."

"I 'm sorry. I knew him well. So did all the Erie folks. His name and his boat stood out in the great days of packet traveling. What are you doing in Rome?"

"I aim to get a job," said Dan.

"Located yet?"

"No. I aim to look around some."

"It 's a good idea to find out what you want. If you 'd like to, I can offer you a job. Come round next week. Butterfield's warehouse. My name 's John Butterfield. I 'd like to help you any way I can. Your father was a fine man."

He shook hands cordially and went on his way, walking sturdily erect.

M. Pantoulenzo, Barber

Following Mr. Butterfield's directions, after three minutes' walking Dan found himself in a street of wooden houses, some with fancy work on the porches, but for the most part severely plain and painted in quiet colors. Over a second-story window of one of these his wandering eye fell upon a sign bearing the name M. PANTOULENZO, ornately scrolled, with the explanatory legend underneath: —

HAIR TRIMMED. EASY SHAVE.
BLOOD LET.
Teeth drawn at Regular Prices.

A door opening on a pitch-dark flight of stairs advertised M. Pantoulenzo again with a card and the words, "One flight up."

Dan entered and, after a moment's groping, found himself on a small landing with a door on the left-hand side. A small pane of glass was let into one of the panels, affording a view of the shop.

Directly before the window stood a barber chair, gorgeous in crimson plush, and at the moment harboring a tall, very thin man with an abstracted expression on his face. He was sitting up straight, with his hands on his knees, his head bent painfully to one side in the manner of the conscientious and anxiously obliging customer. The towel in which he was enveloped had evidently been manufactured by the barber himself, for it reached just below the tall man's waistcoat and formed a chute down which the shorn hair slid to his trousers. Of the barber himself Dan could see no more than the half of a red face, a glancing black eye, and a pair of thin hands stretching spasmodically for the hair above them.

The attitudes of both men suggested so forcibly a precarious equilibrium of mind and body that Dan fingered the latch and opened the door as quietly as he could.

"Goo' morning," said the barber. "Set down, mister. I 'm through in half a mo'."

The tall man did not look up.

The little barber was parting his customer's hair. Then he whipped away the towel, scattering the loose hair broadcast. The tall man leisurely climbed out of the chair and pulled out a bill fold.

"Here you be, Francey."

The barber nodded his head and put the bill in his pocket. The tall man picked a broad-brimmed hat from a peg and said, "Morning," and went out of the room with an easy swagger of his shoulders.

"Next!" cried the barber.

Dan looked round.

"You, mister; you 're next, I reckon."

Dan took his seat in the chair, and the barber deftly slipped the towel over him and pinned it round his neck.

"What 'll you have?"

"Shave."

The sunlight shining through the windows and lighting on his neck made him drowsy, his eyes lazily surveying the varnished board walls, a colored lithograph of the battle of Oriskany their only decoration, the white shelf with its rows of lotions, its two razors and their strops, the worn old mug with a cap of lather gradually settling back into its rimy interior, the kettle of hot water purring on the little corner stove, and all about his feet the shorn hair of former customers lying in heaps like little cords of wood.

The barber set about whipping up a lather. He was a small man, but in spite of his outlandish name there was nothing particularly foreign-looking about him. His pointed face held an expression of keenness, and there was a precocious cock to his head. As he worked, he kept popping questions at Dan.

"Getting warmer?"

"Yeanh."

"I thought maybe it would. We don't get much real cold here till November."

He applied a great deal of lather and then began to strop his razor. He did it with a flourish.

"Stranger?" asked the barber.

"Yeanh."

The barber worked for an instant in silence.

"Well," he said, "you've come to a good place to find work. Rome, New York, is due to become one of the great metropolises." He turned up the left side of Dan's face. "And look where it stands. On the confluence of two canals. Oneida County has just commenced to grow. Look at the timber. Finest white pine in the state. Cribs of timber coming down every spring faster than the locks'll take them. It's right on the trade route to the West. The highroad, the railroad, and the canal right among the streets. You looking for a job on the canal?"

"That's right."

"Well, I wished I'd knowed that. The feller that was in here was looking for a driver. Operates a line boat on the Troy to Michigan Six Day Line."

Dan took an interest. "What's his name?"

"Julius W. Wilson. A celebrated character, now a Roman. Used to belong to Flame and Furnas, the famous knife-throwing team of the American Museum in New York City. Corner of Ann Street and Broadway. If you ever go there, don't miss it. It's one of the wonders of this continent, and if there are any others most likely they're all in it. Every afternoon from four to four-thirty Flame and Furnas did their show. (Flame was Wilson's bill name.) Furnas held the knives and did the talking and Wilson done the throwing. It was a great sight — a cold chill for a thousand people every ten seconds. They had a nine-year-old boy for a target."

"You know a lot about him."

"Why wouldn't I? I'm his regular barber. Most any day he'll tell me all about it; tell me just how close he'd come. Ankle, knee, hip, waist, shoulder (armhole by particular request), neck. Couldn't beat him. It ain't strange, it's the artist temperament."

Dan grunted.

"True as preaching. I've shaved a whole minstrel show; they're all the same.

"Yes, sir," the barber went on, "if you want a job, you go round to Hennessy's Saloon — just round the corner — when you're shaved and ask for Wilson. Probably he'll take you on. He's hauling to Albany."

"I guess I will."

M. Pantoulenzo flourished his razor under Dan's nose and shaved the lip.

"M. Pantoulenzo — quite a name, eh?"

"Yeanh," said Dan.

"A good trade name's a great thing in business. Now, looking at that name, you'd never guess I was born in London, would you?"

"No."

"That's why I picked on it. Real name is Smiggs. That might go in England. Smiggs, barber. But it wouldn't go an inch in this land. Americans are that way. They've got extravagant notions of business and work which makes 'em serious in their notions of pleasure or getting their hair cut, or going to the dentist. My Crikey, 'ow these people do shine to a dentist! If I wasn't a barber, I'd go in for teeth altogether. You can tear out a whole jawful of teeth with them and set up false ones and they'll call it progress."

He reached for a damp towel with which to remove the edges of lather left from the shave, and then, grunting, swung the chair into an upright position.

Dan paid him and made his way slowly down the stairs.

In Hennessy's Saloon

The sun had come out warm, and the air was so sparkling and clear that he stepped out sturdily. Women were going by on their way to market, their baskets on their arms. A carriage crossed the end of the street, and a fast trotter in front of a varnished surrey caught Dan's eye.

Overhead in the cloudless sky he could see a great flock of crows flapping over the town, so high above him that their cawing sounded thin.

There could be no mistaking Hennessy's Saloon; it was so obviously one. Its flashy green doors hooked open, it stood well out toward the roadway; and its two broad glass windows gave it an appearance of extreme open-handedness and sincerity.

Inside the bar, the keep was reading that week's copy of the *Roman Citizen*. There was no one else in the room. He looked up at Dan's entrance, cocking one eye over the edge of the paper.

"What's yours?"

"Is Mr. Wilson here?"

"Come in five minutes ago. He's out back talking to Hennessy. You can see him when he comes out. What's yours?"

"I don't know," said Dan. "I hadn't thought."

"You'll want a bit of a swallow," said the keep. "Julius W. and old Hennessy talk quite a while once they get going. Have a blackstrap?"

"Surely."

The keep mixed a glassful, drawing first the molasses and then the rum directly from the kegs. There was a great row of them behind the bar, which ran the whole length of the room, and over them, on shelves, rows of bottles obliquely picked out the sunny doorway. The keep covered the glass with another and shook the mixture. His hands worked with great rapidity, and when he set the glass before Dan there was a thin cap of brown foam upon it.

"Four cents."

Dan slapped down the pennies and started to sip the heavy sweet drink. It was cool in the barroom, and the shadow was grateful to his eyes after the sunlight in the street. Gradually he became drowsy; the two preceding days had been hard ones. The keep grinned to see him nod and almost lose his hold on the glass.

"Kind of sleepy, eh? Well, Wilson won't be out for an

hour, most likely, and if you want to lie down in the back
room I 'll call you when he comes out."

He pointed his thumb to a door at the back of the bar.
Dan thanked him and picked up his bag.

After he had closed the door behind him, it took Dan a
minute to accustom his eyes to the darkness. The one window
in the room was boarded over, but enough light crept through
the cracks to show him four stout posts, two feet or more in
diameter, rising from floor to ceiling. About each post a circular platform had been constructed with a mattress to fit,
so that as many as twelve men could sleep about a single
upright, their feet to the post and their bodies radiating out-
ward like the spokes of an immense wheel.

Dan stretched himself out with his hands folded behind his
head. He must have dozed for a minute, for he suddenly
became conscious of three voices speaking beyond the door
to the bar; and that strange sense which bridges the gap between sleeping and waking informed him that they had been
speaking for some time. In an instant he had recognized the
bartender's voice; and it occurred to him that he had heard
both of the other voices. And then he caught the names, and
placed them — Spinning, the sheriff of Rome, and Mr.
Henderson, who called himself a horse dealer. Spinning was
talking in his loud voice.

". . . danged near cornered him up by Potato Hill. He 'd
got himself put up at the Morris place. Old man Morris
did n't have no idea about who he was. But he described the
horse to me. He can't see very well, and the feller wore his
hat in the house, a wide-brimmed one, so it was hard to see
his face. Calash had only stayed there overnight. But the
horse sounds like the one you lost. Yes, sir, I 've no doubt
it 's the same. Give us a little more time, Mr. Henderson, and
we 'll have him back for you."

"I don't doubt it." Henderson's voice was harder to follow. "When did he come down this way?"

"That afternoon. We 're not such fools. We had a couple
of people on the lookout. And I know reliable he 's headed
for Syracuse. Nothing more I can do for the moment. I 'm

going to have some rest. We 'll get him, though, won't we, Luke? You know me."

"Sure," said the bartender. "Question of time. You 'll have him, though."

"They 're sending a Department of Justice man up here," the sheriff growled. "But do you think they 'd tell me his name? No, they won't. I 'm to keep on on my own line and help him if he comes to me. Like as not when we 've got Calash he 'll join in on the reward."

"It 's hard," said Mr. Henderson.

"Sure," said the bartender sympathetically.

The voices of the sheriff and Henderson dimmed, as if they had moved to another part of the room. Then Dan heard a new voice, a woman's this time, asking for Mr. Klore.

"Said he 'd be back in half an hour," replied the barkeep.

The young woman's voice replied that she would wait. Quick, light steps came through the half door in the bar to the door of the circular-bed chamber. Dan heard a whisper and the bartender's voice huskily replying, "Just a young lad."

The door opened and Dan sat up and put his feet on the floor.

The young woman was tall and strapping, so much he could see while she paused against the light of the barroom. She wore a red dress and a red hat, from under which a few wisps of light brown hair escaped as though protesting against an unaccustomed confinement. She presented a rather blowsy-looking figure, unaccountably attractive in its blowsiness, with something fresh about it.

When she made out Dan's position, the young woman closed the door behind her and came forward in the unnatural darkness.

"I hope you 'll pardon me disturbing you," she said in a strong, clear voice.

Dan felt stuffy and uncomfortable, and wished she had not closed the door.

"You see," she went on, sitting on the circular bed beside

him, "I 've got to wait for my boater, and I don't like to wait in the bar; and Luke said you was a quiet-looking man, so I come in here."

"I don't mind," said Dan awkwardly. "My name 's Dan'l Harrow."

"Pleased to meet you. I 'm Molly Larkins."

"Pleased, mam."

A knothole in the boards over the window sent a finger of light against her cheek, so that her profile was outlined to Dan in warm sunlight. She had a wide mouth, with full, decisive lips pressed firmly together, and an expressive chin, well rounded. She had compelling hands, long-fingered, which squeezed the handle of a long bag she held on her knees until they took on the shape of a capable pair of fists. Altogether, she did not belong in the musty darkness of the saloon; even there it seemed the daylight had stolen in to mark her. She should have been handling a rudder sweep instead of her little bag, or swinging a scythe.

"It 's a weary place to wait in," she remarked.

"Yeanh," said Dan, trying to guess her age. He had instantly taken a liking to her, for her straightforward manner had put him at ease.

"Be you a-working on the canal, Mr. Harrow?"

It was the first time anyone had put "mister" in front of his name, and he involuntarily checked the "mam" on his tongue.

"No," he replied. "I 'm waiting for Mr. Wilson, to get a job with."

She nodded.

"Yes. I know him. Julius W. Hauling for the Troy–Michigan Six Day."

"He 's hauling down to Albany," said Dan. "I 'd like to get a job with him."

"Well, I would n't want to go there."

"Why not?"

"I don't know. I don't like it."

"You been on the canal long?" Dan asked, after a short silence.

She turned her head toward him, and as the light traveled over her eyes Dan saw that they were deep blue.

"Gracious, yes! I was born on a boat. Dad was a captain for the Old Utica Long and Short Haul Line. After I was thirteen I done the cooking for him. He died when I was fifteen and since then I 've been working mostly on the canal. I ain't got no recollection of Ma. Once a missioner society got a-hold of me and I took a job working in the ladies' ward of the State Asylum. It 's pretty slow work for me and I quit on them. I guess Dad left a bit of Hell in me. He was a big man and never licked. I remember when he fought the Buffalo Bully in Rochester Arcade and licked him after one hour. There was so many people watching I could n't see till a man let me stand on his shoulders. Pa give me a hiding afterwards for yelling when he got knocked down. He said it was n't right for a lady."

She glanced down at her hands.

"I learned to take care of myself pretty good. So I get along. If I don't like the man I hire out with I just quit him and get myself another job through Lucy Cashdollar's agency."

"Yeanh?"

"Yeanh, hers is best. Bentley's Bar. In Utica. Guess I 'll spend a time with her next week."

"Sick of your job?" asked Dan, suddenly.

"Kind of. He 's a sort of bully. I don't have much rest from him. He 's hard to handle. But he 's an easy spender and he 's got good innards for fighting," she added, a note of pride in her voice.

"I seen him in Boonville, if it 's Jotham Klore."

"Yeanh. Did you come down ahead of us?"

"Yeanh. I used to live up above Boonville."

"Is that right?"

Dan began trying to guess her age again; the subject attracted him singularly. Back in Tug Hill country he was considered ahead of his years in figuring a horse's age, and A-1 in the cow line. Yes, he could judge a cow into the right year nine times out of ten. But this was something else, try-

ing to figure a girl's age; there was less to go by; you could
not use your hands, for one thing.

He could not see much of her except her outline in that
dark room; coloring could not help him there. But she had
walked with a straight back; there was no sag in her. And
she had good solid curves in her figure, and as she sat by him
her tight dress showed no softness. He could not see her feet,
either, and that was a point he always liked to go by. He put
a lot of stock in feet. But she walked like a filly, plenty of
lift, and her weight well under her, no forward splurge at the
knees. She was tight in front; she looked sound. He called
her twenty-two.

"Well," said Molly Larkins suddenly, "now you're done,
what do you make of me?"

"Fair, pretty fair," Dan said, still in his professional mood,
"a good buy if the price was right."

She burst out laughing, tilting her head and looking out
at him from half-closed eyes. She had a good whole-souled
laugh, pitched low, with no hoarseness.

"Well," she said, "the price is twelve dollars a month, in
case you want to know."

"Fair enough," Dan said. "If I ever get a boat I'll remember that."

She gave him a quick, square glance; and then smiled
slowly.

"You haven't looked at my teeth, you know. How old did
you make me out?"

"Nineteen," he replied, giving her laugh the benefit of one
less year, and her vanity, in a moment of inspiration, the
benefit of two.

"Eighteen," she said.

"Jeepers!" he said, ruefully. "I need practice in your line."

Molly laughed again.

"Now I'll guess yours."

"Yeanh?"

"You're nineteen. What's more, you're new on a canal."

He gazed at her admiringly.

"You're pretty good, ain't you?"

"It's a thing you get to learn, in my trade. It's a part of the job."

They sat together without speaking for a while, listening to the voices beyond the door, and to the angry buzz of a bluebottle fly against the windowpanes.

"Are you planning to keep on driving?" she asked Dan.

"Yeanh. For a while, I reckon. I'd like to have my own boat."

"Who would you haul for?"

"I guess you can pick up hauling."

"Probably could," said Molly; "but still, you ain't any idea how many people is working on the Erie. Last year they figgered there was twenty-five thousand — men and women and driver boys working on the main ditch."

"Jeepers!" breathed Dan.

"It probably seems a queer place," Molly said, "until you get used to it. People live by different notions there. They're law-abiding by state law; but they've got their own ideas on how to live. The missioners call 'em bad, but I guess a moral is a kind of figure for personal ciphering. Canawlers would say the missioner was unhealthy; he's letting his mind get rid of what his body should get rid of according to nature."

"Who told you that?" Dan asked.

"Friend of mine. An old feller. He used to be a minister himself, and he goes in for ministering now to make money to live with when he needs it."

More people had entered the barroom. The voices of Mr. Henderson and the sheriff were no longer distinguishable. Then a loud hoarse voice sounded close to the panel; the man was addressing the bartender. "Seen my cook, Luke?" "Inside," said the keep. And a hand fell on the door handle. Molly Larkins suddenly stood up. "He's feeling hostile," she said to Dan in a low voice. "Don't mind his talk."

The door swung open and banged shut behind Jotham Klore. For an instant he stood with his back to it, his pale eyes peering into the gloom of the room.

"Come along, Moll," he said, "we ain't any time to lose."

He stopped speaking and came forward a step or two, and saw Dan.

"Say! How long 've you been here, Moll?"

"You kept me waiting a good half hour, Jotham," she said, coolly. "So you need n't talk nasty."

"I 'll talk as I damn please. He 'd better pick up his bag and get out of here. If he wants to argue, I 'm a pretty good hand myself. I won't have no man monkeying with my cook."

"It 's none of your business, anyway."

"What do you think I 'm paying you for?"

"I 'm no slave. I 'll do as I please. I don't have to look hard to get a job."

"You shut up!"

He came over and grabbed Dan by the collar of his shirt.

"Are you going to get out?"

Dan's right hand shot up and his arm straightened; he heard a sudden crack, and felt a shoot of pain run into his hand and wrist. Klore's knees sagged, and his hand fell away from Dan's collar. Molly gave a low cry, deep-toned, with a note of pleasure.

"Quick! Hit him again."

But Dan stood back upon his heels; he had n't thought of hitting him at all; he was completely surprised.

"Quick!" cried Molly, as Klore sucked in his breath whistlingly, his teeth showing white in his black beard.

"Oh, shucks!" she said, and turned away, as if to avoid an unpleasant sight.

"All right," growled Klore. "Try and do it again."

All at once, Dan remembered the grin on the face of the boater in the Lansing Kill, and he felt weak. He wanted to say he would go, but he could n't force the words past his teeth; and he knew anyway that it would n't have done any good. Then he heard an exclamation from Molly.

At the same instant he became aware of a fourth person in the room, he heard a thud, and Jotham Klore's hands leaped past his face and he fell forward limp into Dan's arms.

"Look at the door, both of you."

A man, holding a revolver in his right hand, was standing with his back to the faint stripe of light that came through the window boarding; but a menacing coldness in his tone made Dan fix his gaze on the door. Out of the corner of his eye, he could see that the girl stared as rigidly as he.

"He was set to butter and fry you, young man," said the stranger, almost friendly; then his voice harshened.

"Who was in the bar?" he asked Molly.

"The sheriff," she said, "and Luke and another man. I think his name was Henderson."

"Him!" The man grunted.

"Listen," he said to Dan. "I've just done you a turn; now you can do me one. Go out and get that man Henderson out of the bar for a minute. I've got to get out of here and he's watching out the back window."

"What 'll I tell him?"

"Figure it out for yourself. Only don't start anything funny. I'm watching through the back door of this room; I'll be able to see clean into the bar."

"I'll tell him I seen you coming down the Lansing Kill."

"How do you know that?"

"I can make a guess who you are."

"Don't try. I'm getting out of this room. How about you, young woman? Will you keep shut five minutes?"

"Surely," Molly said. "I'll keep a conversation going with Jotham."

"All right."

They heard him leaving the room, and a gentle draft told them that he had opened the back door. They dragged Klore to one side, out of sight of the door.

"He must've been in here all the while," said Molly in a low voice.

"I guess that's right."

"Are you going to do what he said?"

"I guess so," said Dan. "I guess it's the right thing to do this time."

"If you raised a holler now you'd have enough to buy your boat with, and more besides."

"Yeanh," said Dan, "maybe I would."

"He could n't stop you now."

"I guess he ought to have a chance."

"All right. If you ain't going to say nothing, I won't. You 'd better be going out. Good-bye, Mr. Harrow."

She held out her hand. When he took it he found it hard and warm, filling his palm.

"Pleased to have met you," he said awkwardly, and he went into the bar, closing the door behind him.

Several men stood at the bar, and over in a corner the sheriff was sitting with the horse dealer, Henderson. Dan walked over to them. Both looked up.

"Cripus!" exclaimed the fat man. "It 's the lad I saw in Boonville."

"Yeanh," said Dan. "I wanted to tell you something about your horse, Mr. Henderson."

Henderson drew his cigar from his lips and they followed it out, pursing themselves in their silent whistle. He glanced round him quickly.

"Say!" he exclaimed. "We might as well step outside."

"Yeanh," said the sheriff.

The three of them went out into the street.

"What is it, young man?"

"I seen a horse just like yourn coming down through the Lansing Kill yesterday noon."

"Who was you with?"

"Solomon Tinkle and Hector Berry."

Sheriff Spinning nodded his head. "That 's right. I seen you at the Five Combines."

"We knew he 'd come down. You did n't get a good sight of him?" asked Henderson.

"No," said Dan. "He was quite a ways off."

"Shucks. That ain't no news. I can't do nothing till I know what he looks like," the sheriff complained. "He might be any long-legged feller I had n't seen before. Why, he could be right here in Hennessy's for all I 'd know."

"Thanks, anyhow," Henderson said to Dan. "Let me know, or Spinning here, if you see him again."

"All right," said Dan.

He walked back into the saloon with them. As he entered, he saw Julius Wilson approaching him.

"That 's the young man," said the bartender.

"What do you want?" asked Wilson.

"I heard you was looking for a driver."

"I am. What 's your name?"

"Dan Harrow."

"Done any driving?"

"Some."

"Who with?"

"Mr. Hector Berry."

"That seedless raisin?"

"Yeanh," said Dan, with a grin.

"Well, I 'll give eleven a month driver's wages. But I 'll only hire you in to Albany. I 'll give you one-fifty for the trip."

"It 's right by me."

"Come along with me," said Mr. Wilson.

The Line Boat, Xerxes

Julius W. Wilson walked with a long stride.

"You 're lucky to get a job with me here," he remarked to Dan. "Line boats generally go straight through, and the Michigan Six Day don't hire a captain that 's late. But this trip Wendell, on the western end, shoved a short-haul job on to me, to Rome, so I had to stop over."

He nodded to a boater — and then, with a fine gesture, swept off his wide felt hat to a sharp-faced woman with an outthrust jaw who came striding along the street toward them.

"How d' ye do, Mrs. Quackenbush," he said politely. "How are you this handsome day?"

She swung round at him, and as her skirt lifted a trifle

from the swirl Dan noticed that she wore a man's cowhide boots.

"Hullo, Julius, how be you?"

"You're looking good," observed Mr. Wilson.

"Good yourself! Don't try none of your dandiness on me!"

"Here's a young man come down from Boonville with your sister, Nell Berry," said Mr. Wilson, indicating Dan with a wave of his hand.

"Pleased to meet you. My name's Quackenbush."

She grasped Dan's hand, and her palm felt calloused against his.

"Dan Harrow," he said.

"How is the old hen?" she asked good-humoredly.

"Good."

"She always is. The first time she's sick she'll be underground. Well, I've got to get going. Please to've seen you boys."

"There's a character," observed Mr. Wilson, when she was out of hearing. "You don't know it, Harrow, but you've shook hands with the woman that's pumped the canal dry three times."

Dan stared.

"Oh, I ain't guffing you none. You can ask any boater. She married old Idwall Quackenbush two days afore he died. I reckon she shocked the lights clean out of him. And when she'd seen him buried she took up his boat and she's run it ever since. The danged crate leaks so she's got to keep pumping it; you're apt to see it tied up anywhere with the water tossing out in squirts. Ben Rae, he's my steersman, he figgered one night she'd pumped enough water to fill the Erie three times over."

He laughed.

"It don't faze her. And she makes money. She's raising quite a family, too. Got three boys."

They came down to the docks and walked west along them until they came to a lumber yard.

"There's the old Xerxes," said Mr. Wilson. He pointed out a yellow boat, trimmed green, tied up a little way ahead.

"We're waiting here for some matched boarding to take down to the Oriskany Mills. Then we pick up a load in Utica from the Ashery for Little Falls — a shipment for West-feldt's soap. It's dirty to handle, but we'll have to clean on the way down to Albany. I'm running down empty from Little Falls."

Just as they came abreast of the boat, an immense old Jew thrust his head from the cabin door, came up the steps, and stood beside the rudder sweep, where he stretched his arms over his head and yawned.

"Hello, Ben," said Mr. Wilson. "Got that boarding on yet?"

The Jew turned toward them slowly. He had a great white beard, like the beard of Moses, and when he spoke the end of it jumped away from him in little jerks.

"No," he said. "There was a big line waiting at the yard. We're just due now; we'll get loaded by noon."

Wilson grunted.

"Time enough, I guess. We can get in to Utica by to-morrow evening."

"Sure, that's right. Why n't you go see the missis and meet up with us at 'Riskany? It won't cost you more 'n a dollar."

"I might, at that. Say, Ben, here's a lad I took on as driver as far as Albany. Name's Dan'l Harrow. Ben Rae."

The Jew wrinkled his long nose and grinned.

"It's a pleasure. Come aboard."

"Ben's in charge," Wilson said. "Well, I guess I'll shove along. It ain't often I get a chance to see Aurelia for a night during summer. She won't travel the canal," he explained to Dan, "and she's quite right. It's degrading for a delicate woman. She used to be the loveliest singer on the New York stage. An artist of the first water. Lovely still, but melancholy."

"No blame to her," said Rae, "living by herself so much."

Mr. Wilson waved an arm and walked rapidly away down the dock.

"Come on down," the Jew said to Dan. "William's cooking dinner."

He led the way into the cabin.

The Xerxes had been built to carry twenty passengers as well as the crew. The cabin took up most of the stern half of the boat; freight space lay forward. There was no stable for the horses, as the line companies had their own service stables the whole length of the canal. They handled only the rush freight, and, in spite of the growing power of the railroads, they did big business in carrying emigrants westward.

Under the windows a row of iron-frame bunks, on which canvas was stretched, were hinged against the walls. To the right of the steps a curtain marked the entrance to the crew's bunks, which were built into a cuddy, five feet high, directly under the steersman's deck. In the corner to the left of the steps stood a good-sized stove, at which crew and passengers could take turns.

When Dan and Benjamin Rae entered, a man was peering into the oven.

"Here's a lad Julius W. got for driver as far as Albany," said Rae.

The man turned a pair of mild brown eyes toward them and pushed his hand rapidly the wrong way through his hair.

"Hullo," he said.

He was middle-aged and had a lean, thoughtful face.

"Biscuits coming good?" asked Rae.

"Fair," said the man.

"This lad's Dan Harrow," said the Jew. "Meet William Wampy."

"Hullo," said Wampy again.

He turned back to the stove. A coffeepot spouted fragrant steam, and potatoes and bacon, frying together, sizzled when he turned them with a broad knife.

"Put your bag back there," said the Jew, pointing to the sleeping cuddy. "I'll set out the dishes."

They ate leisurely, and the food was good.

"William's studying to be a cook," Rae said to Dan, as he poured syrup over his biscuits. "He's a pretty slick hand, I'd say."

Wampy flushed with pleasure.

"He's a great hand for a fiddle," said Rae. "He sleeps hearty. And he can work when we make him. But mostly he cooks and eats what he cooks."

Wampy raised his dark eyes to Dan's.

"Eating's fun," he said.

Men stamped on deck. Presently they heard them loading the boarding into the pit forward. Rae shoved back his chair and sighed.

"Reckon I'd better go and get a team."

He went out.

Dan started to follow him.

"No need of you going out," said William Wampy. "We're paid to run this boat, not to fill it full of lumber."

He helped himself to more biscuits.

"It ain't a bad job, if you use your privileges," he observed.

Dan sat down again and watched him eat. He ate long and silently. Once in a while he smacked his lips.

"I married once," said Wampy. "For four years I didn't have no good food.

"Well," he added, after a while, "Benjy'll be coming back pretty quick. We'll have to clear up. Will you wipe or will you wash?"

"I don't care," said Dan.

"I'll dry then. We'll let the cups dreen."

When they had finished, Dan went on deck. The last boards were being handed up on to the boat. The Jew was coming along the dock behind a pair of mules. A man, who had been overseeing the lading, went up to him.

"Fifteen thousand," he said. "You'll sign for Wilson."

"Surely," said the Jew.

He signed the bill, and the men who had been loading got off the boat.

"You drive," he called to Dan.

Dan hooked the evener to the towline and threw the tie-ropes on deck. The mules took up the slack and heaved; the Xerxes groaned against the dock, inched slowly out, and they started down the Erie. As they passed other boats tied up, a man on deck would catch the towrope and pass it across the boat. In fifteen minutes they had cleared the basin, and the mules came out upon the towpath. A hundred yards ahead three other boats crept in the same direction.

"No point hurrying," said the Jew; so Dan allowed the mules to take their own pace, until a little after four o'clock they entered the village of Oriskany and tied up beside the woolen mills.

In the gathering dusk of the cabin William Wampy was fondling notes from his fiddle, making a melody from "The Wind that Shakes the Barley."

"He's got kind of a pretty softness on the strings," said the Jew.

Dan rested his forehead on his arms and closed his eyes. The whirr of the mill machinery and the clack of the looms dimmed as the notes of the fiddle felt their way toward a tune. Boats that passed seemed a long way off. Dan repeated Molly Larkins's name to himself and all at once saw her again, sitting beside him in her red dress in the darkness in Hennessy's Saloon, while the light from the knothole picked out bits of color here and there. Only now they left the saloon together and went down to the docks. . . .

The Jew glanced down at him and smiled in his white beard. "Tired," he said to himself. He pulled a pipe out of his pocket and filled it and put it in his mouth and leaned back against the cabin. But he forgot to light it. And after a while his head bent forward toward his up-drawn knees.

A Sermon by Request

Sunday-morning breakfast they ate at a comfortable late hour. A little after ten o'clock, Julius Wilson appeared beside the boat. He had been given a lift by Mr. Butterfield, who was driving down to Utica.

"Dandiest pair of trotters I've ever sat back of," he said.
He came aboard briskly.

"We'd better start off now; you get the mules out, Dan, but William'll do the first stretch of driving."

Traffic was lighter than it had been on the preceding day. Almost all the boats they met were company boats.

They drifted along placidly, the mules and William Wampy taking a leisurely pace on the towpath. Dan drowsed on the cabin roof and Mr. Wilson steered. The Jew was busy with his Sunday washing. He had a tub just forward of the cabin, over which he bent, dousing his underwear. His long white beard was tied up in a towel to keep it dry.

After they had traveled for a little over an hour, Dan suddenly became aware of a faint sound of people shouting. Far ahead on the right shore stood a small group of houses; nearer at hand a small barn, by itself, with GEORGE HENRY, FEED STORES, UTICA painted in white letters on the end.

Mr. Wilson and the Jew had also heard the noise, for they were looking ahead with their hands over their eyes. William Wampy trudged on behind the mules, and paid no attention.

"He can sleep walking," said the Jew. "He does it so he won't get tired."

The clamor increased rapidly. A bunch of perhaps twenty people were running along the towpath toward them — one man well ahead, then more men, some women and children.

"Wonder what's up?" said Mr. Wilson.

"Some kind of ruckus."

"Wonder what they're a-chasing him for?"

It was obviously a chase. As it neared them they made out the pursued man clearly. He was running in great strides, his long spindly legs stretching out well ahead of him. In one hand he carried a small satchel, in the other a floppy grey felt hat.

"Knee action a mite too high for speed," observed Mr. Wilson, "but he sure is working for it."

They could see the man's face, as red as his scarlet waistcoat. His head was thrown back; his mouth was open; and his long thin moustaches whipped back against his cheeks at every bound. He was holding his own, but no more.

It could be seen now, also, that the pursuers were got up in their Sunday best. Now and then, when he spied a stone in his path, a man would pick it up and hurl it after the fleeing man. Most shots went wide, but occasionally one found its mark, and the skinny man would spring into the air and gain a foot when he came down.

He and the Xerxes reached the barn at almost the same moment, but he paid no heed to the boat. The doors were open, and with a new burst of speed he rushed through them. In a few seconds all of the yelling pursuers had swept in after him, except a small boy who approached at a much slower pace and carried carefully a basket of eggs in his right hand. He had an intelligent face.

Mr. Wilson bawled to William Wampy to stop the mules.

"We might as well tie up and see what's going on."

The barn was well filled with hay, the air drowsy with motes. A small window to the east let in a shaft of sunlight on the head of a ladder leaning against the mow and glittered on the tines of a pitchfork. The boy who had carried the basket was tossing eggs high up over the edge of hay. One popped flatly, and the man in the mow swore in a strangling voice. The congregation at the foot of the ladder gathered the hubbub of their voices into a deep bellow of delight.

Mr. Wilson took a man by the elbow.

"Excuse me breaking in, but what's going on?"

"Why," replied the man, "there ain't enough of us round Maynar's Corners to have a regular church, there being only Hoofman's store and six farms round; but when this feathered snake come in, saying we'd ought to hire a preacher and that he was a good one, we hired him for six sermons at four dollars per and give him free board. We paid him last night, he having give five of them, but whiles he was waiting for service this morning one of the boys seen him sneaking out the back door with his bag in his hand — ready to cut and run, by Jeepers Cripus!"

He was still red-faced from his running, and he breathed loudly through his nose. A little woman in a stiff black dress, black knitted wristers, and upright small bonnet ran over to him.

"Ain't any of you men going to climb that ladder, Nat Wattles?"

"I don't want to run my stummick on a pitchfork, Annie; not me nor any other man."

"Well, by holy, if you men is all scared, the *womenfolk* will climb that ladder. I'd just like to set my hands on that sermonizing Judas man!"

She started elbowing the men aside.

"Come on, girls!"

There was savagery in her shrill cry and the echoing shout of the women crowding behind her. The man Wattles shifted his feet.

"He's to blame for it," he said nervously.

But the man on the mow, who had been lying so coolly behind his pitchfork, heard the cry and got to his feet. He raised his hand into the bar of sunlight, commanding attention. Suddenly, out of nowhere, an egg broke against his palm, and a quiver shot through him while the brown yolk wriggled slowly to his wrist. But he held his posture.

Little by little the people fell silent. The men stared, and the women stopped struggling at the foot of the ladder. Dan noticed one man with the red, crisp-skinned nose and dull eyes of a drunkard, standing mouth agape in a corner. He looked suddenly afraid.

Rage had brought the color back into the preacher's face; and he cried out, hoarsely, "All right! If you want your sermon that bad, by Holy Jesus; I'll give it to you!"

He shook the pitchfork downward.

"Set down!"

His voice thundered along the rafters.

Dan heard Mr. Wilson whispering to the Jew.

"He's a master hand at acting a part, the old renegade."

A thin sighing rose from the people; even the boy who had thrown the egg so accurately set down his basket. There was a gentle rustling of the hay upon the floor as the congregation settled themselves.

In the quiet, the skinny man on the mow picked up a handful of the hay and wiped his hand, back, palm, between the fingers. He did it deliberately; the gesture was a symbol.

Then he knelt, and folded his hands, and prayed: "O Lord God in Heaven, strengthen me, I pray Thee; visit my tongue with fire, I pray Thee, that I may smite these people with it, for I know there is no good in them. Amen."

He rose slowly to his feet, a small Bible open in his hand; and in a fine, resonant voice he read them the text of his sermon: —

"Hell and destruction are before the Lord."

He closed the book and gazed sombrely down upon his congregation. With his white hair, pink cheeks, black moustache, and scarlet waistcoat showing through his old blue coat, he made a glowing patch of color against the brown dusk of the rafters. The sunlight picked out his white hand as it rose again and suddenly jabbed a long forefinger at the people.

At the motion, the red-nosed drunkard closed his mouth; his face went white, and he gulped.

"Hell and destruction are before the Lord," the preacher repeated.

The little woman in the stiff black dress nodded her head.

"Hell is never full," he reminded them grimly.

Again he paused. About Dan the breathing of the people sounded deeper. Suddenly the drunkard groaned. There was sweat on his face.

The preacher moved his left hand slightly, so that the sunlight traced gleaming spots along the tines of the pitchfork.

"Have you ever stopped to figure out what the pains of Hell were like?" he asked them in a lowered voice.

"Have you ever scalded a hog? You could rub the hair off with one wipe. . . .

"You know how fat stinks and starts to roar when it catches fire. There 'll be fires built on your innards down in Hell. . . .

"Think of the red flames gnawing at your feet. . . . Think of the black smoke crawling out your mouths and ears. . . . Think of the boiling water and the tar. . . .

"You 've dropped bullheads into a fry-pan for breakfast and watched 'em curl and hop. What 'll your poor thin naked souls do when the Devil lays them on a red-hot iron skillet? . . ."

The drunkard choked a cry with his hands and hid his face. Even Dan and the crew of the Xerxes stirred restlessly. Out of their own experience he was painting Hell for them until each sense leaped at the word; and then he brought it home to the villagers personally.

"Who can escape the damnation of Hell?"

He lifted a menacing hand.

"Who do you find in Hell?" His voice rose to the question. "Judas Iscariot burns in Hell.

> "Iscariot sold
> His God for gold. . . .

"What man of you told the preacher he 'd give him three dollars a sermon when you all know you 'd give him by a subscription twenty-four dollars to pay the preacher who took the job? Six into twenty-four goes four times. Four times six is twenty-four. He tried to make a profit of six dollars on his own religion. I see him. I see him. But God has seen him a long time. 'The boldness of his face shall be changed.' Look and see!"

The man Wattles drew in his breath, and his face went red and white. But the others did not look at him; they were afraid of their own damnation. Only a grim look came into the eyes of the little woman in the stiff black dress.

The preacher's hand shot out again.

"Who uses doctored scales in Maynar's Corners? 'False weights are an abomination unto the Lord!'

"Potiphar's wife is burning down in Hell. What woman meets a man in Phileo's sugar bush on Saturday nights, or oftener? 'Thou hast polluted the earth with thy wickedness!' Can ye escape the damnation of Hell?"

One by one he fastened on them the stigma of village gossip, until they huddled under the gleam of his eyes.

Through the shadow, through the drowsy smell of summer's hay, the gold-moted shaft of light searched out the preacher's vibrant body, so that in the duskiness he alone showed clear. His white hair glanced as he spoke, and his words, coming down on their heads, were truly the words of God.

He talked of evil, and the methods of evil, and its reward among men, and he talked as if he knew. He spoke of Judgment Day, and he brought them lame and afoot to the Throne. . . . But no mercy lay there for them. "Which of you can claim blessing in the sight of God?" he cried. With a sure dramatic sense he opened the Book again and read, in stirring, measured tones, the Beatitudes.

" 'Blessed are the poor in spirit: for theirs is the Kingdom of Heaven.' You are all set up in envy. You need n't make a claim. God knows your spirit; He has searched them out.

" 'Blessed are they that mourn: for they shall be comforted.' No mourners here. When you do, it 'll be too late. 'And they mourn at the last, when thy flesh and body shall be consumed.'

" 'Blessed are the meek; for they shall inherit the earth.' Woe to the crown of pride! You womenfolk who gossip — 'Thy damnation slumbereth not!'

" 'Blessed are they which do hunger and thirst after righteousness: for they shall be filled.' It 's your bellies you take care to fill, and I ain't seen any man here's thirst taking him to righteousness. Two kegs of rum drunk up last week in Hoofman's store. Who lay on the sidewalk yesterday? 'Strong drink shall be bitter.' O God, how true!

" 'Blessed are the merciful: for they shall obtain mercy.' Who threw stones? Who threw eggs? Who reviled with foul language? What woman wanted to set her hands on me — the preacher?"

His hand rose over his head, and clenched.

" 'Blessed are the pure in heart. . . .' "

His voice tolled on solemnly, irrevocably, truthfully. The evidence was his.

Men and women bowed above their knees. A faint moaning rose with their uneven breathing. The power of the preacher's voice brought their sins upon them; and they saw them all clearly, and knew that they stood clearly before their neighbors, and the women cried, and a weakness came upon them all, as if they had been purged.

The preacher's voice fell silent; the fingers that grasped the Book loosened their hold and let it fall. He stood quite still with his arms at his sides. His face was raised to the bar of sunlight; his Adam's apple worked up and down in his scrawny neck. Even Dan, squatting behind the rest with the crew of the Xerxes at his side, could see the trembling of his lips.

"O God," he said, his voice barely above a whisper, "we are all sinners here, and there is no health in us. Humble our hearts, O God, and let us pray: 'Our Father, Who art in Heaven, Hallowed be Thy name . . .'"

Whisperingly, at first, other voices, one by one, fell in with his.

"'Thy Kingdom come. Thy will be done on earth, as it is in Heaven. Give us this day our daily bread. And forgive us our trespasses, as we forgive those who trespass against us . . .'"

And the barn was filled to the roof with the slow sentences.

"'. . . Lead us not into temptation, but deliver us from evil. For thine is the Kingdom, and the Power, and the Glory, for ever and ever. Amen.'"

He knelt a moment in silence, the people kneeling with him. Then he rose and stretched his hands out over them, and his voice was husky.

"Let us repent and go."

He held his pose until the people began to file slowly through the doors. They went haltingly, and the sunlight outside brought water to their eyes. After the long siege in the barn, some of them stumbled.

The preacher put his Bible back in the small satchel, wiped his hand again with hay, sniffed at it covertly. Then he put on his hat and began to come down the ladder, his

narrow quarters thrusting out between the tails of his coat.
Wattles and one or two of the others waited for him to
reach the floor. They shook his hand solemnly.

"That was as fine a sermon as I ever heard," said Wattles.

"I am glad to hear you say so," replied the preacher. "It
encourages me."

His black eyes smiled at them out of a maze of tiny
wrinkles.

"Now don't you think you 'd better get home? It does a
man good to meditate once in a while. And after this," —
the resonance returned to his voice, — "when you repeat
what I 've said about your neighbors, remember there was
a word said also about yourself. All our hope is in the
Lord."

He took off his hat as he said it, and the men as solemnly
removed theirs, and then filed out. The barn was empty but
for the crew of the Xerxes and the drunkard, who had
fallen asleep in the corner.

Wilson came up to the preacher and shook him energetically by the hand.

"By grab, that was a show! That was a sermon! If P. T.
Barnum could have heard you, he 'd have signed you on
for his museum and your fortune would be made. Yes, sir!"
He raised his right knee and thumped it down. "Thousands of dollars!"

The preacher looked at him slyly.

"Is that a fact?"

"Granpap's gospel — every word. I mean it."

The preacher considered it for a moment. Then he shook
his head.

"I 'm afraid it would n't last. That 's the first original one
I ever preached. Oh, I 've learned sermons. I 've got five
in this," lifting his satchel, "but I bit off more 'n I could
chaw here. The contract called for six."

"Well, I 'd never 've guessed it," said Mr. Wilson.

"I would n't 've myself. That 's why I was cutting away.
There 's just four things 'll make a man preach hard. A

lot of money; being religion-crazy; believing just the opposite of what he's preaching; or being gosh-a'mighty blue scared, like I was."

He chuckled, a sudden musical gurgle in his throat.

"There's a lot in that fact," observed the Jew. "The most powerful evangel I ever listened to started drinking Monday and got the sights by Saturday and woke up Sunday with preachings in his head of the most convincing agony I ever listened to. I danged near changed my faith hearing that man rinse his soul."

He grinned at the preacher and held out his enormous hand.

"My name's Benjamin Rae."

"I'm Julius Wilson. This here's young Harrow. And there's William Wampy."

The preacher smiled round at them as though he felt relieved to be among them.

"My name's Fortune Friendly," he said. "Which way are you folks hauling?"

"Utica."

"Could I go along with you that far?"

"Proud to have you," said Wilson. "Come along."

They walked out of the barn. The mules had found some grass to their liking and were cropping it peacefully. Wampy sighed and went over to them and kicked them in the belly. "Go on," he said.

The others went aboard the boat. The Jew resumed his washing. Mr. Wilson steered. Dan and Fortune Friendly sat down on the cabin roof.

"You look troubled, lad," said Friendly, laying his hand on Dan's shoulder. "Don't let what I say bother you."

Dan stared at him as if he did not understand.

"Don't believe a word of it. I just gave them people what they was looking for. You go along and have a good time. Eat, drink. As long as you ain't dishonest, it don't matter. That's my weakness — but it ain't no robbery from folk like them." He pointed his thumb at Maynar's Corners. "There's a lot of catch-talk in the Bible. But there's one or two things that're mortal true. Here's one for you to get a-hold of: 'And also that every man should eat and drink, and enjoy the good of all his labour, it is the gift of God.'"

He lay down on his back and folded his hands behind his head, and crossed one skinny leg over the other. He turned his head to grin at Dan, and suddenly Dan grinned back. There was something likable about the gnomelike black eyes in the man's pink face, and the unexplainable white hair and maze of fine lines about his eyes and the wrinkles in his scrawny neck.

"Got a good cigar on to you, brother?" he asked Mr. Wilson.

Wilson grinned.

"Sure. Catch it."

He tossed it to Friendly, who caught it, bit off the end, and lit up almost in the same motion.

"I reckon I've heard tell about you," said Wilson. "You're sort of a renegade, ain't you?"

Friendly winked.

"Sure. I was trained for an Episcopal minister. Yale College, by holy. I learned all the confabulations there is in books. But I did n't find it fit."

Wilson's eyes lighted.

"Come here, Dan. You might as well steer. How about a game of pinochle? You're about through, ain't you, Ben?"

"Surely."

"Say," grinned Friendly, "I'm seventy years old, but my luck at cards is good, always good. I figured that was one of the reasons I was n't cut out to be a minister."

He jumped to his feet and clicked his heels together.

"Don't come no religion on us if you lose," said the Jew.

"Religion is a compound of the passions," said the old man seriously; "that's why it puzzles people like you."

Dan took hold of the rudder.

It was straight steering for the most part, and after swinging wide on the first two turns he began to get the knack of the boat. He leaned against the sweep with just enough weight to keep the bows headed straight. And the Xerxes crept ahead.

Down in the cabin he could hear exclamations of disgust from the two boaters, and Friendly's musical chuckles.

Sunday Afternoon in Chancellor Square

Fortune Friendly shook hands with them all.

"Any time you want to make up a hand of pinochle," he said, "you just send out for me."

Rae and Wilson laughed good-naturedly.

"All right, we'll do that."

The old fellow slapped on his hat and picked up his satchel. When his white hair was covered, he looked but little over thirty.

"I've been livin' too strict these past six weeks," he said. "I've got to limber me up. I need a little corn juice for my inwards."

He walked down the plank and waved his hand to them from the dock.

The Xerxes had been tied up at the west end of the basin. Boats lay before them in a long double line. From some of the screw docks they could see smoke rising from the cabin stovepipes. The city basked in its Sunday quiet. The thump of a boater's heels walking over the dock accentuated the stillness.

Wilson came up to Dan.

"Me and Ben's going ashore," he said. "William will stay on the boat. You can come along with us if you like, or stay here, or do what you want. We'll pick up those ashes in the morning about four o'clock, so I guess you'd better be aboard to-night."

"I guess I'll walk round a spell," Dan said. "I'd like to look at some of the streets."

"Go ahead," said Wilson. "Me and Ben'll be at Bentley's most like after six. It's on Liberty Street. Any boater'll tell you where."

They went down the plank.

In the cabin William Wampy had cooked some lunch for himself. He made no comment when Dan sat down across the table, but helped him to food. Dan did not try to talk; neither he nor William wanted to talk; there was no point in it. The flies of the city had found their way into the newly arrived boat; their buzzing was as much as conversation.

Dan went ashore and walked eastward along the course of the canal. Every once in a while he crossed a low bridge under which the canal let into the screw docks by the sides of warehouses. The boats looked deserted for the most part, though now and then he saw two or three women out on deck hobnobbing while they sewed.

He walked as far as the Genesee Street bridge and there turned to the right and went up into the city. The streets, too, were quiet. A couple of gentlemen in high black hats, black coats, and velvet waistcoats and grey trousers, swinging silver-headed canes; a lady ribboned and faintly scented, entering a smart brougham, drawn by a nervous pair of bays, and handsome in basket paneling. He wandered up one street and down another. In the residential district elms grew and the houses stood back behind their brownstone steps. It was quiet there, not with a noonday hush, but with habitual quiet. He tried to visualize the people behind the half-shaded windows, but he saw them only as the two men walking and the lady entering her carriage.

He came to a square which was shady and cool and which had boarded walks running under the trees. There were benches. And all round the square the houses stood on lawns, and the branches of trees showed beyond the corners of their walls, and some smelled faintly of manure spread out in orchards. Dan sat down on one of the benches, where he could drink in the smell, a homesickness in his eyes — not for the meagre Tug Hill meadows, but for a place which, in a way, he could imagine for himself. Now and then a man develops from his labor on his barren land, not an envy of the valley farmer, but an admiration of rich soil.

So Dan's imagined farm was vague in its outlines. But he could see himself feeling of the bags of his cows, hauling his manure, ploughing in the fall, and, when he was done, polishing his plough. He did not see the house, but he had a vague notion of a hip-roofed barn, like one he had seen outside of Rome. . . . And then he started to hear faintly a horn blowing to the north, and he realized that a boat was sounding for a lock.

He was working on the canal. He had left the land. Before him was a product of the life he was to lead. These many fine houses were made possible by the canal. . . .

He was aware of someone walking past him, and then of a catch in the person's breathing, and he glanced up and saw Molly Larkins. She looked very fresh and pretty with the sunlight spilling through the shade on her red dress. And there was a light of genuine pleasure in her dark blue eyes that brought Dan eagerly to his feet.

"Why, Mr. Harrow," she exclaimed in her low voice, "I did n't think to see you here."

He blushed as though he had been caught at some offense.

"I 've been walking round the city," he explained. "I 've been walking quite a while. So I set down here for a while."

"Well," she said, "I come here once in a while, too. I like to see the people that live here." She gave a little laugh, not self-conscious, but with an undertone of irritation in it. "I 'm notional this way, I guess."

They sat down together.

"I did n't think to see you here," said Dan, after a moment.

"I did n't expect to stop here, myself."

She seemed a little depressed.

"Have you quit Klore?" he asked.

"Yeanh. Yes, I quit him. I did n't want to work for him any more. I did n't like him."

"He looks mean."

"He is mean. But not like you say it. He spends easy and he 's a fine powerful man. He 's a good man taking a girl round. I had a lot of fun with him."

"What did you quit him for?"

"You remember he said he'd lace me when he come into Hennessy's?"

Her eyes grew dark.

"Yeanh," said Dan.

"He done it."

His face slowly reddened and his hands shook.

She went on quietly, her voice cold.

"He didn't say anything when he come to. He didn't say anything about the other man. But he said no cook who took his pay could be another man's" — she hesitated and looked at Dan and her eyes held his honestly — "whore and not get a lacing till she learned better or left. I told him he was crazy and to mind his own business. But he grabbed my arm and walked with me down to his boat and took a strap and give it to me."

She moved her shoulders away from the back of the bench. "He's a strong man. He give it to me. I can feel it."

Dan clenched his hands.

"It ain't right," he said.

"Course it ain't. No man can treat a woman that way without she's married to him."

Her eyes snapped.

"I quit him dead in Utica last night."

"It ain't right," he repeated harshly.

She glanced at him. He certainly looked big and strong, and he'd knocked Klore dizzy, but she remembered his expression when Klore came in on him.

"Well," she said dryly, "what're you going to do about it, then?"

He stared down uncomfortably at his fists.

"I don't know."

"Well," she said. "I wouldn't try to do anything."

He was nothing but a country lump anyway; he didn't know a hotel from a hall. She had seen that in Hennessy's, and had stood up for him.

"Don't worry about me," she said. "I can look out for myself. A girl gets the habit living on the Erie."

"Where is he now?"

"I don't know. He generally winds up his likker in Bentley's."

They fell silent. Out beyond the trees they heard the brisk trotting of a pair of horses, and a carriage drew up in front of a house. A gentleman and two ladies got out and went up to the front door. Molly drew in her breath ecstatically and pointed out particular things about the women's clothes.

Dan hardly noticed. To him she seemed as pretty in her plain red dress. It brought out the flush in her smooth cheeks and matched her bright mouth. Her position, leaning back on the bench, moulded her figure under her clothes; and sitting there in the quiet shade with her, with fine houses and strange people about them, gave him a sense of intimacy. His inarticulate anger against Klore was swallowed by a growing excitement.

"What 're you going to do next?" he asked.

"I don't know. Get another job, maybe. I got some money saved; maybe I won't do anything for a little while."

She regarded him with a sidewise glance. He was staring at the toes of his dusty cowhide boots; and his attitude brought out the muscles in his neck, the swell of his shoulders. His hands were heavily boned; she knew he was strong; and his thin face seen in profile with the curved nose and high cheek bones, and the short straight hair on the back of his neck, was attractive.

"I 'll wait a couple of weeks," she said, almost as if it were a promise. "I 'll see what turns up."

He stared out across the square, above the roofs of the houses. Sparrows were circling there in flocks, all jerking as one in their flight, all atwitter. Her eyes softened.

"What 're you planning to do, Mr. Harrow?"

"I don't know," he said. "I 'd scarcely thought. I guess I 'll go on down with Julius W. as far 's Albany. Then I don't know who I 'll come back with."

He looked round at her suddenly.

"But I aim to get a boat some day soon."

"You'll find it hard unless you're awful lucky."

"Maybe. Maybe I could get Mr. Butterfield to help me."

"Maybe you might."

"Listen," he said, "if I got a boat of my own? . . ."

"Yeanh."

"Would you — I'd need a cook," he said.

"That's right," she said, puckering the corners of her eyes. "You'd need a cook and a pair of mules and a driver."

"Yeanh," he said, swallowing.

She laughed, putting out her chin at him a little.

"And you'd like for me to be your cook?"

"Yeanh," he said. "That's right."

"Well," she said, "when you come and ask me, I'll let you know."

"Where'll you be?"

"If I ain't otherwise taken, I'll be at Lucy Cashdollar's Agency. That's over Bentley's."

He leaned back heavily against the bench.

"Mr. Harrow — "

"Yeanh?"

He glanced up; but she was looking at her lap, where her fingers were opening and closing her reticule.

"If you'd ask me, I'd say I'd like to cook for you a lot."

His breath caught. After a while he managed to say, "I aim to ask you, Molly."

They did not speak, but watched the shadows come in under the trees and lights spring up in the windows over the front doors of the houses. A couple walked past them without noticing them. And a flock of sparrows took possession of a tree near them for the night.

"My land!" exclaimed Molly. "It's time I was getting back to supper."

Bentley's

On Genesee Street Molly left him. He walked slowly down the hill to the canal. The moon was still low in the eastern bowl of the great valley, and it sent an uneven thread along the course of the canal. Through the city, the warehouses cast black shadows far into the stream, at times cutting off the thread of moonlight; but every here and there night lanterns hung in the bows of boats pierced the blackness and traced the ripple. A wind was rising out of the northwest, and rumpled clouds were bearing down upon the moon.

Dan paused for a time on the bridge. It was very still there. Close at hand was Bagg's Hotel; but it was quiet — whatever noise issued from its windows was hidden by the slap of the ripple on the piles. He stared away to the east and thought of Molly. "By grab," he said under his breath, "if I had a boat I could have her. She said pretty near that much." But there was small chance of his getting a boat. He could ask Mr. Butterfield for a job, maybe, and make more money than he was making now; but he would be asking in his 'father's name, and he did not want to do that.

"There ain't much chance," he said to himself. "I guess I 'll find Bentley's."

But as he turned to take his course along the canal there was still a glow in him. "Like to cook for you a lot," she had said.

Coming along the dock were two men, one a stockily built boater, the other a mild-looking clerk. They both stopped when Dan asked them where to find Bentley's.

"Keep on how you 're headed," said the boater. "Turn into Liberty Street after you pass Gridley's warehouse. Walk a block to your right, and if you can't detect it by the noise, ask a man and he 'll do it for you."

"It would be simpler —" began the clerk.

"Now you shut up," said the boater. "Don't listen to him. It 's folks educated like him lead people off the track."

Dan went along slowly. The city down by the docks seemed to have come to life. There were few lights, and the warehouses loomed high and dark. But in the streets round them there was a pulsation of indistinguishable sound. When he passed a corner, he sometimes heard voices in loud talk,

or a fiddle playing high and fast, or someone singing a
snatch — a snatch of "Hoosen Johnny," and other voices
coming into the chorus: —

> "Long time ago, long time ago.
> The little black bull came down the meadow.
> Oh, a long time ago."

He stopped to listen to it. While he stood there, a man
passed him, smoking a cigar. The wind brightened the ash,
and, dimly lit as they were, Dan recognized the bulging eyes
and pursed mouth of the fat man, Henderson, who claimed
to be a horse trader. He was walking along slowly, his gaze
on the upper windows of the warehouses.

Dan went on, turned into Liberty Street as he had been
directed. A little way down, an alley branched off on the
right, and from the end of it sounded voices singing, men's
voices, with a swing and bellow that filled the air. It was
a canal song.

> "We were loaded down with barley,
> We were chuck up full with rye;
> And the captain he looked down at me
> With his goddam wicked eye.

> "Oh the E-ri-e was a-rising,
> The strap was getting low,
> And I scarcely think
> We'll get a drink
> Till we get to Buffalo,
> Till we get to Buffalo."

The swing of it took hold of him and drew him towards
the door. He did not need to be told it was Bentley's. It
was a three-story building with an eaveless roof, standing
stiff as a box at the end of the alley. Bentley's Bar, a
boaters' hangout; it had n't had "Oyster Booth" put into the
name then.

Dan pushed his way through the door, and his eyes

blinked. The air was thick with tobacco, the sharp-smelling heat of oil lamps, the heavy sound of men talking in a close room.

"Well, well! Look what just come in! And on Sunday, too!"

Someone guffawed.

Dan paid no attention, but let the door swing to behind him. Running down the length of the room on his left was the bar. Four keeps were working behind it in their shirt sleeves; they worked hard.

Dan wedged into an opening in the line before it.

"What's yours?" asked the nearest keep.

"Whiskey."

The glass slid up to his hand. He paid and made his way to a table in a corner of the room.

He drank his whiskey slowly, and its sting brought water to his eyes. Two boaters at the next table were grumbling over low wages. "Good solid rates, heavy trade, where does the money go?" said one. "We don't see it." The other nodded. He wore a cap tilted back on his head and blew his nose often into a red handkerchief. His forehead bulged like a philosopher's. "The coat and pants does all the work," he observed, "but the weskit gets the gravy."

Dan looked round for Wilson and the Jew; but they were not in sight. As he drank, he lost interest in them, and thought of Molly instead, in her red dress. With the surge of talk about him, the laughter, the stamp of men's feet, the clinking at the bar, he felt the push of the canal behind him. . . .

There was a lift to the floor when he got to his feet and went over to the bar for another glass. But the act of walking gave him a feeling of increased strength, and he leaned his elbow on the bar and glanced round him. It was pleasant for him to stand there, not to feel nervous when a man jostled him.

"Beg pardon," said a man when his heel slipped and he lurched against Dan.

"Surely," said Dan, making to steady him with his hand.

He was getting a gauge of his own strength. "I'd like to see Klore now," he said to himself, thinking of what Molly had told him. "I'd like to see him now."

Down the room someone was stamping on the floor. "Song! Song!"

A man lurched to his feet and a tumbler smashed.

"Abel Marsters going to sing."

Dan's glass came sliding back, and he gazed over the rim at a tall boater who was standing by himself beside the great round stove, and pulling his moustache away from his mouth. Then he lifted his chin a trifle and half closed his eyes and took one hand in the other. He had a fine, moving tenor.

> "Drop a tear for big-foot Sal,
> The best damn cook on the Erie Canal;
> She aimed for Heaven but she went to Hell —
> Fifteen years on the Erie Canal.
> The missioner said she died in sin;
> Hennery said it was too much gin:
> There were n't no bar where she had n't been,
>   From Albany to Buffalo."

The heave, the pull, the plod of the towpath, the people, the men about Dan; all were in the song, all joining the refrain: —

"Low bridge! Everybody down!
 Low bridge! We're coming to a town!
 You'll always know your neighbor, you'll always know your
     pal,
 If you've ever navigated on the Erie Canal.

     "Low bridge! . . ."

The long drag, the meadows, the marshes, the woods and the hills and the rivers, and the canal going through, with the boats, slowly, slowly, one step after another, slow, slow, and the mules' ears flop, and the snake whips crack, and the dust in your throat, and . . .

     . . . "we're coming to a town."

And here they were, after the long week's plodding at three miles an hour, on Sunday night, letting off energy to ease themselves.

Then, as Dan watched, a light sprang to the eyes of an old Irishman, red still in his hair, sitting alone in the corner; and, looking toward the door, he saw the white head of Benjamin Rae over the crowd, and the swaggering shoulders of Julius Wilson, and William Wampy with his fiddle. A cry of "William! William Wampy!" and William was hoisted to a table, and the Irishman called for a jig.

Dimly through the swaying smoke Dan saw William seat himself, and tables and chairs rasped over the floor to clear a space. The lantern over him shed yellow light on his bald head and mild brown eyes as he cuddled the fiddle and talked it into tune. Then his hand and the bow awoke, his shoulders swayed to the left, came up, held still, and the bow flashed. . . . And the old man who had called for a jig was doing it, earnestly, concentrating on his feet, for a moment, till the fiddle gave them the rhythm; and the "Irishman's Shanty" was in full swing. . . . The great Jew slapping his hands on his knees in time. Julius grinning and shouting "Hye!" Men shuffling their feet. . . . Another Irishman on the floor, a young man, springing like a buck deer, a shrill cry from the old man, and an old step of his feet, forgotten, a double tap, a roar of delight. . . . William Wampy shaking the sweat from his face, mild-eyed. . . . The barkeeps snatching a moment's rest. . . . Dan looked on, the blood pounding in his head, singing like the fiddle, an itch in his feet. . . .

The tune stops. William Wampy tears open his shirt, bends over, another rush of notes, quick, shrill — "Jamesville on a Drunk," high laughter, men dance together. . . .

Dan stood at the bar, near the end, staring, half seeing the faces come and go, some old, some young, bearded, smooth, laughing, or serious in liquor . . . and then a face materialized in front of him — a black beard, and pale grey eyes, with white spots made by the lamps beside the pupils — that held him stiff against the bar. He was conscious of his right foot feeling its way from the rail to join his left upon the floor, and he braced himself. Still the faces swept by, back and forth, dimly now behind Jotham Klore's; but the fiddle had a rowdy shrillness in his ears.

Jotham Klore was saying something; Dan could see the words coming through his beard, but they sounded vague, without syllables. Suddenly his face stung where Klore had hit him with his open hand, and then the other side. Dan hit out. His balance wavered, he caught it, but the action brought courage to his fists. He struck again, saw Klore's head snap in toward his chest, and hit his ear, and knew that he had landed twice. Then Klore was close to him, and dull pain entered his stomach, but he found he could hit and land as often as he liked. The pain continued; it did not hurt as badly as he had thought, but for some strange reason it made him drowsy, and shook something in his head. . . .

He was aware of Wilson grabbing Klore's collar, of a roar of voices, and Wilson had vanished. Over a mass of faces he saw the great hands and white head of the Jew coming toward him. But Klore was in again, his teeth showing in his beard, and a bit of blood at his mouth gumming the hair. He pounded back, but the purchase was leaving his toes, and the hands came in against his stomach, one two, one two. The faces behind Klore swept in; he saw the Jew's hands reach forward; but the beat and hammer in his head carried him back. . . . A man grabbed his shoulders, he felt his legs dragging on the floor, the lights swam in the smoke, the roar closed in upon him. . . . The feet of one of the keeps vaulting over him, a big cool man, using a bung starter. . . . The cold, the darkness, and faintly the voice of the fiddle, a soothing tune, "The Little Stack of Barley." . . .

"Sick?"

The sound of water lapping against the piles. He was looking down along a tall man's side. The black water of the canal, and over it a plank as thin as a thread, and boards under his back. The deck of the boat. . . .

"Feel better pretty quick."

He was rolled on his stomach, head over the side, a sharp slap over the kidneys and a pain in his stomach. . . . The water, the black water. . . .

"That sort of evens us up."

The voice was familiar. He recognized dimly. He had heard it always in the dark.

"Got a taste of the canal," said the voice. "You'll feel better now."

He struggled to sit up and saw a man bending over him, back to the faint light of the moon; a wide hat — Gentleman Joe. Suddenly the man cocked his head alertly.

"Working for Wilson?"

Dan managed to nod.

"It's his boat. I've got to cut out of here."

The man moved down the plank and disappeared into the shadows along the warehouses.

Dan sat with his back to the rudder post, the sweep curving out over his head. He felt sore and still sick; but it was not as bad as he had thought it would be. He wasn't afraid. He had tasted the canal; he had become part of it.

He heard a faint whistling moving along the docks, and a man came opposite the Xerxes and paused long enough for Dan to recognize the fat man, Henderson, and then moved on.

Dan got to his feet and went down to the cabin and felt his way to his bunk.

Utica Weighlock

When he woke, Benjamin Rae's hand was on his shoulder, shaking him.

"Hustle up, Dan. We're loading in half an hour."

He helped Dan sit up.

"Belly sore?" The Jew grinned.

"Yeanh."

"Klore sure set out to rangdangle you. What happened to you?"

"I have n't much of a notion."

"I don't blame you."

He passed out through the curtains.

Dan heaved his feet to the floor; his shoes were still on. The bunks swam dizzily from right to left, and he grabbed his head. But in a moment things came steady.

Through the curtain he could hear the others eating, blowing on the coffee and gulping it.

"Come on out if you want to eat," Wilson called.

Dan stepped into the cabin a bit unsteadily. It was still dark, and a lamp was giving a feeble light over the table. Wilson looked up.

"Who brought you back, Dan?"

"Why, I sort of come to on the boat," said Dan.

"Fill him some coffee, William. You took a lot round the stomach — something hot 'll help unlimber you."

"It won't hurt you," said Benjamin Rae. "The best fighter never really fit until he 'd got licked once or twicet."

The coffee eased Dan considerably, and cleared his head, but he still felt sore when he went on deck.

A heavy fog misted the Basin; and when Benjamin Rae went down the plank after the mules his broad shoulders were swallowed up in it before he had passed the bow.

"You get the towline ashore," said Wilson.

In a few minutes Dan heard the Jew returning, the sharp thump of hoofs on the dock, and then the heads of the mules came out of the fog. He hooked the towline to the evener and the mules relaxed their off hips and let their ears flop back against their necks.

There was a roll of wood on wood, and two men appeared rolling barrels across the dock. Another man with a short barrel track jumped into the pit, and the barrels began rolling down. Wilson stood on the edge of the pit, watching, occasionally blowing into his hands.

"We 'll be first out of Utica at the weighlock," the Jew said to Dan. "But if there 's an upstream line we 'll have to wait for them to come through."

Wilson signed the bill of lading and Dan tossed off the

tie-ropes. The loading hands jumped back to the dock, grabbed poles, and pushed the Xerxes out into the current. Wilson passed the towline over the bow standard, so that it would clear boats against the dock, and Ben Rae shortened it at the eveners to avoid the deep sag.

They went ahead. Some of the boats were coming to life, with sounds of crockery in the cabins and smell of smoke from the stoves. But the Xerxes seemed the only boat astir. Ahead of her a black tunnel loomed in the fog. And then boats began issuing on the other side of the canal, the teams' nodding heads visible an instant as they passed.

Lanterns bobbed ahead, crossing and recrossing the tunnel. As they came closer, Dan saw the weighlock, a boat lying in it, heard a muffled voice calling, "Seventy-one, -two, -three, seventy-three-nine eighty-five."

From a lighted office on the other side of the narrow roofed slip a voice answered, "Seventy-three tons, nine hundred."

The boat lay in an empty trough on a ribbed rack, with arms fore and aft extending under the office. At the last words the tender slammed down a lever, water came sucking in, and the boat rose to canal level. The gates opened, the mules took up the slack, and the boat slid through.

Beyond the door, the toll-taker spoke to the captain: "Class of freight?"

"Merchandise. Misc."

The upper lock gates closed, the lower opened, and the tender bawled, "Next!"

Already a boat was sliding in. A man on the bow with a pole to keep it from fending the side. The mules passed on a narrow runway.

"By grab, come slower, Marcy. You're always running in too fast. You'll take off them gates some day."

The tender snatched up a pole and pushed back against the bow of the boat, which was moving with a dangerous momentum. It came up against the upper gates with a heavy thud.

"Gorl!" breathed the tender, running to close the lower

gates. "By Cripus," he cried to the driver, "the next time you come in like that, I'll be danged if I'll let you drive into this lock! What do you think it is, a rubber extension?"

The driver spat into the lock and sat down.

"Oh, go pull up your pants, Buscerk."

Inside the office the toll-taker was making change. "What you got, general merchandise, George?" The captain of the line boat which had passed snorted.

"Swiss! They've brought the hull damn works with 'em. Ploughs! You ort to see 'em. Regular teaspoon trinkets! Every dang little thing. Pitchforks. They've set up a clock in the cabin with a funny set of works. Dangdest racket. And their talk! High jabber, high jabber, jabber-jabber, jabber-jabber-jabber. God! I don't get no rest at all. Jabber! There ain't no sense into it. Jabber this. Yes, mam, it's a mule. No, boy, it's a calf. Jabber that. No, mam, mules don't have any. Jabber! Jesus!"

He stamped out after the line boat.

The muffled voice was calling again: "Fifty-one, -two, fifty-two, even."

"Sold!" cried the clerk, under his oil lamp. "Boat number, name, and cargo."

"Number 1793. Freedom's Flower. Albany. Four bales of 'baccer. Printing press for Rochester, special valuation. All the rest is merchandise for St. Louis. Boots and shoes from Lowell, Mass. Two crates of hats. Haberdashery to clothe the pioneer." He chuckled.

Already another boat was coming in.

"How many boats out there?" the Jew shouted across at the tender, pointing his thumb at the misty entrance to the lock, where the headlights of the boats made feeble smears.

"Expect about forty. Next!"

But the boat was coming in already, deftly, under the guidance of a one-armed man. "Whoa!" he yelled as the bows came into the gates and the boat slid in without a rub and drifted to a stop, dead centre.

"That's Jason Jukes. Handiest man with a boat I ever see."

"Hullo, Ben!" His quick smile showed a flash of gold teeth. "Number 3991. Tammany Hall, Rome. Carrying rope."

He went inside, reappeared, and the mist swallowed him and the faint light of his boat on the far side.

Sitting side by side on the runway, the crew of the Xerxes watched the boats come in. The fog formed drops on their faces and ran down their necks. Boat after boat. Manufactured goods. "Stoves," said Wilson. "Fancy furniture; did you ever see such articles?"

"That's forty-three of them," cried the lock-tender. "Next!"

He waited a second.

"Next!"

He waved his arm at Wilson.

"East-bound boats! Hurry up, there."

Wilson leaped up and ran back and jumped aboard. "Geddup!" said the Jew to the mules. "Whoa!" cried Wilson, and the mules stopped. The Jew jumped aboard on one side as Wilson jumped off on the other and stepped into the office. "Number 1613," he said. "Xerxes short-hauling the Michigan Six Day. Ashes to Schenectady. Fifty bar'l."

"Damn it," said the toll-taker. "What do they got to bother us for with that trash?"

The gates opened. "Geddup," the Jew bawled at the mules. Dan started after them. As soon as the Xerxes cleared the lock they stopped and waited for Wilson. He took a running jump from the towpath and made the deck. Dan heard the scrape and thump of his feet as he scrambled up. "Go on. Lay into them, Dan! We're hurrying now."

The city seemed dead as they passed out of the warehouses into the open country. The mules were nervous in the fog, and kept their heads low to the towpath, snorting now and then. They were a young pair and kept a fast pace. Dan felt the stiffness going out of him as he kept up.

"Don't let 'em burn themselves out," said the Jew. "They're green young."

"All right," said Dan. He slowed them a trifle.

"You can always tell a green young mule by the way he handles his ears," said the Jew. "Look at the fancy twirl they're a-putting on. Now an old mule 'll either prick 'em or let 'em dangle plain. He knows he's got enough to do just keeping the boat moving."

A boat passed on the other side of the canal; and the puff of the horses, and the oily snap of the snake whip, the sound of the wash meeting their own, the smell of wood smoke; and the boat had passed. More went by. Little by little, Dan could distinguish their shadows against the mist. There lurked in it now a restless feeling of motion.

Suddenly it thinned, dropped, and for a few seconds he and the mules were wading in it knee-deep, and he saw the canal marked by teams coming up, and men standing in it steering. The sun was red far down the valley, and a wind began to draw over the hills to the south. Then the mist was all about him for twenty minutes, and but for the momentary droop of it he might have thought himself alone with the mules, pulling mysteriously on a rope. But it lifted again as the wind knifed under, wavered, and went away. And the sunlight swept up the valley, glistening on all things.

They started unloading at Westfeldt's soap factory at one o'clock. By two they had eaten a late dinner and were pushing on, the empty Xerxes light upon the mules. All day, passing Fall Hill and the ancient Mohawk Castle, the East Canada Creek, where the devil Butler had his head chopped off by two Oneida Indians, and Fort Plain, with the sunset red upon it. They changed teams at Canajoharie, and went on in the dark, with thunder overhead and hard rain drumming on the deck. White lights marked the locks, and dozing tenders put them through in silence. When the rain cleared, a stillness came upon them. Farms near the canal brooded unseen, recognizable only by the pungent odor of their barnyards. Once a white hound mourned as they went by, and Dan heard the clink of his chain.

The night swallowed them again. They passed Schenectady in the morning, with the canal once more astir with boats. They went through the cut of the Young Engineer and the Wat Hoix Gap, with the Mohawk roaring through the heavy rapids on their right, and the White Horse tossing his mane of spray.

Then over the long aqueduct and down the locks; early in the afternoon they floated out into the basin, and by six o'clock saw Albany rising on a hill to their right. . . .

IV

THE SARSEY SAL

Morning, Albany

Two days later Dan watched the Xerxes pulling away towards Troy. He was standing on the outer bank of the great
basin, the Hudson at his back. The basin and the canal
beyond it were thronged with boats. Dan could scarcely
have believed so many boats existed. Albany was the eddy
in the long current of trade that swept from New York —
from Europe, for that matter — to the farthest reaches of
the West. Here the long tows of barges came up the Hudson
to dump their freight into the canal boats. Steamers towing
queues of canal boats nosed into the basin embankment;
Dan counted one line of ninety-eight. Men jumped ashore
and went after their horses, left in the great round stable
off the north end of State Street; or they brought their horses
off the boats, stiff-legged from their long ride, the land
uneasy to their hoofs, but rested and fat. Agents for the
steamboat lines ran about with ledgers under their arms
signing up captains for a queue on the Ronan line or the
Swiftsure, or any one of ten. They quarreled among themselves, crying down the other company, fighting sometimes, while the boater grinned as he looked on and signed
with a third man. The blare of voices rose in a long murmur
under the city smoke; the hiss of steam slid into it here and
there from the river, making white cotton-wool patches
against the towering black boat-stacks.

On one side the city rose in tiers of brown-housed streets,
its smokes pulling away westward, a buzzing hive, its crown

of white state buildings aloof above the noise. But, down below, the frayed ends of life were gathered up and loosely
knotted. Here came a line of coal barges from the Delaware
and Hudson; even the washed clothes snapping in the river
wind were grey from the open cargoes of coal. A passenger
train was sliding down the hill from the west, the drivers
of the engine aglitter with speed; and a stately white steamboat far down the river, stretching on the water its clean
white lines, its stacks rolling forth black clouds, sent its
long wail between the hills. Its passengers crowded the forward decks, their gaze on the city ahead, with no eyes for
the murk their passage left on the blue river.

Men jostled Dan, men of all tongues, arguing for passage
money to the West, while their women stayed back with
the baggage and held their wide-eyed children hard by the
hand. It was bewildering to watch, the urge for hurry
begetting confusion which begot again the urge for haste.
All the wide tumult of men who had to be on time, who
learned its value, talked of it in fractions and measured it
anxiously, — clerks getting off their shipments, emigrants
seeking passage that they might be settled for the spring
sowing, trains scurrying on their narrow rails to fulfill their
tables, boat captains sounding whistles for their start, —
and all had forgotten that time had no measure, that it had
no passage, that it was an image of their own creation, built
out of minutes and seconds and purchased with dollars and
cents. On Sundays their ministers called it God. By unconscious irony they had come to call the daily transcript of
their lives a "press."

Far up the canal, beyond the crowded boats, Dan caught
again a glimpse of the Jew's white beard and saw him raise
his hand. Then the bustle and confusion swallowed him,
and Dan was alone, bewildered. The meagre Tug Hill farm,
set between the pointed balsams, had given him no standard
by which he could grasp the great restless haste about him
and make it his own.

He shoved his way among the people until he stood by the
waterside. There he sat down on a short pile, his long legs

dangling. All along the wharf, for the better part of a mile, boats had been tied up. They moved slightly, muttering, with the motion of the water, the noon sun washing their decks and whittling the men and women small with its hot light. Directly before him an old brown boat squatted, its cabin windows on a level with his eyes. A woman was washing clothes on deck. She was heavily built and bent only slightly in reaching into the tub; and when she straightened up she breathed hard and squeezed the suds angrily from her reddened hands.

After a while she caught sight of Dan and fell into conversation with him.

"Hullo, young man," she said.

"Morning, mam," said Dan.

She jerked a man's shirt from the tub and wrung it and shook it and hung it on a line between the cabin and the stable. It shuddered in the wind limply, then tossed out its arms and danced.

"It's a very pleasant day," observed the washerwoman, going on with her rubbing.

"Yeanh," said Dan.

The noise of the wharves tumbled about them, but the woman's voice was clear and pleasant; she did not raise it, but she talked to Dan with no thought of the people bustling by, so that it was easy for him to hear.

"The sun is a pleasant thing, to be sure," she went on.

"Yeanh," said Dan.

"Where do you come from?"

"Tug Hill," said Dan.

"Where is that?"

"Fifteen miles north of Rome."

"That's a long way to be from."

"Yeanh."

She bent to her work.

"A house is a fine thing," she said, straightening up again to wring out a nightgown. "The boat comes and goes. It's always stopping, but it never stays."

"No."

"I married a man once, honey, and had a house and a patch of praties and a fine man to come in for his dinner."

She finished her washing and dumped the grey water of the tub with a slosh into the canal. She stopped for a moment, with one hand taking hold of her hip.

"Are ye working on the canal, honey?"

"No," said Dan, "not now."

"Are ye looking for a job?"

"Yeanh."

She sighed.

"It's a hard thing to find with the years mounting up in a body's bones. But you'd not have much trouble. You're a handsome young man."

Dan blushed.

"I must put on a bit of my best, honey, and go off to my marketing."

She went below, leaving Dan in the midst of the noise, sitting there idly, his eyes on the blue water, thinking of Molly Larkins, and wishing one of all the many boats might be his own.

The Chase Begins

It was with a start that Dan became aware of two men going aboard the boat. The first walked heavily with his chin drawn in, his eyes on the ground. In the second, Dan recognized the man Henderson, who called himself a horse trader.

They went down into the cabin. After a minute Dan began to pick out their voices above the hum round him. The curtains were drawn over the windows, so that they could not see him.

"I've tracked him down here, Samson," said Henderson.

"Where's he now?" the boater asked.

"That's what I wanted to find out from you. Do you know where he'd be likely to hang out?"

"Probably one of the canawl houses — Jason Grew's, or Ficha Thrall's, or in the Bent Window Hotel."

"I 'll look into them," said Henderson.

"Bad actor, eh?"

"On the records. I was sent out from the Central Office. I 'm not in no hurry to lay my hands on him. I 've got his description, and I 've seen him once, not to see his face. I got on his trail in Black Rock."

"Going to snatch him here?"

"Bad place, Samson. If he got away he 'd beat me to New York. Of course, I 'd get word through first, but New York 's an easy place to miss him, and then he could cut out for Europe if he had to. That 'd be too bad."

"Surely," said the boater. "That would be bad."

"I 've been tracking him for two months. He is n't going to break loose here; he wants to hide out and wait for things to cool off. Probably he was born in this part of the country. No, Samson, I aim to wait till he 's in the middle of the state afore I put out my hands at him."

"Maybe you 'll get him," Samson said. "I hope you do."

"Sure, I ought to get him. I 'm good at these things. He don't know who I am. All he knows is we know where he is. That comes in the posting for him. I had that done to keep the people excited after him. They 're beginning to wake up now. When I 'm ready to get after him he 'll be easier to track. Yes. I know some of his hide-outs in the ports now. If he heads to a port, I won't have to lose time looking. He don't know who I am. Thinks the sheriffs are doing the posting. It 's a hot day, Samson."

"That 's right, Sam — real hot; kind of sweaty."

"Makes a man feel dry," said Henderson.

"Yeanh."

There was a moment's silence.

"How about a rum noggin, Sam?"

Henderson cleared his throat.

"Now you say it, Samson, I think it would go pretty good."

Dan heard the boater moving about the cabin.

"Great place for a man to hide out, the canal is," Henderson observed. "There's so danged many boats and so danged many people working on 'em or going through West. The boaters ain't like settled people. They don't keep track of any one place. The only people on the canal I can get anything from is the bank walkers. They've got their patrols to make. But most of them are deef."

"That's probably why he tracked into here," said the boater.

"I guess so. This noggin's pretty good, Samson."

"Yeanh. It's grateful to a man's innards. The lemon makes it kind of blend the stummick, Sam."

"It does, at that."

"Ain't going to make a nab at this Calash here, then?"

"No. Not any chance of getting him. I don't know where he is this minute. I got to learn his habits. Maybe I won't get him till next year. It takes a long time, this underneath working. But it's generally the best way. The bills was marked. But he ain't using them here. He's too neat to do a thing like that. But most likely he'll have to begin using them next year."

"What do you want him for?"

"He's got a list against him other states. He come foul of us last year. Had a gang in Indiana. Once I get on the go, though, I'll have him. — I'll have to be getting along, Samson. Thanks for the noggin. Keep on the watch for him. Anything you see let me know."

"Sure. I'll let you know."

Henderson came on deck and walked off onto the dock. Dan kept his head lowered and the man moved away, shiny brown eyes searching the crowd.

Cholera Rumor

"Well, if it ain't Andy! What're you doing, Andy?"

"Hello, Stark."

"What're you doing now? Balancing the sheet?"

"I'm too old for that, Stark. No, when a man gets old,

he leaves the fancy ways of youth. He gets a job in the street department."

"Well, you ain't cleaning a street. What 're all them figgers on that paper for? Can't tell me I don't know a figger when I see one."

The other pushed his grey hair from his eyes.

"That 's the first four lines of a poem, Stark. It 's going to be a ballad."

"What 's that?"

"Why, I guess you 'd call it a song about something horrid, better spoke than sung."

"Well, it sure looks neat, Andy."

"It 's pretty good," said the writer modestly.

He raised his thin face and looked at the newcomer out of bright, dry blue eyes. His face had an unhealthy pallor, his clothes smelt, not too pleasantly, of his daily work in the streets.

Dan had come into Ficha Thrall's Bankside Saloon after dark. He had not found a job; he was lonely. There were men all about him drinking and talking. Sometimes they dropped a remark to him, but he knew none of them. It was hard for him to mix with them. The old man studying his blank sheet of paper had attracted his attention. In all the clatter he was so absorbed by his work that he scarcely stopped to taste the glass at his elbow.

"That 's Andy Hikes," a boater told Dan. "He 's got education, though you would n't guess it by half. He studies things once in a while and writes poetry. I ain't no judge," said the boater, swigging down a noisy swallow of rum, "I was n't brung up to understand such notions. But it 's got a good hammer into it when he reads it out."

"Yeanh."

The old man ran a hand over his eyes and looked back at his paper. He handled it delicately with the tips of his thin fingers.

"What 's it about?" asked the boater.

"It 's about the capture of Schenectady. I 'll read you the first verse. It goes this way." He cleared his throat and read

it out in a fine voice. The man who had spoken to Dan
thumped out the rhythm on his knee.

> "God prosper long our King and Queen,
> Our lives and safeties all;
> A sad misfortune once there did
> Schenectady befall."

"Listen to that, will you?" exclaimed the man next to
Dan. "Did n't I tell you? You could hammer it out with a
go-devil!"

"What 're you bringing in the King and Queen for? This
is a free country."

"I don't mean nothing by it, Stark," said the old man.
"The editor up to the *Journal* said he 'd give me three dollars for a poem out of history—something folks could get
a-hold of and say it happened in their grandpa's time. So
I bring the King and Queen into the first line to make the
time look proper; and God 's a help anywhere."

"What 's the safeties for?" asked Stark.

"That 's just to show people was scared. It kind of makes
the man reading figure there 's something uneasy going on.
There 's lots of tricks to this business; and this here 's a
neat specimen, if I say it myself. There ain't such a lot of
poets could put Schenectady into a poem under its own
name."

"Why not?"

"You just try."

"Cripus! I could make it rhyme."

"How?" asked the old man, looking up eagerly.

"Well how about Uticy for a rhyme?

> "Schenectady, Schenectady,
> Is halfway up to Uticy."

"That ain't the truth. There was n't any Utica when this
poem is being wrote."

"Who gives a dang?"

"Well, a reader likes to have the truth."

"Not if they read poetry. A man that's reading poetry's lost his principles."

"You got to fool them."

"It's a poor notion, reading poetry is. Reading rots the mind."

"Well, I got to get ahead with this," said the old man. He bent over his paper once more, and the boater left him.

Conversation broke out gustily. One man was trying to sell a mule to another. "Five years, sound as a sand-hill potato, see her yourself." "You don't mean that grey one, George?" "That's the one. Handsome article. That cute she can get by a lock without driving." "Then she ain't safe. I don't like a mule with independent ideas. I had a cook had 'em. She walked out on me with fifteen dollars." "Well, this mule won't. You got a towline on to her, anyways, ain't you? What's more, she's cheap. Sixty dollars for a five-year-old is cheap." "That's your mule, Andy?" asked a third man. "Sure, you know her. Ain't sixty dollars cheap for a five-year-old mule as kind as she?" "Sure. I know her. That mule's been five-year-old three times." "That ain't the one." "Named Andrew Jackson in full?" "Yeanh." "What for, if it was n't for his first in-aw-geration?" "That was her ma." "With the same broke knees?" "Just like 'em. It runs in them grey mules. They're just like a breed."

Dan listened and drank. His face was a little pale and he handled his glass with serious care. . . . He was getting very drunk. He kept his hands on the table as though they alone could keep him in touch with the room. A small, ratty-looking pair of men, at the other side of the room, were watching him. . . . The old street-cleaner glanced up from his paper; his face was sweaty; his mouth trembled. "Hey, Stark!" he shouted. "Hey, Stark, come here. I've finished it." All the boaters turned their heads as if they had been waiting for him. "Read it out, Andy," said the man Stark. The old fellow took a stiff swallow and pushed back his chair and stretched out his legs under the table.

"I'm just going to call it 'A Ballad.' Good honest title. But I've put down a foreword — "

"What 's that?"

"That 's the front end," said a boater. "It 's like the cow-catcher on to a engine. It 's to clear the track, but it don't do nothing but make the engine longer."

"It 's old style," said Andrew, "just to give the notion that this here 's a fact. It says: —

"In which is set forth the horrid cruelties practised by the French and Indians, on the night of February eight last; which I composed last night and am now writing this morning Friday, June twelve, 1690."

"Wait a minute, Andy. That 's good and written fine. Them long words go good there. But you ain't said how long it took to do. If it 's actual, then people want to know how long it took. People always want to know how long a thing takes to do. Why don't you put in 'Wrote in one hour 's time'? That looks as if you knew all about it and only had to figure the rhymes."

"That 's a good idea," said the old man, making an insertion.

Then he began to read: —

> "God prosper long our King and Queen,
>   Our lives and safeties all;
> A sad misfortune once there did
>   Schenectady befall."

The boater next to Dan began beating the rhythm on his knee, a smile of admiration on his hot red face.

> "From forth the woods of Canady
>   The Frenchmen took their way,
> The people of Schenectady
>   To captivate and slay."

"He rhymed it!" Stark exclaimed. "He done a regular rhyme on Schenectady! Can-ady: Schenec-tady. What do you know about that?"

"They marched for two and twenty days,
　And through the deepest snow;
And on a dismal winter night
　They struck the horrid blow.

"The lightsome sun that rules all day
　Had sunk into the west,
And all the drowsy villageers
　Had sought and found their rest.

"They thought they were in safety all,
　And dreamt not of the foe;
But at midnight they all awoke,
　In wonderment and woe."

Between stanzas, the old man would take another drink
from his glass, — which Stark was careful to keep filled, —
shake back his hair, run the back of his hand across his
lips, and fling it out in a gesture. He was unsteady on his
feet; his white hair swayed dizzily to Dan's eyes;

"For they were in their pleasant beds,
　And soundly sleeping, when
Each door was sudden open broke
　By six·or seven men. . . ."

The doors to the street banged open and swung shut; and
a man stood suddenly in the strong yellow light of the bar
lamps. His hand was raised halfway to his mouth to remove
the quid, but he began talking before it was out and his
tongue stuttered under it.

"There 's a case of cholera up above the combines."

They swung round on him like one man.

"Where?"

"Up above the combines."

"Who was it?"

"Henry Hindkopfer. Him and his cook and a driver-
boy."

In the stillness they became momentarily aware of old
Andy's voice sonorously repeating his poem.

". . . They then were murdered in their beds,
    Without shame or remorse;
And soon the floors and streets were strewed
    With many a bloody corpse.

"Oh, Christie! In the still night air
    It sounded dismally. . . ."

"God!" cried the man Stark. "Asiatic?"

"Bad," said the man. "All three of them deader'n turnips."

"I knew him," said Ficha Thrall from behind the bar. "He owes the house four-sixty-three. You can see it wrote there on the board."

"It's going to be another plague. I don't remember it good. I was a lad then."

"I do."

"I don't believe it is cholera at all. It must be the dyree."

"They give 'em green strawberry leaves, but it didn't do no good," said the man, shaking his head. "The doctor said it was a clear case."

"We've been having hot weather, and a lot of rain."

Dan lifted his head to stare at the men's set faces. He had heard stories of the Great Plague of '32. How the cholera came down Champlain to Albany, and traveled to New York along the Hudson, and found its way up the Erie as far as Rome. There had been great fog that summer, and men were struck as they steered their boats to a landing; or as they walked behind their mules they fell without a sound, letting the boat go by, to be found dead when the next team shied. It had been a time of terror; fog — it had been foggy.

The voice of the old man rang out again: —

". . . But some ran off to Albany,
    And told the awful tale;
Yet, though we gave our cheerful aid,
    It did not much avail.

And we were horridly afraid,
    And shook with terror, when . . ."

"I'll tell you one thing right off," said the man who had disbelieved the news. "I ain't starting west to-morrow, nor the day after, neither. I'm going to see what's going to happen first. I'm going to stay right here."

> ". . . The news came on the Sabbath morn,
>   Just at the break of day. . . ."

"Me neither," said another boater.

"It generally comes quick to the cities," said a third. "I'm danged glad I'll be starting for New York on the Ronan's."

"Cripus! It hit New York worst of all in thirty-two. Better 'n a hundred people a day!"

"I'm going to get back to the boat and tell the old woman. It'll tickle her anyway. She thought she wasn't going to have no chance to get her a new hat."

"Guess I'd better move along."

"Me too."

The man who had brought the news whirled and ran out. They stamped after him, the clatter of their quick talking fading down the street. A few remained: the two ratty-looking men who were watching Dan, Stark, Ficha Thrall, at the bar, one or two others, old Andy, staggering, but finishing his piece.

> ". . . And here I end this long ballad,
>   The which you just have read;
> I wish that it may stay on earth
>   Long after I am dead."

The glass dropped from his fingers; it smashed on the floor with a bright glitter; Thrall moved to the board and made a mark; Dan started drunkenly; the old man slumped down on his chair. . . .

"It's all right," he said in a low voice. "It's good. It's pretty damn good, Andy. I liked it a lot."

Andy dropped his face on his loosely folded arms and went to sleep.

"Sure," said Stark. "Surely."

He shook Andy by the shoulder.

"Better leave him be," said Thrall. "When he wakes up I 'll kick him out."

All but the ratty-looking men, Stark, and Dan left.

"I 'll take his paper up to the *Journal*," Stark said. "It 's worth three dollars to any man. Don't he write a pretty hand?"

"Come on, you," Thrall said to Dan. "Get out. I 'm shutting up."

Dan stared at him without appearing to hear.

"Come on, you," Thrall said. "Get out of here."

One of the ratty-looking men touched his arm.

"All right, brother. Leave him be. Me and Frank here 'll take him home. Me and Frank knows him. Don't we, Frank?"

"Sure," said the other. "We know him."

"Sure, we know where he lives. We 'll take him back. Poor feller, he comes from our town; he 's new on the canal. He 's drunk."

"Sure," said Frank. "He 's drunk. We 'll take him back."

Each took hold of one of Dan's arms.

"Come along, Will," they said to Dan.

"My name ain't —"

"Come on," they said. "We 'll take you back."

"My name ain't Will," said Dan. "My name 's Dan."

"Sure, William Daniel."

"Just Dan."

"All right, Dan."

"Thank you," said Dan.

"He 's drunk," Thrall said.

"Sure," said Frank. "He 's drunk. We 'll take him home. Poor kid."

"I ain't drunk, neither; I 'm sleepy. Just kind of sleepy."

"That 's it," said Frank soothingly, "just sleepy."

"Thanks," said Dan. "Pleased to meet you."

They walked him through the door. Behind them they heard the bolt bang in.

It was cool and still. At the end of the alley a light mist trembled on the canal. The feet of the three of them beat

oddly along the board walk. Up over the city a bit of moonlight showed them a roof here and there, glistening as though
there were frost.

"Where 'll we fix him, Jack?" asked Frank.

"We 'll take him over the lock. There might be somebody
coming for him here."

"That's a good idea. Come along, you. Lift your feet
and set 'em down ahead. That's the way a man makes
progress walking."

"They ain't your feet," Dan mumbled. "How can you
tell?"

"Snub him," said Jack.

They yanked him off his balance. Dan stumbled, his feet
trying to catch up. They knew how to handle him.

The great basin opened before them. The boats showed
vaguely in the mist, here and there a blob of light from a
night lantern. The air was fresh. The river lapped softly
against the lower gates of the lock.

"Hullo," said the keeper, coming out of his office, a pipe
in his hand giving out heavy, sweet smoke that made Dan
gag. "Taking sonny home to momma?"

"Just about," said Frank.

They ran him across to the embankment.

"You 're good fellers," said Dan. "I 'm pleased to meet
you."

"Sure," said Frank.

"How about here?" asked Jack.

"Back of the ear, Jack."

"Take his hat off."

Frank took it off. Dan grabbed for it unsteadily.

"Say . . ."

A dull *tunk*. Frank eased Dan down.

"He 's heavier 'n you 'd think."

"Let 's see what he 's got."

Frank bent over him.

"Try the pants pocket."

"Ain't much." He fumbled a couple of bills. "Not over
two dollars."

"Well, come along. We might pick up another."

"Not much chance. This damn cholera."

"Come along."

"Wait a minute. I 'll put his hat on. He might catch cold."

"Oh, come along."

Their feet moved off quietly through the mist.

Hired On

"Hey there, you!"

A big man stood in bare feet on the deck of the old brown boat in the early dawn and stared at Dan.

Dan's fingers caught at the planks, and he hitched himself forward, and then lay still.

"Well," said the boater. "That 's a good thing. He ain't dead. Hey there, you!"

Dan lifted his head and stared sleepily.

"Hey there! Wake up! What 's the matter?"

Dan rolled over and sat up and then suddenly caught hold of his head.

"What 's the matter?"

Dan groaned.

"I guess I got hit on the head."

"Well, there 's worse places to get hit."

"I must 've got drunk last night."

"I should n't wonder. I did myself."

"I feel sick."

"Go put your head in the canal."

"No," Dan said. "I don't want to do that."

"Well, it 's a good thing to do."

Dan let go of his head, shook it once or twice, and looked round.

"Feel better?"

"Yeanh."

It had fallen cool during the night. The dawn wind was lean and fresh. Dan climbed awkwardly to his feet. An idea occurred to him. He felt in his pockets.

"Jeepers," he said. "Jeepers Cripus!"

"Cleaned out, eh?"

"Yeanh."

"You showed the signs."

The boater fished in his pockets.

"Have a chaw?"

"No. I don't want it."

"Well, I find it's good like this. Gives a man to set his teeth again." He bit off a chew, got his jaw going, spat onto the dock. "Well, now you're down to hardpan, what you going to do? Got a job?"

"No."

"Want to hire on to my boat?"

"Maybe."

"Regular wages. Twelve dollars."

"All right. I guess I will."

"She's old, but she's a good boat. I got the best cook on the canal down in the cabin. I'm pulling right out," said the boater. "I've three pair of millstones and mill machinery for Butterfield to Rome, and I've got to get 'em through quick. Cholera or no cholera. I never was scared of no disease. What's your name?"

"Dan Harrow."

"Me, I'm Samson Weaver," the boater said, and held out his hand. "Come aboard. We'd ought to make good time. There won't be many boats till the scare's gone. We ought to get through quick. I ain't scared of cholera."

He turned to the cabin door.

"Annie!" he bellowed. "Hey there! Annie!"

There was no answer.

"Hey, there! Annie! Wake up."

"She's a good cook, but she does sleep hard," Weaver said to Dan. "I'll have to shake her out."

He clattered down the steps shouting, "Annie! Hey, there!"

Dan heard him stamp back to the bunks. Then Weaver swore.

"She's cleared out. She's cleared out clean. Run a regular

rig on me. I did n't notice last night, coming aboard drunk like I was. And I got right out this morning without looking. Well, we 'll have to get along without no cook. Come on down."

The cabin was large for an ordinary freighter; it was nicely fitted out with two comfortable rocking-chairs and an almost new stove, well blacked. Weaver was slamming wood into the stove when Dan entered.

"The old puddery punk!" he growled. "Well, she stocked up anyhow yesterday."

He poured a handful of coffee into the kettle and put the frying pan over to heat, and cut bacon. The fire caught with a roar and snapped briskly. A bit of sunlight found a bright nasturtium on the wallpaper. Weaver bent over to pull on a pair of socks.

"What do you know about that!" he exclaimed. "She went and darned my sock afore she left!"

He stared at it in wonder, rubbing the back of his head.

"Maybe she was scared of the cholera," Dan suggested.

"The hell she was. I seen she 'd took a notion to a tug captain on the Swiftsure. But I never thought to beat it out of her. Well, women are kind of like that. They 'll fool you every chance they get, and if you catch 'em, why, gol! they 'll fool you into thinking they was n't fooling."

He laced his boots and went back to his cooking.

"Got any bag?" he asked.

"Yeanh. I left it at the Michigan Six Day offices."

"Well, we can pick it up when we go by. I 'm posting through to Utica on their line this time. My team needs a rest, anyway. And I can make quicker time that way. The haul on to Rome won't take no time."

He broke two eggs into the pan and slammed the shells into the coffee kettle.

"She made the best coffee I ever got into my mouth," he said.

In a few minutes they sat down to their breakfast at the table hinged against the wall, with the smell of coffee and bacon filling the cabin, and the sunlight finding another window.

"Listen," said Weaver.

Dan held his cup against his mouth.

"Ain't hardly a sound," Weaver said. "There won't be such a lot of boats pulling out to-day. They 're scared. It 's funny how people 'll think they 're better off with a few boards round 'em, hiding the sky. Me, I never was scared of cholera or any damn disease; but I would n't want to wait for it to come in a door."

He ate and drank hurriedly. And every now and then he lifted his head, as if he were listening, his square red face, with its night's stubble, hard.

But when they got up to do the dishes his mind came back to the cook.

"If I had the time, I 'd go after her," said Weaver. "But she 's probably laying low. The Sarsey Sal was a fine boat with Annie on to it."

When he went on deck, Dan recognized other boats; and he realized that Weaver was the man he had overheard Henderson talking to, and that the absent Annie must be the Irishwoman who had been washing clothes on the deck and who had wished for a house and a man to come in for his dinner; and, glancing at Weaver's back and sturdy shoulders, all at once Dan felt sorry for him.

The Burning Boat

At the Troy relay on the Michigan Six Day, they had trouble in getting a driver to take them up to the next change. But Weaver had paid for through horse-and-driver service, and he insisted loudly that he get the full service or have his money back.

He pulled a paper from his pocket and waved it an inch from the man's nose.

"Here 's the bill — horse-and-driver service through to Utica. Where 's the clerk?"

"I act as such," said the hostler. "There ain't a driver here 'll go. Wait a minute, though." He turned and shouted a question into the barn. A voice whined back at him. "Roy's upstairs. Roy's in liquor. He might go if you was to offer him an extra dollar."

"Call him down."

"Roy!" yelled the hostler. "Hey, Roy!"

After a minute a seedy individual, wearing a hat which had lost its crown, appeared in the door, and languidly leaned against it.

"Roy," said the hostler. "This feller wants to go on up. You drive him?"

"Cholera?" asked Roy in a faint voice.

"There ain't much chance," said the hostler. "He's going to give you a dollar extry."

Roy took off his hat and looked into it, as if he used it to keep his thoughts in. Then he spat through the hole.

"A dollar don't show up every day," he said in his thin lazy voice. "So I got to feel it in my pants pocket first."

Weaver snorted.

"That's a hell of a notion. Why, how do I know you can walk that far?"

Roy lifted his eyes mournfully at him, then pointed to the waiting team.

"The off mule's got a tail, ain't she?"

"Yeanh."

"I can hold on to it, can't I?"

"Yeanh. I guess you can do that."

"All right." He reached in the door for his snake whip. "Where's the dollar, mister?"

Weaver gave it to him.

"We make good time with Roy driving," said Roy. "A mule can stand to be licked, but she can't stand to have a man pinching her tail."

Weaver jumped aboard and Dan heaved in the plank.

"You steer first lick," Weaver said to him. "I've got to find where things are. A woman keeps a boat looking neat, but they have n't no sense at all where they put things. A man can't hardly find a thing where a neat woman lives."

He went below, and from time to time as they went on Dan could hear him grumbling to himself.

The boat hauled heavily. But the mules kept up a fair pace, and the walking seemed to be having a good effect on the driver. After the first two miles he was able to get along without holding to the mule's tail; and the animal showed her pleasure by switching it for several minutes with extraordinary rapidity and complication.

At the combines, Weaver came up again.

"Where's the boat?" he asked the lock-keeper.

"Which one?" said the keeper.

"The cholera one."

"Oh. Why, it's half a mile up on the left. You know the Wat cove, set back, where the towpath crosses on a bridge. They took up the bridge and drawed it into there. The doctor said it was best off the canal."

"Disease ain't a thing to be scared of," Samson remarked after a time. "I never had no notions about disease."

"No sense in it."

"No sense at all. Annie used to laugh at it."

"Sure," said Dan.

"I had a cold once into my chest. Regular constricter, but she minded me real handy. She was a queer gal some ways. Knowed a lot. Used to say she thought the Lord loved a drunken man. She said a drunken man never died of no disease. Maybe that's why Roy come along — maybe he knew that."

"Maybe."

"I just had me a good stiff ration of rum. Figure the cholera won't touch a man that's well washed up with liquor."

"Yeanh. I've heard that."

"You better go down and get a drink, Dan."

"Guess I won't just yet. I guess I'll hold off it for a day."

"All right. We ought to be coming up to Wat's cove pretty quick."

They rounded a bend.

"There it is," exclaimed Weaver. "Right there where them people are standing on the bridge. You can see the boat over against them balsams, right there where that cloud shows in the water, see? What in nation are they a-doing?"

"Seems like that man was setting fire to it," Dan said.

"That's right, that's right. Setting fire to it. Good idee. He's got some rags he's putting a light to. Oiled rags by that yeller smoke. They've soaked the deck. See it ketch, Dan?"

A queer, white-faced silence hung over the little group of four men on the towpath as their companion jumped into a rowboat and pushed away. Their eyes followed the heavy smoke upward. Blue-and-yellow flame licked delicately at the planking, ate in, and then caught hotly.

"Hey there!" Weaver yelled at the driver. "What're you stopping for? Lay into them mules there! We've got to get on."

The men on the towpath paid no heed to the passing boat.

"See them three boxes?" Weaver caught Dan's elbow. "Reckon they're burning 'em right on the boat. Ain't that an awful way to have to be buried?"

Another bend; but they could see the flames spouting up against sombre dark balsams. A little farther, and they saw only the smoke mounting up, a bright cinder or two in the midst of it.

"Gol," said Weaver gustily. "Gol, Dan. I'm going to get me another drink."

Poor Samson Weaver

All during the day Samson continued to drink. He would come on deck red-faced and sweaty and bothered with a new worry.

"Dan, I've drank down a terrible lot," he would say. "I've drank more'n a man can to keep sober. But it don't do a thing outside of making me sweat. It ain't right, Dan."

At night Dan could hear him tossing in his bunk. Once he lay still for quite a while, talking to himself, telling Annie about the burning boat. Two things kept eating at him, his fear of the cholera and his lonesomeness. When the cook left, the Sarsey Sal had become a strange boat to him. His continual drinking made even the familiar sights beyond the towpath vague and unreal. Quite suddenly his thoughts had been turned in upon himself, unnerving him.

Halfway through his third turn at steering, he stamped for Dan to come up. His eyes shone feverishly.

"What's the trouble?" Dan asked.

Weaver passed his left hand over his eyes and down his nose.

"Dan," he said, "I like you. That's a fact. There's something wrong with me, Dan. I'm kind of nervous. It ain't like I was scared of being sick. I ain't never been sick, only for that chest-cold I told you about. But it don't seem like I see very good."

"Well, that's too bad."

"Set down, set down," Weaver said irritably. "With you standing up there cutting into my sight, I get nervous.— Dan, I wanted to speak to you. I aim to raise your pay, Dan. You're a good lad. You and me ought to get along good. You're satisfied, ain't you?"

"Sure."

Weaver let out a long breath.

"That's good. Just the same I aim to raise your pay. You're doing a steersman's work. I'll give you twenty a month, for this trip, anyhow. Only I got to get you to spell me more. I don't breathe very easy, Dan. If Annie had n't 've cut along like she did, she could spell you."

"Surely, that's all right, Mister Weaver."

"Just Samson, Dan. Just Samson, to my friends. Plain Samson Weaver. You don't mind taking on for a spell now, do you, Dan?"

"No," said Dan. "I don't mind any."

"All right. I'll go get some sleep."

It was a still night, cold, close to freezing. The stars were mere glittering points. The moon had not yet risen.

The old Sarsey Sal stretched out ahead of Dan in the light of the night lantern, blunt-ended, moving beside the towpath with a faint sibilant whisper against the water. The thin thread of the towline curved on ahead to the mules, plodding patiently with nodding ears, now and then visible over the skyline. A little way behind them walked the driver, his hands in his pockets.

Dan did not call Samson till the sun was up. He was no better; his hands were getting jumpy.

"I dreamed," he said. "I did n't get no sleep at all. Things kept coming in the door."

Dan went forward to tend the team, a thin pair of bays. They were enjoying their vacation and they nuzzled at Dan's hands. He slapped them hearty whacks, and swore at them, though they made all kinds of room for him as he took in their oats. It was good to feel them under his hand, to shove them over with his shoulder when he cleaned the stalls.

When he had finished fixing the horses, he went back to the cabin to cook breakfast, ate it, spelled the driver to let him eat; and then went to his bunk to sleep.

But after an hour Samson, stamping on deck, woke him. His face and neck were covered with sweat.

"I just seen Annie setting there on the cabin," he said. "I ain't notional, Dan. But she set there just as plain. She was darning the same sock I got on my foot, and I cussed her, and she said, 'What an old roarer you be, Sammy!' — just like she always did. I ain't notional, Dan, but it don't seem right. I need sleep. Would you mind spelling me a bit?"

"No," said Dan. "I guess not."

"I 'd lie by for a while, only Butterfield 's in such a hurry for his damned machinery. I 've got to get it through."

"Sure."

Weaver stared at him with a worried expression, sighed, and went down. But he came up again after lunch and managed to fill out nearly four hours at the rudder. Dan slept like a log.

"I reckon I 'll be able to last out most of the night," he said.

There was a stiff frost that night, and the tread of the mules sounded tight and clear. More boats were upon the water than there had been on the two preceding days; but few of them moved after dark.

Down below, in the cabin of the Sarsey Sal, Samson Weaver continued his conversation between himself and the departed Annie; his voice higher than usual, talking fast; then silent while he waited for her to answer. Listening, Dan would feel a stir in the hackles on his neck, and his hand kept straying there to put them down.

Two miles from the relay station between Little Falls and Utica, one of the company mules went dead lame. The driver flogged him ahead for a quarter of a mile and then yelled to Dan to put the boat in shore. He came back, caught the tie-ropes, and snubbed them to posts.

"When a mule can't think of anything else to do, it lames himself," he said. "What would a man want to invent such an animal for is out of my knowledge. Just to see 'em you can tell it 's against nature. It spoils a man's stomach."

Grumbling, he climbed on to the sound mule.

"I 'll be back with a new pair in maybe an hour."

Dan sat down on the deck. The moon was coming up behind him, and for a long way his eyes followed the small figures of the mules along the black ridge of the towpath, the driver sitting sideways on the leader. Directly under him the voice of Samson Weaver broke out in streaks of muttering. Shadows grew and changed with the mysterious swiftness that is theirs by night. There were no boats visible, no farm lights showing against the hills; only the pocket of yellow glimmer cast by the night lantern of the Sarsey Sal.

Then, far back on the towpath and coming forward in the still gleam of the moon, Dan heard the rapid tapping of a galloping horse. Behind him the canal bent round a wide curve, with trees on either bank. Their shadows clung to the water; and suddenly in the heart of them the hammer of the horse's hoofs echoed sharp and clear.

He broke into the moonlight, his grey coat stained with sweat, running hard with a fine drive, a sparkle of silver snatching his bit; the rider hunched forward on his withers, a black shape, as if he had dropped out of the shadows before the horse burst free.

Dan's quick ears caught the clink of a loose shoe as the horse came on; and just as he reached the stern of the boat he cast it. It dropped in a short silver arc, spun for an instant on the towpath, and splashed into the water beside a clump of arrowhead.

Dan jumped to his feet, and waved his arm.

"Say!" he shouted. "Say, mister. You 've dropped a shoe."

He stepped ashore, climbed down to the water's edge, and fished it out, a plate shoe, with light bar calks, as smooth as polished silver.

The rider had drawn in his horse and was returning at a walk.

"Did you get it?"

"Yeanh," said Dan. "I seen it go in by that arrerhead."

"Thanks."

Dan handed it up, looking for the man's face, but all he could see under the wide brim of his hat was a smooth chin and the glitter of two eyes. The man pocketed the shoe.

"Lucky you seen it," he said. "I 'd have had to wait too long to have another made. Them shoes were cut special."

"They 're handy-looking," said Dan admiringly.

"Ain't I seen you before?"

"Once," said Dan. "That was in Hennessy's saloon. I 've seen you twice. Once in Boonville and once in Albany."

"I did n't see you those times."

"No, you did n't."

"Well, we did each other a favor in Hennessy's," said the man.

"Yeanh."

"Well, I 've got to get on. I want to get to Rome to-morrow."

"Close after you?"

"I shook 'em in Albany," said the man.

"You seen a horse trader? Calls himself Henderson?"

"Yes. He 's the man I got you to get out of Hennessy's with Spinning."

"You better watch for him," said Dan. "He 's Department of Justice."

"I 'd guessed it."

The man laughed.

"I don't have to worry about a fat twerk like him."

"He was right behind you in Albany."

The man leaned forward and stroked his horse's neck, and the horse pricked his ears. Dan petted his nose and the horse nuzzled him, blowing clouds of steam against his shirt.

"He likes you," said the man suddenly. Then he laughed again. "I can handle a better man than Henderson. There 's no use worrying about him. I 've got to get on. What 's your name, son?"

"Dan Harrow."

"Harrow," repeated the man. "I 'll remember that. Thanks for spotting that shoe."

He wheeled the horse and went off at a lope. The horse showed no limp.

"Gol," Dan said to himself. "See him nurse that horse! He can ride."

Hoarfrost was forming on the deck when he got aboard the Sarsey Sal. He looked up the canal once more, but Gentleman Joe and the grey horse had passed from sight. The canal was still.

In the bunk cuddy, he heard Weaver muttering. Suddenly his voice became articulate.

"Dan!" he called. "Dan, Dan! Come here, quick!"

Dan ran down. The curtains to the cuddy were pulled back and the brass lamp sent its light directly into the bunks.

Weaver was lying on his back, stiff under the blankets. His face was still very red. When he saw Dan, he lifted his head for an instant, but immediately it fell back on the pillow, and he glared straight up at the planks above him.

"There's something on deck, Dan. What is it on deck?"

"There ain't nothing on deck," Dan said. "I've just come down."

Dan filled the empty glass with rum. He wondered that Samson had not noticed the stopping of the boat, or heard his meeting with Calash.

The boater swallowed noisily.

"Got to keep myself washed out," he said. "Only way to fool this damn disease. I wish Annie was here. You're a good lad, Dan."

He lay still a moment. Then he tossed his head to one side.

"I'm queer, Dan. I'm feeling mortal queer."

"Kind of bad?"

"Bad. I want to see a doctor, Dan. You won't go off leaving me to Utica, will you?"

"No."

"You're a good lad, Dan. We'll get there to-morrow?"

"Yeanh. I guess so."

"Fetch me a doctor, Dan. First off."

"All right."

"You're an honest lad, Dan. You'll need money to fetch a doctor. Doctors look at your tongue, but they like the color of your money better. It's nature, Dan. It don't mean nothing."

"No."

"I got quite a lot of money on the boat, Dan. Banks go bust, so I put mine right into the boat. It's in the beam, Dan. There's a piece lifts out. I ain't got any kin, Dan, nor nobody to look out after me, now Annie's gone. Only you, Dan. You'll let me see a doctor when we get to Utica?"

"First off."

Weaver closed his eyes, and for a few moments he seemed

asleep. Then the lids quivered and jumped up, and he was staring wildly at the roof again.

"It's come back onto the deck. It hadn't ought to be there. Chase it off, Dan. For God's sake, chase it off. I didn't do nothing. I didn't do a thing. It's back there. Go and look."

His voice trailed off into incoherent sentences. "Get on back, Annie. . . . Pa said for you to get the cows, Joe. . . . I always did like buttermilk. . . ."

Dan got up. The cuddy was hot and stuffy, but Samson could not bear to have a window opened. Dan saw to the fire, his mind on Calash, riding ahead of his pursuer. He would never be caught.

Samson's voice followed him.

"It's back again. I can hear it. Chase it off, Dan."

He went on deck. Sam Henderson was sitting with his back to the rudder post, smoking a cigar. The night lantern shone over his plump shoulders, leaving his face in darkness, except for the faint red glow of the cigar end, which was mirrored in his eyes.

"Well," he said, "well, well. Ain't I seen you before, young man?"

"Yeanh, Mr. Henderson."

"Why, sure, that's right. I saw you in Boonville and in Rome. You wanted to tell me about a horse I'd lost, which was nice of you, though Spinning didn't seem to think so. He said this Joe Calash was in the saloon and got out while you was talking to us. But you couldn't know that."

"No."

Henderson grunted.

"What're you doing here?"

Dan glanced out to the towpath where a brown horse stood hitched to one of the tie-ropes.

"Working," he said.

"Yeanh? Who owns this boat?"

"Samson Weaver."

Again Henderson grunted.

"What's that?" he asked suddenly, staring down between his knees.

"That's Samson," Dan said. "He's been that way most of the trip up from Albany."

"Does he do it a lot?"

"He's been that way most of the trip up from Albany," Dan repeated.

Under them Samson shouted.

"Chase it off, Dan! Chase it away!"

The horse snorted and jerked back on the rope.

"Whoa!" Henderson shouted. "I don't blame him, though. I feel that way myself. Poor Samson. He always was a hard drinker. He's got a weak heart. This cholera must have give him a scare. He always was scared of a disease. It's funny thing, a big man like him."

"Dan!" yelled Samson. "Dan!"

"Maybe I'd better go down," Dan said.

"No," said Henderson. "Has there been anybody along the towpath to-night?"

"Not many boats just now," said Dan.

"Listen here, young man. I guess I might as well tell you. See this. I'm a Department of Justice man. I'm after this Calash, called Gentleman Joe. I'm kind of suspicious of you, but I ain't going to do anything if you don't try to head me wrong. Has there been anybody along the towpath to-night?"

Dan gazed at the toes of his shoes.

"Yeanh," he said, after a moment. "Yeanh. He was coming fast."

"Well, I can't catch him now. I'll get into Utica in the morning. He ought to be there. Charley Mack, the bank walker, he'll have heard him go by if he ain't seen him."

"Dan! Dan! Dan!"

"I better go down, maybe," said Dan.

"No," said Henderson. "I'll go down. He's an old friend. He'll be glad to see me. Poor Samson Weaver."

He went down the narrow stairs nimbly for so stout a man.

There was the sound of a striking match, and the sharp sour smell of brimstone came up to Dan on deck, and a harsh scream. The horse jumped again and wrenched against his fastening. "Easy," said Dan. "Easy, boy."

"It 's only me, Samson," he heard Henderson saying, quietly. "It 's only Samuel."

There was no further sound, until all at once Dan could hear Henderson breathing sharply.

The stout man came up again. His face was covered with sweat and his round eyes were glassy.

"He 's took a kind of fit," he said. "He 's stiff as a cherry post. He must 've thought I was somebody else. Poor Samson."

He took off his hat and wiped his handkerchief over his bald head.

"I 've got to get along, young man. If you see anything of this man Calash, write to me. I give you the address."

He went down to the horse and lit a fresh cigar; his hands shook a trifle; but, with the cigar once filling his mouth, he steadied himself and mounted, raised his hand to Dan, and galloped off. The horse seemed eager. . . .

Dan sat by himself. The first grey of dawn and the returning driver appeared together, the mules ambling along the towpath at a good pace.

Dan got up and went down into the cabin. The candle on the stove burned feebly in the grey light, but Dan took it up and went back to the bunks. Samson was lying on his side, his knees drawn up and his head back. His eyes were wide-open, his smooth cheeks a dark, unnatural red.

Dan put his hand down against his side. Then he went on deck.

The driver had cast off the tie-ropes and hitched his mules.

"I took longer than I figured."

"Longer than I figured," said Dan.

"Well, we 'd better get going. How 's the old—?"

He pointed his thumb at the cabin and twirled it between his eyes.

"He 's lying quiet," Dan said.

"It's a good thing," said the driver.

The mules heaved up into the collars, took up the slack, heaved, and the Sarsey Sal groaned a bit and moved sluggishly ahead, with the dawn wind against its bows, and the water muttering on the rudder.

Ten-Dollar Corpse

While they waited outside the weighlock in Utica, Dan searched Samson's clothes for money. He felt that it would take him too long to find the beam which the boater had made his bank. But in the trousers Samson still wore he found four dollars, and in the wallet in his Sunday coat he found five more — enough to see them past the weighlock.

When the Sarsey Sal had been passed through, and Dan had paid his toll, the driver asked him where he wanted to tie up.

"Anywhere'll do," Dan said. "We're hauling out for Rome to-morrow."

"That's funny," said the driver. "A short haul like that. I'd think you'd want to go right on."

"Weaver wants to see a doctor."

"Yeanh? Well, a doctor's a good thing when a man's going to die. He can write the certificate, anyway."

"I hadn't thought of that," said Dan.

"Damndest thing you ever see. A man can't marry a woman without getting a certificate — unless he takes a cook on to the canal. And then people'll have to say, 'My, My!' He can't get born respectable without a man writing a document about him. No, sir, the poor lobster can't even pull in his head to die unless somebody says it's O. K."

"That's right, at that."

"Yeanh. It makes life a tough proposition, all right. — Well, I guess I could take you up to Wheaden's wharf. It ain't in use and it's just above the Six Day. Suit you?"

"Surely," said Dan.

"Ged-dup!" The driver cracked his whip at the mules. *"You* ain't got no certificates. I 'll leather the tar out of you."

They tied up. Dan went into the cabin to get his coat, and when he left he locked the door after him. Utica again. Though he had been there only once before, the basin had a pleasantly familiar feel.

He walked with the driver behind the mules as far as the Michigan Six Day office, where he signed a receipt for service rendered.

"You ain't the man that paid for this," remarked the clerk, comparing signatures.

"That 's all right," the driver said, contemptuously. "Weaver 's sick. How the hell could he sign?"

"Then you 'd ought to put 'per — whatever your initials is,' " said the clerk. "Anybody 'd ought to know that."

"Aw, spit over your chin," said the driver, and he led Dan out, shook hands, and disappeared into the stables.

Dan idly watched the loading and unloading boats, and the boats passing through, the din of voices like a mist beyond his ears. He wondered what he ought to do. He did not know anybody in Utica to whom to go for advice.

After a while he started walking up into the city, eyeing shop fronts as he passed. He did not stop until, in one of the poorer quarters, he came to a store with black curtains at the windows, and a neat sign, white letters on black : —

LESTER CUSHMAN

FUNERAL DIRECTOR

Dan jerked the bell pull and heard, way back in the house, a single soft bell like the stroke of a clock. In a moment the door was opened, and he was confronted by a tall pale man wearing a sober black coat and black cotton gloves and carrying a clean handkerchief in his right hand.

"Step in," said the man, in a cool, soft voice.

Dan found himself in a dark hall, with stairs leading up

from the back and a door on either side. On one of the
doors was printed in white letters:—

BEREAVEMENT PARLOR

"Walk into the parlor," the man in black said quietly.
"No, not there, young gentleman, — not yet, — the door
across the hall, if you please."

He held open the door. Dan walked stiffly into the room,
which was fitted out with grey curtains and black haircloth
furniture.

"Sit down," said the man in black, and he took a chair himself, carefully pulling his coat tails over his knees as he did
so. Dan sat down and placed his hat beside his feet and took
out his handkerchief to wipe his face.

"Too bad," said the man in black, scarcely above a whisper.
"High and low, it finds us all; better so, perhaps."

"I guess that's right," said Dan. "I'd like to see Mr.
Cushman."

The man in black made a slight, stiff bow.

"I am Mr. Cushman, at your service, Mister — ?"

"Harrow," said Dan. "Dan Harrow."

"Thank you, Mr. Harrow. I shall do my best for you. I
have a very creditable name in this city, I assure you."

"I guess that's right," said Dan, swallowing.

"Too bad. Just tell me where and I shall take everything
off your hands. Details are hard to mind in a case such as
this is."

"Yeanh," said Dan. "That's what I come to you for."

"Yes, yes, Mr. Harrow, and that is what I am here for,
to relieve sorrow of its burdens."

"I'm afraid," Dan began.

"Certainly, certainly, I shall be glad to suit your needs.
Something economical, simple, but dignified. Plain pine,
perhaps. Pine, stained, looks very well. And is inexpensive,
relatively speaking. Not cheap. At such a time we do
not want cheapness, do we? I can show you some very nice
coffins if you would care to see them — about twenty-five
dollars, say, lined nicely in white satin?"

"No," said Dan. "It would n't do."

Mr. Cushman regarded him for an instant out of cold, fortified eyes.

"No," he agreed. "Such things are trying. Sister, might I ask?"

"No," said Dan. "It's a man."

"Dear me, a friend. Very hard."

"Well, I've known him four days," said Dan, "but he was all right."

He looked down at his shoes, his cheeks flushed.

"Mr. Cushman, I come in to get advice. He's a boater, name of Samson Weaver, who I hired on to in Albany and he died just outside of Utica. He's down on the basin on his boat, and he ain't got any kin, and I ain't got any money, and I come to see what I ought to do about it, and I thought maybe you could tell me, and I guess that's the whole of it."

Mr. Cushman coughed and took off his gloves.

"What did he die of?" he asked.

"I would n't say. He was scared of cholera. There's been a scare."

"Sure," said Mr. Cushman. "I heard about it."

Dan gave him the details.

Mr. Cushman took off his coat and hung it over a chair. His sleeves were rolled up, showing strong forearms, light-colored from indoor work. He unbuttoned a pair of cuffs.

"Hmmm," he said. "Hmmm. It sure was n't cholera. So you don't know what to do, eh?"

"No," said Dan. "That's what I come in here for. I can't pay for no funeral, but I'd ought to get a certificate of death."

"That might be arranged."

He glanced sideways at Dan.

"You and I might do a dicker on him. He was n't a close friend, you say."

"No, I would n't say he was; but there was n't anything I had against him."

"Well, I know a doctor that might want to take him.

Sometimes I 've been able to supply him with a specimen. Suppose I saw to the certificate, et cetera, and took him off your hands, would ten dollars do?"

"I ain't got even that much."

"Ten dollars paid to you," said Mr. Cushman.

"Why, I don't know that that 's right," said Dan.

"Why not? He won't know anything about it."

"I guess that 's right."

"He 'll be serving a useful end of science."

"Surely."

"Then he goes on the books as buried in the public grounds. It 's all very proper when you look at it correctly. Where 's the boat?"

"Wheaden's wharf. It 's the Sarsey Sal, a brown one."

Mr. Cushman rubbed his hands dryly together.

"Well, you can look out for me about eight." . . .

Dan stopped in at a waterside bar and had a drink. There were no familiar faces there, so he walked back to the boat. Once in the cabin, he began to worry about Samson Weaver. The boater's presence was about him, vaguely. The tobacco box, and the charred clay pipe on the shelf with the clock; the clock itself, black marble, a prized possession of Weaver's, with a small silver horse prancing on the top. Once, at the beginning of the haul from Albany, he had said to Dan, "When I hear the tickin' it sounds like he was galloping out the time, and when it strikes, then I think he 's crossed a bridge." But the most bothersome thing was his suit of Sunday clothes. Dan could see one elbow of the coat between the curtain and the wall, a dark green cloth with a red hair stripe, if you looked at it closely.

A fly buzzed along one of the windowpanes. Dan watched it idly. He wanted something to smooth him down; he looked at the pipe and tobacco, Warnick and Brown Tobacco, made for boaters. He had smoked some once, heavy, sweet, soothing stuff. He got up suddenly and filled the pipe and lighted it. It tasted good. A blue cloud of it floated up to the wall and the fly came buzzing through it to dart for the other side of the cabin.

But the Sunday coat kept catching Dan's eye, and little by little the smoke began to lose its flavor.

"Cripus!" he exclaimed after a while. "It ain't right."

He got up, knocked out the pipe, and went into the sleeping cuddy. When he returned to the cabin it was so dark that he had to light the lamp. The clock struck six.

He sat down again under the lamp and pulled the boater's Bible from its shelf. For an hour he thumbed the pages, reading here and there, but the Book did not hold his interest. The cabin hemmed him in. On the wharf outside, sounds of passers-by became less frequent. A boat passed occasionally, but the voice of the driver was dim.

Dan replaced the Bible and went into the sleeping cuddy and fumbled in his bag. When he returned, he had the volume of Shakespeare's plays the peddler had given him on the road from Tug Hill.

He opened it haphazard and began to read, " 'A made a finer end and went away an it had been any christom child. 'A parted even just between twelve and one. . . ." He did not understand it all; but the old man lay before him, plucking the sheets and calling, "God, God, God!" and he knew at once that it was real. . . .

It seemed no time at all before he heard a man thumping on the deck.

"Gol," he said, and sighed, and shut the book.

Mr. Cushman came in, dressed in a pair of overalls and a flannel shirt, and accompanied by a sharp-faced little man with red hair.

"Evening, Harrow. This is my friend, Mr. Nidds. Where's the body?"

Dan pointed his thumb.

They went in. "All curled up," said Nidds. "The doctor likes 'em straight."

"We only promise delivery," Cushman reminded him. "Wrap him up."

He came out to Dan. "Here's the money, Harrow. All right?"

"Yeanh," said Dan, fumbling the bills.

"All right, then. Any fuss, refer them to Lester Cushman. Ready, Nidds?"

"Sure. He weighs like cement. What's he all dressed up for?"

Dan mumbled.

"Well, they're too big for me, anyways," said Nidds.

They pushed their way up the stairs, the sack between them scraping on the steps and bunting the sides. As they dropped it on deck to catch their breaths, there was a click of breaking clay.

"Must've been a pipe on him somewheres," said Nidds. "That's too bad. I needed a pipe."

Dan put out the lamp and followed them.

"Get along," said Cushman.

They carried it out to the dock and heaved it into the back of a light wagon. There was no one to notice them. The watchman was way down the wharf under a door lamp, whittling a toothpick.

"See you again some day, maybe," Cushman said good-naturedly to Dan.

Dan raised his hand. The wagon clattered ahead and turned down a street. When it disappeared, Dan drew in his breath. The air was freer now that Samson had gone to see the doctor.

The Cooks' Agency

Later in the same evening Dan walked through the doors of Bentley's Bar. The big room was full of boaters sitting at the tables, the hubbub of their voices striking his ear heavily. But he had no intention of drinking.

"How do I get to see Mrs. Cashdollar?" he asked one of the keeps.

The keep pointed to a door at the end of the bar.

"Right through there, mister. Turn right down the hall and go up one flight. It's the door right opposite the stairs."

"Thanks," said Dan.

He followed the keep's directions. The hall was lighted only by a small lamp set on a corner shelf halfway up the stairs. The boards under his feet creaked; there was a smell of oldness in the walls; and as he climbed Dan could hear the whisper and stir of rats behind the lathes. An old spotted tomcat, who was watching a hole in the corner of one of the treads, glanced up at him with a harassed expression.

At the top of the stairs, a door opened into the front wall. A card was tacked to the centre panel. It was smudged by fingers which had traced the painstaking printing.

MRS. LUCY CASHDOLLAR
COOKS AGENCY
FOR BACHELLOR BOATERS
KNOCK

Dan took off his hat and knocked.

"Come right in," said a woman's voice beyond the door.

Dan found himself in a large bedroom, colorfully got up in wallpaper patchings of red and blue, yellow curtains at the window, and green rag rugs on the floor. On his left stood a monumental walnut bed, with medallions of fruit in high relief on the head and foot boards; on his right was a Franklin stove bearing a copper kettle which purred lazily, a glass with a spoon in it, and half a lemon. The air smelled sharply of the lemon and heavily of rum. Before the snapping fire a plump woman, rather pretty, in a scarlet Mother Hubbard and a bright yellow wig, stretched scarlet stocking feet to the warmth. She was smoking a large meerschaum pipe, the stem of which lay along her breast, and blowing smoke rings at the toe of her right foot, which was curled back through a hole in the stocking.

"Set down, young man," she said, motioning to another chair beside the stove.

Dan sat down, holding his hat with both hands. The warmth of the fire beat upon his face and showed it flushed. The plump woman gazed at him with a quiet smile. Her face was high-colored, and the edges of her broad nostrils were red, as though rum noggins were a habit.

"Well," she said, "what can I do for you, young man?"

"I come to see if Molly Larkins was here," Dan said.

"What's your name?"

"Dan Harrow."

"So you're the lad! Well, I ain't surprised," she said, looking him over carefully. "You're a well-set-up young man. If I was as young as I used to be, I might want a job with you myself."

Dan felt the blood in his face.

"She said she'd be with you if she was in Utica," he mumbled.

"That's right, Mr. Harrow. She's staying here."

"She ain't gone?"

"No. But she ain't in now. She will be later."

Dan's hands squeezed his hat, and a slow smile came over his face. The corners of Mrs. Cashdollar's eyes crinkled; she smiled back at him.

"Feeling strong about her?"

"Kind of," said Dan.

"I don't blame you. I can't say as I blame you at all. She's real pretty. I made two good commissions on to her. Fat ones."

Dan looked puzzled.

"Oh, you won't have to pay none. She's been expecting you. She was going to stay another week. I'd hate to charge you any, anyhow. It ain't often I can fix up such a pair. When I can, most generally I charges light — for old time's sake."

She settled her wig on with both hands and sighed.

"Yes. Old times. I was as pretty as she was, once; not so long ago, at that. Yeller hair and a tidy figure. Men would look around on the street when I laughed. Oh, well, the world goes by a person and they get left after a while."

"I wouldn't say that, mam."

"You're a nice young man, and you're a lucky young man, too, to get such a pretty cook. You'll make a smart-looking pair if she takes care of you right. She's a good

gal, a good cook. She's willing and kind and honest; but
there's times when she's hard to hold. I know her right
through. I've took special care with her. Yes, sir, I've
turned down bids when a man wanted to get her, by telling
she had a job already. Jotham Klore turned out a kind of
error. But he's a good man, in a way, a fine free spender,
and he gives a girl a good time, and Molly'd took an affection to him. There's times, young man, when you'll have to
bear right down on her and make her mind. That's the
kind she is. She's got to feel a bit all the while."

She leaned forward, her Mother Hubbard wrinkling tight
behind her arms, and took a coal out of the fire with a little
pair of tongs. When she had her pipe drawing again, she
asked Dan how he was fixed. He told her about the boat
and Samson's death.

"Poor Samson Weaver," said Mrs. Cashdollar. "He was
a nice man. I made quite a bit of money through him, but
Annie always was that way. Lucky I don't guarantee my
gals'll stay, unless I get a wife proposition. There was an
old feller came in a year ago. He had a farm up by Steuben.
Used to be a boater and he come down to me to get him a
cook. He wanted a young gal, so I give him one and told
him the gal wouldn't stand for it. Well, she was gone in a
week. Back she come, and back come the old feller. White
was his name. He was all cut up. He wanted another, when
I told him the gal wouldn't go back. So I let him have
another. He tried three. The last time he come in I says to
him, 'Mr. White, you don't want a gal that's pretty,' I
said. 'You want a woman that knows that sowing means
reaping.' Oh, I talked to him right like a mother. 'I got a
woman here — she's the best cook in Utica,' I said. 'She
ain't pretty; she's forty. But she's about ready to tie up,'
I said. Well, even then he didn't want only a gal. He thought
he was a boater still. So off he went and I called up the
woman, and I told her, 'Hermy, there goes old man White.
He's a good man, but he's notional. He's got a good farm.
You get ahead of him and get a good meal. I'll loan you the
money to get there — five per cent profit. If you can't get

there and stick, you ain't the woman I think you are, with your powers for food. That man don't know it, but he's fonder of his insides than a hen is of corn. That's the way a man gets when he gets old; with a gal the trouble comes outside.' So off she went, and she beat him back and had his supper frying for him; and two weeks later, when it was time to pay up, I was sitting here one night thinking she might pop in, and getting ready to tell her she needn't hang round my agency if she hadn't settled down, when in comes White. He fishes the money I'd give her right out of his pocket, with the per cent with it, and he says, 'Mrs. Cashdollar, here's your money, and thank you,' he says. I counted and told him it was right. 'Yeanh,' he says, 'my wife give me the account.' Well, she'd knowed where she stood all right; they're real happy. I got her off my hands and made a profit. It was good all round."

"Yeanh," said Dan.

"That kind of a woman won't give you no bother," Mrs. Cashdollar said. "Give her a little honey-love once a day, and she's fixed. But a gal like Molly Larkins has got to be rode steady. She's notional."

"Yeanh," said Dan. "Thanks."

"Course you ain't paying a bit of attention to what an old woman tells you. Well," she sighed again, "I was that way once."

"When'll Molly be back?" Dan asked.

"Pretty late. Shall I tell her you're waiting for her?"

"Yeanh," said Dan. "Please."

"All right, where's the boat?"

"Wheaden's wharf. It's the Sarsey Sal."

"All right. You're certain you want her? I've got a pretty, dark-complected girl here, just in from the country, if you're taken that way."

"No, thanks," Dan said, getting to his feet awkwardly. "I think I'd better be getting on back."

"All right, young man, good luck to you. If you don't have it, come back here and I'll see what I can do for you. I'd enjoy having your trade."

"All right. Good night, mam."

"Good night," said Mrs. Cashdollar.

He walked slowly down the stairs. The spotted cat was still at the same hole; and it looked up at him with a disgruntled air at the sound of his heavy tread.

Dan did not notice the cat. He went out through the bar and into the street and headed back for the Sarsey Sal. There was an odd feeling of suffocation in him as he went along the docks. Under a light he passed the watchman he had seen earlier in the evening, twirling a toothpick back and forth across his lower lip. The lapping of the water came upon his ears with a clear insistence; the wind was sharper; and the tread of his heels over the planks rang hard. Above him the stars clustered in a clear sky.

In the cabin he lit the lamp, and looked round him. His blue-green eyes shone and his tanned cheeks were flushed. He changed triflingly the position of the two chairs and pushed a stool back into the corner. Then he went into the cuddy. As in some of the older boats, it had a partition dividing the double bunk from the single. On the walls hung odds and ends of Samson Weaver's clothes — a pair of overalls, deeply kneed; an old hat, the brim of which was pulling away from the crown in front; a pair of boots hung on a nail by their laces, the mark of the boater's feet evident in their worn leather. Dan gathered them up and took them forward to the stable. The horses were lying down, but they turned their heads toward him, their eyes glowing warmly in the light of his lantern.

He dropped the clothes in a corner and grinned at the team.

"You old devils, you," he said to them, his voice thick, "what 're you thinking about?"

They did not get up; but as he went out again one of them nickered whisperingly.

In the cabin once more he sat down; and then got up to put another stick in the stove; and then sat down with his book on his knee. But his eyes could not follow the letters through the short lines. It was warm in the cabin; the kettle was purring, hiding the mutter of the water outside; the air was dozy with the smell of past cargoes, of sweet apples, the choking smell of grain, the clinging, solemn smell of potatoes. A mist was closing on the windowpanes, shutting in the lights. A horn blew flatly far out along the water. Forward, one of the horses shifted its weight. . . .

Dan heard light footsteps on the dock, on the plank, on the deck of the boat just over him. He sat still for an instant, his hands gripping the arms of the rocker. The steps started down the stairs; the door opened; Molly Larkins came in, in her red dress and hat, carrying a carpetbag.

"Hullo, Dan."

Her face was a bit flushed; but her dark blue eyes were cool. He got up slowly to take her bag.

"I 'll just drop it inside," she said, and she carried it into the sleeping cuddy. His eyes followed her in and out again. She stood close before him, taking off her hat, her skirts lifting a little at the sides of her ankles.

"Hello, Molly."

She gave him a wide smile.

"Just to think of you getting a boat so soon."

"It ain't actually mine."

"Mrs. Cashdollar says it 's as good as yourn. She 'd know."

"I ain't got any money yet. I won't be able to get a driver for a spell."

"Well, I guess I can steer, Dan."

He glanced approvingly at her strong hands.

"I 'd ought to get trade from Butterfield," he said.

"Sure," she said. Her blowzy bright hair hung down in a loose coil over one ear. She poked at it.

"My gracious, I can't never make it stay respectable!"

She laughed and shook her head, and the coil slipped out to fall forward over her breast. Dan drew his breath and looked away suddenly.

"Samson said he had money hid on the boat, into one of the beams."

"Goodness," she exclaimed, her eyes shining. "We'll have to look to-morrow."

"I think we'd better wait till I've seen Mr. Butterfield, Molly."

"I don't see why."

"If he says it's our boat," he said almost shyly, "it'll be like looking for our own money."

"It'd be fun to look to-morrow. Why, we might even find it to-night."

He glanced down at his hands and shook his head.

"No, I don't think we'd want to."

She laughed again, low and clear.

"It don't make much difference."

She got up suddenly.

"I've got to nose round," she said. "I always was nosey getting into a new boat."

His eyes followed her here and there as she opened the cupboards and poked into corners, giving little exclamations, or wrinkling her nose as she found dust.

"I'll have to clean up good right away," she said. "My heavens, you could tell just two men had been living on this boat."

He grinned with a warm feeling of pride in him. When she bent over, the loose strand of hair would brush her chin and she would catch it back with a pleasant sharp snatch; but it always curled forward again across her shoulder.

The clock whirred and rapidly beat out the hour.

"Goodness," she exclaimed, looking from it to him. "I'd scarcely noticed it! Ain't it a cute pretty horse prancing like that?"

The lamplight picked out the muscles in the arched neck of the little animal. He looked alive.

"It'll be nice to have him there prancing with his feet," she said. "There won't be no drag in the time."

"Molly," he said.

"Yeanh?"

"Molly," he said.

She came to him and stood by the arm of the chair.

He wanted to speak, but the word snagged in his throat.

Suddenly she reached down for his hand and pulled his arm round her waist. Her eyes were bright and large and a little misty, and there lurked in the long corners enough of the devil to make them sweet, and a dimple poked into her left cheek.

"Gracious me," she said. "Ain't a man a silly thing!"

She spun away from him suddenly, her skirt lifting about her knees, and laughed and went into the cuddy and drew the curtain.

Dan sat by himself a while, listening to the soft stirring beyond the curtain. The fire lulled in the stove; the kettle ceased its talk with a few light tinkles of the dying steam; the lapping sound of the ripple closed in round the boat. The clock struck the half hour.

Dan got up suddenly and turned to the cuddy.

"Land!" said Molly, a low, soft kindness in her voice. "Ain't a man silly? You 've forgot to blow out the lamp."

Rome Haul

When Dan woke, he heard Molly moving round the cabin. He could hear the stove roaring and the fat hopping in the pan, and the warmth and the fry smells were already coming in to the bunk. The early morning sunlight, shining against the curtains, traced the barred frame of the cabin window. Dan stretched and yawned silently, and lay still with lazy contentment. His hand could still feel the warmth in the blankets beside him.

Overnight a new atmosphere had stolen into the Sarsey Sal. As he lay there, Dan could feel it all round him. On the wall to the right of the curtain three print dresses hung, and beside them a cotton bag out of the top of which poked a bit of the collar of Molly's red best dress. Her hat lay on the shelf above the nails; two pairs of shoes sat side by side in the corner. And Molly herself was humming a little tune in the kitchen, over and over, in snatches as she went about her work. Like many women whose speaking voice is strong and low, she sang in a small voice, almost shyly: —

> "Down in the valley,
> The valley so low,
> Hang your head over,
> Hear the wind blow."

Dan swallowed hard, as if he would have liked to cry, and sat up suddenly. Molly came to the curtain and put her head through. Her hair hung forward on her shoulder in a big loose braid, making her look ridiculously young. She was wearing a thin green print that brought out the bright flush in her cheeks; and her blue eyes, seeing his tousled hair and the patient, bewildered pleasure in his face, grew dark with tenderness.

"Get up, lazy Dan. Come and get your breakfast."

She tossed his trousers onto the bed and went back to her work.

> "Hear the wind blow, dear,
> Hear the wind blow,
> Hang your head over
> And hear the wind blow."

He pulled on his trousers and laced his boots; his fingers were clumsy. Then he went on deck and drew himself a bucket of water, washed, and went to the stable. The horses were up and eager for their feed. He got them a bucket of water from the butt and stood by their heads watching them drink. The offhorse lifted its head when it had drunk and brushed the back of his neck with its cool damp muzzle. Dan swore and thumped it with his fist, and the horse laid back its ears and pretended to nip him. Dan laughed at it and slapped its neck; and the horse pricked its ears suddenly and stamped. The other, impatient of the byplay, whickered into the belly of the manger for oats.

Dan brushed them down and grained them. They were a fairly good team, a little lighter than he liked a horse; but they were fattening from their week of rest. He put on their collars and adjusted the hames and went back to the cabin.

Molly had let down the table from the wall, and now she sat at one end, the coffeepot before her. The sunlight coming through the window caught in the edges of her hair.

"Good morning," she said, her eyes on the high color the cold water had whipped up in his cheeks.

"Morning," said Dan. He went over to the sink, felt for the comb behind the mirror, and ran it through his hair.

Molly laughed.

"It don't do a bit of good to do that."

"No," he said. "I guess it don't."

"Come and set down, then. Here's your coffee," she said, pouring him a cup. "Whatever woman was on to this boat before you men tried to run things certainly knowed coffee. She stocked up good. There's enough of everything to last us till we get ready to leave Rome, except for eggs and butter and milk."

"Yeanh," said Dan, starting in on his bacon and potatoes with relish.

She eyed him dubiously.

"I haven't had time to make a pie," she said. "But I'll whip up something to-night."

"This is good enough for me," Dan said, looking her over with a broad grin.

Her eyes smiled to watch him eating.

"It's an old boat," she said. "But it's real nice. It's fixed out about the most comfortable of any boat I've lived on to. The china's pretty, too, white and red like this. Just my color. But I'd like to clean it out good."

"We can when we quit Rome."

"It ain't that it's so awful dirty," she went on. "But I don't like to live in it with the old man dead the way he is, and not clean up all round."

She wrinkled her nose.

"He was all right," Dan said. "Samson Weaver was a good man."

"I don't doubt he was all right. It's just a feeling."

"Mrs. Cashdollar said you was notional."

"What did she say?" Molly asked quickly.

Dan grinned.

"Please tell me."

"No, I guess I'd better not."

"It must've been bad."

"No, I wouldn't say it was bad. She seemed to like you all right."

"She's been nice to me," Molly said. "She's a pretty nice old woman."

"I like her a lot."

"She is nice. It's too bad she's getting so fat. She has to wear a wig, too."

"I didn't guess it."

"It is. It's a pity, too. She looks awful with it off her."

"Well, it looks all right on."

"Men don't notice. I'd rather lose my teeth than my hair."

"You've got enough to last a while, if it's real."

"You'd ought to know it was real. I had to pull it out from under you a dozen times."

"It's pretty, such a lot of it," he said, his eyes shining. The dimple stole into her cheek.

"I wish it was yellow."

"I like it just how it is," said Dan, seriously.

She smiled to herself.

"When do you want to start?"

"Just so soon as you're ready."

"I want to hang the blankets outside anyway to-day."

"All right. I'll rig a line while you're washing dishes."

He felt as if he could sit there for hours just watching her, as she bent forward, her elbows on the table, her chin cupped in her hands. There was no denying she was pretty, when you looked at her fresh coloring and the feathery curl of her light brown hair. The sunlight dusted her skin with a luminous bloom and picked out a shadow between her shoulders.

"Dan," she said suddenly.

"Yeanh."

"Could I get a bigger mirror? I can't hardly see to do my hair in this one."

"Why, yes, I guess I could, after Butterfield pays me off."

She sighed, as if relieved.

He pushed back his chair.

"I reckon we'd ought to get ready. I'll hang out them blankets."

"There's some pins in that bag hanging on the door. I found them this morning."

Dan stretched a line between the cabin roof and that of the stable. There were two notched uprights already cleated in place within easy reach of the left runway, as though Annie had superintended the operation. The iron-tipped boat pole, one end against the bottom of the pit, could be used as a brace.

It was a bright windy morning, with white clouds tumbling high up. The blankets whipped and shivered. When he had hung them, Dan raised the half hatch of the stable and laid the gangway for the horses.

In the cabin Molly was drying the dishes, her hands and wrists red from the water. Dan took the dishpan out to empty it.

"It's kind of cold," he said, when he came in again. "You'd better dress up warm."

She nodded, her mouth full of pins as she began twisting the braid round and round her head. It made a heavy coil. When she had finished, she gave her head a little tentative shake.

"Have you got something warm I could use, Dan?"

"Yeanh. There's a blue shirt in my bag."

"I'll get it," she said. "You'd better get the horses out."

The team came down the gang eagerly, but rather stiff from their long ride in the stable. He rubbed down their legs with his hands, while they drew trembling long breaths and bent their knees as he finished.

Molly came on deck. The tails of his blue shirt flapped loosely over her hips.

"All right," she said, swinging the rudder out.

He let down the stable hatch, drew in the gang, tossed off the tie-ropes, and spoke to the team. They settled down willingly under their collars. Dan saw that he would not need to use the reins or Samson's heavy whip.

They were a good pair, active walkers, but too light and quick to do much hauling without another pair to relieve them. Dan decided that he would want another team, and, if he got another team, that he would buy a good one.

The Sarsey Sal swung out from the wharf into the basin. They cleared it quickly and came into the open canal. A cold wind snapped across the water when they passed the last street; looking over his shoulder, Dan saw it drawing Molly's skirts snug about her legs, fluttering it behind her. She stood with her weight on the hip nearest the rudder, both hands on the sweep, her face turned sidewise to meet the wind. A strand of hair whipped her lips, and she caught it suddenly with her white teeth and grinned ahead at Dan while she held it.

He warmed to see her there, on his boat, wearing his own shirt, a heavy woolen one with the collar standing up against the back of her hair. The awkwardness of its fit made it curiously becoming to her. His boat — the water cuddling the clumsy old bows; his cook; his heart rose in him and he turned his head into the wind to feel it beating on his skin, and he smiled to himself.

There were not many boats heading west that morning. The press of the emigrant season was over. Most of the west-bound boats were freighters like the Sarsey Sal, heavy-laden. But there was the autumn push of crops coming east. Grain from the lakes, boat after boat; and potatoes coming down to the cities all along the line; and apples, with their sharp sweet smell. Every few minutes a boat passed him.

At noon he put the horses on board for an hour to feed and rest. Molly got a quick lunch of potatoes and eggs and tea; and she begged some apples from a boater as he passed. He tossed them onto the Sarsey Sal and took off his hat to Molly; and, standing beside her, Dan flushed with pride. His boat, his cook; forward in the stable his team munching their oats; he belonged to the canal.

"Maybe we'll go down to New York next spring," he said to her in the cabin.

She caught her breath.

"I'd like to."

"Ever been down?"

"No. But I'd like to see it. It's a great city, and the streets full all the while. And theatres and museums."

All at once Dan felt a little afraid of it, so many people. He had not liked Albany, and Albany was a small place alongside of New York, by all accounts.

"You can see boats from four canals, there, all to once," Molly said.

He watched her biting out of her apple.

"Seen anything of Klore?" he asked after a while.

She took another bite without looking at him.

"Yeanh," she said, with the apple against her mouth. "He's out hauling to Buffalo."

"Yeanh."

"He come around to Mrs. Cashdollar a dozen times looking for me," she said.

"Yeanh."

"I wouldn't have nothing to do with him. Not any more."

"I'm glad he's away."

"He's looking out for you, Mrs. Cashdollar said. He's mad about you and me."

"I don't want to fight him."

"You'll have to sometime."

"I probably will," Dan said seriously.

"You ain't scared of him?" she asked with a quick sidelong look.

"I don't want to fight him."

"You'll have to lick him if I stay with you. It's got to

come," she said, with a definite cold prescience in her tone. "I can see it."

"Yeanh," he said, moodily.

She gave him a long frank look.

"Any kind of a man can get a-hold of something, Dan; but it's keeping it that counts."

They went on after the meal. For an hour Molly walked with the horses and Dan steered.

"Keep 'em slowed down!" he shouted to her.

She nodded her head. She had a free, swinging stride which he liked to watch. He could see that the horses liked her; and that was a good thing, he said to himself; you could trust a horse or cow's opinion better than a man's or a dog's.

She came nimbly up the boat ladder when he swung it in to the towpath, and he caught her when she came over the side and held her in his arm. She was flushed from her exercise, and he could feel her drawing herself in hard against him.

"Get ashore, lazy Dan," she said, kissing him.

He gave her a squeeze.

"Dan!" she gasped. "Lord! You can lick Klore any time, if you have a mind to!"

For a while he felt as though he could.

"What a thing it'll be to watch!" she said to herself, looking ahead at him where he walked beside the horses, his heavy shoulders bent. "He needs to be stiffened, but it's got to come."

They hauled into Rome at four o'clock, and tied up at the Butterfield dock.

Samson's End

Mr. Butterfield rose from behind the cherrywood desk that faced the door.

"Good afternoon. What can I—"

His grey eyes brightened.

"Why, it's young Harrow, is n't it? I'm glad to see you. Come in and sit down."

He stepped forward, smiling, and shook hands.

Dan put his hat on the desk and looked down at his fists. It was cool in the room. The chairs were black-leather-seated, and a dark green rug lay on the floor. Two small windows high up on the left wall let in the afternoon sun to fall in two squares on the varnished sealing of the opposite wall. Facing Dan, Mr. Butterfield sat erect in his well-fitting black coat, the tips of his fingers touching across his lap, a kindly look in his grey eyes.

"I come to ask you something," Dan said somewhat diffidently.

"I 'll give you the best advice I can, Harrow."

Dan swallowed. Even in the office there were traces of the dust of the new grain, with its sweet, musty smell.

"Where have you been since I saw you?" Mr. Butterfield asked.

"Utica and Albany and back to Utica," said Dan.

"Who did you come in with?"

"I come in on the Sarsey Sal."

"Why, that 's Weaver's boat. Did you bring up my machinery?"

"Yeanh."

"I 'm glad it 's here. I expected it yesterday. Did Weaver come into the office with you?"

"No, that 's why I come to see you, Mr. Butterfield. Samson 's dead."

"Good Lord! What happened to him?"

"I reckon he was scared of the cholera."

"Yes, I heard there was a case. Strange at this time of year, but we 'd had a good deal of hot foggy weather. Tell me how he died."

Dan told him how he had signed on in Albany, how they had passed the cholera boat burning, how Samson had been worrying, how Henderson came aboard.

"It must have been his heart," said Mr. Butterfield. "It was a hard trip for you, Harrow. I think you did well to come through so quickly. What did you do with the poor fellow?"

"That's partly what I come to see you about." And Dan told him in detail of his deal with the undertaker.

"I did n't know rightly what I ought to do," he said apologetically. "I had n't had no experience. When Pa died Mr. Breezy done the job."

"Well, Samson Weaver was a good man. I would n't want him to go that way."

"It did n't seem right," said Dan. "But I had to have some money. And I did n't know nobody in Utica to borrow from."

"You ought to have written up to me."

"Weaver said you wanted the machinery right away."

"That's true enough. Still, I don't want to leave him as he is."

"It don't seem right," Dan agreed, wiping the sweat from his forehead with the back of his hand.

"I guess I know the doctor the undertaker was taking him to. He's a first-rate surgeon, and I suppose he has to have a study once in a while. I won't mention his name. There's a good deal of prejudice against the practice, though I don't see anything wrong in it. But we ought to consider Samson. I don't think he would have liked it, Harrow."

"I guess that's right, Mr. Butterfield. He had a kind of horror."

"Well, then, suppose I look up this surgeon; I've got to go to Utica to-morrow anyway; and I'll have the body buried decently and have a stone put up. Don't you think yourself that would be best?"

"Yeanh," said Dan, "it did n't seem right letting him go to the doctor that way — seeing as how I was n't in Samson's family."

Mr. Butterfield looked grave.

"Yes. I agree with you, Harrow. Seeing he has n't any family, it's a sort of double obligation to us to see he's treated decently. He was a very decent man."

"Yeanh."

"I 'll be glad to pay for the headstone, but maybe you 'd like to contribute something, Harrow."

"Yeanh. That 's what I come to see you about, Mr. Butterfield."

"How about ten dollars?"

Dan drew a breath of relief.

"That 's just what I 'd ought to give, I think."

He took the ten dollars Cushman had given him from his pocket and pushed them across the desk. Mr. Butterfield put them in his wallet, took a cigar out of a drawer, lit it, and leaned back.

"What are your plans now, Harrow?"

"That 's what I come to see you about, Mr. Butterfield. I wanted to see you about the Sarsey Sal. Samson said he did n't have any folks. I was wondering if you 'd know if anybody else had an interest in the boat."

"I happen to know that nobody has."

"I was wondering who 'd own the boat then, Mr. Butterfield."

Mr. Butterfield examined the end of his cigar.

"I should think you had as good a claim as anybody, Harrow. You took good care of Weaver on the haul up."

"I did n't have much time to take care of him. I did n't feel right about letting the doctor have him."

"We 've straightened that out. I should n't worry about it. I don't see why you should n't go on with the boat, Harrow, just where Samson Weaver left off. He was very fond of that old boat. He said to me once, 'I 'll bet she 'll keep on moving as long as there 's water to rub her belly on.' I think he 'd like to think of the Sal still going along. I had his boat and him working for me regularly. Would you like to sign up with me?"

"Yeanh."

"I want to send a load of corn and oats up to Ney's in Carthage to-morrow. Will that suit you?"

"Yeanh."

"How are you fixed for horses?"

"There 's a pair on the boat, bays — six and eight, I 'd

judge. They're good walkers, but kind of light to suit me. I don't think they're a lot over twenty-three hundred."

"Well, you won't have much more hauling to do this fall. But next spring you'll need a second pair."

"Yeanh, I'd thought so."

"There's going to be a fair on the second of November at Whitesboro. Horses will be cheap in the fall. If I were you, I'd buy then and hire them out during the winter. I send grain and supplies in to the Goldbrook camps in winter. I'd be glad to hire a couple of teams and a pair of drivers. You could tie up at Utica for the winter."

"That would be fine," Dan said.

"All right, then. I'll see to changing the Sal's registration at the Rome lock to-night. How about a driver?"

"I hadn't thought to get one this fall. I've got a cook with me; she's sort of a nice girl," Dan said shyly.

Mr. Butterfield looked at him a moment as if he were about to say something, but evidently changed his mind.

"If she's young and strong she can help you out. I won't ask any rush hauling from you this fall."

"She's real willing to help out."

"That's a good sign. Now let's see your bill of lading."

Dan handed it across.

"I'll have it checked to-morrow morning when we unload. But I know it's all right, so I'll pay you now — Weaver's terms, naturally."

"They suit me," Dan said. "They'll suit me right along."

"All right."

Mr. Butterfield went to a door in the wall, unlocked it, and with a second key unlocked the safe inside.

"Eighty-five dollars?"

"That's right," said Dan.

"Here's the receipt," said Mr. Butterfield, handing him a pen.

Dan signed.

Mr. Butterfield held out his hand.

"You've made a lucky beginning, Harrow. I'm glad of it. I think you deserve it."

He shook hands. Dan went out of the office and crossed the wharf.

The Sarsey Sal lay squat and heavy on its brown reflection. Boats passed just beyond it, but Dan had eyes only for its brown hulk. It was his boat.

V

THE CLOSING SEASON

Fortune Friendly

WHEN he boarded the Sarsey Sal, Dan found it empty. For an instant a fear that Molly might have cleared out gnawed at his insides. Her hat and red dress were gone, and her narrow shoes. It was only when he noticed her comb and brush sticking out from behind the mirror that he took comfort. She would n't have gone off without them, he told himself; her hair gave her too much bother for her to leave them behind.

So he went up on deck and sat down to wait for her. He listened to the horses munching forward with a sense of pleasure; they were his horses. But he was anxious for the time when he could get the team he wanted. Maybe he could pick them up singly; match up a team, and save money that way. If he bought at all, he would buy good ones.

The long basin was a-crawl with boats. Round from the Boonville feeder a chain of them came one after another, stacked high with firewood — twelve-inch lengths for stoves. It was the first tangible sign of winter. There were times when the canal froze early in December — two years ago it had frozen in the first week, catching many boats. Dan was anxious to get going. The Carthage trip would take better than a week. A great flock of crows which flapped across the valley sounded as if they were talking snow.

Clerks were coming out of the warehouses at the end of the day's work. The docks were crowded. Men from the granaries moved past him, spanking the flour mist from their trouser legs with whitened hands.

A man was standing opposite the bow of the old boat. He wore a wide grey felt hat and a black coat, and his narrow trousers were strapped under his shoes. There was something familiar to Dan in his attitude, and when he pulled a watch from his waistcoat pocket to read the time, Dan recognized the flaming red front. At the same moment the man looked up and met his eye.

"Why, hello, young man," he said, coming forward with a grin wrinkling the corners of his eyes. "Were n't you on Julius Wilson's boat that I went to Utica on after preaching a sermon at them hellions in Maynar's Corners?"

"Yeanh," said Dan. "You 're Mr. Friendly, ain't you?"

"I am, but I 've forgotten your name."

"I 'm Dan Harrow."

"Harrow! That 's right. How 's Wilson and that old Jew? Have they learned to play pinochle any better?"

"I don't know," said Dan. "Won't you come aboard?"

Mr. Friendly glanced again at his watch.

"I don't know but what I might as well. Thank you."

"We 'll step down in the cabin," said Dan, very much tickled at the presence of his first guest.

He poked up the fire and motioned the ex-preacher to the rocking-chair.

"Who 's the boater?" Fortune asked.

"Me," said Dan.

"You?"

"Yeanh. Boater, owner, driver, the hull works, all but the cook. Want a job?" he asked, making a poke at a joke.

Fortune laughed; then he sobered down, and a frown appeared on his smooth, child's forehead.

"Serious?"

"It 's a gospel fact," said Dan. "This boat 's mine and I 'm going to haul for Butterfield."

"Where 's your next haul?"

"Carthage."

"When you hauling?"

"To-morrow morning first thing."

"Got a cook?"

"A-1."

"Sold!" said Fortune, holding out his hand. "It's the first time I ever hired on to a regular job. What am I going to do?"

"Drive and steer."

"How much do I get?"

Dan scratched the back of his head and looked serious. He began to realize that the ex-preacher was not joking. He would have to be careful now, and hire the man on as cheap as he could.

"You ain't done any driving before, have you?"

"Not to speak of," said Fortune.

"Well, a driver-boy ought to get ten a month, by rights, but I'll give you eleven. How'd that be?"

"Surely. That'd be all right with me, Dan."

The old man hooked his feet in the rungs of the chair and rocked comfortably.

"I don't mind telling you, Dan, I was broke again. Busted bare. It wasn't my fault. I'd done a good haul on the Rome sheriff playing euchre. There was a lot he didn't know about that game. So when he was cleaned out he got sore, took my money and his'n, and said I was cheating and if I was in town next morning he'd lock me up for a public nuisance. You'd think I'm old enough to've known better than play cards with a sheriff."

"Was you cheating?" Dan asked.

"It depends how you look at it, Dan."

The ex-preacher ran his hand down over his smooth face. "How'd you come to get the boat, Dan?"

Dan told him the story. When he had finished Samson Weaver's death, Fortune Friendly clucked his tongue.

"Poor devil."

"He was scared all right," said Dan, and he told about the undertaker and his interview with Mr. Butterfield. Friendly snorted.

"Undertakers! I'd call 'em overtakers. They've got everybody buttoned right into their gloves, and they know there's nobody dares say no to 'em. And when the time comes to themselves, they get a good discount for a trade courtesy!"

"I believe it," said Dan.

"Who's your cook?"

"Why, I got her in Utica. She ought to be back pretty quick."

Dan lifted his head.

"That's her coming along the dock. I can tell her walk. She's kind of a pretty nice girl."

Molly Larkins came into the cabin, carrying a market basket and several packages.

"Hello, Dan. I did n't expect to be so long."

"That's all right, Molly. This here's a driver coming along with us. Mr. Fortune Friendly."

Molly poked her head over a bunch of carrot greens and gave him a bright smile.

"Why, Mr. Friendly. When did you go in for boating?"

"Just fifteen minutes ago, Molly. Lord, girl, you look pretty! What's come over you?"

Her color deepened, and Friendly drew in his breath.

"Well, I don't rightly wonder," he said softly, his black eyes moving from one to the other. "I knew I was going to like driving for this boat, even if it was steady work for a man like me, but I did n't know how much."

He settled back in the chair and smiled happily.

"I'll be a sort of un-hindering pa," he said. "So I'm going to say right off I'm hungry for my dinner."

Molly laid down her purchases.

"I've bought a regular outfit of food. Turnips, 'tatoes, eggs, butter, and lard. We did n't need sugar and salt and pepper. And I've got the dandiest pork chops you've ever seen."

She went into the sleeping cuddy.

"Dan, have n't you brought in those blankets?"

"No."

"Maybe you and Fortune'd better get 'em right away. They'll get damped out in the dew."

"I'll get them," said Fortune.

Molly poked her head through the curtains while she buttoned on a work dress.

"What did Mr. Butterfield say?"

"He said the boat was mine. I'm to haul for him. We'll make the Watertown haul to-morrow morning early."

"It's our boat," she said.

"Yeanh."

"Dan, I've got you a kind of a present."

She held out a clay pipe. Dan took it and slowly turned it over.

"Thanks," he said; but there was tremor in his voice. He felt all at once very kind toward her.

"There's some tobacco in the basket," she said shyly. "I thought maybe you'd like it."

Friendly came bunting through the door, his arms stuffed full of blankets.

"Where'll I put 'em?"

Molly came out of the cuddy, flinging the curtain open.

"Stretch them on the bed," she said.

It was grown dark. While the chops were sputtering in the pan and Molly was setting the table, Dan, with his pipe lighted, went forward to feed the horses and hang out the night lantern. The old ex-preacher, sitting in the rocker, watched Molly moving about, his nostrils widening now and then to the fry-smell.

"How did you come to hire on with him, Molly? Through Lucy Cashdollar's?"

"No. I seen him first in Hennessy's."

"Oh, you did, eh?"

"Yes," she said, with a little nod.

"You made up your mind right then, I guess."

She nodded again, with a rather shy smile.

"Where's Klore?"

"I left him," she said, poking sharply at a chop. "I was sick of him."

"Did he take it kind?"

"No. He gave me a licking first."

"He'll lay for Dan. Do you think it's right by Dan?"

"He knows it," she said, turning on him.

"Then they 'll have to fight it out," Fortune said. "Is Dan afraid of him?"

"I don't know," she said in a small voice. "But he 's terrible strong."

"It ought to be a dinger," said the old man, his eyes gleaming.

"I hope Dan 'll lick him. He 's got the strength. I hope he 'll lick him down."

The ex-preacher glanced at her sharply.

"Well," he said after a moment, "it 's a good sign. Do you love him, Molly?"

She caught her breath, and made eyes at him without speaking.

"Lord," he said, "you 've got pretty, Molly. Lord! If Klore saw you now he 'd go crazy."

She smiled to herself.

"It generally happens once," said the ex-preacher. "I guess it 's best for you both to go through with it this way; but the end of it 's likely to be hard for you both, Molly. I got to thinking a little while ago that Dan would n't last on the canal. Getting this boat and all is good, but he don't look like a boater; he don't talk right; he 's half asleep, Molly."

"Asleep!" she cried. "I know better!"

"He has n't found out who he is; he has n't shook hands with himself," said the ex-preacher moodily.

Molly turned, her hand holding the fork on her hip, a loose strand of her hair caught in her white teeth.

"Look at me, Fortune. Do you think he 's going to go away without me?"

"No — hardly!"

"Well, then!"

The old man's smooth face became sober and wise as he looked at her.

"That 's the hell of it — going in for it hard this way. It ain't natural and proper for you and me, Molly. We 've just gone along rubbing elbows with folks, the way boaters do, and seeing things, and learning things; and they're so many they don't matter. But when a man like Dan wakes up to what he wants it's a hard thing. He's got the whole of everything inside of him. He does n't move light enough to let them go out. That's the hell of it, Molly. You'll want to quit him."

She laughed, throwing up her chin.

"Lord!" said the old man.

"Yeanh? You don't know nothing, Fortune."

"I know you, Molly. I've taught you a lot. I've taught you what I think. And now you're busting right out against everything. But you're built like me. There's no profit doing things hard, Molly."

"Go along with such talk."

"You're in for it now; you could n't get out if you tried. It's bright all over you."

"Why should I leave him?"

"I don't know," he said, feeling of his hands.

"He's big and he's strong, and sometimes he don't seem only a baby to me; and then again he scares me, just setting there looking at the wall with them eyes of his."

Fortune nodded his head.

"But he's handsome!"

"Yes," said Fortune. "He's about as fine-looking as they come."

She bent over and kissed him, and the loose strand of hair brushing along his cheek tickled him.

"Lord!"

"Fortune," she said, seriously, "can't you see I can't leave him? I would n't want to. Not him! Why I can't get him out of my sight!"

"You mean you love him."

"Yeanh. That's why I could n't leave him. It would n't be right!"

"Of course, you could n't," he echoed her. "It would n't be right."

"That's the hell of it," he said to himself, as he heard Dan's heavy tread on the deck above them.

A Mirror and a Pair of Shoes

"Are them the only shoes you 've got?" Molly asked Fortune Friendly.

He was sitting facing the stove, his heels resting on the corner, his thin shanks sharply outlined through his trousers.

"They are. What 's the matter with them?"

"Gracious me! Those won't hold out for more than two days. They 're so thin you can do everything but see through them."

The old man cocked one eye whimsically.

"Well, I ain't got the cash just yet; but I 'll get a pair when wages come."

"Dan," said Molly, "you take him up and get him a pair of boots. Go to Lerba's — you can get good ones there cheap. If you let him go alone, he 'd go and get to playing cards. He 's such an old rascal."

"Well, it 's too bad to get Dan out so late. The stores 'll probably be closed," said Fortune, with a sigh over his supper. "It 's real comfortable here."

Molly flicked the top of his head with a dish towel.

"It 's Saturday night. Go on, now, you won't have time in the morning."

"Yeanh," said Dan, getting up and stretching his arms out sideways.

The old man sighed.

"Well, I guess it 's wiser."

He and Dan went out, leaving Molly at work on the dishes.

They walked slowly through the dark streets; there were few lights.

"Lord," said Fortune suddenly. "If I had any money on me, I 'd hate to meet this Gentleman Joe on a night like this."

Dan turned on him, but it was too dark to see the old man's face.

"What do you know about him?"

"Two thousand dollars reward for information leading

to the capture, dead or alive," replied Fortune. "I got a job yesterday tacking them bills up all over Rome. I could say the danged things backwards. I got one of them in my pocket."

"Who 'd you do it for?"

"Sheriff Spinning. That 's how I came to get into a game of euchre with him."

"Spinning 's no good," said Dan.

"No. That 's true enough. I 'd like to get a chance after this Calash. He ought to be hanged up. He does n't belong here on the canal."

"That 's right," said Dan. "Do you know where Lerba's store is?"

"Yes, it 's down here."

Fortune turned off to the left down a narrow street, and stopped before some steps leading down to a cellar. A window letting above the level of the ground gave them a view of a little man hunched over a form, a short squat hammer in his hand. He looked up as they entered.

"Hullo," he said. "What can I do for you shents?"

Fortune sat down on a box and crossed one leg over the other.

"This young man brought me in to buy a pair of boots," he said, waving his hand at Dan.

"It is a good place to buy shoes, Lerba's," said the cobbler, packing a quid of nails into his cheek and laying down his hammer. "I will get out some boots, hey?"

"Heavy cowhide," said Dan. "Double sole."

"Here is some good ones," said the cobbler, bringing out a bunch of them. "Five dollars, with lacings."

Dan undid the knot of laces and selected a pair.

"Kind of stiff," he said.

"They work smooth," said the cobbler, disgorging a nail. "It is good leather in them boots — no scraps in Lerba's five dollars. Just the best all the time, like tenderloin to the butcher's, only cheap."

He smacked the nail in and rolled another off the end of his tongue.

"Try 'em on," said Dan.

Fortune took off his shoes and rolled his trousers up along his shanks.

"It fits all right," he said, stamping his foot on the floor.

"Sure," said the cobbler through the rat-tat of his hammer.

"Try the other one," said Dan. "When you buy a team, you look at both horses."

"The young man is right," said the cobbler; "only at Lerba's you don't need to look at both — it is all tenderloin, not?"

The dim lamplight cast his shadow grotesquely against the leather stacked by the wall, where it did a pantomime of hammering, and the nails rolled down from a pendulous lip, larger than life. The whole little underground shop smelled strong of leather, with a sharp damp odor mixed in. There were traces of mould on the walls.

Fortune got up and walked round. The shoes squeaked protestingly.

"I said they was stiff. You'll get sore feet with them, I guess, Fortune."

"Noo," said the cobbler, laying down his hammer and disgorging a handful of nails over his tongue. "It is just the leather is so lively getting acquainted."

"I don't know . . ."

"It is good shoes," said the cobbler. "I give them away for four dollars and half."

"I guess they ought to be all right," said Fortune.

"Sure, the old shent wears them. He should know."

"All right," said Dan.

"It is good," said the cobbler, pushing his hands down his leather apron. "It is fine. I am an honest man and it is fine."

Fortune took them off.

"I go find some paper," said the cobbler.

His bent back disappeared through a door and they heard him creaking up some stairs and calling, "Rachel, come quick! There is paper for shoes sold."

"He's a funny old turkey," said Fortune. "Him and his

wife sell furniture upstairs and take in a lodger once in a while."

"That is right," said the Jew from the top of the stairs. "Would you shents have furniture?"

"No," said Fortune.

"It is good furniture, bargains. There is bedroom crockery with pansies, and some good quiltings, and some mirrors . . ."

Dan started.

"Gol," he said. "I might get a mirror, at that."

"Sure," said the cobbler. "A pretty mirror very cheap."

"I guess I 'll go and look at it."

"All right," said Fortune.

They felt their way up the narrow stairs, the cobbler looking over the rail at the top and guiding them with his voice.

"It cannot fall, them stairs. But don't step on the next one to the top one. It is n't."

Dan and Fortune found themselves in a fairly large first-floor room with two windows facing the street. The ceiling was high for so small a house. Chairs, beds, tables, wash-hand stands, were piled along the floor in complete disorder, with crooked spaces between through which a person could barely walk. Dishes and crockery sets "with pansies" were scattered over all objects with a horizontal surface. In the doorway stood a dark-haired woman in a loose brown dress which kept falling away from her right shoulder, showing a smooth pale skin. The lamp she held over her eyes swayed a little from side to side, so that there was a constant slow procession of shadows back and forth across the wall.

The cobbler held his apron tight to the sides of his legs and picked his way between two rocking-chairs.

"Here is the mirror, mister. See. It is pretty, with the carving on the wood all around."

"There 's a chip off it," said Dan.

"Secondhanded goods has chips," said the cobbler stoutly. "That is why they are secondhanded goods. Such a mirror is four dollars at Lerba's. You take it with the shoes, it is eight dollars for the combination. Look, it is a good mirror.

You can hang it two ways — up, so, or sideways, so. Whichever way you hang it, it makes the other way look not right. It is a good mirror."

One corner of the glass was freckled, but except for that, and for the chip, it looked very respectable to Dan. Broadways it would be just the thing to hang in the cabin. It would please Molly.

As it lay against the arms of the chair, Dan caught in it a glimpse of the ex-preacher staring nervously about him, and of Mrs. Lerba's thin hand holding the lamp.

"Hey, Lerba," asked Fortune in a friendly voice, "got any lodgers now?"

"No, no lodgers any more."

"I thought you always kept lodgers."

"No, mister, it was one kept, but not no more."

"That's funny," said Fortune. "I thought I heard somebody moving around upstairs."

The apron rattled in Lerba's hands and the lamp swayed, and suddenly beside and behind the reflection of it, looking over a stair rail outside, Dan saw the tall figure of a man peering in from under his wide hat brim. While Dan watched, the figure moved softly down, and he thought he heard a quick closing of the outer door.

Lerba cleared his throat loudly and said seriously to Fortune, "No, it is the Missis says there is a baby, so we put a nursery in the lodging room and don't paint it with paint this year. No. There is no lodger."

"Hey, there!" called a voice from the foot of the stairs up which Dan and Fortune had felt their way.

Again the lamp swayed suddenly.

"Make a light steady, Rachel," said the cobbler. "You will take this mirror?"

"Yeanh."

"All right, we take it back down with us."

"Hey there, Lerba!"

The voice had a cavernous echo, coming from the cellar shop.

"Yes, yes," cried the cobbler. "I make a hurry."

He caught up the mirror and picked his way quickly to the head of the stairs.

"Get paper, Rachel," he called to his wife, and then, to Dan and Fortune, "Make care about the steps."

They came back into the shop. Henderson was sitting on the cobbler's stool, his fat short legs crossed, his hat on the back of his head, pulling at a big dead cigar.

"Hullo!" he said on seeing Dan. "You here?"

"Yeanh."

"The shents came to buy boots and a mirror — good ones, a bargain," explained the cobbler.

"I 'll bet it was a bargain, all right," said Henderson.

Lerba nodded his head with a pleased smile.

Henderson nodded affably at Fortune Friendly.

"I just dropped in, Lerba," he explained. "Just a friendly visit."

"Sure," said the cobbler. "What is the name? Boots is cheap."

There was a sudden scratching and rustling down the stair treads. "It is paper," exclaimed the cobbler. "It is paper from Rachel."

He ducked out to get it.

"Got a lodger, Lerba?" asked Henderson when he came in.

"No, not no more at all."

"You used to have one."

"No more no lodger, not at all."

"Did he leave?"

"Yes, it is. There is a baby, Rachel tells — the shents say so. It makes a nursery."

"Well, I want to poke round the nursery," said Henderson.

"These shents tell . . ." protested the cobbler.

Henderson looked at the end of his cigar; then with his left hand he pulled his suspender through the armhole of his waistcoat.

"Sure," said the cobbler, at once. "Rachel, there is a shent wants to see the nursery. Show him with light."

Henderson got up and disappeared through the door, whistling "Walky-Talky-Jenny." They heard him climbing the stairs behind Rachel. Lerba went about wrapping the boots and mirror, using his teeth as a third hand in tying the string. By the time he had finished, Henderson was coming back.

"Well, well," he said pleasantly. "It 'll be a nice nursery. When do you expect the new Lerba?"

The cobbler spread his hands.

"It is not my business; how shall I tell? Rachel makes it."

"All right, Lerba. I won't bother you any more to-night. You gents walking back towards the canal?"

"Yeanh."

They went out.

"How 's Samson?" Henderson asked Dan.

"He 's dead."

"I guessed he would. He looked bad when I seen him that night. Who 's got the boat?"

"Me."

"You have, eh?"

"I asked Mr. Butterfield about it. I 'm hauling for him."

"Well, I guess it 's right if he says so. Seen any more of Gentleman Joe?"

"No."

"I expected he might be lodging at Lerba's here. I guess he 's cleared out. I know where he 's gone, though. Who 's this gent?"

"Fortune Friendly," said Dan. "Know Mr. Sam Henderson."

The ex-preacher shook hands.

"He 's driving for me."

"Where are you bound for?"

"Carthage," said Dan.

"Well, you may run into me up that way. If you do, I 'll probably have Calash with me."

He put his hands in his pockets and turned aside down a street.

"Who 's that man?" Fortune asked.

"He 's Department of Justice," said Dan. "He calculates he 'll get Gentleman Joe."

Samson's Bank

"I 'm tired," said Fortune Friendly, when they got back to the cabin of the Sarsey Sal. "I think I 'll go to bed."

Molly glanced up from the toweling she was hemming. "Did you get the boots?"

"Yeanh."

"They 're regular bullhead boots," said Fortune.

He got himself a dipper of water from the water butt under the stairs and then went to the single bunk and drew the curtain. Dan sat down, refilled his pipe, and lit up.

"Is it a good pipe?"

"Yeanh. It 's breaking in real handy."

He stretched out his legs to the stove and tilted the chair back. Molly bit off her thread, close to the toweling, pressing the cloth tight against her cheek.

"I 'm going to look at Fortune's boots."

She squatted down on the floor before the package, like a child.

"Let me have your knife, Dan."

He tossed it to her.

"Ugh," she exclaimed, pressing her upper teeth down on her under lip. "I can't open it. You open it, please."

He grinned and handed it back to her.

"They 're good boots, I guess. My, they 're heavy!"

"Yeanh," said Dan. "They 'd ought to exercise him good."

"Poor old man," she said softly, "he ain't going to like driving for very long."

"I don't know. He seems to like you a lot, Molly. How 'd you come to know him?"

"Pa used to let him travel a lot on his boat. He used to say old Fortune was a gentleman for all his ways at cards. Fortune never did a lick of work, but he 'd used to sit on deck when I was a little girl with my hair in a ribbon, and he 'd tell stories. And Pa would listen just as hard as me. He 'd tell stories all about witches and such things, and Pa believed 'em as much as me. And when Pa died Fortune asked me did I want to stay on the canal. And then he took me down to Lucy Cashdollar's and told her to look out for me careful."

She pushed the boots to one side.

"What's in the other package?" she asked.

Dan pressed down the tobacco in the bowl of his pipe with his thumb.

"It's an article I bought to Lerba's."

"What is it?" she asked again, looking back at him over her shoulder, and squinting a little against the light.

"I got it for you," said Dan, awkwardly.

She flushed.

"Oh!" she exclaimed as she pulled away the paper. "Oh! Ain't it pretty? Ain't it big? Why, I think it's real pretty, Dan."

She stood up lithely, her eyes shining.

"Why, Dan."

Dan gave an inarticulate grunt and leaned forward to open the draft of the stove, his face red.

She caught him by the shoulders and held him down, shaking him.

"Why did n't you tell me right off?"

"You did n't ask."

"You old surl," she said, stooping to kiss him. Then she jumped away from his arm and picked up the mirror. "There's a wire on to it to hang it broadways, Dan. It 'll just fit over the table."

She took down the little mirror that had been Samson Weaver's and hung the new one in its place.

"Now I can see to do my hair."

She took out the pins and shook it down over her shoulders. He stood behind her and gathered it into a handful and pulled her head back against his chest, grinning at her. She pushed his face away.

"Don't, Dan. Not now." She turned her eyes to the sleeping cuddy. Dan laughed. "Listen," he said.

Fortune Friendly's deep breathing purred suddenly, unmistakably.

"Let's look for Samson's money," Dan said. "It'll be our money when we find it."

She put a finger to her lips, and smiled behind it, a conspirator's gleam in her eyes.

"Fortune's a good enough body," she whispered. "But it's just as well he didn't know."

Dan nodded.

"Where'd the old boater say it was?" she asked.

Dan lowered his voice.

"He didn't say — only that it was in a beam, and that part of it lifted out."

Together they looked round the cabin from the middle of the floor. There was a beam across the middle of the ceiling, and one across each end, and a heavy beam sill jutting out of each rear corner. Dan began running his finger along the middle beam.

"It would be on the back side," Molly said. "The light wouldn't hit there."

They found no crack in the middle beam, and Dan began feeling along the end ones. Molly began to examine the corner sills. Suddenly she made a little crowing noise, and, looking round, Dan saw her hunkered down in the corner. She had lifted out a false front close to the floor and was holding out to Dan two limp rectangular packages wrapped in dirty brown paper.

Dan took them back under the lamp and sat down in the rocking-chair, and Molly perched herself on his knees. The packages were tied with red cord, a bowknot directly at the crossing, the ends corresponding exactly with the loops, as though old Samson had taken care and pleasure in wrapping them. The paper was thumb-marked and stained, and when Dan opened the first package some tobacco ashes slid down on the back of his hand.

Molly drew in her breath and looked down at him. There was a friendly feeling in the touch to Dan, and he held his hand close to his eyes. Spidery long ashes, made from Warnick and Brown, that Samson had smoked.

"He was a nice feller," Dan said seriously. "I think he

was a good man, though he was bothered with Annie's running off."

Molly blew off the ashes suddenly. They rose in a burst, and scattered in an indiscernible fine powder. She leaned closer and kissed his hand.

"Let's count it, Dan."

He stared at her as if he did not quite comprehend.

"Let's see how much there is," she whispered again.

He tossed both packages into her lap. She took out the bills and started laying them down one by one on her knee.

"You'll have to steady them," she told Dan.

He pressed his hand down on them and lifted it when she put down another bill. It became a kind of game for the two of them to play, like children stolen out of bed when the house is sleeping — a fugitive, trembling sort of game, requiring a touch of hands. Molly frowned and kept the tally with silently moving lips, heedless of Dan's watching gaze on the curve of her cheek and the soft mass of her hair.

Finally she stacked the bills together with firm little raps on her knee.

"Dan!" she exclaimed softly. "There's eight hundred and thirty-five dollars. Eight hundred and thirty-five dollars. My, that's a lot of money for a man to have!"

She caught Dan's left hand and brought it round her waist, and let herself lean back against his shoulder, her face close to his cheek.

But he was staring at the opposite wall. Eight hundred and thirty-five dollars — it was a lot of money. It represented many things. With it a man could start a farm, a small farm. As he sat there with Molly against him, he seemed to see again the hip-roofed barn, and himself behind a heavy team going out to plough long furrows in rich earth. He saw more than he had seen before; he saw Molly churning on a kitchen stoop. He heard the lowing of cows; and he saw himself and Molly moving from one to the other in the hay-smelling shadow to milk them.

"What're you going to do with it, Dan?"

He took hold of her hands with their strong long fingers.

She watched him carefully, almost jealously, and cast a worried glance at the side of his lean head, tracing the curve of his ear. Beyond the curtain they heard Fortune Friendly's even, sure breathing, purring a little now and then at the end of the breath. The canal beyond the curtained windows was silent and dead.

The stillness was very close to them.

"What 're you going to do with it, Dan?"

"It 's a lot of money," Dan began uncertainly.

Suddenly, thin and faint, they heard the blast of a horn, blowing for the weighlock; and when the silence came again they were conscious of the ripple of the water. The horn sounded a second time — louder.

Molly sighed and stirred against Dan's shoulder, and he twisted his neck to look at her.

"I guess I 'll buy a good team," he said. "A good heavy team. I 'll want 'em in the spring for heavy hauling."

She drew a deep breath of relief.

The clock whirred and rapidly beat out ten strokes.

"Good land! Dan, it 's time we went to bed."

They returned the money to Samson's bank and blew out the lamp; and when the east-coming boat passed they were asleep.

Ecclesiasticus

Five days later the Sarsey Sal was nosing along southward up the Black River behind a string of four boats. Leading the string, the sidewheel tugboat smacked the river with her paddles and belched a line of dark smoke in which hot wood cinders swirled. The northwest wind blowing on their backs carried the smoke free.

It was mid-afternoon. Small cold showers coming with the wind at intervals of an hour all day had washed the air clear under the tumbling grey sky. Once in a while a spot of sunshine running across the valley would cover the boats for an instant with a bright warmth; but the cloud-shadow swooping down after it immediately brought back the darkening chill.

"It feels quite a lot like snow," said Dan, who was steering.

"It does, at that," said Fortune Friendly. The old man was stamping up and down the deck beside the cabin windows, smoking at an alder pipe he had cut and baked himself. The wind had whipped a bright red into his cheeks and nose, and his sharp eyes glistened.

"This is the good part of boating," he said. "The walking ain't so bad now my boots are broke in," — he glanced down at them, — "but I like riding the river this way, when all I've got to do is take a turn at steering."

They were almost opposite Lowville, now, on their way back from Carthage. To the west, the great hogback of Tug Hill began climbing over the bank-side trees. As they went on, the edges of the nearer hills crept up against it, until they were winding through a flat deep valley.

The hardwood was turning to sombre browns and yellows; even the maples were rusty; there was no brightness in the leaves. The poplars on the hilltops shook and leaped in the pitch of the wind; but the great pines on the valley floor stood straight, only their tops stirring with a slow lifting of arms. The entire land brooded before the solemn approach of winter; it appeared to be breathing the clear bite of the air; and on it, with the rolling sky above their heads, men and animals moved with circumspect minuteness. A woman stood in a yard, pumping glittering water; two dogs stalked a woodchuck taking his final meal of the year; two men spread manure, tossing forkfuls first on one side, then on the other. Back and forth across a slope a farmer moved behind a dappled team, uncovering dark threads with his plow.

"It's a fine land for farming," Dan said.

The old man knocked out his pipe and sat down on the cabin roof, clasping his knees with his smooth hands.

"I was born in this section," he said.

"Yeanh?" said Dan. "Was it good for dairying?"

"Sure, as good as any land. My folk were related to folks at Lyons Falls. We had a good farm. And then Pa come into money from some city kin, and Mother said I'd ought to be a minister. So I went to college."

"Yeanh," said Dan.

"I learned a lot it wasn't good for me to learn," said the old man. "But my pa had money, so it didn't do no real harm. But when I come back I didn't go to preaching, as I might have if I'd growed up here. I'd learned a lot to make a man afraid of preaching."

"Yeanh."

"I come back and said I'd settle down. I married and I lived on a farm my wife's kin owned by Lyons Falls. I built barns and I planted an orchard, and I dammed a brook and made a fishpond. I had three men working for me, and there was a maid in the house. And when my pa died and the money come to me I got a good dairy started and my wife was happy."

"Gol!" said Dan.

"But it was the same thing every year. First the winter, and then the summer; calves dropped, and growed and milked, and the crops sowed and harvested. And the field ploughed in the fall, when the ducks went south. I finicked with my orchard, and I raised some good horses. I was a regular farmer. And the second year Hester had a child. And she did the third year. It became a habit with her."

"Yeanh."

"Then one day, when the canal had been put through, I saw a girl on a boat. She had hair as black as a crow's, and she had an orange-colored dress on, and she waved her hand when she went by. And I went home that evening. It was in August, near the end, and the men were drawing oats. I saw nothing in it, just the bundles staggering up on the forks. So I said to my wife, 'Let's quit this country. There's no profit in just farming. We'll go to the city; I've got money enough. We'll live in New York.' And she said, 'Fortune, I wouldn't want to move the children.'"

"Yeanh."

"It don't count, farming, or anything else a man does. Where does he get to? He works his fields and gets crops and raises cattle and builds a house, and he says it's his. It's the same way in everything. There's nothing we've got under the sun. We haven't even got a hold on our selves. We're just a passing of time. So next morning I got up early and took a hundred dollars and cleared out, and that was twenty years ago. I've been on the canals, I've been out West, I've been on the sea and sailed in ships. And it's just the same as if men were asleep, making a dream with their business. And it don't get them anywhere, does it?"

"It's how you look at it, I guess," said Dan.

"They learn new names to call things," said the old man. "But they always call the new names by the same old one. They say progress is what they're making. But progress is like time. It's just the same from beginning to end, because it can't move. 'As it was in the beginning, is now, and ever shall be, world without end, Amen.' And that's true, Dan, no matter what you say it about. All we've got is the working of our own minds."

He refilled his pipe.

"I went down the canal, Dan, and when I was hungry I played at cards. A man I lived with at college had taught me the tricks of that. And once in a while when I needed money real bad I'd preach, which is another kind of game, only the preacher holds the trumps and the temptations are very strong. I saw people fold their hands round a prayer on Sundays, Dan, as if they were doing business; but there's a peculiar comfort in it for some people. And I've preached funeral sermons for people I never saw the face of, for a meal and five dollars. I did it once for an Oneida half-breed for a glass of liquor and a venison steak, and the men's kin were real pleased with what I told them. Only his wife went off in the woods when I was done and mourned. There ain't anything new under the sun, Dan."

Molly, who had been listening at the cabin door, came up on deck, and the wind caught hold of her dress and hair.

"Did you ever see the gal again with the black hair, Fortune?"

The old man looked at her, sombrely.

"No," he said. "I was telling Dan that."

He went down to smoke his pipe in the quiet of the cabin.

Molly sat down in his place, drawing the collar of Dan's shirt up about her ears.

"I was talking with a woman on one of the boats." She nodded ahead at the string. "We'd ought to get into Lyons Falls this evening."

The queue of boats followed the tug round a wide bend to the right. The brown-and-gold tints of the sunset merged into a pale green twilight, with copper edges to the lower clouds. The beat of the paddles slackened and the roar of falling water increased in volume. Still, through heavy mutter, Dan's ears caught the clear ring of cowbells, and looking away to the left he saw a great farm opening out through the pines, a long herd of cows tailing through a pasture, the pale light washing the white on their bodies to silver, and, against the faint glow of the eastern slope, the white skeleton of a rising barn.

"Look at them cows, Molly."

"They're pretty, Dan."

"That barn they're building there's the biggest barn I ever see."

"Why should anyone want so big a barn?"

He did not answer her.

Little figures of men in blue overalls were coming slowly down the ladders, backward, their faces turned on the work they had done.

"It's as big as a church," Molly said.

"It's bigger," said Dan.

Then the river straightened ahead of them, and the tug swung in by the side of the lock that let the canal into the river. A string of boats was forming to go down-river. Another tug, beside the pier, was spouting up columns of oily smoke, a white hiss now and then escaping the valve. Men were loading five-foot logs aboard for the fires.

Visitors

Down below, Molly got supper. When they came into Port Leyden in the darkness, Dan called to Friendly to tie up behind a squat white boat.

Just as they were finishing their meal, they heard footsteps on deck and a rapping on the cabin roof.

"Come in," Molly called.

Before Dan could go to the door, footsteps clattered on the stairs, and a hearty voice called, "My, my! Where's Dan Harrow?"

There was a familiar ring in the voice. The door was flung open and a little man wearing a cap, with the ear mufflers up, peered in.

"Dan Harrow aboard?"

"He ought to be if he ain't," said the hearty voice from behind. "It's the Sarsey Sal, ain't it?"

"Hullo," said Dan. "Hullo, Mr. Tinkle."

The little man beamed and stretched out his hand. Then he put his head back through the door and shouted, "Come on, Lucy!"

They heard her puffing down the stairs.

"She's getting awful fleshy," the little man confided. "Don't know but what she's getting wheezy."

"I ain't neither. Sol, that's a lie. I don't tell tales on to your rheumatiz, do I?"

The fat woman came breezing in, her hat a little on one side from bumping on the stairs.

"My stars, Dan, ain't this grand?"

She swept over to him and enveloped him in her arms.

"To think of you owning a boat, being a regular boater! I always let on to Sol you would be, but he'd shake his head, when the rheumatiz wasn't bothering him too much, and he'd say he guessed not. Mr. Butterfield told us about you. We're hauling for him now."

She stepped back and cast her bold eyes round the room.

"It's real comfortable and homey, ain't it? These old boats are nicer, I think. They've got a better feel into them. You don't feel so old in them. And it's clean, too. And curtains on the window. My! Ain't it a nice boat, Sol?"

The little man was holding his cap in both hands, the lamp shining on his bald head, a grin of pleasure puckering his face.

"Listen to him!" exclaimed Mrs. Gurget. "Just standing there and looking round as if he'd never been out of Stittville all his life. You'd hardly think but what he was a deef-and-dummer. Can't you talk, Sol?"

"Once in a while I edge in a word, Lucy."

"Fresh," said the fat woman, tossing her head. "Well, how be you, Dan? You look thriving. Don't he, folks? Introduce me, Dan. I always feel itchety till I know who folks are. Gives a person a handle for conversation."

She drew herself up with a smile.

"Now's your chance, Dan," said Solomon.

Mrs. Gurget tossed him a frown.

"This here's Fortune Friendly — he's driving for us. And this is Molly Larkins. Mrs. Gurget and Mr. Solomon Tinkle," said Dan, the blood bright in his cheeks.

Mrs. Gurget gave the old man a smile and beamed at Molly.

"I'd knowed there was a woman on board as soon as I laid eyes on them curtains, fresh ironed. A man alone might as well hang up a dishrag."

"Won't you set down?" said Molly, pushing forward the rocking-chair. Dan watched her with open admiration. She was very cool about it.

Mrs. Gurget sank down and threw back her red shawl to show the locket on her bosom.

"Well, it feels good to set down. I've been steering all day. We unloaded in Lyons Falls this afternoon and Sol said we'd ought to start right back. Mr. Butterfield asked us if we knowed you, Dan, and then he told us you'd got a boat. It gave us a start. I thought Sol'd spit right there in the office. So when we see your boat coming in a while ago Sol wanted to go right on board, but I told him to mind his manners and give you folks time to eat. That's the way men are," she said to Molly, patting her hand; "so long as they see smoke in a stovepipe, they think there ought to be food set right out to feed a circus. How do you like cooking for this man, dearie?"

Molly smiled.

"He's a real nice man to work for."

Mrs. Gurget gave her another pat.

"I think so myself. Dan's all right — yes, sir. Oh, me," she sighed, with a smile at Solomon, "we're all young once. Don't you find it so, Mr. Friendly?"

The ex-preacher leaned back on his stool, his hands clasped over one knee. He had been smiling ever since Mrs. Gurget entered the cabin.

"Well, some of us never lose it, Mrs. Gurget."

The fat woman laughed delightedly.

For a minute or two the conversation hinged on minor gossip, on the triplets borne by Mrs. Scroggins on the Pretty Fashion while the boat was going through Lockport, — a child for every other lock, as Solomon said, — and a new cure for consumption, and the "Rheumatic Amputator" Solomon had bought at a horse fair out of Syracuse from a traveling surgeon. He pulled up a trouser leg to show it to them, a thin lead band that fitted just above the calf of his leg. "Careful," Mrs. Gurget admonished. "We're in company." "It burns the rheumatiz right out," Sol explained. "See them little teeth on the inside? Well, you soak them in sour cider and that generates the beneficent electrical that balances the blood by getting it to proper temperature. It helps a lot. Why after I've wore it an hour I can feel the heat a-swarming in to beat the cars. Yes, sir."

"It only cost seventy-five cents," Mrs. Gurget said. "Ain't it wonderful the progress that science can make for the money?"

Fortune Friendly nodded gravely.

"It's as good as God."

"It's better for the rheumatiz," said Solomon.

"Hush, you," said Mrs. Gurget.

Molly smiled.

"You'd ought to get out that rum you got in Carthage, Dan. Unless you prefer cider, mam."

"No — no, thanks." The fat woman laughed. "Rum noggin's a healthy habit with me."

Molly got the glasses and Dan brought a small keg out of the sleeping cuddy.

"Here, Sol, get up and help Dan. He's a great hand at driving a bung, Dan. Sol's the handiest man at it I ever see. Let him do some work. Dearie, can't I help you with them glasses? Mr. Friendly, it's nice for old folks to be waited on, ain't it? I don't count Sol as only a child. There's times, seeing him with a bottle, I think he still ought to be sucking."

The kettle was purring full on the stove, and the sharp odor of lemon that Molly was cutting mingled with the smell of rum. Mrs. Gurget spread her nostrils over her glass.

"It's a regular party. Well, here we be. You're a lucky man, Dan, though I don't know if you know it."

She drank it down to "Dan and Molly and getting together."

"Now Lucy's got her belly warmed, she may soother down," said the little man. "Butterfield says he wants for you and me to get potatoes in Denley, — there's a load there, — and to Boonville, Dan; but while we're waiting here along you come; so here's how."

He drank, and broke into conversation with Fortune Friendly. Mrs. Gurget was occupied with Molly. The cabin looked very homey all at once to Dan; and Molly, with a bright look on her face, bending toward the fat woman, was prettier than he had seen her. He felt a little nervous, but very happy, and Molly's collectedness gave him a sense of comfort. Now and then the two women glanced his way, as if they were talking about him, a sort of smile in their eyes. The kettle steaming, the warm light of the lamp, the scent of rum coming after the day in the cold air, brought an air of establishment to the Sarsey Sal. His guests, his boat. . . .

Solomon turned back, laying his hand on Dan's knee.

"I've been talking to Mr. Friendly, Dan," with a pert nod in the ex-preacher's direction, "and I've got an idea. All at once, like, there's been a lot of talk coming up about this feller Calash. I've kept my eyes looking out and my ears listening, Dan, and I reckon he's up here, especially after what Mr. Friendly's been saying about Henderson in Rome. I think he's up here."

"I guess that's right," said Dan.

With elaborate nicety, the little man tapped Dan's knee with the end of his forefinger.

"How would two thousand dollars, split three ways, go between us, Dan?"

Dan was uneasy.

"Why, I don't know."

"Two thousand dollars!" exclaimed the fat woman, glancing up. "Where's two thousand dollars?"

Solomon pointedly ignored her.

"This feller Henderson's up here, but he won't ever get him. He don't know where he is. But I'll bet I do. Why don't me and you and Mr. Friendly round him up, then?"

"Why, I don't know," repeated Dan. He felt suddenly uncomfortable and worried. It would mean seven hundred dollars to him, a lot of money. But he had a liking for the man, somehow; he did not know why. He had seen him once in Boonville when he came on the canal, and once on the haul to Rome, and twice in Rome; and the man had put him aboard his boat in Utica; and he had petted his horse, and the horse had liked him. It was a lot of money. He did not know why he liked him. There seemed to be a lot of things tied up in the man. . . .

"He's a criminal," said the little man. "He's wanted dead or alive. He ought to be caught afore he breaks loose here."

"My land!" exclaimed the fat woman, settling her hat straight. "He ought! It ain't safe with him roaming around like a bug on a hot night; there's no telling where he'll bump into. I get a start every time I hear a team on the towpath!"

Solomon Tinkle nodded approvingly.

"That's it; there's no telling what he'll do. We'd ought to go after him. It's a duty."

"That's right," said Mrs. Gurget. "It's a duty."

The ex-preacher nodded gravely.

Molly was regarding Dan with a queer questioning light in her eyes.

"I don't know," he said uneasily. "How'd you go about it, Sol?"

"I've figured out just about where he's liable to be. You know, down by Denley, where the road crosses to the river. There's an old brown house down there."

"Yeanh, it's the Riddle house," said the fat woman. "I know it. It's eight-sided."

"Yeanh," said Solomon, leaning forward, his glass clasped in both hands. "It's got eight sides. Old Riddle built it when he got off the canal. He was born in these parts, so he come back to build. Wanted to get away from folks, so he built him a house down in that God-sake hole. He was born deef, and they say from living alone that way he lost the power of speaking. Used to bring his order into the Denley store on Saturdays, wrote out on a paper. It's the dangdest house I ever see. He lived by himself, and two winters ago he died into it."

"He always liked chocolate cake," said Mrs. Gurget.

"I heard tell of it," said Molly. "They found him after a heavy blizzard. He was sitting dead in a chair."

"He was a funny old bezabor," Solomon continued. "Well I mind him on his boat in them canvas pants he used to wear, snarling his horn in his chin whiskers and blowing like they'd reëlected Jackson. They say he used to blow it some down to his house. Once in a while Murphy tells me they still hear it blow."

"I heard about him," said Fortune Friendly. "He had the horn in his hand when they found him."

"I've always wondered if the rooms was shaped like pieces of pie," said Mrs. Gurget. "Having eight sides to a house would make a person think so."

"I don't know," said Solomon. "I ain't never been inside. But I'll bet who is inside right now. It's a comfortable house and a good place for him to stay while he's up here. I reckon we three might edge in there to-morrow night and see."

"I don't see how we could handle him," Dan said.

"I'll take my revolver," said Solomon. "I'll hold that on him till you get your arms round him, Dan. Then we ought n't to have no trouble. When you hold him, I'll knock him on the head."

"He's a menace," said Fortune. "If we can get him, it's our right duty to get him; and we'd ought to be able to collect the reward."

"Well —" Dan began; but they were all looking at him, Molly still with that queer worried expression. Maybe they thought he was scared.

"All right," he said.

He did not wish to go; but at the same time he felt an irresistible desire to see the man's face. . . .

Riddle's House

They hauled into Denley in the afternoon — a bit of a village with the store and post office in one building, and two houses, and a small cheese factory, all in a row facing the river valley. Lumber wagons loaded with potatoes from neighboring farms were waiting on the towpath. The boats tied up, and Solomon and Dan took their teams aboard for the night. By five o'clock the boats were loaded; by six they were all eating in the cabin of the Nancy. Mrs. Gurget had insisted on that, so that Molly could keep her company while the men were away. Solomon put his revolver in the pocket of his coat, where it made a heavy bulge, and he and Dan and Fortune went on shore. The little man was white with suppressed excitement.

It was quite dark, and a rain was falling. There was no wind. Solomon carried a lighted lantern in his hand.

"We might as well stop in at Murphy's and have a sniff first," he said.

"Suits me," said Fortune.

They tramped down the towpath toward the square of light cast by the store window. Against it they could see the rain falling in grey streaks, and drops twisting down the glass. Inside, Murphy, the storekeeper and postmaster, sat on a stool before the round-bellied stove and smoked his pipe at a saturnine man, with black hair, a thin face, and bat ears.

"Hullo," he said, when the three entered.

"Evening," said Sol. "We just come down to get a glass of strap and see how you were making out."

"Pretty good," said Murphy. "I seen you loading your boats."

"Yeanh. We loaded 'em."

Fortune nodded to the bat-eared man.

"Evening," he said.

"Let me make you acquainted, gents. That's Reuben Doyle, gents. He drops in in an evening to make me some conversation."

Doyle returned his nose to his glass and grunted.

Murphy drew them glasses of strap and then leaned against the counter to make some exchanges on the weather. Fortune sat down on a wooden box and Dan lingered by the door, shaking the rain from his hat.

"I hear old Riddle's dead," Solomon remarked after a while.

Murphy started, his thin mouth opening with surprise.

"Why, yes, he's been dead two years, Solomon. I thought you knowed about it."

"Well, I'd heard a remark here and there," said Solomon. "But not enough to pick up and believe."

"He's been dead two years now. He died after a hard blizzard. Rube, here, found him."

"Stopped in to get the loan of a chew," said the bat-eared man.

"Yeanh, Rube found him sitting in his chair, holding his horn, and dead. Did n't you, Rube?"

"Hard as a post."

"He saw he was dead right off."

"Whiter 'n cheese."

"So he come right along."

"Was n't a chew in the house," explained the bat-eared man.

"It was awful cold that week," Murphy went on. "But we turned out and had a funeral and buried him. It was hard work digging his grave."

"Got up a sweat at twelve below," said the bat-eared man.

"Rube used the pick," said Murphy. "I can remember him down in the snow and the pick head coming up and glancing and going down. *Tunk!*"

"A handy tool," observed the bat-eared man.

"So we shoveled in the dirt and locked up the house."

"Been down there since?"

"Once," said Murphy, a little white. "Went down with Rube to borrow a chair my old lady 'd took a fancy to. Just to borrow it against some of Riddle's folks turning up. Just a loan it was to be. But when we turned into the holler we heard a horn blow out loud. It was his horn and blew out loud, did n't it, Rube?"

"Dismal," said the bat-eared man in a low voice.

"So we come away."

"How 'd you know it was his'n?"

"Why we buried it with him. Who else's could it be?"

"Had it in his fist," said the bat-eared man.

"Heard it again?"

"Rube heard it last week."

"Fact."

"Anyone seen round the house?" asked Solomon.

"That 's what give me such a start," said Murphy. "There was a man here this afternoon, just afore you come in, wanted to know about the house. Said he was going down to look it over. He said he was going to buy it, maybe, off'n the estate."

The three boaters perked their ears.

"Yeanh. What did he look like?"

"Fat man. Had on a hard hat. Said his name was Henderson. He smoked a cigar."

"Gol," said Dan.

Solomon swore.

"What's it all about?" asked Murphy.

"Nothing," Solomon said. "I used to know Riddle, the old bezabor."

"Well, it's all right by me," said Murphy.

"We'd ought to be getting along back," Fortune said.

"That's right. Lucy'll be getting nervous. Good night."

"Fifty cents will cover it," said Murphy.

They paid and went out.

"What do you know about that?" Solomon exclaimed, as they paused on the stoop to turn up their collars. "The fat little twerk. No, sir. I wouldn't have guessed it."

"We ought to go down and see if he's all right," said Fortune, "even if we don't come in on the reward."

Solomon nodded sharply. He took the lead, carrying the lantern under his coat to protect the chimney from the rain. A dim rim of light was cast about his heavy shoes. Now and then it glistened on a puddle. It was raining harder; the drops had begun to bounce on the water of the canal; they could hear the heavy roar of it out of sight upon the hills.

Except for the little spot of lantern light that marked Solomon's feet, squelching along the road and picking up great clouts of mud, the night closed in on them, as black as tar. In intervals in which the rain appeared to be catching its breath, they could hear the river, far down on their left, muttering over the rapids.

The Sarsey Sal loomed up beside the towpath, its windows dark; but Dan heard one of the bays grunting as it lay down in the stable. Then a little way ahead the lights from the cabin of the Nancy poked out onto the towpath. As they passed, Dan had a glimpse of Mrs. Gurget playing solitaire at the table, and of Molly knitting beside the stove, a yellow glow on her brown hair. She looked up, as he came abreast, but her eyes were on the wrong window to see him.

They turned down a road toward the river, the rain roar-

ing on invisible trees to their right and left, and stirring a
heavy smell of rotting leaves out of the ground. Dan's feet
kept slipping in the mud; he followed the jerking patch of
light blindly. The little man stepped sturdily on, as though
he were well acquainted with the road, and Fortune, treading at his heels, made easy progress.

After a while Solomon stopped, scattering a rim of drops
from his coat and holding up the lantern. The light picked
out their faces redly, a-shine with wet, against the dim veil
of rain. They looked at each other, counting noses.

"I'll bet he did n't go down," Solomon said.

"Maybe not," said the ex-preacher.

"He probably went back after help."

Dan did not feel so sure; he had a growing respect for
the fat man — he had seen him so often on Gentleman Joe's
heels.

"I don't want no share of the reward," he said suddenly.

Solomon stared up at his big bulk, then shifted his gaze
to where a little channel of rain ran off his hat.

"What?"

"I don't want no share of the reward."

"You're coming with us, ain't you?"

"Yeanh."

Fortune's smooth face poked close to theirs.

"What do you know about that?" exclaimed the little man,
snatching the trickle from the end of his long nose.

The ex-preacher grinned.

"It makes that much more for you and me, Tinkle."

A drop pinged against the glass, and Solomon hurriedly
lowered the lantern.

"It ain't natural."

He took up the lead again, and for a while the others
found it hard to follow the feeble light about his feet. The
lantern had left a red glow in their eyes.

It was perhaps ten minutes later when Solomon stopped
again, and again they stared at each other in the close light
of the lantern.

"Riddle's road branches off on the right pretty quick,"

said Solomon. "You want to keep watching for it and let me know if you see it afore I do."

They pushed on. Dan became conscious of the weight of his hat and of the beat of rain upon it. The ex-preacher's trousers were soaked through and moulded close round his thin shanks. He walked with a long, lurching stride, his hands in his pockets. Now and then he chuckled as though he were enjoying himself. Dan's hands swung limply from the wrist, close to his legs. Solomon's feet, leading the way, went with a martial tread. Once in a while one stumbled, or slipped over a stone; and then the light would escape from his coat for an instant and shine on the twisted branches of the trees.

Suddenly Dan caught hold of Fortune's shoulder. The ex-preacher whirled round, and then laughed under his breath.

"Hey, Sol!" Dan called.

"Yeanh?"

"Ain't that the road?"

Solomon walked back.

"I don't see how it could be so soon."

He was disgruntled.

He swung the lantern up, and great shadows were evolved against the rain and fled away. He lifted the chimney and blew the flame off the wick. The darkness struck them, leaving an ache under their eyelids.

"It's all right. Take hold of my coat, and, Dan, you take hold of Friendly."

He began to move into the side road marked by two ridges of grass between the ruts and the horse tread. Fortune shuffled along at his heels, Dan behind him; the three bent over, moving stealthily in the invisible rain, like monkeys holding each other's tails.

For a hundred yards they went ahead at a fair speed, the road easy to their feet. Then Solomon stopped and they felt for each other and laid their heads close together.

"The ruts has stopped," the little man said in a low voice. "We must be in the yard."

Dan and Fortune lifted their heads, but saw nothing.

"It ought to be dead ahead," said Solomon.

"How 're we going to do it?" Fortune asked.

The little man took hold of his long nose in the darkness. Dan kept his eyes searching for the shadow of the house.

"First," Solomon said, "we 'll get up close to the house. If he 's inside, he 's asleep. If we don't hear nothing, we 'll open the door if we can, and I 'll sneak inside on my stummick with my revolver. I 've got a-hold of it now."

To know that somehow comforted all of them.

"Don't be scared," said the little man. "I 'm pretty good at using it. When we 're inside, Dan goes left and Friendly goes right; and when I thump, you stop. There ain't any back door and the stairs comes down facing front. Then I 'll light the candle I got in my pocket and we 'll wait under the stairs for him to come down."

"What if we can't get in the door."

"We 'll have to find another way."

"It sounds all right to me," said Fortune.

"All right."

Once more taking hold of each other, they crept ahead. The rain found the collars of their coats now, and ran down inside, but they did not notice it.

Then Solomon's outstretched fingers bumped against clapboards.

"We 'll try left," he whispered. "Look out for the well. It 's got boards on it, but I would n't trust a trained flea on to them."

Again they crept forward. Dan's ankle scraped against a board, and a loosened bit of wood struck water somewhere far down.

"Shhh!"

Solomon was crawling up the stoop steps to the vague grey blur of a white door. His hand reached up and found the latch. It lifted silently, and to their surprise the door swung gently open. Wriggling, Solomon crawled inside. After a moment Fortune followed him. Then Dan started.

Through the front door he turned to the left, keeping close to the wall. He came to a shallow corner and went on. Then there was another shallow corner, and he realized that the ground-floor room must be eight-sided, like the outside of the house. A little farther ahead his hand came against the belly of a stove. It was still warm, but the fire must have died down two or three hours before.

He crouched beside it as a thump on the board floor sounded back by the door. A plank creaked faintly as Fortune stopped opposite him. For an instant they all lay still in the darkness, listening. At first, through the monotonous drum of rain on the roof, the silence seemed breathless; then Dan became aware of a fourth person in the room. He was not sure of hearing anything. It was impossible to see. He could not be certain of the position of the fourth person; but he was convinced, suddenly, that it was not Gentleman Joe. For he smelled a faint, stale smell of burnt woolen.

A spit of blue fizzling burst out beside the door, turned into a cloud of greenish biting smoke, caught in a yellow flame upon the candlewick. The flame lowered, then climbed up, tremblingly. The candle balanced on the floor, stood upright, and Solomon Tinkle scurried to one side, his blinking eyes on the stairs.

Water filled Dan's eyes for a moment; he noticed Fortune staring foolishly at the lone candle in the door and the grey rain beyond, drumming on the mud of the yard; Fortune, with his back to the stairs, squatting, his hands on his knees, helpless if Gentleman Joe had been in the room. Only Solomon Tinkle was looking in the right direction, and his gun was wavering in his hand, and his staring eyes wept after the darkness.

"Jeepers!" he said.

Dan felt the blood in his face, and turned round from the door. In a rocking-chair against the wall beyond the stove sat Henderson. A revolver, in his hand, rested its muzzle on the floor. A fat cigar had caught in his lap, and the ashes were smudged all over his waistcoat. He was slumped down on the small of his back, his fat legs sprawled out in

front of him. He seemed to be sleeping; his tight little nostrils stirred to an uneven breathing very faintly. His coat
on the left side was wet and dark, and there was a small
pool on the floor, spread out.

Fortune chuckled ridiculously.

"You shut up!"

Solomon moved forward to the stairs. Hunkering down,
Dan watched his small bowlegs out of sight into the shadow.
His feet trod forward over their heads, sending down a faint
silt of dust through the board ceiling.

Then he came down.

"I knowed he was gone," he said, pocketing his revolver.
"I knowed it as soon as I saw that twerk. Is he dead?"

Fortune stepped forward and pushed his hand against
Henderson's side.

"No. It's lucky it wasn't one of us. Calash could have
nailed Dan and me and then knocked you on the head afore
you could 've seen him."

"Cripus!" snorted Solomon. "I'd have nailed him first.
I'd have screwed the lid on him right there."

He pulled a red handkerchief out of his pocket and wiped
his face.

"What 'll we do with him?" he asked, nodding his head
at Henderson.

"He's hit pretty bad," Fortune said. "But he ain't bleeding now to speak of. We'd ought to carry him back."

"He's heavy."

"I guess I can shoulder him part of the way," Dan said.
He felt relieved; he had not wanted to find Calash. Now
that the man was safe away, he had nothing to worry about.

"We could go back and get a wagon. I'll go back," said
Solomon, "and you could stay here."

"It would take too long," said Dan. He wanted to get
back to the boats, to see Molly. An unexplainable enthusiasm
took hold of him. "I can carry him all right."

"It's better than half a mile."

"Let him try," said Fortune, looking at Dan's big shoulders, "I'll bet he can."

Solomon went out for the lantern. When he had lit it, Dan picked Henderson up across his shoulders. The man's head swung sharply down and bumped against his cheek. They blew out the candle and closed the door. The house faded behind them, eight-sided in the rain.

It was easier walking with the lantern only partially shielded, but Dan's shoulders ached by the time they got to the towpath.

"Had we ought to take him on the boats?" Fortune asked.

"Why not?"

"It might scare the women."

"It'd take a fatter dead man than she's a woman to scare Lucy," Solomon said.

The women had heard them, for they came on deck.

"Lord, what rain!" Mrs. Gurget exclaimed. "That you, Sol?"

"Yeanh."

"Is that him?"

"No, it's the Department of Justice man. We're going to bring him on board."

"Say," she cried. "Spinning's down by the store. He'd got a letter from him to be here to-night. You'd better fetch him down there. I'll come along with some whiskey and a towel."

Dan carried Henderson on down the towpath to the store. A buckboard stood in the light, which also picked out the wet and glistening rumps of the team. The horses stood quietly, but they looked fresh.

"I'll bet he did n't founder 'em trying to get here," said Solomon.

They barged into the store. Spinning was standing straddle-legged, his back to the stove. The bat-eared man still regarded his glass, and Murphy was whittling a chew from a plug of Hammer Brand. All three started, and Murphy and the bat-eared man got to their feet.

"What in hell?" said Murphy.

"That's what I'd like to know," said the bat-eared man.

"It's Henderson," said Dan, easing him down on the counter and rolling him over on his back.

"We found him down in Riddle's house," said Solomon. "He must have gone down there alone. Calash shot him, I reckon."

"What in glory was he doing down there?" demanded Spinning, with a bluster in his voice. He bent forward, suddenly. "Why, it's the horse trader. What was he doing down there?"

"He got shot," said Fortune Friendly.

The bat eared man bent over Henderson's stout stomach and poked his coat open to look at his waistcoat.

"It's the truth," he said solemnly.

Henderson's face was pasty white.

"Is he dead?" asked the sheriff.

"No."

"That's a blessing," said Murphy; "we won't have to dig a hole for him, anyhow."

"It's damned funny," said the sheriff, taking off his hat. "I got a letter from the Department of Justice man that was working on the job. He wanted me up here with a rig at eight to-night. I threw a tire coming into Boonville and it took three hours to get it on again. Gol! If it had n't been for that we might have got him."

"Gol!" echoed Fortune. "I guess you might. There was n't no other rig in town, I suppose."

Spinning flushed.

"Hold your jaw, old man. You're a bad character. I'll take you in with me if you don't shut up."

"Now, now!"

Mrs. Gurget came rushing in, the rain streaming down her cheeks. In one hand she carried a bottle of whiskey, in the other a towel wrapped round some strips of clean linen. Molly was at her heels, and Dan instinctively moved toward her. Her hair was soaked through, and dark, and tight curls were stuck to her forehead. She gave him a glance, and smiled to see how bright his eyes were. He was still panting from his heavy load and he kept stretching his shoulders to ease the stiffness out of them.

Mrs. Gurget bustled over to the wounded man.

"Heat some water, dearie," she said to Molly.

"I 'll get some. The kettle 's full."

Murphy disappeared into the kitchen.

"Shall I get the old woman?" he asked, as he came back with the kettle.

"No," said Mrs. Gurget, shaking a spray of drops from her hair. "I don't want to be hindered. You men go and set somewheres and leave him to me and Molly."

They took their seats round the stove, and Spinning transferred his attention from Molly to the inside of his hat.

"I got a letter from Jones, telling me to meet the Department of Justice man here at eight. Here it is." He pulled a damp envelope out from the sweatband. "I wonder who the hell he is and where he is now."

Dan pointed his thumb in the direction of the counter.

"That 's him there."

Spinning swore.

"I don't believe it."

"It 's him," Dan repeated.

"That 's a fact," said Fortune.

"I don't believe it," said the sheriff, angrily. "Why, that feller 's been along with me a dozen times. He 's just a horse trader. I told him all about this Department man, and told him just what I thought about this Department man. He did n't say nothing. Calash had stole his horse. That 's what he was after."

They looked back to the counter. Mrs. Gurget handled the fat man as if he were nothing at all. She had pulled off his waistcoat and shirt and was bathing the wound in his side. Then she rolled him on his back.

"Come out clean," she said. "It 'll lay him up quite a spell, but I don't think it 's done a lot of damage. He 'd ought to see a doctor, though, as quick as I 've bandaged him."

"I 'll take him back," said the sheriff, "as soon as I 've found this Department man."

"It 's him."

Spinning glared angrily at Dan.

"My," Mrs. Gurget said to Molly who was helping her, "you 're real handy bandaging a man. I got too many thumbs to do it proper. Get a dry shirt, Mr. Murphy. And don't tell Mrs. Murphy. She 'd have a hollering fright. They always come easy to her."

She forced some more whiskey down the man's throat.

"There. Now you can see he 's the man."

Dan pointed to a suspender strap that fell off the counter, swung, and bumped against it with a smart rap.

The sheriff took it in his hand and his face became crimson.

"The son of a bitch!"

"It 's all right," Fortune said. "He can't hear you."

They bundled him up in blankets, put him in the wagon, and the sheriff, still swearing, drove rapidly off toward Boonville.

Potatoes for Rome

Next day the Sarsey Sal pulled out of Boonville, leaving the Nancy to go up the feeder after her load of potatoes. Even in those days Boonville potatoes were favorably known in the New York markets and fetched a high price.

The fat woman stood on the steersman's deck wrapped up in a great cloth coat, the collar turned up at the back of her neck. It was a man's coat, so that her bulges came all in the wrong places. The wind blew the tails down against her barrel-like legs; and when she lifted her arm to wave to the Sarsey Sal the back puckered between her shoulders and crept up into a small hump.

She had waked that morning in a panic, wondering if the dye in her hair would hold after the wetting it had got. But, once she saw it in her mirror as red as a carrot, her relief had expanded into uproarious humor. With Molly to keep her company, she had joked all the way to Boonville, old jokes that Molly could hardly follow. But just before they parted Mrs. Gurget said, "He 's a good lad, Molly, dearie. Stick to him. It ain't often a girl gets such a fine-looking man."

Now, as she looked back at the Sarsey Sal drawing out of the basin, she let out a gusty sigh. "Young. Ain't they pretty? They go good together—same height, same color, a matched pair. He's heavier-built, but that ain't no more 'n right."

She looked ahead to where Solomon walked behind his mules, pulling reflectively at his pipe, the smoke popping past his ears.

"Ain't you going to wave good-bye, Sol?" she called.

He turned round, took off his cap, and the sun glanced on his high bald poll. Mrs. Gurget smiled to herself.

"A matched pair," she repeated, to herself. Then she saw that the Sarsey Sal was drawing away out of sight round the hill, Molly and Dan standing together on the stern, and Molly waved, but her face was turned away to Dan's.

"Young," said Mrs. Gurget again, in a low voice; and then she snorted and began singing the weaver's song in her full hearty voice.

"They're real nice, I think," Molly was saying to Dan.

"Yeanh," said Dan. "They was good to me."

The bays had pulled clear of the docks with their sharp stride, and behind them Fortune Friendly was tramping along the towpath, the broad brim of his hat curling up behind. Now and then he threw a glance over his shoulder at the river valley they were leaving; but with a little shake he set it forward again, a grin on his smooth face.

"I'll be glad to be getting back," Molly said to Dan. "I don't like it up here."

He said nothing, but kept his eyes on the towline. She watched his big hands on the rudder sweep, and turned her eyes to the hard high line of his cheek — brick-red from the sun and wind. His blue eyes squinted against the sunlight on the water. But they were bright and eager. She thought he looked happy. Standing beside him, she swayed a little to let her shoulder touch his.

"Aren't you glad to be getting back?" she asked.

"Yeanh."

He glanced sidewise at her for an instant. The collar of his shirt rolled up against her face, and her hair, whipped forward by the wind, caught here and there on the rough blue wool.

They swung southward, heading for the Lansing Kill.

"I come onto the canal, to Boonville," he reminded her.

She slid a hand inside his arm. He was remembering his strangeness; she could see the half-timid look on his face.

"You belong on it now," she said.

"Yeanh."

"You've got a boat and team, and you've got quite a lot of money, Dan."

"Yeanh."

He was staring ahead along the towpath, Fortune treading in the shadows of the team. The trees were coming bare, only the beeches carrying their bright rust of leaves.

A boat was creeping up heavily against the current. The driver's whip cracked and hissed, the mules were lathered. Fortune slowed the bays and Dan swung the Sarsey Sal to the far side of the canal. The steersman of the other boat shot a squirt of tobacco juice through the reflection of a window and wiped the back of his hand across his mouth.

"Say!" he said. "Heard the news?"

"What is it?" Molly asked.

"This Calash laid out a marshal up to Denley. Just missed his lung. I seen him in Western. He looked bad."

"Yeanh."

"Funny you didn't hear about it. I guess Spinning took him out too fast. I'd seen the feller before, but I'd never guessed he was a marshal. Little fat feller. His head was rolling all over his shoulders like an old apple in a wind. He sure looked bad."

He got his jaw going and spat again.

"Seen anything of this Calash?"

"No," said Dan.

"Most likely not," agreed the other. "He's cleared out. They say he's back on the main ditch. They'd ought to get him. Folks is beginning to talk."

"That's right," said his driver. He stung the mules, and they lurched ahead into their collars. The boats drew apart.

"So he got away again," said Molly.

"Yeanh," said Dan. He was remembering now how he had first seen Calash on the Boonville docks, talking to Jotham Klore; and how he and Solomon and Hector Berry had had a glimpse of the man riding down the Lansing Kill. He would be riding ahead somewhere now.

"They won't get him this winter," said Molly. "It was that little fat man who could have caught him. I felt sorry for him lying there in the store. I really did. Now he's out of it, it'll be just luck to catch him."

"Yeanh."

"You're glad he got away."

He kept his eyes on the team, and Fortune walking with his hands in his pockets.

"Yeanh."

"Then I'm glad, too."

She stepped round in front of him, so that he had to look at her.

"I don't see why you like him. You don't have anything to do with him, do you, Dan?"

"No."

"I can't see why you like him, then. He's a bad man all through; he's got to be, or they wouldn't be after him."

Dan was silent.

"Everybody says so."

"Yeanh."

"Why do you like him, Dan?"

He avoided her eyes.

"Just because he helped you out in Hennessy's? He wanted you to help him, that's why he did it."

"Maybe," said Dan. "I don't know."

He let his eyes meet hers, with their bright frank look. To her he seemed a little bit ashamed.

"Why do you like him, Dan?"

"I don't know, Molly. I seen him there in Boonville talking with Klore, and then later. He done a couple of things for me. He put me back on my boat in Utica." Dan was breathing hard.

"Yes," she said.

"He's been all along the canal. I 've seen him everywhere I 've been to." He talked awkwardly. "He helped me out twice, like I tell you. You seen him fix Klore."

A slight frown wrinkled her forehead. Then she smiled.

"I don't care," she said. "If you like him, I 'll like him. I won't say anything."

She turned and went below, leaving Dan puzzled and uncomfortable. How could he explain to her? Or to himself, for that matter? Why should he have to? He did n't see. It was n't the man's clothes, or his fine way of talking. Anyway, Dan knew he was a criminal. There had been a lot of talk round the docks in Boonville. People were on the watch for him now. He would stand a small chance up in this country. Dan had seen him first on the Boonville docks, — Uberfrau's, — and he had made no move to stop him. He was a stranger; so was Gentleman Joe. He had never seen his face, even. Yet he felt a definite friendliness for him, as if in some way they were both involved together. . . . He could not explain. He wished he could see the man's face and talk to him. . . .

At Westernville a man came out of Han Yerry's Hotel and signaled them in to the dock.

"Sorry to stop you," he said. "We 're looking over every down-boat."

He pulled open his coat and showed a badge.

"Can't tell where to expect this Calash."

"He ain't here," said Molly.

The man gave her an admiring grin.

"I don't doubt it, girl. I 'm acting on orders."

He went over the Sarsey Sal quickly but thoroughly. There were not many places to look.

"Where 're you bound for?" he asked Dan.

"Potatoes for Rome. Hauling for Butterfield."

"All right. Sorry to bother. You 've got a nice boat."

He gave Molly another admiring glance and went ashore.

On the dock Fortune was talking to an old man fishing for sunfish.

"Not any luck," the old man said, gumming a pinch of snuff. "It's getting too cold nights for fish to bite good. The worms is dozy. It's the winter coming. See there!"

Overhead, a line of geese pricked the sky.

Getting up a Party

It was Friday morning in Utica. The Sarsey Sal lay tied up beside the Wheaden dock, which was now, as Solomon called it, a Butterfield proposition.

"It'd be a good place for us to tie up at for the winter, Dan. Though I guess probably Lucy'll want to be farther downtown."

The little man was sitting on the side gang of the Sarsey Sal, his thin bow legs hanging into the pit.

"I guess we'll tie up here," Dan said. "Molly likes it all right, and I'll be stabling the teams in the barn back."

"Put your grease on upwards," Solomon said suddenly. "Then rub it down."

Dan glanced up from the trace he was greasing.

"I don't see why."

Solomon leaned backward to spit overside; then he poked the stem of his pipe in Dan's direction.

"There's a lot of things you don't know the why of in this world, but that ain't saying they ain't true."

Dan grunted and went on with the greasing. The headstalls and collars hung from spikes he had driven loosely into the wall of the pit, and the traces hung down from the hames.

"You going up to that fair?" Solomon asked, after a while.

"I guess so," said Dan.

"Aiming to buy horses?"

"I want a good team. I'll need two next summer."

"Well, I guess I'd ought to go along and see you don't get squeezed by one of these damn dealers. You're still kind of new on to the canal, Dan, and they 're sharp-edged."

"I know what I want," Dan said, picking up the rubbing rag and watching the leather soften and come out black under his hand.

Solomon nodded.

"That 's the hell of it. Once they know what you want, you ain't got a chance. They c'd set up a bar'l on four sticks with a brush broom for a tail and make you think it was Lexington himself. But when you got home with it you 'd most likely find the contraption did n't even have no bung in it."

"I know a horse," said Dan.

The little man cocked his head and peered at Dan out of his bright blue eyes. For a moment he sucked some poison out of the clay stem of his pipe and sent it overside. He picked at it critically with a splinter and tried to look into the bowl.

"We could hire a rig," he said. "We could start early. They 're going to hang Mary Runkle to-morrow morning."

"I don't know as I 'd want to see that."

"No, but the crowd 'll get there early. Nothing to see. They 're doing it inside of the jail. Folks always come around if a woman 's going to be hung. She strangled her husband."

"How 'd they come to find it out?"

"A cigar peddler discovered it," said Solomon. "She strangled him in bed one night and told her daughter to come and hold his feet as her pa was having a fit. Then she let on he 'd died of pneumony. The cigar peddler 'd sold him some cigars two days afore and he found the butt ends of four cigars in the ash pit of the stove. Made him suspicious. A sick man 's got no pleasure in smoking."

It was a cold, clear day, but the sunlight in the sheltered pit of the boat was warm and pleasant.

"What come of Mr. Friendly?" Solomon asked.

"I paid him off," Dan said. "I guess he got tired of driving. He was headed down for Albany. Aimed to spend the winter there."

"He's a queer bezabor," said the little man.

Dan finished the harness, and then leaned back against the wall and lit his pipe. Solomon came down and sat beside him.

"Trade's falling off," said Solomon. "Some people already tying up for the winter. Line boats are going, though."

They listened to the horn of one coming down. The team tramped by above on the dock and the rope crossed over their heads against the sky, while its shadow crept along the pit, climbed to the stable, and vanished. They heard the low swish of water against the boat, and the ripple shoved the Sarsey Sal against the wharf, where it rubbed with a high-pitched squeak.

About noon they heard Mrs. Gurget's voice break out on deck over their heads.

"There they be, setting alongside of each other just like two toads."

Her bebonneted red-haired head was thrust out over the pit; and suddenly beside it appeared Molly's face, smiling, and a sharp, dried woman's face under a bristling hat, and the pompous round face of a man.

"Look what we run into, Sol," cried Mrs. Gurget. "Walking along as large as life."

She patted the man so forcibly on the shoulders that his hat bobbled forward over his eyes, and he clutched at it frantically. Solomon grinned.

"Hector Berry! Gol! And Mrs. Berry along with him. Looking younger every minute!"

Hector waved his hand in a magnificent greeting, and Mrs. Berry worked her wrinkled lips into a smile.

Solomon scrambled up the cleats on the stern wall of the pit and reached down to take the harness as Dan handed it up. In a minute they were all in the cabin, the womenfolk on one side, the men on the other.

"Dan and me have decided to go up to that horse fair to-morrow," Solomon announced.

"Where?" asked Hector, perking up.

"Whitesboro. Dan allows to buy a team."

"Is that right? Well, I guess maybe it would be a good thing if I was to go, too. I was calculating to, anyhow. It takes more 'n one man to buy a team of horses. Bad time to buy, too."

"Yeanh?" said Dan.

"Yes, sir, they 're trying to get the lumber-camp trade, and matched teams will fetch high."

"I 'll buy single," said Dan. "I 'll do my own matching."

"It 's a good idee if you 're any good at it," said Berry, leaning his chair back against the wall, hooking his legs through the rungs and his thumbs through his galluses. "Yes, that 's right — match 'em yourself. But it takes judgment. I 'm allowed a good hand at it. I 'd better come along with you."

Dan dropped his eyes to the floor. He was nettled, for he wanted to do his trading by himself. But he could see no way out of it. He realized that he had already proved himself a fool by telling even Solomon he wanted to buy a team. Fortune Friendly had told him that. "A man's best friend 'll see him cheated on a horse deal," he had said one morning. "Everybody in the world likes to see a man pay money for a horse." So Dan nodded.

"Well, well! My!" exclaimed Mrs. Gurget. "Listen to them boys talking, and not one thinking of asking the girls. Never mind, dearie, you and me and Nelly, here, we 'll get up a shindig of our own. I know a grocerman."

"No, you won't," Solomon said quickly. "I got it all planned with Dan you 're coming along with us. We 'll hire a rig."

"So long as I can wear my new dress somewhere, it don't matter." The fat woman rolled up her eyes and passed her hands down over the front of her, smoothing her skirts. "It 's real pretty, ain't it, Molly? You ought to see how it 's going to hang — so. Right in style."

She posed herself on light feet, as though she were examining herself in a mirror, and turned slowly round before them, pointing out the merits of the new dress. It did not seem to matter that the material lay wrapped up in brown paper on the table.

"What you wearing, Nelly?"

"I don't know," said the wizened little woman sharply. "I don't bother over such light notions. Dressing pretty's just nothing to an honest woman."

She cast a supercilious glance at Molly, and Hector wiggled his hams uncomfortably on his chair.

"I don't know as I'll go, even," she said.

"Yes, you will," said Hector suddenly. "We're going to start in good time, too."

Solomon turned a questioning glance on him.

There was an unusual and determined gleam in Hector's eye, as he snapped a cigar into his small round mouth and cocked it towards his eye.

"I want her to be outside the jail when they're hanging that woman," he said in a low voice that the women could not hear. "I just want Nelly to be there for a while to think it over. That woman always bossed her husband."

The women would not have heard him, anyway. They were discussing what they would wear and what they would take to eat. Mrs. Gurget promised her new dress and sandwiches, Molly a cake, and Mrs. Berry a pie.

"Well, you're in luck, Dan," Berry said. "You're in luck all around. A good boat and a good cook. But don't let her get her chin up high. I'd heard about you out in Manlius. Ran across Jotham Klore; he was out there. He said some hard things about you. I'd look out for him, if I was you. He says you took his cook away from him, but he says he'll get her back. I never seen him act that way. He used to get riled easy, but he didn't look riled then. Seemed kind of steady and sour inside. He says when he finds you he'll give you the dangdest licking a man ever got."

"Shucks," said Solomon. "Molly cleared out on him of her own accord."

"He don't look at it that way. No man will," Hector said sententiously. "It ain't in nature."

Dan glanced across at Molly, sitting under the window

with the light coming over her shoulder, and found her eyes on his. Her gaze was searching, and he felt uncomfortable. Then Mrs. Gurget swept her off on a point of dress.

"There ain't anything for you to worry about now," said Berry. "Klore's tied up out there for the fall and he's got a contract working his team on the railroad this winter."

"Yeanh."

"He's a regular bear for fighting," Berry said. "I've seen him three times. That time he licked O'Mory of Little Falls was the worst fight I ever see. I had five dollars on O'Mory."

"Cripus! When him and Dan hooks horns, I'll put my money on Dan. He's got the heft. It's a sure thing."

Berry raised his brows and made a silent whistle round his cigar.

Dan glanced up to see Molly looking at him again.

"I guess that's right," he said, suddenly. Her eyes brightened, and her head lifted with a sudden wildness, like the lift of a mare's head. Dan felt the blood in his hands. Outside a horn was blowing for the weighlock — a flat, harsh, ringing note, stirring him.

Mrs. Gurget got to her feet. "Come along," she said. "We've got to eat, Sol. And I've got to make me up that dress."

When they had all gone, Molly set about cooking dinner. Dan sat smoking, with his eyes upon her. She moved easily from table to stove, aware of his eyes, not noticing them. When she spoke her voice was low and full. She told him about Mrs. Gurget's shopping.

"My, she was funny, Dan. I declare I think she wrapped herself in twenty different colors for me to see how they matched her. She bought a yellow silk—it was pretty expensive, and she was awful fidgety coming back home. She was kind of pretty all flushed up."

She put the food on the table.

"What time are we going to start?"

"Sol says we'd ought to get going about eight. He's going to bring the rig around to the dock."

"You'd ought to get you some new clothes, Dan."

"Maybe I'd ought not wear 'em to-morrow. Not if I'm going to buy a team."

"It don't make any difference. You ought to have a new suit. You can afford it, Dan. I'm going to get you some shirts this afternoon. How does it pay a woman to keep looking pretty if the man she's going with don't dress up to take her? You're rich enough."

"I don't see any point in it."

"Sometimes a man can be too close with money," she said, giving him a steady look. "Then he finds it's all he's got."

Dan was silent.

"The others'll be wearing Sunday clothes," she said.

"I guess that's right," said Dan. "I don't know much about buying clothes."

"Then I'll go along," said Molly.

After they had finished their meal, Molly put on her hat again and the dark brown cape she wore on cold days, and they set out to a tailoring establishment, where, according to Molly, men's clothes could be bought at a fair price.

"Ready-cut?" asked the tailor's clerk.

"Yeanh," said Dan.

Now that they were at the point of buying, Molly seemed ill at ease, and Dan found that he would have to do the talking. The clerk wiped imaginary water from his hands and looked Dan over with an appraising eye.

"We don't run much of a stock of ready-cut," he said dubiously. "What would you want, a tail coat?"

"Nothing fancy — just a suit."

Through a door in the back they got a glimpse of an old man, wearing square spectacles, who was examining a piece of broadcloth with all the force and concentration of a preacher considering a text. His great brass-bolted shears were held open in his right hand, and now and then the points traced an imaginary pattern.

"What size, William?" he asked, without removing his attention from the cloth.

"Forty-four, p'r'aps," said the clerk.

"Show the brown suit made up for Mr. Potter."

"By jiminy, that might do."

The clerk disappeared headfirst into a wardrobe and came out again holding a dark brown homespun coat and trousers. He held up the coat.

"It ought to just about do," he said. "Try it on, mister."

Dan slipped into it. The clerk led him to the mirror, where he examined himself nervously.

"It 's smoother 'n honey. By jiminy, there 's what I call a fit. Ain't it, mam?"

It did fit well. In his enthusiasm, the clerk began to praise the cloth.

"Hard as iron, wears like steel, and there 's no chance for its getting a shine on it. Just the thing for you, I 'd say. Quiet and sober and looks rich. It 's a gentleman's coat. And the cloth is very especial. Imported out of England. Yes, sir. It goes elegant into a pant. We made some of it into pants especial. Right there, mister," holding up the trousers, "is an elegant pant. There is n't a pant in the store — or in the city, for that matter — to come up to it. You don't have to try 'em on to see they 'll fit."

It was just about what Dan wanted. He liked the color. So did Molly. It was becoming to him.

The clerk went ostentatiously to one side to look for more coats.

"What do you think of the cloth?" Dan asked. "It seems all right to me. It 's good and heavy."

Molly fingered it.

"Yes, I think it 's good, Dan. It looks good on you, too."

"Yes, it 's good cloth. Can't be beat," said the clerk, returning.

"How much?"

"Well, it 's good cloth, but it 's been made up. That would cut it down. Twenty-five is a cheap price. Your wife can see what good stuff it is, I 'll bet."

Dan started slightly, but Molly, watching him closely, saw no change in his expression. After an instant of feeling the trousers, he said, "Got anything cheaper?"

She let out her breath slightly.

The clerk ran his hand down over his face.

"Well, I dunno. Maybe."

Through the door the tailor said, "Twenty-one we let it go for, William. No less."

The clerk stared over his shoulder and let out a low whistle.

"That is low," he said, as if to himself. "Well, Mr. Perkins is the boss."

"I don't know," said Dan, still fingering it. "What do you think, Molly?"

She had him step over to the window to get the light. It did look well on him.

"I'd take it," she said.

"All right," said Dan, relieved that it was over. Through the door the tailor was focusing hard on the broadcloth. As soon as Dan spoke, the difficult pattern must have appeared to him, for he began to cut.

The clerk wrapped up the suit and took the money, and Dan and Molly went on to a haberdasher's. She walked vigorously beside him, saying little, and whenever Dan glanced at her she was looking straight ahead. Now and then men turned to look at her as she passed, and he felt a glow of pride. It was a great credit to him to be walking with her.

They bought a couple of shirts, and Molly fussed over some ties until she found one that suited her taste, a dark green, flowing silk one.

"It'll make your eyes bluer," she said, holding it up to his chin. Dan flushed uncomfortably, and the clerk smiled.

"A woman always likes to buy her husband's neckties," he said.

This time they carried it off well; but once they were outside the store, they went nervously again, like conspirators. If Dan had asked her then to marry him, she probably would have said yes.

But, back on the Sarsey Sal once more, there seemed to be no point in the question. Dan said nothing.

Buying a Team

Dan and Molly had no more than finished clearing away breakfast than they heard the trotting of a light team coming along the dock. Then the horses stopped, and they heard Solomon calling to them to hurry; and all at once there was a burst of hearty laughter.

Dan slipped into his new coat while Molly pinned on her hat before the mirror; and they grabbed up the cake on a plate and ran up the steps, locking the door behind them.

Mrs. Gurget looked at their flushed faces and began laughing again good-naturedly. Hector, with his hands folded on his waistcoat and a new cigar upended in his mouth, said sententiously, "Spooning never made for spinning," which made their faces even redder, at which Mrs. Gurget started laughing again on the rear seat, while Mrs. Berry sniffed and pointed her sharp nose in the direction of the horses.

Solomon had scrambled down over the wheel, after passing the reins to Hector, and he was now rearranging the luncheon baskets under Mrs. Gurget's seat.

"Molly," he said, "seeing you 're thinnest, I guess you 'd better set here with Lucy. I had to put her in the back to bring her as close over the rear ax' as I could."

"That 's a lie," the fat woman said with a broad smile; "he did n't want to talk to me. I made him shave."

The buckboard was a light three-seater, and the team looked uncommonly well for livery horses.

"I thought I might as well get a decent pair," Solomon said to Dan as they climbed into the front seat. He picked up the reins, took out the whip, pulled his hat down over his eyes, and looked over his shoulder at the others. Mrs. Berry was got up in a bombazine dress, beribboned and black, and Hector wore a pot hat on the back of his head. Behind them Molly, in her new hat, was talking to Mrs. Gurget. The fat woman felt Solomon's eye.

"Go on, Sol," she said.

The team, which had been lifting their forefeet nervously from time to time, started off with a lunge and broke into a smart trot.

"My gracious!" cried Mrs. Berry, clutching her bonnet. "Be they safe, Hector?"

"All right till we make the turn to the bridge," said Hector, swinging his cigar across his lip.

She braced her feet and sat back rigidly, her tense mouth bringing her chin up towards the end of her nose.

"You persuaded me, Hector," she said, and thereafter she preserved an ominous silence.

"It's all right, Nell," Solomon cried over his shoulder. "The hind wheels 'll stay down, I guess."

"You shut up!" called Mrs. Gurget.

The rig rattled over the planks, and Solomon made a smart turn over the Genesee Street bridge. They turned west into Whitesboro Street, and the team settled into a flinging trot. There were several wagons on the road ahead of them.

"Getting out to see the execution," Solomon said. "Not that they'll see it; it's coming off in jail. I remember the Peters case in 1810. I was just a boy, but I remember it real clear. They hanged him on the hill west of the town. The sun come up just when he stopped kicking. It was a high gallus, and there was a drunken man kept a-wondering and a-wondering if Peters had seen it come up. He was ten feet higher than what we were. It's queer how people will go to see somebody hanged. But they do it in the jail now. It was a clever notion to have the fair there that day. A lot of folks that wouldn't have come to a fair 'll stop to look at them horses; and looking at a horse is next to buying."

As they swung past the last houses of the city and saw fields beginning to appear, they felt the sun warm on their necks. Mrs. Gurget wiggled the shawl looser and straightened up on the rear seat, so that Molly had to grab the rail to keep from being jogged off.

"Your hat's real pretty," she said to Molly. "And don't Dan look nice?"

"I made him go out and get some clothes yesterday. He

was getting ragged. I had an awful time arguing with him. He's kind of close with money."

Mrs. Gurget smiled, and let her eyes rove the road. She began commenting on the turnouts, on the women's clothes, pungent words popping out of her plump mouth, her face warming with laughter. Molly laughed with her and watched Mrs. Berry wincing whenever they passed another wagon. Dan was silent, but, as they slowed down behind a string of five horses which a gypsyish-looking man was leading from the back of a wagon, she saw his eyes on a big black horse with a white blaze and muzzle. Even when they turned out to pass the string, Dan kept his eye on the black horse.

The gypsyish man, who wore a red shirt and a heavy sheepskin waistcoat and sat with his legs hanging over the tailboard, grunted something to the man who was driving the wagon — a seedy, thin man, who wore a high-crowned hat and chewed tobacco with a speculative swaying of his jaw. At the other's grunt, he lifted a languid pair of eyes at Dan, nodded, spat, and went on chewing.

It became quite warm. By the time they entered the village of Whitesboro and turned out before the jail, Mrs. Gurget had taken off her shawl altogether. Molly herself felt warm, and even Mrs. Berry perked up and jerked her bonnet straight.

"I don't see why we come so early," she said to Hector, "and I don't see why we had to stop here. The fair's up behind the hill, ain't it?"

"Yeanh," said Hector, humbly. "But I ain't driving this rig, Nelly."

"What's all these wagons here for, and people got up so for?"

"That's right, Nelly. They do seem to be wearing Sunday clothes."

"What for?"

"Well, it's Mary Runkle," said Hector, managing to tip a wink at Solomon with his off eye.

"What about her?" demanded the little woman angrily. She scented a conspiracy.

"Nelly talks so she ain't had time to hear the news, I reckon," explained the fat woman kindly. "You see, Nelly, it was whiles you was up to Westernville, Mary Runkle killed her husband."

Berry produced his ponderous watch from his waistcoat pocket.

"That's it, Nelly, and in five minutes they're a-going to hang her. She had it coming, I guess. She used to bother her husband a lot, bossing him all the while, I've heard."

"That's right," said Mrs. Gurget.

The wizened little woman suddenly drew herself up, slapped Hector's face, jumped out of the wagon.

"You're mean, you're all nasty-mean, all of you!" she cried, and her voice choked and she ran away round the corner of the jail.

Berry stared after her with round eyes. He touched his cheek with the ends of his stubby fingers and drew in his breath.

"Well, damn me," he said. "Who'd have guessed it? It was your idee, Sol."

"Yeanh," said Mrs. Gurget, hedging herself a trifle. "You got it up, Sol. You'd better go after her, Hector."

But Hector had already jumped to the ground and run after his wife.

"Nell, Nell!" they heard him shout.

"I declare, Sol," said Mrs. Gurget. "What did you have such a notion for is beyond me. Right here in all these people. Why I can't hardly think how to look."

Solomon was the most amazed of them all.

"Why, Lucy, I didn't have no idee. I didn't say to do this."

He glanced at Dan for support, then pushed his hat over his eyes to scratch the back of his head. "I didn't have no idee."

Mrs. Gurget laughed suddenly.

"It got her sudden. And her nose was awful red to start with. I'll bet she's a sight. She's a good body for such a measly woman."

"I think she's nice," said Molly.

"Too nice," said Solomon. "She makes it awkward, being that way."

He switched round and leaned to the left to get his watch out.

"It ought to be going on now."

The space in front of the jail was crowded with wagons. There must have been thirty or more, mostly farmers, who could take the morning off. They stared at the expressionless front of the jail with sombre eyes, talking now and then in low voices so that a breathing murmur seemed to hang under the bare branches of the elms. Some stood among the wagons, and a couple of old men sat with their backs to the trunk of a tree and drank out of a glass bottle and looked at their watches between drinks. Between 10 A. M. and 2 P. M. had been the judge's sentence; and Sheriff Jones would put it through as soon as he could.

Tied to a hitching post, the doctor's horse dozed in the shafts of his buggy, one hip slung for comfort. He looked like a fast trotter, but he had learned to take what rest he could when he could, no matter how fresh he was. A big farmer in a pepper-and-salt suit was driving a pair of colts in a surrey up and down the street. Every time they came opposite the old men sitting against the tree they shied and bolted, and it took the farmer two blocks to turn them and bring them back. He seemed to be afraid to take the time to unhitch them and leave them in a shed.

The bell in the schoolhouse clanked once to mark the end of an hour, and a complete hush fell upon the crowd. One of the old men against the tree untied the tobacco-pouch strings under his chin which held on his straw hat, so that he could take it off in an instant if it should prove to be the proper thing to do. And through the stillness they heard the farmer swearing at his colts when they started to bolt for the third time. He looked up as he passed and saw everyone's eyes on him and flushed deeply. Glancing back, Dan saw Mrs. Gurget obviously holding her breath, a dazed, awestruck expression sucking dimples into her fat cheeks, and

Molly looking white, her eyes dark. He took out his new handkerchief and wiped a cold damp from his neck.

A bit of blue flashed over the heads of the people, and, lighting on a branch, a blue jay began to squawk profanely at them. Instantly a red squirrel answered him angrily. And the people watched them. All at once the noise ceased, the attention of both squirrel and jay being caught by the opening of the jail door. The doctor came out, dressed in black, carrying his bag in his hand. He paused a moment to talk to the sheriff, who had come out after him.

"Good-bye, Sheriff," they heard him say. "I 've got to get along. Man at Oriskany caught his hand in a loom belt."

"Bad?"

"Probably lose a finger."

"A thing like that 's apt to be serious," said the sheriff.

He watched the doctor get into his buggy, wheel the horse, and go rattling up the valley. His jaw was set grimly. All at once he became aware of the people watching.

"Get out of here!" he shouted. "Get out! Do you think this 's a circus?"

They grinned at him shamefacedly. One of them called, "Morning, Mr. Jones."

The sheriff raised his hand.

"Get out," he said again, and wheeled and went into the jail, banging the door after him.

Solomon shook the reins.

"We 'll hurry to get a place in Finkel's shed," he said to Dan.

In the shed they found the Berrys waiting for them. Mrs. Berry looked very red about the nose and eyes, and Hector was wearing an embarrassed expression. For once he did not have a cigar in his mouth. Mrs. Berry gave Dan a conversational smile.

"So it 's done, is it?"

"I guess so," Dan mumbled. A hearty man was lifting his daughter over the wheel of the buckboard next to theirs. He looked round.

"It 's the first execution I ever got close to," he observed, "but for downright push and horror, give me the wind colic. Out there all you did was set and watch your watch."

Mrs. Berry was straightening Mrs. Gurget's shawl, while Molly was getting out the lunch basket.

"Coming to buy?" asked the hearty man.

"Yeanh," said Solomon.

"Well," he said, "it ain't much of a fair. No fancy stock, anyway. But we might poke around together. Jed Johnson might have some good teams. He generally has. What are you looking for?"

"Me?" asked Solomon. "I ain't looking for anything. It 's my friend here." He pointed his thumb at Dan.

"Pleased to know you, gents," said the hearty man, shaking hands with Dan. "My name 's Brackett — just Bill Brackett — a plain, honest man."

He gave himself a light pat on the chest and nodded his head at his daughter, a little girl with two braided pigtails of yellow hair, blue ribbons in each, blue serious eyes, and a very freckled nose. "Daughter Nancy. Likes to set on the back of the buckboard and lead home pa's horses. Can't leave her home."

The child dug her toe into the ground and stared upward from under her lids, blushing furiously. Suddenly she caught the fat woman's eye and smiled.

"Why don't we take her with us?" said Molly. "That will leave you men free."

Brackett took off his hat.

"That 's downright kind of you. Since you offer, I accept. Maybe I can put you in the way of a good deal," he said to Dan.

The girl bashfully joined the three women, but when they came out of the shed she was holding Mrs. Gurget's hand.

"Me, I 'm looking for a light horse," said Brackett, fishing a stout stick from under the seat of his wagon. "What are you after?"

"I want a pair," said Dan. "About thirty-three hundred."

"Matched pair, eh? Well I 'll bet my friend Jed Johnson will have just about what you want. He always has three or four pairs of real handsome horses he brings up from the South. Suppose we go and see what he's got."

"I don't know as I'll buy a team outright. I guess I might match a pair."

"That's a good idea, young man. It's good if you know enough to do it. Buying from Johnson, you're sure of a good team, though."

They sallied out of the shed together, Brackett with his left hand on Dan's arm, his right swinging the stick. He wore a light brown homespun coat and black trousers and a scarlet tie, and stuck his legs out handsomely as he walked.

Solomon and Hector kept in the rear.

"How's Nell?" Solomon asked.

Hector let out a long sigh. Then he turned on Solomon with a shamefaced grin.

"Me and Nelly ain't talked the way we just did since we been married. She allowed she'd been mean, but that she hadn't meant anything by it; and then I said it wasn't right the way I'd treated her; and she said she'd stop naggin'. Can you beat that, Sol?"

"No!" said Sol. "Did she, though?"

"Yes, sir! She admitted it. But it was worse than that. It was worse than seeing an execution."

"Yeanh?"

"By Cripus, I'd got so wound up, I said I'd give up cigars."

Even to recall his promise petrified Hector's round face.

"That's too bad," said Solomon, judiciously. "You hadn't ought to have done that."

"Well, I done it. We was so loving all to once, I couldn't think of anything else to say. And when I said that, Nelly kissed me right in the shed with all them horses, and then made me say it over. She's been pert as a squirrel ever since."

They found that they had lost sight of Dan and Brackett, but on looking round they sighted the fat woman before a gypsy's tent, with the gypsy woman, her head covered with a red handkerchief, talking to her through the opening of the tent, one brown hand stretched out, palm up, gracefully. A little behind the fat woman stood Molly, with the little Brackett girl, who was carrying the lunch basket. Farther down the line of tents they saw Mrs. Berry, her small bonnet bobbing from right to left as she tried to fool a pea-and-thimble artist.

"She will try it," said Hector sadly, "and she's close-sighted too."

Shivers of superstitious delight were passing up and down the fat woman's back. Now she drew herself up with a shuddering breath as a keen deduction of the gypsy woman went home, and then she leaned over chuckling outrageously over some revelation for the future. All the time the black eyes of the gypsy kept glancing up from under her brows at the broad red face.

"Let's sneak up to the back side of the tent," Solomon whispered. "Maybe we'll get a gossip on to Lucy."

But, before they could start, the gypsy woman dropped the fat woman's hand and held out her own again, palm up. Mrs. Gurget giggled like a schoolgirl as she dropped a quarter into the hand.

"I sure got my money's worth," she chortled. "See what she says about you, Molly."

The two men saw the girl leave the child and step up to the gypsy. Her fresh, bright coloring made a vivid contrast with the gypsy's brown skin and black hair. The palmist let her bold eyes rove over Molly, trying to learn what she could from her general appearance. Then she took Molly's hand and slanted it to the sun. For an instant the two heads bent over it; Molly bending easily, the short tails of her jacket flaring upwards; the gypsy leaning forward from her seat, her black eyes glittering. Once in a long while a palmist sees a hand which makes clear sense according to the laws of the science, and which can be read without invention. She glanced up at Molly's face, said something in a low voice, then drew her shawled head back through the flap of the tent. To the amazement of the others, Molly followed her.

There were a dozen or so of tents set up opposite the hitch-racks and shed; and most of the people seemed to be interested in the attractions they offered. The gypsy fortune tellers and palmists were popular, and the Egyptian phrenologist, K. Kopulos, who was just starting a vogue in the Mohawk country; and the glass blowers, making magic with their breath and fingers — they could always be found at any such gathering. In this instance they were a Swiss family, who had found the fortune they sought in their old profession. Little white glass bucks and bluebirds could be found in half the corner cupboards of the river counties. At the end of the line a quack had set up a booth from which he hawked, in a thin, monotonous voice, rheumatic belts, stone water for gall stones, smallpox antitoxin, and the inevitable panacea for man and beast, claiming even that it stopped the roup in poultry. His tall, bony figure in the black pipe hat and black coat, the velvet collar of which had long since turned a rusty green, caught the eye and held it. He had an interested, kindly face and knew a cure for every ailment. Across the way the reputable agent for Dr. Brandreth's Pills, a jolly, healthy, stubby man, himself a product of the medicine he offered (according to his advertisement), writhed impotently as he watched the quack's sales. Even the famous *Symptom Diary, or Invalid's Almanac* he carried as a side line went poorly. He looked too healthy to be sympathetic.

Behind, under a long shed, or tied to a hitching rail outside, stood the horses, their manes and tails stirring on the slight north wind, some fidgety at the noise and bustle, some trotting round the rings behind a boy as the dealer stood beside the expected buyer, cracking his long-lashed whip and pointing out what virtues the purchaser might miss. Like a refrain to the rise of human voices came the stamp of hoofs and the rattling of halter rings.

The morning sun washed over the crowd, picking out here and there the bright red and green of gypsy dress, or the pearl grey of a gentleman's hat or the gloss of his tile. The old grass was a dull green underfoot, and at the entrance to the grounds and in the ring, where horses' hoofs had loosened the frost, the dark mud showed through.

For a minute, with all the bustle round them, Hector and Solomon watched the flap of the gypsy's tent. Then Solomon swore.

"She 'd ought to have more sense than to do that."

They joined the fat woman and the little Brackett girl, who was eating her way into a pink nest of spun sugar.

"Well," Mrs. Gurget admitted, "it is queer, Sol. But I don't see as anything can rightly happen to her so long as we watch till she comes out."

"Guess I 'll go round back," said Hector. "If there 's any monkey business, it 'll show there."

But a few minutes later Molly appeared in the door of the tent. Her face had lost some of its color, and her hair, escaping from under its bonnet as it always did, hung lifeless. Her shoulders slouched. For an instant she did not appear to see Mrs. Gurget and Solomon, but stood with dull eyes.

The fat woman drew a sharp breath.

"My gracious!" she said sharply. "Open your eyes, dearie."

Molly glanced at her and lazily pulled a wisp of hair from in front of her eyes. She smiled, but it was a lifeless smile.

"Shucks!" snorted the fat woman. "What 's she been telling you?"

Molly looked down at her hand, then wiped it down over her hip.

"She said it was a true hand."

"You 'd ought n't to go believing an ugly witch like her," said the fat woman. "It 's just a game for making money."

"She said it was true," repeated Molly. "She asked me first if I wanted to hear."

"What did she tell you?" asked Mrs. Gurget, drawing her out of earshot.

Suddenly Molly laughed.

"It don't matter — it 's nonsense. You 'd laugh to hear it. I ought to go back where I can do up my hair."

"All right," said Mrs. Gurget, patting her arm. "We 'll

go look for a place to eat, and leave the men find Dan. He's off buying horses."

"No," said Molly, suddenly. "Let's all go look for Dan."

"Surely," said the fat woman.

They picked up Mrs. Berry and Hector.

"What did she tell you, Molly?" Hector asked.

"Oh, nothing. It's all lies, that talk," said the fat woman, but she frowned aside at Hector and put her finger to her lips. He stared at her, then winked and said solemnly, "Sure, all lies. They told me I was going to marry a pretty, red-haired gal."

"Well, didn't you?" asked the fat woman.

"It was too white to tell when I did. But the temper was there."

"You shut up," said his wife, angrily.

The little Brackett girl had finished her sugar. Her eyes were shining and the corners of her mouth and the end of her freckled nose were grubby and sticky.

"Let's get some more," suggested the fat woman.

The child gave her a glance of mute admiration.

"Vi'let," she suggested in a small voice. . . .

Mr. Brackett had started to lead Dan down the line of horses before the shed. He walked slowly, swinging his stick with gusto.

"Jed has his horses at the bottom end of the shed," he explained. "We might as well head there first."

Dan said nothing, but kept running his eyes over the horses. Most of them were work teams, generally looking puffy as if they had been greased and heavily corned for a short while. He mistrusted all such horses.

Now and then Mr. Brackett would nod to a dealer. The dealer would nod back at him as though he were an old acquaintance.

"Got some good-lookers there," Brackett would say, and the dealer would nod and put a cigar in his mouth or a chew, according to his disposition, and cross one foot over the other in preparation for making a trade. But Brackett would pass on.

"Jed's reliable," he said to Dan. "Let's see what he's got. You've got to watch these fellers."

"Suits me," said Dan.

But then, just as Mr. Brackett was about to wave his hand to his friend Johnson, someone touched Dan's elbow.

"Looking for a horse?"

Dan saw the gypsy whom they had overtaken earlier in the morning driving his string to the fair. His eyes languidly surveyed Dan's waistcoat buttons, and a long straw drooped over the middle of his lower lip.

"Yeanh," said Dan.

Mr. Brackett turned an indignant gaze on the gypsy.

"Who are you?" he demanded.

"Who are you?" the man echoed in a mild voice.

"Brackett," said the farmer. "Just Bill Brackett. There's plenty to vouch for my character."

The gypsy raised his hat delicately by the crown half an inch off his head and let it drop back. Then he took his straw out of his mouth, examined the chewed end critically, and put in the unchewed end.

"Pleased to meet you."

"Get out," said Brackett. "My friend wants to buy a team."

"That's what I was asking him."

"He's going to deal with Mr. Jed Johnson, a reputable dealer," said Brackett, throwing out his chest. "I vouch for Jed Johnson's character."

"I don't want to show my character," said the gypsy. "I want to show this gent my horses."

"Sure," said Dan, "let's look them over."

Mr. Brackett grunted savagely and then strode behind them, a look of determination on his red face. The gypsy led them to a corner of the lot, where five horses were lined up under the care of the red-shirted man. Most of the horses were light, carriage weight. But Dan's eyes lighted again at the sight of the big black with the white blaze and muzzle. He was dirty and looked thin. Mr. Brackett let out a gust of air through his teeth.

"You ain't looking at that, be you, Harrow?"

"What?" asked Dan.

The red-shirted man winked, ostensibly at Dan, but including everybody within reach.

"Gent means a horse, probably. Don't know the name."

Brackett swore.

"Horse! That, eh? You ain't looking at that bald-snouted brush-harrow, be you?"

"Yeanh," said Dan. "I kind of like his looks. He's a bit high to match, though."

"Sure," said the owner, taking out his straw to point with. "But his shoulders is set on straight. He's short-backed. He's a fast walker. Sam, show him round."

The red-shirted man unhitched the halter rope and walked the horse up and down. He had a good stride.

"Trot him," said the dealer.

The red-shirted man jerked the rope and the horse threw up his head and trotted in a circle.

"Limber," remarked the dealer. "He's kind and sound. He's a good horse."

"How old is he?"

"Five."

Brackett snorted and said, "Five!"

"Why don't you look at his teeth?" suggested the dealer.

"I would n't get in reach of that animal's eye, let alone his teeth. He's vicious."

"Well, I would n't then. Sam, open the horse's mouth so the gent can look without getting breathed at."

The red-shirted man led the black over to them, caught his off ear in one hand to hold the head down, and pinched the lower jaw. The horse flared his nostrils, but his mouth opened.

"Twelve," observed Mr. Brackett. "Look at them rings."

"Sure," said the dealer. "Three on each."

Dan ran his hands down over the horse's legs. The horse stood easily. There was no sign of ringbone.

"Sound," remarked the dealer.

"Spavined," said Brackett. "I thought I'd noticed."

"No," said Dan.

"He's had a fall," said Brackett. "Ain't his nigh knee broke?"

"How much do you want for him?" Dan asked.

"Ninety-five, cheap."

"Yes, it is," said Dan. "Was he stolen?"

The gypsy let his languid eyes drift over the skyline. "No," he said.

"Where was he raised?" asked Dan.

"Man I bought him off did n't mention."

"Where'd you buy him?"

"A pasture lot in Round Top."

"Where's that?"

"Tioga County, Pennsylvania."

"All right," said Dan. "Can you keep him here for a while? I want to match him up. When I get the horse I want, I'll fetch him and pay you."

"Option?"

"Five dollars?"

"Sure."

Mr. Brackett seized Dan's elbow.

"Boy, boy. You want to look out. Of course he was cheap. But them'll stick you, them gypsies."

"Yeanh?"

"You'll have a hard job matching him. But I heard Jed speaking about a grey roan he had might do."

"Might as well see," said Dan.

At the end of the line in the shed a puffy-looking man leaned against a hitch-post. He wore a long coat and high leather boots and had a dirty fawn-colored hat on his head. At sight of him, Brackett waved his arm.

"Hey there, Jed, how be you?"

Mr. Johnson uncrossed his legs, looked up, said "Hello" in a hoarse voice, and crossed his legs again. He was chewing tobacco, and Dan could see by the way he could spit through the hitching ring on the side of the shed that Mr. Johnson knew what was where.

"Jed, here's Mr. Harrow come to buy a horse."

Johnson ran his one eye over Dan, and then seemed to perk up a little. His heavy cheeks collapsed on the heels of a long spit and he wiped his mouth with the back of his hand.

"How big?" he asked hoarsely.

"Not over seventeen hundred, fourteen to fifteen and a half hand," said Dan.

"Not notional in color, be you?"

"No," said Dan. "But black would go best."

Mr. Brackett thought it was time to put in a good word.

"Granting you could find the ideal horse," he said in a confidential tone to Dan, "I bet your neck Jed will have it."

"I 'll show you what I got, young man," said Jed.

He stowed his quid behind his nigh back teeth and put two fingers on his tongue. His cheeks filled like a balloon and he whistled.

"That was for my man," he said, when he had listened a moment. "He ain't going to answer. He never does. He 's lazier 'n a beef cake. Reckon he 's sleeping off some likker. God damn him, anyway."

"Ain't sleeping, ain't drunk!" cried a high voice. "Ain't a cow cake, neither. Go to hell."

A skinny man with a grey beard and big hands drew himself out of the manger in front of the horses and looked them over owlishly.

"What 's the trouble, Jed?"

"Gent wants to see a horse."

"Thar 's seven," said the old man, pointing down a line of friendly snouts. "He can take his pick, can't he?"

"Get up," said Jed hoarsely. "Get up, will you?"

"Sure."

He clambered out, clouted a horse's shoulder for room, and joined them.

"What 'll the gent see first?"

"Wants seventeen hundred, fifteen hand," said Johnson. "Black."

"Why, bless his brisket, we 've got the picture of it right here."

"That's what I was thinking," said Johnson. "Lead her out, Jimmy."

While Jimmy was getting a big black out of the string, Johnson said, "Five-year-old mare, kind and honest. Real pretty. I'd call her better than seventeen hundred now, but she's in heavy flesh. She'll train down. There she is. Good head and neck, well set on, not a scar on her feet, heavy quarters — a good hauling horse."

Jimmy walked her round. The horse was loggy, Dan said to himself, stiff. Her size was right, but she was too long in the back. She would n't keep up with the other horse for more than a mile. She lost motion every step.

"Nice horse," he said. "How much is she?"

"Well, I'll tell you, Mr. — "

"Harrow," said Brackett, putting his hands in his pocket and striking a critical pose as he watched the mare.

Johnson spat and began again in his hoarse voice, "It's this way, Mr. Harrow. There's a five-year-old mare, broke double or single, active worker, handsome shape, if I say it myself. None of your Southern horses, not her. Raised on my farm to Canandaigua. I'll tell you about her. Her own sister was matched up with her, the neatest spitting picter they made. You could n't tell one from the other, I'll swear it, except by the way they'd hold their tails in dropping. Fact, ain't it?" He turned to Jimmy. Jimmy halted the mare, looked round her and under her, said you could match hairs on them. "Sure," continued Johnson, "that's how they was. I aimed to sell 'em as a pair. But a gent came and offered me a hundred and fifty dollars for that other one. But I held out for two hundred and he was glad to pay. This one I'll sell for one-fifty, seeing it's late in the season and going single. I was to ask four hundred for the team. I was a fool to sell the other."

Dan went over to her and looked at her neck. Her mane was trimmed cleverly, but he had been right at first. Her neck was set too low on her shoulders. A week of heavy hauling and she'd have sores.

Out of the tail of his eye he kept watching a brown. The

horse was thin and out of condition, but he liked its set. It stood easily in the line and kept its head up. It looked clever. Dan turned back to the mare.

"Let's see her trot."

Johnson uncoiled the lash of his whip and cracked it. Jimmy yanked on the lead. The mare lumbered heavily. Then she stumbled.

"First time she ever done that," said Jed.

"I ain't sure I like her," said Dan. "Got anything else?"

"There's a grey roan. Not so slick an article. But good. All my horses are. Take him out, Jimmy."

While the old man was bringing out the grey roan, Johnson ran through his catalogue of virtues, named one twenty-five for the price, and declared that the horse was seven years old. Dan decided that the horse was fourteen.

"You're making a mistake to look at this one," said Johnson. "That mare's what you want. Still, for a steady horse, this one'd do a man proud."

"First-rate horse," said Jimmy, with a grin in his beard. "He's a regular odacious clever one, he is. Name is Ponto."

Dan went over him carefully.

"He looks pretty good to me," he admitted. "What's wrong with his left eye?"

"Wrong?" asked Johnson hoarsely.

"Eye?" asked Brackett.

Jimmy grinned again.

"I ain't told Mr. Johnson," he said. "That's a most odacious clever horse. He's got the moon-eye."

"Moon-eye?" asked Dan.

"That speck you seen," explained Jimmy. "It grows along with the moon. In a couple of weeks you'll see it going down. It commences with the new moon. If it's rainy when the moon commences, you can look at his eye and see what the weather's going to be like. It shows like a new moon, wet or dry. You can make money betting on the new moon."

Johnson spat a long squirt.

"I've heard tell of the moon-eye," he said with hoarse frankness, "but I never seen one. Why didn't you tell me,

Jimmy? I'd have put the price up. Won't now, though. Jed Johnson never put a price up'ard on any deal he makes to offer."

"That's honest gospel," said Brackett. "I vouch for it."

"What's the good of the moon-eye?" Dan asked.

"Don't you know that?" Jimmy asked. "Gol! And you out to buy a horse?"

"A horse with moon-eye don't need no light for traveling," Johnson explained, winding the whiplash round his thumb. "He can see in the dark."

"Well, he looks good," said Dan, "but I ain't sure."

"I don't know as I've anything to offer that'd suit. You can look, though."

Dan went down the line. He had a chance to see the lean brown, and the horse looked good to him. He guessed he was not over seven, and he saw that he was healthy.

"I tell you," he said. "Let me go and get my other horse and see if the black or the grey goes best."

"Sure," said Johnson. He sat down on a bucket and took another chew, and began talking to Brackett.

"Well, Bill," he said, "I guess I'll owe you a commission for that one."

"I think so myself," said Brackett. "You'd ought to stick him high."

"I aim to," said Johnson.

Halfway back to the gypsy's string, Dan saw Solomon and Berry and the womenfolks coming down the line towards him. It had begun to get colder again, and the northwest wind was bringing clouds over the valley. Once in a while a horse would snort and rear over a swooping shadow. Molly saw him first and waved her hand. When he reached them, she put her hand inside his arm and walked along beside him. The wind, which fingered her loose hair, had brought a color up in her cheeks.

"What luck?" Solomon asked.

Dan told them about the black horse he was about to buy from the gypsy. Then he spoke of trying to match it, and Mr. Brackett's enthusiasm for Mr. Johnson's horses.

"I think Brackett and Johnson has a deal on between them for trade," Dan said. "They're trying to get me to buy a black mare that shows she's a cribber and broken-winded, and a fourteen-year-old grey with the moon-eye. I let on to like them. But they've got a brown horse in the string that'd match up with the black better 'n any horse I've seen to-day. I didn't let on I seen him. I figger Brackett must get a piece of all trade he brings. I think he's foxy."

Brackett's small daughter pulled her freckled face out of the nest of spun violet sugar and wiped the stickiness off her lips. She smiled at them proudly.

"My pa's slicker 'n polish," she said. "He says so himself."

They all started to grin, and Mrs. Gurget swept up the child, sugar and all, for an enormous hug which made her squeak with terror and pleasure.

"I'll bet he is," said the fat woman.

"I was thinking," Dan went on, "how it would be for Hector, maybe, to go down and buy that brown horse for himself. He's awful poor and Hector'd ought to get him cheap. Then I'll bring the black along to match with the grey."

"How much'd you want to pay?" asked Hector.

"Not over a hundred and twenty, with the poor flesh he's in."

"I'll pay for everything he costs over one hundred and ten," Berry promised.

"Hector!" exclaimed Mrs. Berry. "Ain't that betting?"

"Kind of." Berry grinned.

"Well, you ain't going to bet no money, see?"

"Why not?"

"I said so. You shouldn't ought to go betting our money that way."

"Well, I won't lose."

"Shut up. You heard what I said."

"Quit your nagging, Nelly."

"I won't quit. I won't have you betting our money. Why'd I ever marry a gambler," she wailed rhetorically.

"Did n't know no better. A sheltered honey like you would n't," soothed Mrs. Gurget.

"Quit nagging," said Hector.

"I won't."

Hector gave a jubilant shout.

"She ain't going to stop nagging! You all heard her say it. Then I might as well smoke."

He poked a cigar between his lips, and the enlargement of his button mouth brought back a jolly good-humor to his face that had been lacking all morning.

"Now," he said to Dan, "I'll pay you every dollar that horse costs you over one hundred."

He strode off with pompous quick steps of his tubby legs, spouting great clouds of smoke down the wind ahead of him.

"Hector's a great hand to make a bargain," Solomon chuckled. "He can find more things wrong in a horse than there is in a horse to be wrong. I'm going down to the back side of that shed to listen to him talk."

"Come on," said Mrs. Gurget.

"I'll go with Dan," said Molly.

They went slowly, to give Berry plenty of time to drive his bargain, and Molly kept close to Dan.

"Is he a nice horse?"

"He's a dandy," Dan said. "Him and the brown 'll look good on the towpath hauling the old Sal."

She smiled and squeezed his arm. He looked down at her.

"What's the matter, Molly?"

"Nothing, Dan. I'm kind of tired, I guess."

"You ought n't to be tired. Wait 'll you see my team."

They found the gypsy and Dan paid him the money. The man took the money and then lifted his languid eyes and looked from Molly to Dan.

"That Brackett's slick," he said. "He gets trade for Johnson. Better watch out."

"Thanks," said Dan.

The red-shirted man gave him the lead rope.

"You won't have no bother with him. He stands easy. He's a clever article."

They went slowly back down the slope with the big black at their heels. When they came in sight of the end of the shed, they stopped in to see how Berry was coming on with his bargaining. They could see Jimmy trotting the horse round. Dan nodded.

"He looks as if he'd match up proper."

"My, he's big," said Molly. "Look at his feet."

Just then the black head with a white muzzle was pushed between their shoulders and the black horse snuffed at Molly's bag for sugar. She started and looked up to see Dan grinning at her. "He's took a notion to you," Dan said. She smiled and put her hand on the horse's crest. He pricked his ears and swung his head gently closer to her.

"He's nice," she said. "What's his name?"

"You name him," said Dan.

"Let's call him Prince."

"I'd thought of it myself," Dan said admiringly.

Down ahead, they could see Berry running his hands over the legs of the big brown. At every joint he shook his head and counted on a finger. Brackett and Johnson were looking on gloomily, and Jimmy did not seem to take much interest in the proceeding. Then Berry started to walk off, his plump legs rigid with simulated disgust.

Johnson lifted his head and sent a long squirt ahead of him.

"Ninety dollars," Dan heard him say.

Berry turned back, fished out his wallet and paid out the money like a shot.

Then Dan and Molly came up. Behind the dealer they saw Solomon waving his arms and grinning ecstatically at the corner of the shed.

"Here's Mr. Harrow," said Brackett.

Johnson looked up.

"That the horse?"

"Yeanh," said Dan.

"Trot out the grey, Jimmy."

"How about that brown?" Dan said, pointing to the horse Berry had just bought.

"Sold," said Johnson.

"I'd like to try him with the black."

"Go ahead," Hector said affably. "Maybe there's a deal somewhere in it for us."

He slipped the lead rope through the halter ring of the black, and took both ropes in his hand. The horses walked off stride for stride. They were a good match.

"Trot 'em," said Dan.

Berry managed to run for a few yards and the team trotted without breaking stride, eyeing each other warily and keeping fairly well apart.

"If they make friends," Dan said, "they'd ought to make a good pair."

"Sure," said Berry.

A premonition of evil had sobered the faces of the dealer and Brackett, but Johnson managed to swear.

"Say," he said, "how about trying that grey?"

"I only want two horses," Dan said. "Mr. Berry, here, bought the brown one for me."

"Cheap, too," said Hector, proudly. "Ninety dollars."

"My God," said Jimmy. "I'm going to get some sleep."

He crawled back into the manger.

Brackett's jaw dropped.

"I don't think it's nice, Harrow. It wasn't honest."

"He's slick," said the little girl, looking at Dan admiringly.

"You're a swell man to get trade," Johnson said to Brackett.

"It amounts to the same thing," Brackett said. "The party bought the brown one. Where's my per cent?"

"It was another deal," said Johnson.

"The little fat man bought him for Harrow, and I brought Harrow here to you," Brackett maintained, his voice rising angrily.

"Go spit in the river," Johnson growled, and turned his back, and got out a fresh chew.

The rest moved off, Molly and Dan bringing up the rear with the two horses.

"Let's eat lunch now," Mrs. Gurget said. "I'm all hollowed out with hunger."

They ate in the shed, to escape the rising wind.

"They'll make a good team," Berry said.

The horses were looking each other over carefully; after a while the black lifted his muzzle to the other's ear, then they touched noses, and afterwards, when Dan grained them lightly, they ate contentedly side by side.

"What'll we call the brown one? We named the black one Prince."

"Call him Earl," Solomon suggested.

"Those are good names," Hector said nodding. "They'll make a good team."

"Well," said Mrs. Gurget, starting to open the second pickle jar. "Their bones look good."

VI

THE WINTER TOGETHER

It began to snow that afternoon; it snowed all night. The next morning it was still snowing, small flakes drifting lazily through a bright sun. It stopped at noon, but the temperature sank in the first cold spell of the year. In the afternoon, word was given out at the weighlock that the canal was shutting down. Dan and Molly noticed the dropping of the water that afternoon.

The old Sarsey Sal groaned during the night, waking them, at first, until they became used to the sound. A stiff wind was drawing down the valley, and a smart ripple slapped the hull. Dan went to sleep again with the sound of it in his ears.

But later he woke suddenly, stiff in the bunk, with a cold damp on his face. He lay quite still trying to determine what was wrong. The clock in the cabin whirred and struck rapidly, three notes. Then there was dead silence in the boat. Outside he could hear the shrill whistle of the wind.

He shifted slightly, and became aware that Molly was awake, as tense as he. For an instant neither of them spoke; then he asked, "What is it, Molly?"

She did not answer.

It occurred to him that someone must have come on board. But he felt sure that he would have heard the creak of the cabin stairs; and the wind would have rattled the door. But, with the idea, Jotham Klore's face, black-bearded, had come back into his mind, for the first time in many days.

He got up slowly, cautiously, letting his weight come gradually on each foot. Little by little he edged into the cabin. A faint moonlight, white and brittle as it was reflected from the new snow, lay in two bars across the room. In a moment he was able to pick out the familiar shapes, the chair, the stove now dead and cold, the mirror with an unreflecting pallor in it, his own hat and Molly's coat hanging side by side on the door.

"There ain't anyone aboard," he said in a low voice.

In the cabin he heard Molly stirring. Presently she came out quietly, about her shoulders a pink Mother Hubbard she had recently bought, mysteriously colorless in the stillness. Her face was vague, and her light hair had acquired shadows. Only her eyes, dark and large, seemed real to Dan.

There was an unreality in the world for both of them, as if they were ghosts — they made no sound, their voices were inarticulate whisperings, like the touch of flakes against the windowpanes. They stood facing each other in a silly, breathless hush.

Then Dan drew a deep breath; and the faint food smell in it, and the cold in his lungs, reassured him. He could hear Molly's even breathing.

"What woke you up?" he asked her.

"I don't know."

Her voice, too, was low. He could catch her uneasiness in the sound of the words. Again he felt a terror overwhelming him. He would have welcomed a sight of Jotham Klore opening the door and standing there with his black beard and heavy fists.

"I don't know, Dan," she said again, almost plaintively.

She kept her eyes on the door as if she also expected someone to come in. He knew she was afraid of Klore. He did not know how badly. Ever since he had met her coming towards him with Mrs. Gurget, the Brackett girl, and the rest at the fair, she had been uneasy, paler than usual. She had smiled to watch him with his new team, and she had gone with him to see them stabled in Butterfield's barn back of the wharf. She had kept close to him the rest of the day. He had felt an insecurity in the old Sarsey Sal, which he dared not admit to himself.

As he stood opposite her there in the dim light, his

flannel nightshirt rubbing on the backs of his ankles, he realized how pleasant she made living on the old boat. For the first time he took her into the personal account of his own life. Before, she had been a matter of course — essential to the Sarsey Sal as the rudder and the towline. Seeing her now with her deep broody eyes staring at him out of the paleness of her face, she became important to him; but it was hard to say how.

Things had come upon him since he had left the Tug Hill country. They had come by pieces, here and there, almost without his seeking; certainly without his knowing that he sought. And as each came he had a dim awareness that he had expected its arrival, as the jobs he had got, as the Sarsey Sal, as Molly Larkins. It was hard to see where they might all be fitted in.

Behind it all there had been the moving figure of Gentleman Joe, with a price upon his head, as strange to the canal as Dan himself, who seemed to keep tabs on Dan's journeying back and forth, and who yet was followed step by step by the fat marshal, Henderson. It almost seemed as though they traveled the same road. He could not see where it would bring them out, for Gentleman Joe had Henderson to reckon with, and Dan had Jotham Klore. But for the winter, by all accounts, Henderson was out of the picture, and by all accounts Klore was also. But Molly stood in front of him, between sleeping and waking. He was puzzled. He rubbed his hair back until it stood on end, tousled and ungainly. He did not know what had waked him; Molly had said she did not know.

Then she laughed and came over to him. There was a high note in her laughter, but even so it comforted him. She led him to a window on the canal side of the cabin and stretched on tiptoe beside him to look out.

The wind was blowing swirls of snow off the roofs; a white moon glittered. It was silent but for the breath of the wind.

"See, Dan, that's why we woke up."

She pointed to the bed of the canal, where the low water

should be lying, and he saw that it was still in the wind, with a dark unruffled lustre.

"It's frozen over, Dan."

"Yeanh."

He put his arm about her and felt her draw in close to him. She was laughing to herself; he could feel her shake. But when he lifted her chin to look at her, he saw her cheeks glistening.

Now that the stillness was explained, he felt it close about them both. It had a comforting touch. He put his haunting uneasiness behind him, for though he knew that he must make up his mind about where he was to take his stand in the path sometime, and choose his way, he knew that the winter lay before them. The canal had frozen in.

They woke next morning with the run of sleigh bells in their ears. The sound had a closeness and intimacy, coming and going quickly, with no echo, that caught Dan's ears.

"More snow coming," he said to himself.

Molly was already stirring in the kitchen, and the smell of coffee was coming in to him, with the humming of a little tune.

> "If you don't love me,
>   Love who you please;
>   Throw your arms round me,
>   Give my heart ease."

There was plaintiveness under the light dance in the tune. Though he could not see her, the humming brought to Dan's mind Molly's face as he had noticed it at the horse fair — pale, anxious. And it brought back her face as he had seen it the night before, in the dark, with the winter coming in round the old boat. . . . Afraid — she was afraid. Jotham Klore was safely out of the way, working his team on the railroad between Rochester and Syracuse. When they had heard the news of him, Dan had covertly watched her face. He had noticed that she listened breathlessly; then she had dropped her eyes to something else. Her expression had made him think of her as he had seen her for the second time, just after she had run away from Klore, after Klore had given her her licking. He had felt, as he could feel it now, the same hot anger coming up in him, and he wanted the boater in reach of his hands. He had toughened during the fall; the easier winter would build him up. His shoulders had thickened through; he was putting on weight. Molly had noticed it in the mornings when he shaved, with his shirt hanging from his belt.

He got up and greeted her in the cabin, went up to wash. There was a grey film of cloud hanging over the roofs of the city; the morning smokes spread out under it mushroom-wise. The air was quite still, but heavy to breathe. It seemed strange not to see boats stirring in the basin, not to hear horns blowing for the weighlock. Boats lay tied up to the docks, resting low down, like the Sarsey Sal, with just enough water to keep them off the bottom. Smoke came from the stovepipes of some, feebly against the grey air, and it hung low over the bed of the canal. The boats seemed sleeping — on the verge of death; and yet they were in the heart of the city, which was full of life, going about with its accustomed activity, on its morning chores. The sounds of wagons on the docks were muffled; there were few now, anyway. But across the canal Dan caught glimpses, between the warehouses, of city bucks racing their trotters in cutters up and down Canal Street. They went by with a flash of bright red and silver, and a jingling of bells that burst out and faded away all up and down beside the course of the canal. And a smell of more snow coming hung over the city.

As he shaved in the cabin, he caught glimpses of Molly out of the tail of his eye in the mirror. Once or twice he surprised her watching him with a speculative glance, doubtful; the same expression he had seen upon her at the fair. It worried him; he wondered what she was afraid of, with Klore out in Rochester.

The second time he caught the look on her face, he asked her flatly, "What's bothering you, Molly?"

And she said, "What would be bothering me?"

"I don't know," he said.

She brought up a smile for him.

"You hadn't ought to talk till you've had breakfast."

He looked at her awhile, till the bright color came up to her cheeks, and she busied herself with the dishes on the table. She was wearing a bright pink gingham with short sleeves and a low neck, and she needed color to set it off.

"Ain't you going to get harness for your team?"

"Yeanh," he said, buttoning his shirt. "Sol knows a man. I'll take them round with him."

"I like them," she said. "I like the black one with his big white nose."

"He's a good horse," Dan nodded. "But he's got an awful thin hide. I'd ought to have some hemlock syrup to rub his shoulders with till he gets hardened up."

"I'll make some to-day," she said.

His mind full of the team, he ate his breakfast quickly.

"When will you commence hauling up to Goldbrook?" Molly asked.

"First of the week, I expect. There ought to be good snow then."

The team went well. As soon as he had seen them making friends in the shed off the fair grounds, Dan had said to Molly, "I could take them just as they be and win a prize in a ploughing match." He could believe it himself, now, watching them walk. Their stride was so well matched that they kept step as a natural thing. They would, he felt sure, turn in two miles better than the bays in their trick on the towline, for all the others appeared to move faster.

The bays were ahead now, drawing Solomon's sleigh, and on the down grades they broke into a smart trot and drew away from Dan. But on the up grades the long, even-tracking stride of the big team caught up with them, and, looking round, Solomon would see their noses close to the tail of his sleigh.

They pulled without strain, though they were hauling by far the heavier load, close to two tons; they gave no evidence of the weight at all in their even stride; only the puckers in their haunches showed deep. Dan did not need to hold the lines. After the first mile he kept his hands inside his coat; and Solomon, watching them over his shoulder, called back, "See them keep a sight on where they're going. After a couple of trips you won't hardly need to be on the sled."

The little man had the horse blankets round his knees, and he wore a horsehide coat with the high collar turned up. Even when he turned round, all Dan could see of him was his thin nose, red as a strawberry, poked between the edges of the collar, with a white patch of frost under it, and his protuberant blue eyes, water-dimmed with cold.

Crouching behind the barrier of boxes and barrels he had constructed round his seat, Dan had nothing to do but watch the sky and the woods. The scrunch of the travois runners on the snow, the insistent, light jingle of the trace chains, the squeak as the bobs tracked round a turn, merged into an unheard monotone. As even as their stride, the breaths of the team spouted in four puffs ahead and whitened on their withers.

The road led them past farms, at first, and then into the woods round the base of Deerfield Hill. At times they tracked over corduroy stretches. And once they crossed a small brook on a high narrow bridge, from which the woods had drawn back, so that on a dark night it would almost be invisible.

It was slow going, and on windy days, with the temperature way down, Dan let the team drive themselves, and made it his business to keep warm. He had nothing to do but think of the warm comfortable evenings in the Sarsey Sal. Three nights a week he stayed in the camps, hauling out from Utica three days and three days hauling in. But three nights he spent aboard the boat and he had his Sundays off.

Those were pleasant evenings: he and Molly, sitting together in the cabin of the old boat, the fire roaring till the draft holes and the belly of the firebox reddened, the kettle purring on the stove and spouting its stream of steam. Behind them on its shelf, the clock ticked the minutes out and beat the hours rapidly.

Molly had fixed over the cabin until it seemed like a different place. It had taken on a clean, healthy smell; there was no dust. She had made new curtains for the sleeping cuddy, heavy green ones that kept out the light in the morning, so that he never woke till she had his breakfast ready.

Now and then Mrs. Gurget breezed in with Sol to pass an evening, or they went to the Nancy. More often they were alone, and then Dan sat in a sort of comfortable daze, listening to her voice and watching her; wondering in a vague way where they would be next winter. He never thought of that long; this winter was enough for him.

Once in a while they went out to dinner with Mrs. Gurget and Sol, to eat at Baggs's or some other place; and on Sundays they went to church — to different churches, for Molly liked the variety. She was interested in the clothes of the women; but she had real devoutness, and Dan enjoyed seeing her kneel beside him. He liked it also when people turned to look at her, to catch a friendly smile from an older woman; to listen to the sermon and to take the benediction, solemnly and seriously, with Molly; and then to walk out into the fresh air with the other people and slowly to take their way back to the Sarsey Sal, squatting low and ungainly beside the dock with the ice round about her and the snow drifted up toward the outer windows; to go aboard and start the fire in the stove, while Molly pinned an apron over her Sunday dress; to tend his horses in the barn and chat with the stableman on feeds and liniments and the price of oats in the dim, musty-smelling shadows by the hay chutes;

to go inside the cabin and take off his coat and sit at ease, smelling the cooking food and listening to Molly dressing the sermon with observations on millinery. Lazy, comfortable days were Sundays, between the long drives up to the lumber camps on Goldbrook; something to look back at. . . .

In the lumber camp he and Solomon unloaded their sleighs at the storehouse and took their teams into the long log barns. Here in the woods the snow hardly melted during the days. The road leading in was feet about the earth, packed hard on its double tracks; and the snow had drifted up against the buildings till the windows on the northern walls had tunnels dug down to them to let the light in.

The stable had a line of long single stalls running down one side, and a space at the end for hay. It was dark inside, and the unfrozen earth just under the board beds of the stalls smelt fresh and strong. At night, with the teams all in, it was as warm as the bunk house, and the air was thick with steam, choking with the smell of sweat and sharp ammonia. It braced Dan like a tonic after the long cold ride.

Then he and Solomon sat in the cookhouse, with their backs to the great stove, where the cook worked in an undershirt and apron, his blacksmith's arms hot and red from baking, his quick stiff fingers white with flour. He could bake twenty pies at a time in the great oven; he had eighty men to feed all at once. It was a man's job. Yet all the time he gave them gossip over his shoulder and asked for news of Utica. And when the talk went low he told them how he lost his foot on a steamboat, when a connecting rod broke in a race down the Hudson; and how he had a wooden foot made in its place and took to cooking.

"I couldn't keep away from a fire. Feeding pies to jacks is just the same as raising steam in a boiler. It's harder work on your arms, but not so hard on the foot."

It clacked and banged on the planks as he moved back and forth.

"I had it carved in the shape of a shoe," he said. "So I only have to get one real shoe made to a time. And it don't squeak, nor does it need a shine — only once a year."

He pulled his moustache away from his mouth, leaving the end white with flour.

The men came in and lined at the tables, and the cook's helpers put the food in front of them. They did not talk as they ate; they were too tired. Now and then the cook made a snatch at conversation with Dan and Solomon in an effort at hospitality. After the meal he cleaned his skillets and pans, leaving the dishes to his helpers. The men went to sleep in the bunk house early, and Dan and Solomon went after them. A single lantern burned by the door, making a feeble glimmer in the long room with its double rack of bunks. Beyond it in the shadows the deep steady breathing and heavy snores mingled with a hum and drone like twelve-foot band saws ripping virgin pine. It was a heavy sound, beating upon Dan's ears, and it brought into his mind, each night he spent there, the quiet of the cabin on the Sarsey Sal. He turned in his sleep on the narrow mattress and fought the wall. Or he lay awake for a time, his eyes on the small square window at the far end, where the moonlight cut a slice through the darkness and showed a glimmer on the snow outside. Once he heard wolves running.

Then, next day when the lumbermen were at work in the woods once more, the cook made them up lunches and he and Solomon harnessed their teams and took the road back. All the long ride, his mind went ahead to the Sarsey Sal, where Molly would be getting his supper when he arrived, and where he would have his hours of ease, to stretch the stiffness from his back, to eat hot food that made him sleepy just to eat it; to have the deep quiet night of sleep.

The days and weeks went by like a dream; and he felt lazily contented. The routine absorbed his consciousness, with the nights on the boat and Sundays to keep track of and remember. Molly, in a print dress and fresh apron, at the cabin door to greet him and and look him over with her frank blue eyes. Sometimes she came out along the road on fine days to meet him, when he could be expected early; and they rode into the city together. The smoke rose up against the gathering darkness like a shelter from the snow. Molly, Sunday mornings combing her light brown hair in front of the mirror, with the sun against it, glowing on her shoulders; and he sitting there looking at her, pulling at his pipe now and then, taking pride in her while she made talk.

It snowed heavily in February; there were four feet on the level in the open valley; and in the woods, if a man jumped from his snowshoes, he went in up to his neck. The snow was piled higher than Molly's head along the sidewalks. The city went about its daily life with a curious hemmed-in feeling in the air.

Few minstrel shows traveled during the cold months. What entertainments there were had been got up by church workers. Generally they were given for special audiences. But even so Dan did not care to go to them, for they were apt to come on Saturday nights, and he was tired after his day on the sleigh. He preferred to sit in the Sarsey Sal, to listen to what Molly would tell him of her doings. Her accounts of marketing, of shopping for dress goods, of a hardware sale, of a walk in the streets, never seemed to him to be the same. It was enough to hear her voice.

When he talked, himself, he talked about the team.

"They're good, Molly. They couldn't be better-matched if they was own brothers."

"Yes," she would say, with her eyes on the cap she was crocheting.

"I'd like to see 'em working on a plough."

His eyes were fixed on the windows with a far-away glance when Molly looked up at him. She had seen him so more often lately. It was the time of year.

"I'll be glad when the canal opens," she said. "I can't hardly stand waiting for spring."

"Yeanh. Men'll be going over their seed potatoes soon."

They were silent.

"What've you been doing?" he asked.

"I've been working on a rug," she said, with a sudden lifting of her head. He caught the strain in her voice. "I got some odd pieces yesterday."

She got up to show them to him.

"They're pretty," he said, scraping the bowl of his pipe.

"Me and Mrs. Gurget went after some red flannel in the afternoon. We didn't get any. She couldn't find none with a yard and a half in a piece, and she needs all of it in a petticoat."

"Yeanh."

"Eggs have dropped two cents," she said.

"Pullets commencing to lay," he said. "I thought they'd be coming in about now."

They talked on, in odd sentences, Dan watching her out of the corner of his eye, and she him. When their glances met, they dropped them. She did not seem natural to him; ever since the fair she had acted queer. It was the wear of the winter, perhaps.

"What's the matter with you, Molly?" he asked, suddenly, when their silence had left the tick of the clock to itself for several minutes. His voice sounded harsh to his own ears.

She looked up swiftly, her eyes shining as he had never seen them. He thought she was going to cry; he hadn't meant to speak so roughly. He stared out of the window, waiting for her answer.

Suddenly she forced a laugh.

"There's nothing the matter with me. Is there?"

He did not look at her, for his ears had noticed the catch in her voice.

"Well," he said heavily, "I guess I'd ought to fix the team for the night."

He got up, put on his hat, and went out. On deck he paused, wondering to himself. Then he glanced in the windows. Between the curtains he could see her. She had broken down, crying. He wondered whether he should go back; then he decided she would not want him to see her. He grunted and went to the barn.

There he fussed with the team for a few minutes, slapping their bellies after he had taken up the blanket straps, and grinning when they humped themselves.

"Only a month and a half," he said to them, "and you'll be sweating on the towpath."

When he came out of the barn, he paused, glanced at the Sarsey Sal, and then went swiftly along the basin until he came to the Nancy. Mrs. Gurget told him cheerfully to come in. She was sitting in a rocking-chair, with her feet against the stove, her red hair in a thick braid round her head. She was alone.

"Hullo," she said. "Come in, Dan. Where's Molly?"

Dan took off his hat and sat down.

"She's on the Sarsey Sal."

Mrs. Gurget rocked jerkily back and forth. After a while she remarked: "Sol's gone up to Bentley's for a snort to soak his nose in.

"What's the trouble?" she asked.

"I don't know," Dan said. "Molly seems to act queer. She's crying now, to beat all. And there ain't anything to cry about I can see."

Mrs. Gurget watched her toes as she rocked. Then she said, "Reach me that pie on the table, Dan."

There was one piece left, and she held the knife over it with a firm hand.

"Have a piece?" she asked.

"No."

She sighed, picked it up deftly in her fingers, and began to nibble it.

"I always did like cold pie," she remarked.

She watched her toes over the piece of pie as she rocked.

Dan said, "She's been queer off and on since she was to the fair. When I ask her what's the trouble, she don't say nothing."

Mrs. Gurget nodded her head and munched.

"I noticed that, Dan. I'll tell you. She had her fortune told there by a gypsy. It give her a turn, I think."

"She ain't been singing lately," said Dan.

"Don't get worried," said Mrs. Gurget, smiling at him and running her tongue along her lips. "She's young, and young gals is notional."

"What did the gypsy tell her?" Dan asked.

"She won't say. I've tried to edge it out of her a lot of times when she'd be aboard here to spend the day. She won't tell. I've told her all such ideas gypsies has is untrue nonsense. But she'll just set there, and then after a while she'll perk and laugh."

"I've noticed it," Dan nodded gloomily.

Mrs. Gurget studied him with a kind light in her eyes.

"Don't you worry, Dan. Gals is notional at times. There ain't anything you can do if she's getting notional. I'll bet when you go back you'll find her all perked up. She'll have rinsed herself all out."

Mrs. Gurget put the last of the pie into her mouth, munched it deliberately, swallowed it down. She sighed and licked each thumb.

"How long've you and Molly been living together?" she asked.

Dan reckoned up: "Four months."

Mrs. Gurget pulled her shawl up round her neck.

"That's just about time to get to know each other, ain't it?"

"Lord!" said Dan. "I know her all I need to know her. She's a good gal."

"Yes," said Mrs. Gurget. "I think she is."

Dan felt comforted. Then, mulling on her words, he was startled.

"You don't think there's another man she's took a notion to?"

Mrs. Gurget dodged the question momentarily.

"The gypsy's talk upset her, didn't it?"

"Seems so," Dan admitted.

Mrs. Gurget nodded.

"All gypsies has two lines of talk," she said. "If it's a gal they're a-reading for, they talk about a journey and sickness, or about a dark and a light man. You're light. I'll bet she's worrying about you. She'd ought to know better, but in the winter little odd notions get growing. But she's good to you, ain't she?"

"You ain't any idea," said Dan, earnestly. He was thinking: a dark man or a light man — a journey and sickness — a dark man and a light man. "You're light," Mrs. Gurget had said. Maybe he was. And Jotham Klore was the dark man.

"Well," said Mrs. Gurget, "you don't need to be worrying about anybody else only you two. Molly wouldn't hold to but one at a time. Should she change her mind, she'd leave like knocking a bung; all in one rap. Don't you worry, Dan. There ain't anything you can do."

"Do you think she'd want me to marry her?"

"Well . . ."

"I'd thought about it," Dan said.

"You can ask her," said Mrs. Gurget, "but I don't think it would help. And if you ask her, it's like saying —" the fat woman shied clear of her words. "Mostly there ain't anything wrong in not being married on the canal. As long as you're honest there ain't any real sense in it. It's different if you're going to get off the canal. Then you've got to act like other folks. But here living's just a working agreement, and if you want you can get a minister to lick the revenue stamp to seal it with; but it don't add a lot. And a gal's free to back out. Sometimes it makes it hard for her, but if she wants it that way, it ain't any bother of yours. Unless you want to take her off'n the canal. Be you going to stick at boating, Dan?"

"Yeanh," he said.

"Then don't you worry, Dan. I'll bet when you get back to the Sarsey Sal you'll find Molly's all chippered up."

The fat woman drew in her breath. Her deep bosom arched, and a little locket hanging there caught the light.

"I used to be young and pretty like her, and have notions," she said. Her fat fingers opened the locket and she turned it to the light.

Dan glanced at a crude pencil drawing that looked as if it

had been taken from a lithograph. It was the head of a very pretty girl on a slim neck, with a gay upward curve to the chin. The fat woman chuckled somewhere deep down in herself.

"Ever see the face afore?"

"No," he said.

"Well," said Mrs. Gurget, "that's me. I was a notional gal and I turned down Sol, who wanted to marry me — such a wizzen of a man, I thought. I went West with another. But when I came back on the canal, looking like this, he was looking for a cook, and I took the job. Sometimes he asks what's in the locket and then I put him off and say he'd better not know, and he pesters, and I laugh. And nighttimes he talks about Nancy when he's sleeping. It knocked him bad to lose her."

Suddenly she laughed, and her voice rang true.

"It's funny my telling you, Dan," she said. "I never told anybody else but you, but you won't tell anybody. Sol's asked me to marry him; but I said no. It wouldn't be fair to him now; and there ain't any sense. We both have a good time, living along."

She laughed again, leaned over, and kissed him.

"Run on back, Dan. You'll find Molly's chippered up expecting you."

The light still burned in the cabin of the Sarsey Sal. Molly was not there, but when he opened the door she came out of the cuddy in her night clothes. He looked at her covertly; her face was fresh and clear again, and she smiled, and her eyes were tender as he had seen them when she first came aboard his boat. By secret consent, neither said a word, but when Dan sat down Molly sat on his lap, her feet curled up on his knees. He took them in his hand to keep them warm.

It was dead still, a quiet night. They kept silent with the march of the clock in their ears, the breathing of the kettle. Her hair, braided for bed, hung over her shoulder and swung back and forth against his waistcoat as she breathed; and he felt each touch against his heart.

Monday Sol and Dan pulled out from the city under a leaden sky. The low-hanging city smoke behind them looked white. Now and then the horses snorted and shivered their withers as they walked. The air was breathless, and Dan felt the skin on his neck tingling.

"It smells like a blizzard coming," Solomon said. And Dan agreed.

Before they reached the woods, snow began to fall; here and there a flake, drifting straight down. When one lit on his cheek, though the day was not cold, a chill touched him.

Behind them the great Mohawk valley dipped, then mounted to the sombre arch of the sky. There were no clouds, but an even darkening, out of which the flakes stole downward. The snow on the ground shone with a miasmic pallor. The runners of the bobs scraped on the snow with a hollow sound, and the clink of the trace chains was small, dull, and struck the air a close note that died instantly. There was no echo.

After his one remark, Solomon hunched down inside his coat and said nothing. For all the stillness, it required effort to speak; the air was heavy in the lungs, and words clung to the teeth. To try to make the voice carry, a man had to shout his words, as though he were battering a wall with them. His only refuge was inside himself.

A week had gone by for Dan since his talk with the fat woman, and the quiet night with Molly. The happy life had come back to them. But now, with the darkness closing in, he remembered Mrs. Gurget's words — a light man and a dark man. Untrue nonsense. But the words revolved in his mind, and he saw himself and Jotham Klore. Even at the beginning he had seen Jotham Klore; even the old peddler who had brought him down to the canal had warned him against the man. A big bully, in his last fight he had licked the Buffalo man, they had heard; he was cock on the canal. . . . A light man and a dark, and Molly in between. . . .

When the wind came, it came stealthily. A cold breath from the north, unnoticeable except for the drift of the snowflakes. Now and then they lifted just before they came to earth, and drifted southward a few feet before settling down.

So slowly did the wind take hold that before it found its strength the sleighs had entered the woods, tiny figures in the stillness, crawling along the winding track, with the snow feeling its way through the branches to light upon them. Gradually the loads whitened with a thin powder. The big flakes were thinning out.

With the new snow, the gleam went out of the ground; a dullness enveloped the world. Space closed in, distance became an illusion. Time was measured by the steady stride of the horses, the faint sound of trace chains clinking. Light spread through the flakes and thinned and died. Dan traced patterns in the falling snow. The cold crept closer.

As the wind grew, there came a sigh out of the trees. When they passed spruce clumps, Dan saw the upper branches lifting and falling in a monotonous ritualistic rhythm. Down on the road they could not feel it. They would hardly have known it was storming, had it not been for the mounting snow in the tracks. It lay soft and thick and powdery.

An hour passed. Then, with no warning, the sound of their passage was snuffed out. A great hand rocked the trees; the snow smothered the sound of the runners; the mounting roar of the wind, so gradual, had taken possession.

When they came into the first long clearing, the drive of the gale struck them. The tails of the horses before Dan whipped back straight at him like flung spears; it seemed that he could see the skin on their quarters pulled tight; their heads dropped as if they had been malletted. For a second they stopped, then lunged on the collars and fought ahead. The snow drove on them so fast that Dan could not say how it blew, up or down; there was a thick mist between him and the trees; and he felt the cold cutting past his coat into his stomach.

He had a glimpse of a group of ancient pines on the hill on his left. Their old stalwart trunks were bending; their great branches stretched southward, as if they had turned their backs to the wind.

Then once more the forest, and the roar of wind in the trees, and a lightening of the pressure on his breath. The teams picked up pace and forged ahead, eager for the camp. The snow deepened. The horses had to lift their feet.

Hour by hour, with no knowledge of the time. It was early afternoon when they entered the camp and saw dim lights behind the snow. Both teams were white with frost and snow; the sleighs were coated. Dan was so stiff he could hardly fight to his feet; he felt as if he must break to do it. Gradually he thawed in the kitchen; then went out again to rub his team down. Solomon sat by the fire, stretching out his hands as if he begged a precious thing, and the cook clogged back and forth with his wooden foot, making great kettles of coffee, for the men would be coming in early.

"This ain't going to stop," he said. "It's got a tail hold on all the winds in time, and it's out to travel somewhere."

Wind gripped the roof of the cookhouse and shook it. It found the doors and beat upon them till they groaned like living things. When a man lifted the latch to open them, they were snatched from his hand and cracked against the wall so that a murmur broke out on the shelves of kettles. The man came in hunched over and fought the door to shut it. He was white over, though his red face sweated.

"Palery's hurt," he shouted to them, and he shook his fists, as if he thought they were not listening to him. "Him and Franks was cutting a four-foot spruce," he cried, "when the wind took hold afore they was more than half through. It buck-jumped right across his legs, right here." He smashed his fists across the front of his thighs. "He's a mess!" he shouted. "Can't you hear me? He's just a mess. They're fetching him in."

Six men broke through the door, carrying a man on a stretcher of poles and coats and put him on the table and looked at him and drank coffee. He was unconscious, his face a dead white like rotten snow. The manager came in ahead of more men. He looked him over.

"Don't take his pants off," cried a man shrilly. "Don't take 'em off, for God's sake."

The manager felt of the man's legs. "No use," he said. "He ain't bleeding, but we can't do anything. He 'll have to see a doctor."

"You could n't get him down through this," the cook said, passing out sugar.

"We 've got no team knows the road enough," the manager said. "A man could n't see."

He forced whiskey into the man's mouth. After a while they brought him to, and he screamed at them.

The manager turned to Dan. "Could your team make it?" he asked. "They know the way."

"They 've had a hard haul," Dan said.

"They 'll be going light."

"He 'd freeze," said a man.

"We can rig him a tent back of some boards and put lanterns under the blankets."

Dan hesitated. His team was tired. The track was sheltered in the woods. If the snow was not drifted too high in the clearings, they might make it. He nodded. The black would smell out the track.

"One other man, to help in a drift," he said.

"I 'll go," said Franks. "I was with him — I 'll go."

He was a huge fellow, smooth-shaven, with a low forehead and dark sunken eyes that gleamed.

"All right," said Dan.

The hurt man heard them, for he began to curse them and beg them to let him stay.

In the barn, Dan harnessed his horses, talking to them in a low voice. The black nuzzled him inquiringly, but the big brown merely stared at the wall and shook the harness down comfortably. They had put on flesh since Dan had bought them.

"They 're fine horses," said the manager. "I 'd like them here."

At the entrance to the stable the black snorted, but the brown pushed out uncompromisingly, walking to the sleigh.

"Second link!" Dan shouted to the men who hitched them.

Palery had been loaded aboard under blankets. The lanterns under them were bringing out the smell of horses. Dan squatted down in the lea with the big man Franks at his side. "Ged-dup!" he shouted.

The team looked round, then lunged into the darkness, walking slow. At the edge of the woods they reared slightly to break the drift. Behind, the camp was swallowed from sight. Then they entered the woods and the wind passed over their heads, shaking the trees on either side, where branches shrieked as they fought against each other. There was a wild tumult in the storm, now, a hideous uplifting of voices as it beat the woods, and the old great pines groaned in the darkness. Only the road had comparative quiet, running under the uproar, like a tunnel of silence.

Once inside, the team broke into a trot before Dan's urging. He had never trotted them before, but he knew they must make their best speed to get into the city before the deepening snow stopped them altogether. Once stopped, there was no exit. The road would be a coffin and the wailing trees the mourners.

Once in a while, during the first hour, when the wind died down to let them listen, they could hear the hurt man jabber and shout. At first Dan feared he might throw the blankets off; but when he touched the blankets to see how the man was, Franks caught his arm in a great hand and shouted close to his ear.

"Leave him be! He 's tied."

There was a gleam in the big man's eyes, a green glow in the dark, like an animal's, as he crouched beside Dan. Now and again he would lift his face at the wind and shake his fist. But the cold, striking his throat, would make him duck down again.

The rumps of the horses were snow-white. The deepening snow had slowed them to a walk, but they made good time. The cold came under the howl of the wind to freeze the sweat as it formed.

At the first clearing they stopped. Then they went ahead

slowly. The snow was over their bellies and they gathered their hind legs up under them until their haunches sat on the snow, and then jumped like rabbits. Between each thrust, they stopped again, panting in racking gasps, and lowered their noses, as if they smelled for the track. Then they jumped again. Once in a while they seemed to dispute a turn and stood with their heads close together. When they moved next, they would lean against the snow at their chests and push their feet forward to select the track.

It took them fifteen minutes to buck the clearing of a hundred yards. In the shelter of the woods Dan stopped them and let them breathe a minute before he walked them ahead.

The feeling of night came over them with added cold, but no darkening beyond the snow. The power of sight had been taken from them; Dan and Franks glued their eyes to the rumps of the horses and trusted to them. The lines were frozen in Dan's mitten; the lids of his eyes had stiffened. He had to rub them to keep them open. But his companion sat glaring ahead from his sunken eyes, and now and then he appeared to laugh at the howling wind and the wild thrash of the trees.

The third clearing they were barely able to win through, and the horses shook and staggered as they burst into the shelter of the woods. From here each step was a task. Gouts of snow were snapped from the branches, building the road up in lumps, and the sleigh bucked over them in jerks and shunted from side to side.

They came to the edge of a ravine, and Dan shouted suddenly, "There's a bridge!"

But the fury of the storm was in the horses. They did not stop. The sleigh lurched drunkenly into the open, slipped sideways. Franks leaped to the far side and caught the tail end in his hands and drew it on with a gigantic heave; and then the team found the corduroy under their shoes and stamped as they crossed it. Franks leaped on again, his eyes gleaming, laughing and throwing his arms at the storm. He reached under the blankets and felt beside the hurt man and drew out a huge dinner bell which he swung back and forth over his head. The wind took the sound as it was born, but they could think of it rushing miles away across the valley. The team heard it, and pricked their ears.

"Three miles!" shouted Dan.

They struggled downhill through the drifts into the valley. On and on; it took an hour or more for each of those last three miles. But the team were roused and battled the snow with a steady strength. . . .

Windows lighted with warmth blossomed out of the snow beside them. In the street they heard the clamor of their bell; and the team shuddered and stopped and tried to shake themselves. Dan wrenched the lines apart in his hands and felt his mouth crack as he grinned at the bald face looking round and the great head of the brown stretched forward, waiting to be driven. Franks grabbed his arm in a monstrous mitten and rang his bell at the horses, and shouted in his ears, "The dirty sons of bitches, look at them stand there!" and he burst out crying, letting the tears freeze on his cheeks.

They drove to a doctor's and carried the man in. He was still alive.

"Come and get a drink," cried Franks, "on me, on the camp."

"I got to go home," said Dan. "I've got to mind the team."

They shook hands, and, still ringing his bell, Franks went lurching through the snow to Bentley's to get drunk. But no liquor could make him drunk now.

Dan drove the team to Butterfield's barn. He turned in by the Sarsey Sal and saw a faint light burning in the cabin windows. He unhitched the horses and led them to the barn and rubbed them down. He felt weak and staggery, and they were spent.

He pushed the cabin door open. The lamp had been turned low.

"Molly," he called.

He was weaving on his feet when she came out of the cuddy, but a light of achievement burned in his face. She stood looking at him, pale in her nightdress, feeling suddenly small before him. He had acquired stature.

Her eyes lighted.

"Dan!"

He sat down heavily, too tired to take off his clothes.

"Where 'd you come from?"

He grinned, and said stiffly, "Goldbrook. There was a man had his legs broke. I brought him down with a man called Franks. I think he 's crazy."

She stood off a little way. Then she said, as if to herself, "It ain't possible."

Both of them listened to the wind, the menacing whisper of the snow on the frosted windowpanes audible in lulls of the wind. He looked at her seriously.

"If you 'd see the horses now, you would n't think it was possible. It 's a wonder they were n't killed. They 're a team, Molly. They 're the only team I know could have done it."

He let his head back with an infinite satisfaction and went to sleep. She stood looking down at him, pride suffusing her, as a mother might feel who sees her son grown up.

A knock sounded on the door, and Mrs. Gurget burst in.

"He 's here!" she cried as she saw Dan. "A man came around from Bentley's to tell me. A man came in busting for drink a while back saying they 'd come down through the blizzard. Folks would n't believe him till one of them went to the doctor. They can't hardly believe it now. My land! There must be twenty of them out there looking at them horses, late as it is."

She shed her wraps right and left.

"How is he?" she asked, her hearty voice sinking to a whisper.

Molly said, "He just come in. He went right to sleep there."

Mrs. Gurget stepped forward, put her hand on his forehead.

"I don't want to advise, dearie, but I 'd get some blankets

out and heat 'em and take his clothes off and wrap him up and feed him hot tea. And if you don't do it I'll do it myself."

Molly nodded, "It's the best."

They worked over him quickly, the fat woman puffing loudly through her broad nostrils. He only half woke to take a cup of tea, grinning at them foolishly.

"Now he's sweating you'd better put him to bed, dearie. He's all right — only played out. I'll stay with you."

They sat together before the stove.

"They must be a great team," said Mrs. Gurget. "It was a fine thing bringing that feller down, poor man. They say he'll live, but I don't doubt he'll be a cripple."

Molly nodded.

"He's a good boy, dearie," said Mrs. Gurget, after a time. "Don't you love him?"

Molly nodded again.

"You were a lucky gal," said Mrs. Gurget. "I love him myself."

Molly said a strange thing.

"I know how you mean."

The fat woman looked at her speculatively. "Such a pretty," she said to herself. Then she nodded. "Dan's a good boy."

"Yeanh," said Molly. "He's an awful good boy. Sometimes I think he don't know what he wants. He just sits there looking out the window seeing things to himself. He's so good-looking. The big shoulders and neck and them blue eyes of hisn. It scares me sometimes." She folded her arms round her knees and leaned her head back as if she were tired. The fat woman breathed hard.

"You started it," she said accusingly.

"I played up to him," Molly said. "I let it catch me."

"What're you going to do now?"

"I don't know. I love him. Honest, I do. If he wants me to stick, I will. It's only fair now. But I couldn't stand it off'n the canal."

The fat woman's broad face worked into a smile.

"Poor pretty," she said. "I don't blame you. When did you find out?"

"That gypsy told me partly. She did n't know very good herself, I think. I 'd been wondering afore."

"That 's how it was?" The fat woman mused. Then she sighed.

Molly spoke softly.

"He was so big and so nice. Right away I liked him. He did n't seem to know nothing, and I wanted to see him take hold. I thought I could make him."

"It 's what you 've got to do now. He don't know where he 's standing," said the fat woman.

Molly nodded.

"He 's thinking what he wants to do. When he knows, he 'll do it."

"If he stays here on the canal, you 've got to stay with him," said the fat woman grimly.

"I could n't go with him anywheres else."

"If he sticks, he 'll have to fight Klore."

Molly nodded.

"It 'll be a big one. Dan 's awful strong."

"Right now he 'd want to dodge it," Molly said.

"Not now," said the fat woman. "He 's commenced to wake up. I could see it on him sleeping there."

"If he fights Klore, he 'll lick him."

"It would be a good job," said the fat woman.

Molly stared at the clock striking three. At times she felt as if she expected to see the horse start galloping.

"I tried to make him have a good winter," she said.

Mrs. Gurget patted her hand. "He 's had it, dearie."

She cleared her throat.

"We 've got our own lives we 're born with," she observed. "Once in a while we reach outside of it, but there 's only something that 'll fit. It ain't in us really to pick and choose like men. When it comes to the finish afterwards, you 've got to do the best you can with it. I 've seen women fixed like that."

Molly drew in her breath.

"I do really love him."

"I know it," said the fat woman.

Toward the end of the month they began to get rains from the southeast and the roads became bad. Dan and Solomon traveled early every morning to take advantage of the frost. A thinly veiled excitement began to show in people's faces, and one morning the fat woman came bursting in to show Molly some cotton crêpe she had just bought for summer nightgowns. That day, coming down from the camps, Solomon, who was leading, stopped the bays until Dan had caught up. Close beside them in a sugar bush a man was tapping maple trees and hanging buckets out.

"Look," said Solomon, pointing the stem of his clay pipe and loosing a ring of smoke.

Mist was hovering all along the riverbed, and it wavered with a delicate lifting motion. While they sat there with the red sunset glow on their faces, — Dan watching the mist, not knowing what to see, for he had not lived by a river, — the horses, all four of them, suddenly pricked their ears.

"I thought so," Solomon said, a tremble in his voice; and he took off his hat and wiped his high bald head with his red handkerchief. "Now look at it, Dan."

Gradually a motion became apparent in the mist, a pulling away upstream. As the dusk settled and the violet shadows came into the valley with grey darkness on their heels, the mist stole off over the river, faster and faster, until they saw the last of it, a single streamer, vanishing.

The tapping of a man's hammer in the sugar bush ceased. He came out to the road.

"If it goes up three nights," Solomon said, "we'll have spring."

The man nodded.

That night Dan found a new excitement in Molly, a shine new in her eyes, in the place of the broodiness he had seen there all winter.

When they crossed the river in the morning on their way

into the woods, they heard the water talking under the ice. Just below the bridge, where the wind had swept snow clear, they saw bubbles passing under.

The next afternoon they stopped again on the edge of the sugar bush. The farmer was collecting buckets with his two boys. They had worn hard trails in the snow going from tree to tree, and a small path came out to the road, from where they could see the valley. Now the man walked out, and he had to step over the top rail of the bordering snake fence.

"The snow's melting underneath," he said, and he sat down on Solomon's sleigh and took a chew.

"Did the mist go up again last night?" Solomon asked.

"Yeanh," said the man.

"Two nights," said Solomon.

"I've seen it lack the third in March many a year," the man said. "I ain't expecting it now."

"Let's wait and see," Solomon said.

Dan nodded.

The horses shook themselves with a jingling of traces, and the bald-faced black pawed at the snow and snuffed up deep breaths.

From where they sat the men could see the valley spread out below them, the city small and flat in the perspective, and the farmhouses dots upon the grey snow. The farmer licked his thumb and rubbed the edges of his nostrils and drew deep breaths.

"There's a sour smell to the snow."

"I'd noticed it already," Solomon said. "The tracks are running wild all through the woods."

"The river's been talkin' all day."

A deep silence brooded.

"I had my cows in the barnyard this morning," the man observed. "My wife'll turn them out soon for a spell."

Even as he spoke, out of sight beyond the woods on the right they heard a cowbell ringing. The sound brought a lump into Dan's chest and he stared as if he would pierce the trees to see the spotted figures.

Beyond the river the railroad tracks ran straight in a narrow black band. Along it a train swooped, the engine a bright glitter of blue and silver, spouting a trail of smoke. As it passed, it gave a long whistle, then two short; and the sound crept up to the two boaters until it seemed to lie at the feet of the horses. In all the scene the train was the only moving thing. The farmer pointed it out and gave a long spit of brown down the road toward the valley.

"They're going to kill the canal."

The little man snorted.

"Them dinkey wagons," he said.

"They make money in the winter," the farmer said. "In summer now they can cut their rates for competition. They go fast."

"Cripus!" said Solomon. "Let 'em try."

But it came to Dan that the farmer might be right. And the farmer said, "People like things to come quick. Mail, and freight, and money. It saves a bother of thinking."

As the sun set, the same soft colors they had seen before were evolved on the hills, shades of vermilion, and violet, and cobalt blue. A cloud of rolling masses of grey reared up in the south, with a warm look of rain in the depths of it. Far down on a farm, dull sappy chunks of sound broke out; a man was splitting firewood. His axe glittered in front of the shed, flashing a speck of gold.

All at once, in the snow round them, they heard a pulse begin to beat, a faint slow ticking, as if a clock, dusty and forgotten in an attic, had suddenly begun to run. Without warning a blotch of gold broke out in an open space beside the road, and spread upon the snow and began to move toward the river.

They stared at it unbelieving.

"I never knowed a brook ran there," Solomon said. "I'd never guessed it."

"Yeanh," said the farmer. "There's good fishing into it. My boy caught a trout weighing better than a pound last May."

Suddenly he pointed, his arm rigid.

"Look!"

The mist was being born upon the river. It spread rapidly. Feelers of it began to creep up from the valley, winding in and out among the balsams, bringing the perfume of the trees with it.

For a breath they watched it.

"It 's moving up," Solomon said. "Look, you can see it down there against them elms."

"Yeanh," said the farmer.

He got to his feet.

"I 've got to be getting back. I expect a heifer due to-night. She might be coming in early."

He went back into the sugar bush, calling his boys.

Dan and Solomon still lingered. "It 's spring," the little man said. Each began to see in his mind's eye the canal coming to life, the long lines of boats moving east and west. The strokes of the axe sounded like the crack of whips. They heard a wail like a horn, and for an instant they were tense, looking for the boat. But it turned out to be a train of cars, running in from Albany, and the engine blew again on a flat whistle.

"Ged-dup," said Solomon.

The teams started on into the dusky valley. Both men felt the spring stirring, and the brook on their right went with them toward the river. They thought of the boats, and the sound of water, and Dan had a picture of the big teams pulling the Sarsey Sal, and Molly on deck in his old blue shirt, with the wind fingering her hair.

Then also he saw a picture of the farmer in the shadow of the barn, with his wife holding a lantern while he helped the heifer with his hands.

Word was given out from the weighlock next morning that the canal would open early the next week. In the basin a new life had entered the boats tied up. Men were oiling harness and going over their towlines foot by foot. A woman was putting a patch on a grey canvas pit-covering. A little man was painting his boat — a gay pink-salmon shade —

while his wife looked on with a voluble friend and considered the color of the trim; and he brushed away with his hat over his eyes, his eyes furtively watching the docks for men who might guy him for his wife's artistic tastes.

On the Sarsey Sal, Molly gave Dan a letter from Butterfield. It ordered him to report to Rome as soon as the canal opened.

"It 'll be good to get free," she said, her eyes dancing.

That evening she and Dan roamed here and there over the boat, trying the stable hatch and gazing at the heavy coil of the towline.

"I 'll order feed to-morrow," he said.

"I wonder where we 'll haul to first?" she said. "I 'd like to go west again."

"We 'd likely meet Klore out there, Molly."

She looked at him.

"We 'll have to sometime," she said, her face brave.

He felt the spring growing in him.

"Yeanh."

He had beaten out the blizzard; he could take a chance at Klore.

He worked over the towline next morning.

A voice hailed him from the dock. He looked up to see a fat man in a dark suit and pot hat and high cowhide boots smoking a cigar.

"How be you?" asked the fat man.

"Good," said Dan. "How 're you, Mr. Henderson?"

The Department of Justice man grinned.

"Fine. I 'm back at work now. Say, I 'd ought to thank you for fetching me out of that house to Denley. Spinning 'd never have gone down that night."

"It 's all right," said Dan, affably. At that time he could not help feeling a liking for the fat marshal. The sun was too warm in him.

"How 'd you come to find me?"

Dan glanced down.

"A man I was hauling with figured Calash might be there," he said.

"I wish I'd knowed as much as you seem to."

"He just guessed," Dan said. "I didn't know he'd be there."

"I don't believe you did. But you're friendly for him, ain't you?"

Dan said nothing.

"I can see why," said the fat man. "But don't you get mixed up with him. I'm going to get him this time," he said grimly.

Then he smiled, taking his cigar out of his mouth to do it.

"I heard how you brought Palery down. It was a fine thing. I've been looking at your team. They must be extraordinary good ones."

"They be," said Dan.

"Well, good luck."

The fat man put his cigar back and waved his hand.

That night the Sarsey Sal began to groan. Now and then the ice cracked in the bed of the canal. Dan and Molly lay awake, listening, feeling the boat shift under them. Now and then the timbers squealed as she lifted.

"It's the water," Molly said. "They're letting it in, Dan."

Then there was quiet, until they began to hear a thin ripple washing the side of the old boat. They seemed to feel it themselves, a slow soothing touch, and their bodies relaxed, as if it were taking the winter from them.

On the planks over their heads a gentle sound increased to a whisper, a mutter, and they heard rain falling, loud drumming rain, grey rain washing the air.

Dan found Molly's hand in his.

"I wonder if Fortune'll be back in time," she said. . . .

But when they were eating breakfast in the early morning the old ex-preacher put his thin head through the door.

Molly jumped up with a cry of delight, and Dan pumped his hand. Fortune lifted his thin nose to the smell of the coffee.

"I guessed I'd get here before it got cold," he said. "I needed it. My luck's been bad at cards."

There was an affectionate pucker at the corners of his eyes as he looked at them.

"Bad at cards?" The fat woman's voice broke out beyond the door. "My land! I like to hear that. Mine's just dandy."

She bustled in, bringing a breath of spring air with her in the swirl of her skirts. Her laughter was gay and warm as the morning sunlight.

Solomon, in a new grey flannel shirt, stepped in behind her.

"I'm hauling for Rome in an hour," he said.

"So'm I," said Dan.

VII

THE LAST HAUL

Open Canal

It was a typical March sky; grey clouds on the rising edge of the valley to the south and east, with the sun breaking through in golden showers. There was a sweep of wind upon the hills, so fresh that it seemed to acquire visibility and color — a wind of silver in the morning.

It blew upon Dan and Molly on the stern of the Sarsey Sal, whipping her skirts toward him, until he felt them brushing his ankles. She had turned her shoulder to the wind; she had the sun and the wind in her hair; she had a warm light in her eyes, like the glow of the sun in the open sky; and the spring warmth brought the color to her cheeks, after winter's paleness.

The valley stretched westward under a still white carpet; but on the edges of the woods the balsam pitch had made the snow black; and they saw it black and old on the white feet of a hound trotting home after a night of chasing rabbits. It was old snow, dying, and it put its own peculiar sour smell on the wind; a tang like vinegar, urging the lungs to deeper breaths.

The valley had come to life overnight. The rain had swelled the brooks; they were bursting free on the slopes and eating out their channels to the river. They made bright gleams on the old snow; and when they reached the river ice they spread out eagerly in glittering pools.

As yet the river slept; but it was stirring. Where its course came close to the canal, they could hear it muttering,

taking in sobbing breaths at the air holes, like an old man
struggling to wake after a long night of sleep.

But the canal, in the midst of silent farms, led straight
away westward with a blue darker than the skies. The boats
had rushed to meet it that morning. At the weighlock they
cleared as fast as the men could put them through; empty
mostly, going after cargoes, of wood, of flour, or spring
machinery. Some would leave Utica later in the day with
loads. But the first boats traveled light on their first haul,
as if their owners had sent them off merely to see them
moving on the water.

They came behind the Sarsey Sal making a tumult in the
valley; horns blowing when there was no need of horns,
blown merely for the blowing; long wails that went ahead
upon the wind to the far southern clouds to bring the rain;
men and women laughing, jollying, red-faced after their
warm breakfasts, turning their faces to the wind; children
large-eyed, running in the tracks of the horses, shouting in
the empty pits until the plank walls boomed. Some boats
came out with bright new paint upon them, gleaming blues
and yellows and colors more fantastic, nourished by the dark
hours of winter and brought into the sun.

Even the horses partook of that first ungovernable flush
of spirits, tossing their heads, bringing them down to snatch
at the snow with vicious snaps of their brown teeth, wriggling their withers to settle the collars that later would bring
sores. Solomon's old mules, opposite the stern of the Sarsey
Sal, came along with nervous lifting feet. They had had an
easy winter; they were fat as butter tubs; and they twirled
their ears like three-year-olds. The little man walked behind
them with a sprightly step, a wide, unmeaning grin on his
thin mouth. Back on the Nancy, the fat woman in a flannel
petticoat more red than her dyed hair cocked her head to
listen to the blowing of the man behind, grinned, and put her
own horn to her lips and mastered all sound in a wail that
woke the hills. Her breast rebounded after the blast; she
waved her fat arm over her head, brandishing the horn
like Michael's sword, and blew again.

A flock of crows came flapping over the valley to see what had disturbed them. They lit in some poplars and watched the fat woman past. She blew again on her horn, pointing it toward them, and they shrieked with pleasure, giving stiff-legged hops off the branches, swooping up, and turning over.

Up ahead, Fortune Friendly was walking behind the big team. They hauled on the boat as if they had done just that all their lives. They had started it easily with a handsome upward pull in the collars. The black kept looking round at first, to see what this odd wheelless vehicle might be. He pricked his ears to see Molly. But the brown kept his head forward. He had business to do. As Fortune had remarked, he took work the way a Quaker took religion.

The ex-preacher was glad to get back. His luck had held good for the first part of the winter, but with the new year had come a change for the worse. Eventually he had had to get a job on the docks — hard work. His cheeks were thin, a little hollow, as if he had had poor food, and the seat of his pants was worn through. Molly had been obliged to put a patch on them that morning. "A lucky thing," Mrs. Gurget said when she saw it. "It wouldn't have been polite for me to set here steering."

Sitting by the stove drinking coffee in the early morning, Fortune, with a blanket round his bare shanks, while Molly mended his trousers, had gossiped. He had seen Henderson a month before. The Department man had two deputies with him. A big man one of them was, with a down-South way of bringing out his words. You could tell him by his long light moustache. The other had a slight limp, and a bullet scar on his right temple. He slicked his hair down like a foreigner. "Regular pomatum by the smell of it," Fortune said; "but I'll bet it's lard with a drop of perfume thrown on after. Smells like violets."

Dan had gone out to get the team and uncoil the towline. The old ex-preacher had sat there smoking a pipe, his fine smooth-skinned face and twinkling eyes turned toward Molly. He had looked her over searchingly. She caught his gaze in glancing up when she stopped to bite off her thread.

"Did you have a good winter?" he asked.

"Yeanh."

"How was Dan?"

"He was good."

"Oh, I don't mean was he sick."

"Did you hear about him bringing that jack down through the blizzard, February?"

"No."

She told him.

"It was a fine thing to do," said Fortune. "There are n't many would have done it."

"No," she said, proudly.

The old man drew his ideas into himself for a minute. He sat there looking down at the blue socks on his feet. Molly thought he was handsome, with his white hair and red cheeks and black moustache.

After a while he raised his head.

"He 's a good lad, Molly."

"Yeanh," she said with a smile.

"You 've changed."

"Getting old already?"

"Don't nonsense," he said. "You 're just as pretty. You will be."

"Fat?"

He looked at her again.

"Not a mite."

"No," she said.

"I 'm like your pa," he said.

"That 's what you always say when you been hungry."

"You 've changed," he said. "He has, too."

She caught in her lower lip against her teeth.

"Oh, no, he still 's keen after you. Not that way. He 's catching on, that 's all. He looks more like he knew what he was doing."

"Yeanh. He 's been that way more since he come out through the blizzard."

"Molly, do you still love him like you did?"

Her stitches were careful, very neat.

"Did you have a good winter?" he asked when she did not answer.

"He was real good," she said in a low voice. "He was good to me, Fortune. He's a good boy."

His face was sober.

"Are you going to marry him?"

Her head lifted like a doe's and there was a sudden flight of amusement through her eyes.

"Gracious me! You ain't preaching!"

"No," he said, "I ain't preaching. I'm just asking."

"Why do you ask it?"

"I think he'll ask you to marry him."

"Land!" she said, and dropped her eyes.

"There ain't any hiding it in you," he muttered. "It isn't bright on you the way it was."

"No," she said, her eyes following her swift needle. "It ain't that I don't love him, Fortune. Only he's just a boy. He's handsome to see; I like to go out with him. But he don't talk. He's a farmer. He's close with money, not like —"

"No," said the ex-preacher.

"Maybe when we get to moving on the canal it'll come back."

She said it without hope.

The ex-preacher sighed.

"You're like me, Molly. You just want to move around. You'll never want to owe nothing to anybody."

"No," she said seriously. "It ain't that, Fortune. I'd as lief owe myself to a man. But I don't want it way off on a farm. I can see it coming in him. Last night he was late coming to supper, so I went to the stable and the man said Dan was to the granary. They'd been bagging seed oats and he was setting there by himself with a lantern just picking up handfuls and then letting 'em run out through his fingers. I could see it in the set of his shoulders."

"I don't think he'll get off the canal if you stick with him. I wouldn't if I was Dan — or any other man. By gadger,

I would n't, not even if I was Fortune Friendly himself."

"Go on," she said with a slow smile. "Go put your pants on."

She handed them to him.

"Then what 're you going to do, Molly?"

Her voice had a note of plaintiveness.

"I don't know, Fortune. I love him, that's the truth; but the burn's gone out of it."

"Yeanh. But no burn, less scorch. You might marry him, at that."

"Would n't he get tired then? It would n't be right for him."

"Maybe. What 're you going to do? If he stays, he's bound to run foul of Klore. Then what?"

"He 'll lick him. I 've been hoping for him to do that. That was one reason I wanted him. He could have licked Klore to Hennessy's if he 'd had a mind to. He 's got it now."

"Molly, what 're you thinking about Klore?"

Her lips sprang open, then changed to the square grin the old man was so fond of. She tilted her head and laughed. "Go put on your pants, Fortune."

Holding the blanket up with one hand, he had shuffled in to the cuddy. She had done it well, he said to himself. He peeped at her through the curtains. She had gotten herself into something beyond her strength of heart; getting out of it would leave a mark on her, he was afraid; and he was very fond of her.

She was braiding her hair and putting it in a coil round her head. . . .

Now, standing beside Dan on the stern deck, she drew deep breaths of the bright March wind. Her breast arched finely. The loose man's shirt could not hide the strength of her figure, but it made her seem more slender, brought out the suppleness of her hips. Above the up-turned collar the feminine lines of her face had a quaint softness, appealing to Dan. As he watched her breathing in the wind, her frank blue eyes on the far western notch of the valley,

he felt himself older and stronger. For all the long winter
together she had not been so intimately near to him as she
was now, with the boats before and the boats behind, the
rush of the coming spring in the air, the rising and falling
notes of the horns. She breathed deeply through her nose,
her lips equably closed, giving her an added appearance of
vitality. It stirred him; he took the air in quietly and felt
it in his lungs. It had a mysterious intoxicating quality that
traveled to all parts of his body, until he felt it in his
fingers, and his toes curled in his boots to grip the deck.
There was no need of speech for him; it was enough to be
out at last, with the blue water coming towards them, with
the hurry in the sky, with the white banks passing on either
side.

The boats wound on beside the towpath, one behind another. Sweat had come out upon the teams, as the morning
grew, and the snow turned soft underfoot. The hoofs of the
horses picked up great clots of it, which they kicked free.
Seen from across the valley they appeared to the farm folk
an orderly procession, creeping with the slowness of an
ancient habit, as boats had passed, year in, year out, as long
as they remembered. For now the boisterous blowing of the
horns had begun to fade out.

But in the faces of the people the unpent joy of moving
shone as freshly. Their own lives had been given to them
again. Winter had died. For the farmers it still lay upon
the fields; for the boaters it had gone. The canal had opened.

Haircut

In a day, life on the Sarsey Sal had reassumed the pleasant routine of the preceding autumn. All day long they were
hauling now, alternating the two teams in three-hour shifts.
The first night in Rome the big horses had been nervous
about going aboard. The black, which Dan had taken first
to the gangplank, hung back, distrusting its narrowness. So,
after a minute, he had tried the brown. The big fellow was

eager for his stall, and, once Dan had stood upon the planking, he set his own forefeet upon it, slipped them forward inch by inch, and then, with a deep, satisfied grunt, went aboard, turning round inside to face the hatch. The black had looked on anxiously, but, once the brown was inside, no living power could have kept him on the dock. When he crowded round he found the other already started on his supper. After that they needed no leading, and the black somehow managed always to be the first on board. He found that, if he was, he could snatch at least one mouthful from the brown's manger.

In the gorge of the Lansing Kill they came against shrill winds with a breath of ice out of the woods. The Kill roared in its course under the trees with a deep power that reverberated on the snow. The high falls at the head leaped far clear of the overhanging lip.

Old Ben, at the Five Combines, went about his duties with a subdued fury, swinging his long staff and shouting militant hymns over the gorge, where his deep voice met and mingled with the uproar of the falls. The cold days reddened his hands and brought blue chapped patches on his cheeks; but his long beard had a warmth in its whiteness against the blue shadows of the snow.

At the next lock Ethan Allen McCarthy came out, wearing mittens. He nodded his head toward the Five Combines and told them, "Ben thinks it's spring come when the boats commence to move. His religion's festered his mind all up. I tried to get him to wear a hat, but he told me to get out. The poor old rooster ain't even got room left in his head for a cold."

The Sarsey Sal went on down the gorge. The sound of Dan's horn was thin through the cry of the wind and the roar of the Kill. They stopped at Delta, late one afternoon, to get a load of plows from the factory.

The shipping superintendent gave Dan his orders. The ploughs were to go through to Buffalo. They tied up for the night at the Delta dock. Sleighs brought the plows in crates from the factory — a mile haul. The arm of the feeder had not yet been built to the village, so that all boats loaded here, which made good trade for Denslow's Delta House.

Fortune Friendly wheedled all through supper for an advance on his wages. A quack doctor, peddling gout removers and corn cure, had put up for the night. There was a chance for pinochle. Denslow had a great thirst for the game.

"But he never won nothing off me," Fortune said. "The doctor thinks he's a master hand, but he ain't never come up against me. Come on, Dan, don't be a tight-fist farmer."

Finally Dan let him have the money, and within five minutes the game was under way. Dan looked through the door after supper. Denslow was nursing his cards in both hands, frowning at the corners, his lips forming figures to himself; and by the look of him Dan judged that the figures were small ones. The quack leaned back in his chair. His high black hat stood bottom up beside his feet, and his face wore his customary encouraging smile. He played as if he had a faith in better things. The old ex-preacher sat between them, his thin nose drawn down, his manner sober; but when he looked up Dan saw a gleam of seraphic happiness in his eye. His luck was in.

Dan went back to the Sarsey Sal. The night was blustery, a cold wind under stars and no moon. The waves slapped sharp along the shore and chugged against the side of the boat. The teams were restless; he could hear one of them stamp.

Buffalo — he was hauling to Buffalo. Sooner or later he had known that he must stand up to Jotham Klore, if he was to hold Molly. It seemed that the time would be at hand. He wished, however, that it had not come so soon. He was not afraid, but he was not eager. Though Molly had been happier in the last few days than he had ever seen her, he had felt a change in her kindness for him. Her happiness lay in the breaking of winter, as if she were leaving it behind; and the winter had been the happiest time he had had. He felt a new strength in himself; but at the same time he was aware of an aloofness in Molly, not physical, for the spring was in her, but mental, as if she stood aside to watch the spring. It roused his hunger, but strangely it did not make him anxious to find Klore and settle her between them. It was as if he smelled defeat, as he could smell the old snow on the earth. He knew that there was one way in which the question could be settled.

When he went into the cabin, he found her drying her hands after finishing the dishes. Her face was flushed from bending over. As soon as he entered she read the question in his eyes, and a dread bordering on panic swept her down. But she rallied.

"Do we start early?" she asked.

"To-morrow morning first thing."

"Buffalo?"

"Yeanh."

The blood came into her cheeks again; her eyes were frank with pleasure.

"I always like going out there, Dan."

"I 've never been," he said.

"Where 's Fortune?"

"Pinochle."

He sat down and looked at her.

"Molly . . ."

She had turned to the mirror and was poking a wisp of her hair back into place. Now she wheeled round with the lithe motion he loved.

"You did n't get your hair cut, Dan, when we was in Rome. It looks awful. I declare I 'd be ashamed to have a friend see it. What would Lucy Gurget say?"

He fingered the back of his neck and said seriously, "I guess it is kind of long. I did n't have no time."

"You won't have time going out, either, and when we get to Buffalo it 'll be as long as Ben's."

He grinned sheepishly.

"I 've got a mind to do it myself, Dan."

"Well, it could n't look no worse."

"Don't sass."

She gave one of her small decisive nods.

"I will do it, too."

"All right."

She laughed.

"I 've got a pair of scissors I keep for myself. Bring the chair under the lamp, Dan."

He did as she told him, and she covered him over with a pair of towels, tucking them into his shirt collar tight enough to choke him. She pulled her sleeves back over her round forearms; he could see the soft brown down on them in the light of the lamp; and then she tilted his head forward with a sharp push.

"Thank you, mister," she said, for all the world like a barber.

Her fingers were clever; she cut quickly.

"Molly," Dan said again. Now that she was occupied near him, she would find it difficult to turn a question.

"Yeanh."

She turned up the wick of the lamp. In the interval they both heard the wind and the water, and, as it often had before, that peculiar, almost suffocating sense of intimacy entered the old boat.

So close beside him, the feel of her arm touching his cheek, the swift clipping of the scissors in her fingers, her steady, gentle breathing, the warm lamplight over them both, he felt his question rising up in him without his control.

"I want to marry you, Molly."

He heard her breath catch, but, with her woman's instinct urging her hands, the scissoring went on. She had thought she could keep the question away from him.

He sat staring toward the window with the quiet preoccupation which she had learned to expect, but which always made her uneasy. Only now the stiff tilt into which she had forced his head made it foolish and somehow whimsical.

"When, Dan?"

Though she had dreaded the question, now that it had come she was pleased with it.

"Right away."

"But we've got to go out to Buffalo. There would n't be any chance."

He considered this. They would not have time in any port.

"When we get back," he said, "I'll take time off."

She snipped up the back of his neck and followed the curve of the hair over his ear.

"I'm well fixed, Molly, you know that."

"Yes," she said. "Put your head over. — It's awful good of you, Dan. I want to thank you. But there is n't any call for your breaking your hauling. It don't bother me, our being this way."

He realized, as he felt her hand on his head, that she was taking the seriousness from his question.

"I want to," he said slowly.

Just to see the bend of her elbow made him want her.

"It is n't as if we needed it on the canal," she said.

"I 'd feel better."

"Why? If I like it this way, why do you want to change, Dan?"

He could n't tell her that.

"Will you stay on the canal?" she asked. There was a challenge in her words which he could not accept honestly.

"I don't know," he mumbled. "I had n't thought about it."

The scissors clicked sharply.

"You been thinking about it right along lately," she said. "I could see it on you."

He did n't answer.

"Will you stay in a city?"

"I don't know."

"No. You don't know. Do you like it, Dan?"

"Yeanh," he said, slowly.

"Then what 're you worrying about?"

"I thought you 'd like it if I asked you to."

She worked in silence for awhile.

"I do like it, Dan."

He could feel her fingers running in the hair on the top of his head. She was not cutting; she was just letting her fingers run through his hair.

"I like it a lot, Dan. I don't think there's anybody I'd like better to hear say it."

She took up the job again, letting him ponder her words.

"I thought you loved me, Molly."

He did not say it accusingly; but he felt her fingers stiffen. Then, suddenly, she came round in front of him and pushed his head back, the heel of her right hand on his forehead. Her blue eyes were very kind.

"I do love you, Dan. Can you doubt it?"

Looking at her then, he could not doubt it. He saw her as he had seen her in the fall, when she had first come aboard, with all the familiar details of the stovepipe, and the ventilators, and his hat hanging on the door behind her. The clock whirred to strike nine. Involuntarily they both glanced at the proud little figure of the prancing horse.

"No," he said.

His quiet face, earnest now, and his steady blue-green eyes must have brought back the first days to her, days she had found sweet, when she could see him take what she had to give him and grow stronger for it. She felt her own weakness as the light brightened in his eyes, and she pushed his head down as he settled his feet to rise.

"Just a minute, Dan, don't get grabby. I ain't quite finished."

She brought his hair forward on his forehead and trimmed it back close in a rounded bang, letting the ends fall down on his eyes. Then, as he shook it off, she stepped back laughing, low and husky, as if she were feeling her way toward mirth. As he got to his feet they heard Fortune walking down the dock, whistling "Gamboleer's Pay."

They looked at each other silently, her laughter still on her lips. He kissed them and grabbed his hat and the night lantern.

"I want to rub some more hemlock syrup on Prince." He turned to the door as Fortune came in looking very guileless and satisfied.

"Well!" he exclaimed. "We've got a regular barber!"

Dan went forward to rub the black, to prod him with his

elbow and slap him good-naturedly and call him all kinds of a loafer.

Fortune hung up his hat, smiling to see the kindness in her eyes.

"The cards liked me, Molly. All the queens kept coming right to me, and the kings came after them to see where they were." He chuckled.

"I reckon that medicine peddler's still scratchin' his head, wondering about the phenomenons of nature," he went on as she swept the floor. "You'd ought to've seen him. I wish that fat woman had been along. For all she's so lucky, she wouldn't have stood a show-in. You look pretty well happy yourself, girl. Has Dan been telling you things?"

She nodded, the glow still on her.

"Wants to marry you?" he asked, his shrewd black eyes twinkling.

She nodded.

"What did you do?" he asked anxiously.

"I said we'd leave it be awhile. He's an awful good boy, Fortune. I almost thought I'd tell him I would. I don't know; maybe I will yet."

"He was looking happy, all right, when he went out," he said.

"Yeanh."

"But it's better to leave it be." He began counting his winnings. Then he looked up. "You certainly did a good job cutting his hair."

She smiled.

"He looks nice with it cut short that way, don't he?"

"He does. Where did you learn to cut it?"

Her body sagged and she leaned on the broom heavily.

"I learned it cutting Jotham's hair."

They stared at each other hopelessly. Then, mechanically she stooped to sweep the loose hair up in the dustpan. She slid it into the stove, where it fizzled a moment. Then she put back the lid, hung up the dustpan and broom on their respective nails and went to bed.

"You poor fool," Fortune said to himself. "You old gibbering rooster. Oh, lord!"

He put his money back in his pocket.

Coming in later, Dan found the cabin empty and silent. He sat awhile, as if he expected Molly to come out. But she did not come, and when he went into the cuddy she was lying quiet on her side, as if she slept.

The Chase Westward

Cold winds still blew out of the north, reminding them that winter was still hard in the mountains.

The Sarsey Sal made good time westward. The big team were fast walkers, and the bays, getting a proper share of rest, kept the boat moving at a good pace when they were on the towline. Traveling beyond Rome, they found the towns sparser and smaller. Dan began to have a better idea of the greatness of the canal. Mile after mile, heading southwesterly, to Lenor, and then due west to Syracuse through sandstone country.

Dan took turns relieving Fortune on the towpath. He preferred the long stretches of walking. Since the long haul had started with that night at Delta, he had had a growing excitement. He had seen Molly roused again for a moment then, and though he had found her subdued the next morning, with that same haunting watchfulness in her eyes, he had felt that perhaps he might yet bring her back to him. At times she seemed closer to him than before, but she always kept some vital part of her just out of his reach. The exercise of walking helped to alleviate a growing urge in him for speed. He must get west and find Klore. For he was convinced that he and Klore must settle her between themselves before he and Molly could come together in the old vein.

Then, too, he had a feeling that he and Gentleman Joe would see each other again. It was a meeting that he looked forward to with a mingling of fear and excitement. Whenever he felt the spell of the canal, it was wound up for him in the figure of the mail robber. The man was so sure of himself, so able to preserve himself, that even the marshal, Henderson, who trailed him, gave him a grudging admiration. The more Dan found his own way muddled, the more he found himself regarding the image he created of the criminal riding the towpaths and roads on his fine grey horse. That he had never seen Calash's face added to the illusion. When he had seen it once, he felt that he would see his own way clear. Perhaps he would find a secret there of the man's strength. In his brooding way he tried to imagine the man's features, but he could find nothing in his mind to build them on. The man was associated with action, with Dan's first night on the wharf in Boonville, his first day on the canal, with his getting his own boat, in his very life with Molly. Even when he had bought a mirror for her, he had first seen the man's reflection in it. . . .

In the morning, when they had hauled out of Delta, the first word of the chase had reached them. The night before, Henderson had been seen in Rome, outside the jail, talking to Sheriff Spinning, while his two deputies had stood by the heads of their horses in the street. Then the three had mounted and ridden south out of town.

At a canal tavern in East Boston they had tied up for the night. Here Fortune Friendly, in the process of cards, learned that Henderson had been in the village the night before — "A little fat twerp chewing a cigar like honest-to-God tobaccer," the owner had described him. But this time he was alone. He had talked to the bank walker in his cabin, and the bank walker had refused to say anything about the interview, beyond telling them that the man was a Department man on the heels of Gentleman Joe. "Him a marshal!" the owner snorted, dealing the cards. "No wonder they can't catch the rat." Fortune remembered his very words because, when he picked up his hand, he had found double pinochle looking him in the eye.

The canal was alive now with heavy trade. They had the familiar sight of boats hurrying ahead, passing during the night when they tied up. The relay stables on the tow-path were a-scramble with teams going in and coming out. In the early morning when they went by they could hear the *siss* of men brushing down the mules like the whisper of bees.

The Sarsey Sal pushed on. They stopped in Syracuse next day for a little while to have one of the bays reshod. The blacksmith did a quick job, and while he worked he told Dan how he had made a shoe for a road horse. "A big grey," he said, "and the dandiest plate shoe I ever worked out. A tall feller brought him late in the afternoon just when I was shutting shop. But trade is n't so heavy just at this season, so I took the horse in."

"Yeanh," said Dan.

"I made a good penny out of it," said the blacksmith. "It was a special job," he added quickly. "I charge regular rates on work horses."

"When was that?" Dan asked.

"Day afore yesterday," said the blacksmith, sticking the hot shoe into the hogshead while a wisp of steam coiled out of the black water.

When Dan started to lead the bay out, he saw a man walking down the street leading a saddle horse. The man had a long yellow moustache, and Dan heard him say to the blacksmith that he wanted the nigh front shoe reset on his horse. He spoke with a gentle slur and drawl. Dan remembered the description Fortune had given them of Henderson's two deputies. He had n't a doubt that this was one. He wondered what the blacksmith would say about the good penny he had made when he learned the tall man's identity.

They passed the vast Montezuma swamps, where the tow-paths rose like dams on either side, and the canal ran like a waterproof trough in level country. Here and there patches of black water showed, and the only growth was alder brush and gaunt cat-tails, broken over by the winds, or occasionally thin tamaracks, or clumps of cedars, or the skeletons of ancient trees. Fortune told him that in the early days the highwaymen who covered the western roads hung out here safely.

Only they knew the winding trails by which a horse could pass the bogs. Even the Doanes and Tomblesons had used it in their day. If the great swarms of mosquitoes made their stay miserable, at least they knew no man could get at them. It was a melancholy stretch of thirty-five miles to haul through; it wore an aspect of death. The broken flight of low-hung clouds served only to heighten the sombre spirit of stagnation; and the blue open water of the great canal, with its slowly moving boats and horses and bright-faced people, held the eye with a promise of escape.

They hauled on. Twelve miles out at Geddes, where the salt works were, they saw Henderson riding along the tow-path. He kept opposite them for a short time; he was a poor rider, his fat body thumping his horse unmercifully. The pot hat on the back of his head seemed perpetually on the point of sliding off, but he paid no attention to it. His cigar stuck upward from the corner of his mouth as rigidly as if he were standing on a street corner. . . .

As they entered Weed's Basin, a man held them up to ask if they had seen anything of a man on a grey horse. The questioner had a scar on his temple, and when he took off his hat to Molly they saw that his hair was slicked down with some 'kind of grease and a smell of violets came to their nostrils. But they had no news for him. He stopped several other boats, and a little before dark he rode on westward.

"It's queer," Fortune said as they ate supper. "We keep seeing them all the while, here and there, but we don't never get a sight of Calash. Nobody appears to. It makes me feel I'm dreaming."

They came into Rochester, the Flour City, with the houses close to the towpaths and the roar of the high falls in their ears. At the Water Street turn two men stood talking, Henderson and the deputy with the long moustache. But the Sarsey Sal pushed on toward Buffalo with her load of plows, across the aqueduct, under the Exchange Street Bridge and the Main Street Bridge and on through the basin. . . .

John Durble's Story

Dan sat on the edge of a dock at Buffalo; the Sarsey Sal was to take pork back to Rochester and there pick up a load of flour for Rome; they would start back in the afternoon. It was warm and dry where he was sitting. The raw, growing city with its high wooden buildings, some of the houses carrying triple porches, lay at his back, with the hill rising behind. Before him the canal ran into the open lake. A schooner was coming in on a brisk wind, heeling over toward the curve of her great sails, like the bend of a woman's hip. But the bows caught snatches of diamond foam out of the water and shook them after her. Streaming out behind, and with thin cries to the wind, a flock of white gulls rose and dipped with the motions of the boat.

In the shelter of the warehouses, the sun had melted away the snow. A dry dusty summer smell rose out of the planks. Boats were coming and going at the far end of the basin. Teams worked back and forth along the wharves. Where Dan sat, it was quiet; he barely caught the hum of the city.

While he was watching the schooner drawing in, he became aware of a man standing within a few feet of his shoulder. He was sturdily built, with big, blunt-fingered hands, smooth-shaven but for a white goatee on his chin. Suddenly his brown eyes turned to Dan. His square face broke in a smile, and he came over and sat down beside Dan on the wharf.

"I like to see the gulls," he said; "they're the most beautiful fliers in the world."

"Yeanh, they be pretty to watch, but they don't fly as keen as a hawk does, mister."

The stranger took snuff from a square silver box.

"That's true," he said. "Maybe I like to see 'em because they hang round people."

"Yeanh."

"Do you work on the canal?"

"Yeanh. I work a boat."

The other glanced at Dan.

"You 've done well to get a boat so soon."

"I was lucky," Dan said.

"The canal 's the greatest thing this country has done; it 's the greatest thing it ever will do."

"It must have been a big job," Dan agreed.

"I saw it finished," said the man. He sat with his hands on his knees, looking out to the west. "See there," he pointed to a lake boat up whose gangways immigrants were crowding. "They all come by the Erie Canal. They may go clear to Ioway, but what they grow will find its way back through the Erie."

"Yeanh."

"I saw it finished," said the man. "My name 's John Durble."

"Mine 's Dan Harrow."

They did not shake hands. There seemed to be no need of that.

"I was a carpenter, forty years ago, when I come to this country. I got work in New York and New Jersey. I made money fast. I was a master tradesman. I spent five years building houses for other people."

"I 've never been to New York," Dan said.

"It was a growing city, but they say it 's grown a lot faster since the canal went through."

"Yeanh."

"I worked at the carpenter trade. It was good pay, but it seemed I was getting tired of it. I wanted to settle down on a place of my own."

"Yeanh."

"One day I was working on the roof of a house on Abingdon Road — fifty-three was the number. I 'd been reshingling a patch; and I was coming down for the end of the day when I saw a girl no more than twenty coming out the door. She was looking white, and she was carrying a bag in her hand. I was a likely-looking lad and she a girl, so I asked her what was wrong, and she told me she was looking for service, but had n't been able to get any. Her money was running out, and she'd come over from England with her mother and her mother had died on the way, and there she was alone. So I said, 'Come along to Asa's,' where I had a little cubby room on the top floor, and where I knew she could get one for but a little, and so she did. When I'd left my tools and put on a coat and washed my hands, we had a meal in the back tap, cheese and beer and a slice of cold beef; and, watching her, I saw the color come back. She was a very pretty girl. So after supper we walked out Love Lane and down by Lepner's. It was a warm evening; there were a lot of couples out, but nobody paid no attention to us. Couples were never noticed in Love Lane. I told her how I was fixed; and I was proud about it, and had a right to be so, for, though I was a young lad, I was a master carpenter and earned my dollar with the best of them. Perhaps I said I had more money than I had, but that was only a natural thing, I got to liking her so. Her clothes was worn, but they were neatly sewed and I could see how clean she was.

"We sat in the meadows and watched the sun down over the river. So I told her how I had saved money and how I wanted to go up the state to the great Genesee Valley I'd heard of, where the land was so rich, and take to farming the way the folks had in England — Dorset; I remember the sheep, and the oil smell in the house at shearing. And I said I had planned to go before the month ended, but that a man settling a country alone did a poor job, because it took more than a man to settle. Still I said I did n't know but what I would go. She asked where I went to get there, so I told her by boat to Albany, but after that I was vague about it, only mentioning Rochester, which was that year only a village. But I did n't know that. In truth I had just only got the idea of being a farmer at all. Then she told me again how she was just alone and right at the end of everything, and we sat watching the sun down over the river and I as dumb as an owl at noon.

"But in the dusk we went round about back, all the way out to Kissing Bridge."

The old man paused, took the silver box from his pocket, had his snuff, and watched the boat and the gulls. His face never changed expression.

"I took her there, for she was strange to the city, but after all I think she had a better acquaintance with the bridge than I did. We got married the next morning, and a month later we managed to reach Rochester. It was not more than a thousand people big. I doubt there were more than fifty buildings, all in all, built all on the west side of the river, and no more than a light bridge thrown across. She'd stood the trip dandy, but when she saw what a little place we'd come to I think it closed her up a little. But I'd got the fever then for getting my own place. They said land was high in the Genesee Valley, and I'd got the urge for gettin' westward. We'd picked up a couple of cows in Rochester, and a pair of horses and a cart we'd got in Utica. I bought a plow and grain and flour, and we went on to the Tonawanda, where I'd been told there was good land much cheaper. It took a week nearly to get out, she driving and I bringing on the cows.

"We came in one night on the valley and we found a house there in meadows cut out and burnt by a settler. It was a log house, just one room and looking small in front of the woods, but there was a light in the window and I got a smell of pigs from a pen out back. A man came out wearing a coon cap and leaned on a gun and just looked at us. It was the only farm we'd seen in two days. Just someway it was neither of us spoke, and then his wife came out of the door and right away mine got down and the man shook hands with me. We spent the night there. There was a good fire and the woman gave us bacon and tea. The woman and my wife slept in the bed bunk and he and I slept on the floor."

The old man took snuff again. He looked over the lake as if he saw the cabin, and not the schooner, now so near they could make out the people on deck.

"Next morning," John Durble went on, "I told the man — his name was Cutler, James Cutler — that I was aiming to settle down here. I asked him if there was land. He did n't say anything. He just waved his hand right round. Then he said would I want to buy improved land. Pretty soon I figured out he wanted to sell his farm. I could see it was good soil, and I liked it being close to the Creek. Running water 's a great help — just to see it and hear it. We made a deal. Then we went in to the women. My wife did n't say anything — but I think she was pleased to be living where there 'd been other people living, as long as there were n't going to be any neighbors. But the woman's eyes sort of glassed — as if there was something curling shut inside of her. She looked older than her husband.

"He took me outside and we spent the morning walking the place — a hundred acres, and I could have more after I 'd been settled there for a year or so; but now I had enough cleared meadow and all. I paid the man dollar-down for the land, for six hogs, two cows, and three sheep. There was a couple of chickens, too, but he throwed them in on the deal. We took two days off riding down to Black Rock and making the papers over, and then me and Ellen, my wife, settled in for the winter. There was wheat and oats to be got in, and still the firewood to cut for winter. I was busy. Ellen worked into the house and tended a bit of a garden the other woman had kept there. Just when she left, the other woman had dug up some daffodil bulbs; but she left us one to grow. That was all she done — she did n't speak about leaving. But my wife said she 'd been on six different places since she had married. Her husband did that, cleared and sold improved land. He could n't abide."

Nobody looking at Dan and John Durble would have guessed that the old man was talking, he spoke so quietly. Or, if they had known that, they would not have thought that Dan listened. Both men sat in the same position, backs to the wall, hands on knees, both looking out over the lake. The schooner had come in now, and the wharf hands began to unload her. She carried fur from the winter's trapping —

"The nearest person to us was eighteen miles down the creek toward Black Rock. In and about the creek was heavy timber. We did n't get the full smash of winds off the lakes. But I think it commenced to wear on Ellen, just the shadow of them and the wind-shriek in the branches. Our boy was born that summer. We were lucky. A man wagoning west had his wagon-reach break half a mile from the house, so him and his wife came in and I mended his wagon and the wife minded Ellen.

"But I 'd become a farmer. I 'd done well with crops and my sheep had lambed and I had three litters of pigs. We were n't troubled during the summer. But late in the fall the bears come after them.

"It 's the second winter comes hardest; but Ellen had the boy to fuss with, and so did I. I 'd built onto the barn that fall and put a storeroom on the cabin; but now I got to planning that when I 'd got settled well, maybe in two years, I 'd set right out to build a big house — that is, if there was a way I could get lumber. There was n't no mill yet on the Creek. I 'd even gone and spotted the place I 'd build at. On a rise down the Creek, where a kind of flat land came in from the north. You could see quite a ways from there — pretty near to the lake. But it snowed heavier and heavier that winter — the worst I 've seen. And I took sick, and my wife had to do the whole job. Lucky I 'd got my wood in.

"But I 'd generally had to go down about the January light-snow time to Black Rock for stores. This year I could n't. Our tea give out. Worms got into the flour. I was getting bad, and I could n't only lie on the bed bunk. My wife kept up pretty good. She always had a smile. And she still looked pretty in her eyes and hair; but the worry was making her thin. We knew we was in for a bad time.

"Then one day, when it was all-harry cold and the wind cracking the trees like rifles, somebody knocked on the door. My wife opened it and in come an old feller, brown as an Injun, with white hair. He had a long-eared hound dog with him. He set down on a bench and kind of looked us over, and my wife said 'Hello' to him and talked about the winter,

watching his face close. He set there looking at us; he had a
hooked nose and his eyes was so light they looked white
alongside of his skin. After a while he grinned at my wife
and he said, 'Don't you worry.' And right away she smiled at
him. Then he come over to me. I had n't been able to speak
none at all. He sat down and took a-hold of my hand. I 'd
been figuring and figuring how to get to town, but I could n't
get no sleep for worrying. And right off, when he took
hold of my hand, I went to sleep. When I come to, it was
sun shining through the winder right across the blankets,
and I thought I could feel the sun through them. My wife
was cooking tea. I asked her where the old man was. She
said he 'd gone to town. I asked her where she got the tea,
and she said he 'd taught her to make it out of white-pine
bark. It was good. I had a cup. Then I went to sleep. It
had frozen solid, so he 'd gone with the two horses down
the Creek. Someway I knew he 'd come back right enough.

"He did. After that he come round regular till I 'd got
well. Seems like he 'd had a cabin back in the woods about
four mile. He 'd knowed all along we was there, but had n't
come till one day he 'd been by and seen my wife going out
to mind the barn. After that he come round again to make
sure. Then he 'd come in with some rabbits and a bird, and
then gone off to get our flour. He was a trapper. All his
life he 'd been in the woods. He 'd seen three wars come and
go through these woods, but he had n't mixed. He kept by
himself off in the woods. There was n't much trapping
through these parts, but he done well enough for him. He
could n't read nor write, but he knew a lot of great men by
the way of his talk. His name was Parchal Smith.

"But he never stayed long. Till I got well, he brought in
game twice a week and stayed for a meal. After that he
only came round once in a while. The winter dragged
through. We 'd see him once in a while in summer. He 'd
bring fish. He 'd took a fancy to Ellen, I guess. But if there
was anybody with us he 'd leave the fish by the door, and
we never knowed he was there till we went out and found
him gone.

"That summer word come through that they was planning to start the canal. People talked about that like it was Judgment Day getting close. They'd commenced to dig in Rome. People said it would be fifty years by the time it got to Black Rock, and others said it would be three. We'd hear from time to time how it was getting along. The first year they did fifteen miles. The next year there was three thousand men working on the line, by all accounts. In '19 they turned the Mohawk water in at Rome and ran a boat to Utica. That was late in the fall. We heard about it a month later where we were.

"There had been two farmers moved in within walking distance of my place. I helped them build. My wife went over to help in their houses. She'd got a loom now and was handy at making cloth. In '19 a mill was built up above us on the Creek. The man that built it was looking forward to the canal. I did the work and hired a man to mind the farm. I made money, but I worked on half pay, meaning to take the rest out in lumber. I'd got it fixed I'd build a real house and barn. And after planting, next spring, I commenced the work. The rest come round and said I was building too big, but me and my wife knew now that we had to settle there for good or give up the country. It was a notion I had that that would be the last carpenter work I'd do. I wanted to build my own house. Ellen and me'd dreamed about that house, just how we wanted it — two stories with a peaked roof and dormers.

"It took me a year to build. It was right on the rise I told about, and I'd put a long stoop round the side facing out. There was more people going through. By this time the canal had opened beyond Syracuse, so there was less space for them to haul across in wagons. I made money selling them food and grain. My wife was handy making cheese. That sold well. Only now and then she'd go give a cheese away. Just when she saw a young wife that couldn't buy it. Them would look at the house I was building like it was the last they'd ever expect to see.

"Old Parchal Smith come round less. Three other families

had moved in, — but none more, — but that was too much for him. He only come in the middle of winter or late at night in summer. He was getting restless. He'd leave his hound outside, and as soon as he'd hear the dog growl he'd go out. He didn't like the talk of the canal.

"It was easier for Ellen now, with three other women round. They'd hold parties 'mongst each other, and make us get dressed up to go. They'd send round letters by one of the children, when they could have walked as well themselves. They figured out a lot of manners that way. And they was particular about them.

"We'd talked about the canal. It didn't seem like it would ever get to us. They'd surveyed in '19, and the route would come close to my place. We knew it would be good for trade, and Winster, who had the mill, figured he would sell planks for boats.

"It was different with the women. They watched the news; they got it out of everybody that come along. They wanted the talk about it, I guess.

"I'd moved into my big house, though I had n't enough to furnish it decent, and the neighbors had said I was foolish to build so big. But me and Ellen did n't care. We guessed they'd wished they'd builded that way to begin with. It was the finest house west of Rochester.

"Then, first thing we knowed, in '23, men commenced working on the route between Black Rock and Lockport. Black Rock figured they would be the port, and Buffalo figured they would. Once a month one of them would hold a celebration, according to the news. We'd hear the guns and fireworks clear to Tonawanda Creek. The men that worked was Irishers mostly, though we hired out teams.

"I remember, two springs after that, how me and Ellen sat on the big stoop in June. A warm afternoon. The word come the water would come in from Erie. And after a while we seen it come. Brown and muddy, very slow; so's not to rip the banks. It went by us in a little creek. We watched it rise all day. At night it was still getting up. Brown and muddy. Me and my wife just set there holding hands, and

we dass n't try to speak. It seemed like the garden would
have more flowers that year — there 'd be people to look up
and see them on the rise. Then she put the children to bed,
and come out again. We did n't have no supper. We did n't
want it. We 'd listen to the water eddy down below all night.
In the morning it had come off blue in the sun — pretty
near that color."

The old man pointed.

"We had n't realized the water would come so close —
but now it was there we liked it. People said there would
be noise, but we liked it. They finished Lockport that fall.
Tolls was taken on the first of October. It had been a fine
farming summer. I 'd had more money in than I 'd expected
for a single year. Then on the twenty-sixth the opening
come."

He stopped again, his eyes far off, as if he listened.

"It was a masterful event. The leaves had turned late
that year, and there was still color to the woods. Wednesday
night, me and my wife was waked up by a knock, and, going
down, there was Parchal. He 'd heard. He 'd been down to
the water of the canal. He had a pack on his back and his
long rifle in his hand. The dog looked gay. He knew he
was going on a hunt.

"They had put cannon — you know how — all along the
canal and down the Hudson. There was an old ten-pounder
mounted on my rise of ground, its snout pointing west, and
there was one of McDonough's sailors — an old horny man
snoring upstairs in the best room — there to touch it off.
The neighbors came next morning early. Ellen and the women
had gotten up a big feast, and a lot of the Irishers had
come in from Lockport, remembering us, to get the food.
Old Parchal that night took us out and showed us a doe
deer, fat and prime, he 'd brought for us. 'I had my eye
on her all summer,' he said. But his eyes was cold and kind
of still.

"That next morning we got up and the women went to
work. The men sat on the porch, looking down the canal
to the lake. I had some Jamaica and Golden Medford for

them — it was a brisk morning. Cool from frost at night, but no wind at all. The smoke from our pipes hung under the roof. The children played round — noisy. The cook smells came out to us. The sailor, Benjy Wright, sat on the cannon's butt, patting her once in a while, and telling us how he used to shoot her. Parchal stood off by himself on the grass, leaning on his rifle, the hound dog sitting right in front of him. Both their heads was still, but they both looked westward. And the hound was working his nose. Some of the men laughed at the lean old feller and his big dog, but when I told 'em how he 'd fed me and my wife one winter, they stopped.

"About nine o'clock Benjy cut him a hard plug with his sailor knife. He had a tail of hair on his neck, and he 'd oiled it that night, staining the piller till my wife could have cried. He wore a red-and-white striped shirt and had pressed his pants himself. They was wide pants. Now he petted the butt of the old cannon and he says, 'Lilah, when it comes your turn to talk, you talk out loud.' He lighted his match and we stood waiting. Then a cannon sounded down by Buffalo. And Benjy touched the match to the fuse and in a minute the old gun bucked and roared, and a glass broke in the window of the parlor. The Irishers jumped up cheering, and the little girls commenced to cry. And the women come out. They was n't crying, but they had wet eyes. Then we sat down and watched Benjy load up the cannon. And an hour and forty minutes later there was a cannon faint to eastward of us. And our gun bucked and shot again and we heard a gun boom in Buffalo. But with that sound from the eastward of us we knowed that New York knowed. The sound of it told us that.

"All to once we knowed there was other people back east who knowed about us. We were in a country as big as half the world, but with that shot it all come closer together. We were n't alone.

"My wife," said John Durble, "come and sat in my lap and cried."

"Yeanh," said Dan.

For a while there was silence.

"Clinton's boat come along a while later when we were eating dinner. The food got burnt somehow. But we cheered him by and his four grey matched horses, and he waved to us. And we cheered the other boats. We finished eating. But it was only when my wife and I put the children to bed that night we noticed Parchal Smith was gone. When the shot sounded eastward he must have gone. Him and the hound both. I never heard of them again. But nights now me and my wife hear the boats once in a while — a horn, maybe — or, when it's still, the clink of a trace chain. Or we see the night lanterns. The railroads come in time. But here it did n't make so much difference. They come too easy and quick.

"The canal brought us money, and built great cities along the line — it's building this one. But it brought something better to me and my wife. I could n't tell you, son. We hear the horns."

After a while he said, "I got to get home."

And he went away.

But that evening, as the Sarsey Sal moved eastward by the intake gates of Tonawanda Creek, Dan looked up and saw a house on the gentle rise of ground. A white house, peaceful, comfortable, two stories, with dormer windows on the peaked roof. He blew his horn, softly. It sounded gentle on the air. Molly, who was standing close beside him, asked, "Why did you blow it, Dan?"

Dan pointed to a lighted window. The shadows of two figures appeared standing together. Then one opened the window and leaned out, to follow with his eyes the light of the night lantern along the velvet water. The light caught a red glow in Dan's high cheeks and traced golden threads in Molly's hair as she combed it out and braided it there on the deck.

It was very still; it was spring. Tree toads lifted clear treble voices against the black sky; and the chirrup of tiny frogs along the canal went with the Sarsey Sal in a rising throaty song.

In Erlo's Boarding House

The horses had the rhythm of the long hauls. They went with a plodding stride, and Fortune went slowly behind them, head down and hands in his pockets.

It was a warm April morning, and the sun had just cleared the light mists from the meadows. Tendrils of it still lingered where the balsams shaded the canal. A flock of ducks scrambled out of a setback, leaving a white trail of foam over the water, and started out again on their northward journey. A little later Dan heard a distant murmur, a cry taken up by twenty voices, and thrown back and forth between them, singly and in a swelling chorus. Fortune, too, heard the honking and kept his eyes on the sky. Dan called Molly on deck. Soon they saw them in the liquid, early morning sky, high up, a line of geese rippling northward.

At Lockport they caught up to a long line of boats going down. Far below, the canal shot straight away, out under the high bridge. On their left the water thundered over falls. Boats, like tiny chips pulled by ants on a cobweb thread, moved out at measured intervals from the downward flight. All along the locks tenders worked quickly at the levers, their shirts soaked with sweat. Regularly, life-sized boats issued from the top lock of the upward flight and hauled past the waiting queue. Dan sat on deck by the rudder and watched them pass. The immigrant season had started. A line boat came by, bright yellow, one of the Michigan Six Day, with an old German smoking a porcelain pipe, his stocking feet straight out on the cabin roof in front of him, the soles turned to the sun. Women's voices rose from the cabin, and the sound of a fiddle wheedling at a tune. Steering was a tall upright old man with a long white beard.

"Ben!" Dan cried. "Ben Rae!"

The Jew turned his fine face toward the Sarsey Sal, a puzzled light in his eyes. Then he recognized Dan and waved his arm.

"Hullo, Dan. How be you?" He turned to the cabin door, his deep voice booming, "Hey, Julius! Julius! Here's Dan Harrow."

The lanky black-haired Wilson sprang out on deck.

"Hello, Dan. Glad to see you. Who're you boating for?"

"*My* boat," Dan said proudly.

"Say," said Wilson, "I met Berry back in Rochester. He said to tell you Jotham Klore was hauling east, working on the Boonville feeder. He said you'd want to know."

Fortune had turned to see who was talking. He recognized the Jew.

"Hey, there, how's pinochle?" he shouted.

"How's preaching?" cried the Jew.

Wilson laughed, shook his fist, and Fortune chuckled. The boat drew away. Line boats worked on schedule. Their crews could not stop to talk. Dan felt sad.

The Sarsey Sal sank down between the stone walls, and down again when the gates closed, until it came out once more on the smooth flow. The big team waited for it, with their heads turned round, and stepped out on the towpath of their own accord as Dan tossed the towrope to Fortune. They heaved and went on.

They kept the teams at a good pace that day, and late on the afternoon of the next they saw the roofs of the city ahead of them in the southeast. The windows were afire with the sunset, and, as the boat pulled forward, the red light moved from pane to pane along the entire city front. There was a slight haze of flour dust over the roofs of the mills. On their left the thunder of the swollen falls beat heavily.

There was an empty berth for the Sarsey Sal just under the Main Street Bridge. They ate in the cabin with the shadows stealing over the canal. Boats passed in each direction. But the shouts along the dock, where men had been loading, grew fainter, thinned out. The boats passing now were bound straight through.

After supper, in the cool of the evening, Dan sat awhile on deck, smoking his pipe, while Molly cleaned the dishes.

It was a peaceful scene he looked out upon from under the rafters of the bridge. The boats lay still all along the banks in a double row; smoke and the smell of cooking rose from their cabins. A horse stamped in his stall, and sighed over his oats. Along the wharf a few men moved leisurely; and a couple loitered on the bridge over his head, their voices falling toward his hands in a soft murmur.

Fortune had gone off on his eternal pilgrimage to cards.

Molly came up after a while in her street dress with its tight-waisted jacket and flaunting hem. At the news of Klore's being on the Boonville canal, a worried expression had left her eyes. She had been quietly happy that day. Now she was smiling when she took Dan's arm.

"Let's walk around a little, Dan, if you ain't too tuckered."

They stepped to the towpath and made their way up to the bridge by a little flight of stairs set in against the wall. For a while they strolled up Plymouth Avenue and through the streets of the third ward, past the fine houses with their lawns under towering elms. There was a misty vagueness in the line of the trees against the twilight, and the dusk about their roots was deep.

They made their way down again toward the canal along Exchange Street, getting glimpses of the dark water of the river between the mills. The night had closed in. Lights came in windows on their left; roof lines were lost against the sky until the stars came out, when, gradually, they were born again.

They went down to the canal and walked out along the towpath on the aqueduct. They leaned on the parapet, looking downstream. Here and there were lights in the dives on Water Street, and the reflections of them seemed to be running on the river. The thunder of the falls below came to their ears in a steady muttering and made speech an intimate thing.

"I wonder where Gentleman Joe is," Dan said after a while.

Molly was standing close to him, her hand still in the bend of his arm. Now he felt her turn.

"If he was here, he 'd be in one of them houses, I guess."

She pointed to the row of houses on their right, rising three stories high, their foundations licked by the river. Their clapboarded sides, even in that dim light, had a neglected look, and their odd, old-shingled roofs made an unkempt line against the stars. The nearest of the row, not twenty feet from where they stood, showed no lights; but a wisp of smoke floated upward from its chimney. The windows of its second story, close to the aqueduct, were not more than three feet above the parapet.

Dan and Molly, taking up their stroll again, moved under it. As they passed, they heard a guarded voice call to them.

"Say!"

They both looked up. There was no one visible in the window, and the voice seemed to come from above it.

"There 's a dormer set back on the roof," Molly said suddenly. "I remember noticing it before."

Dan stepped back until he could see the dormer. He could barely make out a man's figure leaning out of it.

"Hello," he said quietly.

He caught a movement of the man's head.

"It 's all right," he said. He had guessed who the man was. "It 's me — Dan Harrow. There ain't anybody around."

He thought he caught a sound of sharply indrawn breath.

"Say," said the man, again.

"Yeanh?"

"Henderson 's watching all along the street. The only way I can get out 's by this window. Can you bring me up a line? They won't be keeping people out of the houses. It 's people coming out they 're watching for."

"All right," Dan said.

"Listen. Do you know where Jannard's stable is?"

Dan felt Molly at his side.

"I do," she whispered.

"Yeanh," he said.

"Then go there. I 'll make it worth while for you. The horse 's in the back box stall, saddle by the door. There 's a line hanging from the hook next to it. I seen it yesterday.

Bring the horse here and come into the house. The horse 'll
stand. It 's straight up at the top — three flights."

"All right."

The man drew back. Dan turned to Molly. She was looking at him steadily. Then, as if she knew what she had
read in his face, she took his arm. A block back across the
river, down on Front Street, they found a small stable. A
lantern burned dimly in the harness room. Dan took it. In
a moment he had found the big grey, the saddle, and the coil
of rope.

The grey snorted at the strange hand, but gave himself
readily to the girth. Running his hands down the clean fore-
legs, Dan could feel the trembling of the horse.

"He knows what 's up," he said softly.

"He ought to by this time," Molly said.

The horse walked gently behind them. At the door Molly
stopped.

"Wrap that line round under your coat," she said. Dan
gazed at her a moment with admiration.

"Hurry up, Dan," she said. Now that she had made up
her mind to help him, she thought clearly. He had n't asked
her to help him, she was doing it because she wanted to.

On the towpath again, she stopped.

"I 'll stay here with the horse. You go down over the
aqueduct. It 's Erlo's boarding house. The door 's on Water
Street."

Dan went ahead alone. There were no lights in the dingy
street, but he kept close to the walls. He thought he saw a
movement three houses ahead of him, and he paused. But
there was no further indication of a watcher. Relieved, he
turned into the doorway by his left hand. It was pitch-dark
in the narrow hall. In a room over his head he heard a man
snoring. Then the creak of a bed. There was a sour smell
of old carpet. In the back, a whisper of the river running
by. He felt his way cautiously up the stairs.

On the landing he paused. He had heard no sound, but a
cool breath of air told him that the street door had opened.
He tried to reassure himself by thinking that he had failed

to latch the door after him in his care to be silent. But he was sure he had latched it.

There was no sound, no creak of boards. He held his breath. But he heard nothing but the trip of his heart. Still he stood quiet. After a few moments he began to think that no one had come in. He was just putting out his foot for a step along the hall, when something made him stop. It was nothing he heard, nothing he could see. But up the stairs was stealing an odd perfume, a faint smell of violets.

At first he thought a woman had come in. Then before his mind's eye was flashed a picture of a man with a bullet scar on his temple and slicked black hair. The hair had smelled of violets.

Both men waited — an interminable time. The rush of the river was in the ears of both. The ticking of a clock back in the kitchen crept into the silence. The man in the bedroom snored on.

After a time, Dan heard a creak below him. Then again the breath of cool air came up to him. Again it was shut off. The man had left.

All over him Dan felt the sweat breaking out. But he went on now more confidently. In a moment he came to the door of the attic room and rapped gently. It swung open. All he could see was the pallid patch of the window. Something was poked into his back.

"It's me," he said quietly.

The pistol was taken away.

"Got the rope?" Calash asked.

Dan unwound it. They tied it to the knob of the door.

"Where's the horse?"

"My cook's got him at the other side," Dan said. "I did n't want to leave him alone."

"All right. You'd better come down after me. They'll stop you if you go out how you came in."

He put one leg over the sill and began to lower himself. Dan saw his tall thin silhouette sliding down. Then he stopped, his face against the shingles, lying breathlessly still. Round the bend in the towpath came the jingle of trace chains. They heard the breathing of mules harsh above the mutter of the distant falls. The boat went by with a ripple along its sides casting a bright patch on the water.

"Evening," they heard the driver say. Dan knew he must have seen Molly with the horse.

"You 'd better hurry," he said.

The man slid down, his face turned away from the light. The rope tightened on the shingles and moved half an inch from one side to the other, with tiny squeaks. Then it jerked, and Dan went down slowly.

When he reached the towpath, he found Calash mounted. Molly was standing by the horse's head.

"It 's lucky the driver did n't see that rope," Calash said.

He bowed over the horse's withers to Molly.

"It was mighty fine of you to bring the horse," he said to her.

She did not reply.

He leaned down to shake hands with Dan.

"I owe you a lot."

He put his hand in his pocket.

"No," said Molly suddenly, in a firm low voice.

"I was n't going to," Dan said.

"Not money," Calash said. He put something in Dan's hands. "You can have this to remember by."

"Thanks," he said again, his voice odd, harsh.

Then the grey horse leaped forward.

Molly caught Dan's arm.

"They 'll hear him," she said. "Come quick, Dan."

She hurried back across the aqueduct. Before Dan could move, two men came out of Front Street. They were mounted.

"Did you see a horse?" they shouted.

Dan waved his hand eastward.

"He turned off," he cried.

They dashed into the darkness.

Molly met him on the far side.

"If he crosses the canal beyond the Wide Water," she said, "he can lose his trail in the woods by Cobb's Hill."

Slowly they went back to the Sarsey Sal. In the cabin, with the lamps lighted, Dan sat down and opened his hand. Gentleman Joe had put a small pin into it, shaped like a running horse.

"I wonder if they're diamonds," he said.

Molly turned from brushing out her hair.

"It's pretty," she said. Then, "Dan, don't help him again. Keep clear of him."

"Why?"

"Did you ever see him?"

"Why, sure," he said. "I've seen him a lot of times."

"His face, I mean?"

"No," he said, "I never seen it. I'd like to."

It surprised him to have to say it. He knew perfectly well that he had never seen Gentleman Joe's face, but his impressions of the man were woven in so closely with his life on the canal, that to hear his admission in plain words was startling.

"I saw it against a window light," Molly said.

He did not hear her; he was looking at the horse again, shining on the callus on his palm; he was happy.

To Boonville

Henderson and his deputies had missed Calash in Rochester. After Dan's brief glimpse of them there, the chase vanished again, as completely as if they fled behind the moon.

The Sarsey Sal took up her appointed journeyings; back and forth between ports, from Albany to Buffalo. Life in the cabin ran smoothly. But once more Dan detected a cool aloofness stealing into Molly's kindness. His mind returned to Klore. They had heard of him. He was doing job hauls on the Boonville Canal. Sooner or later Butterfield would have to send the Sarsey Sal up the feeder, where she could not be missed.

Dan had grown heavier during the summer. His skin had

taken on the warm brown shade the sun and wind give to light-haired people. He walked now, or stood beside the rudder, with a new erectness. He seldom had men dispute his place at a lock. Once in the night at Number 54, another boat had tried to overtake them and hold them from going through the lock. Dan called to Molly to pole the boat in; the horses knew enough to wait at the upper end; and at the lower, in the light of the lock-tender's lantern, Dan and Fortune settled the other crew. Fortune returned breathing war and nursing a black eye with the palm of his hand, but Dan went merely to the team, hitched the towline on the evener while the big black looked over his shoulder, and took up the trail again.

Back and forth, back and forth, in hauls of varying length, the life which the boaters loved for its variety, the different places to tie up, the waterfronts of different ports, Dan began to find monotonous. After the first sight, the rush and hurry at the locks, the gush of waters, the lifted voices in the long basins, the line boats passing with their noisy immigrants, the crack of whips, were all the same to him. Yet he still held to the canal. For one thing, he liked to watch his big team overhaul another with their long stride. For another, he had Molly. For a third, the wail of the horns at night.

Then, one morning in August he hauled into Rome and went to the warehouse office for shipping orders. Mr. Butterfield was reading a letter at his desk. He merely nodded to Dan, pointing out a chair. Dan sat down, put his hat on the floor, and glanced round the cool room, then at Butterfield's handsome white head.

Mr. Butterfield had been kind to him. They liked each other.

After a minute the older man folded the letter with his clean fingers and rapped it gently on his desk.

"Harrow," he asked, "do you intend to keep to canawling right along?"

Dan glanced at him curiously.

"I ain't sure, Mr. Butterfield. I had n't really thought."

The cool grey eyes looked across at him thoughtfully. "Some like it," he said.

"Yeanh."

"I should think a man like you would get tired of it. Just hauling another man's goods back and forth between cities."

"Well, I do sometimes, Mr. Butterfield."

Mr. Butterfield continued gently tapping the letter on the desk.

"This letter's from a friend of mine," he said. "He wants to know if I know of a good man to take charge of his dairy. That is, really, he wants a superintendent for his place. Would a job like that interest you?"

"Where is it?"

"Lyons Falls. He has the finest farm in Lewis County. Maybe you saw the barn he was building last fall."

Dan remembered the ribs of the great structure rising on the meadows, as lovely to him as a cathedral.

"Yeanh."

"He has a fine herd," Mr. Butterfield continued.

"I saw it," Dan said.

"Have you had any experience?"

"Not with fine cattle," Dan said. "But I'm pretty good with cows. I admire good cows."

"He says he does n't care for too experienced a man. He wants a young fellow willing to learn."

Dan remembered the wide meadows on the river bottom and the long herd winding in. Above all, he remembered the great barn rising. "You 'll get three hundred a year to begin with, and keep. And if you work out right, the salary will go up."

"It sounds like a good proposition," Dan said, slowly, looking down at his hands.

"He wants a man in the fall, in time for fall plowing."

It seemed to Dan that he could feel the plow helves on the heels of his palms.

"And he wants a single man," said Mr. Butterfield. "So right away I thought of you."

Dan looked up.

"That might sort of stop me taking it, Mr. Butterfield."

"Why?"

Dan was embarrassed.

"I'm sort of bound up here. I couldn't take it single."

"Do you think she'd go with you? She's nice for a canal cook, I know that; generally they won't leave. They've got a taste for travel in them."

"I'd like to talk it over with her," Dan said.

"All right. There's no particular hurry. I'll write Mr. Wilder and see what he says. I think it would be a good place for you, Harrow. And I think Mr. Wilder would find you a good man for him."

They turned to business abruptly. Dan was to take a load of corn to Boonville. . . .

That evening Dan told Molly and Fortune that they would be heading for Boonville in the morning. Her face paled slightly.

"Klore's up there," she said.

"Yeanh," said Dan.

"Well, it's got to come to a wrastle one way or another," Fortune said.

They started out of Rome in the grey before dawn, when the mist lay on the water and the air was still. Dan was steering. It was on such a morning that he had entered Rome the year before. Under his feet his own boat moved; his team went along the towpath; and his own cook worked in the cabin. He had all these. They would be worth fighting for. He knew that Klore stood between him and all his life on the canal.

Molly had said little during breakfast. She was having one of her moody days. Later she came on deck and stood beside him in the stillness, her eyes on the towline stretching into the mist; ahead the clink of the traces, and occasionally, as the mist swirled, a sight of the rumps of the team and Fortune's thin shanks walking. Drops formed on her hair and crept slowly over her cheeks.

Just as they cleared the basin they met a boat coming in. The other team stopped and the Sarsey Sal went over the tripped rope. As the rudders passed, a harsh voice hailed them.

"What boat's that?"

"The Sarsey Sal," Dan said.

The heavy voice swore a hard oath; and, as if the mist cleared before it, they had a glimpse of Jotham Klore, black-bearded, looking after them. He did not try to get ashore; he said nothing further; he just looked after them. He would be on the up trip before they could come down.

Then the mist closed in between him and Dan, and when Dan turned to Molly she had gone below.

When the mist burned off, they saw men reaping oats in the fields, men in a line, swinging the cradle scythes in beautiful rhythm, while women and boys walked after them tying bundles.

Molly came out again into the warmth of the sun and sat opposite Dan with her basket of sewing, mending the collar of one of his shirts.

For a while Dan said nothing, but he let his eyes roam over the meadows where the wind made waves in the grain and the corn lifted its leaves and whispered. Finally they came to rest on her, on the light hair at the nape of her neck, and the print dress tight over her bowed shoulders.

"Mr. Butterfield says there's a job for me up at Lyons Falls — superintendent of that big farm where we saw them building the barn."

She kept her head bent.

"It's three hundred a year, to start with, and keep."

"Yeanh?"

Her voice was toneless.

"Yeanh," he said. "It's a fine dairy."

A note of enthusiasm crept into the words.

"It's a fine job to start with."

"What did you say, Dan?"

He grew moody.

"They want a single man."

She looked up at him quickly.

"What did you say, Dan?" she asked again.

"I said I could n't take it single."

"Yeanh."

"Mr. Butterfield said he 'd write and see. I could n't take it single. I could n't leave you, Molly."

Her eyes were wet.

"Molly, will you come with me if they 'll take us double?"

Her face bent toward her work again.

"Dan, why don't you want to stay on the canal?"

"What 's the use? Just going back and forth — all places the same. There ain't any interest into it."

She drew a long breath.

"Will you come, Molly, if I get the job?"

She did n't answer.

He looked at her a long time.

"Will you marry me if I stay on the canal, Molly?"

She kept her eyes on her hands, but there was a slight heave in her shoulders, and when she finally looked up he saw that she was crying. Eventually she went below without having given him an answer.

He brooded as they went along, steering by instinct. He knew that even if Mr. Wilder offered the job to him, as a married man, he would have to say no. His eyes followed the reapers and rested on a wagon being loaded with bundles, jumping up on the underhand swing of the forks. He turned his head to get a last glimpse of them, as if he were saying good-bye. His emotion ran so deep that he could scarcely feel it. After all, he would have the boat and his two teams and Molly.

The hills closed in. They entered the Lansing Kill, and began the long slow climb through seventy locks. . . .

In Boonville they met the Nancy. The fat woman was in high good humor. She had learned a new recipe for cheese pie.

"It 's good," Solomon said. "I don't deny it 's good, but when you get it seven days in the week the boat smells so even the rats get out."

"Go along," said Mrs. Gurget.

"It troubles the digestion," Solomon said.

"Sol!" cried the fat woman.

"It's true," he said grimly. "It segashuates right —"

"You shut up!" she said. "Where's your manners?"

Fortune broke in tactfully.

"I wonder if we might n't get a game of cards?"

Mrs. Gurget snatched her breath.

"My stars! Cards! Pinochle! I ain't played in a week."

She hitched her chair forward to the table.

"Show me a pack."

Dan looked questioningly at Molly.

"I've got a pack," said Fortune, "only they're kind of dirty."

"That's all right," said Mrs. Gurget in her hearty voice. "Sol ain't washed his hands. He says it spoils his luck, but he's a dirt-easy proposition anyways. How'll we play?"

"I'm no good at it," said Molly.

"Me neither," said Dan.

"It ain't right. One of you ought to play. Still," the fat woman comforted her conscience, "three-handed pinochle is a lot better game than four-handed. Ain't it, Mr. Friendly?"

"Yes, there's a kitty three-handed."

Molly cleared off the supper things, and the game started and went on while Dan helped her wash the dishes.

The fat woman played with gusto; one end of her shawl, trailing over the back of the chair, twitched like a third monstrous arm as she put her card on a trick. She would hesitate an instant, then put forth the card, snapping a corner down sharply, and whenever she took the trick she would break into her hearty laugh. As the playing progressed, her laughter became more frequent and good-humored. The melds she declared were extraordinary; four times she held a hundred aces, with an extra ace or two at that, and she seemed to be able to fill one hundred and fifty of trumps whenever she liked. Even double pinochle came to her hand; and the kitty always favored her.

"Some day she'll get a thousand aces," grunted Solomon; "and that will serve her right, too. There's three people I've heard tell about getting a thousand aces, and they all had their hearts stop."

"Mine would n't," chortled the fat woman. "I'd be too anxious to see it again to die."

Fortune Friendly said nothing. But he watched the fat woman's playing and followed her luck with eyes as rapt as Jacob's must have been in his dream. When he shuffled with his quick fingers, he got himself good hands, but all the other good cards went to the fat woman; and when she or Solomon dealt, her luck was monolithic.

Solomon was like the fly between the two irresistible forces.

Molly and Dan sat down on the far side of the cabin, listening to the click of the cards and the remarks of the players, and Solomon's intermittent groaning. Whenever the fat woman leaned back in laughing, the lamplight glittered on her locket and fell full on her broad red face. And Dan thought of the face in the locket, and looked at Solomon sitting across the table from her, his thin nose beaded with sweat as he concentrated on his cards. But then the fat woman would straighten up and settle her hat with both hands and go about the business of dealing.

Dan leaned back and drowsed with the sound of the playing in his ears. Content in each other's presence, he and Molly did not talk; but now and then she glanced up at him with a smile at one of Solomon's groans or Mrs. Gurget's delighted shrieks. They were all his friends, Dan thought, and it was pleasant to have them there together; and he forgot Jotham Klore coming up from Rome.

The fat woman's voice broke in upon him, as she made conversation in dealing.

"Do you know Mrs. Quackenbush?"

"The woman that pumped the canal dry three times?" Fortune asked.

Mrs. Gurget laughed.

"That's her. Nell Berry's sister. Well — " She was swept into a paroxysm of laughs, her sides lifted, her face reddened, and she clutched at her bosom with a fat hand.

Solomon looked up from picking up his cards with an air of disgust.

"It's funny," he snorted. "Jeepers, it's the funniest story you ever heard."

The fat woman was not at all disturbed.

"Sol's right, at that. Mrs. Perkins up to Slab City gave Mrs. Quackenbush an order for a hat like hers last month. One of them strawy ones with decorated pansies onto it. But the old woman got to Utica and she couldn't recollect which woman had asked her. So she went off and bought a dozen just alike. She buys clothes for a lot of them women up there, so she knew the sizes. Then when she come up she sold each one of them twelve women a hat. They was pretty, and the women was anxious to buy them; and each one figured she'd be right up in the top of style and show up in church next Sunday with a new hat right before the rest, and show off on to the others. None of them said nothing: they wanted for it to be a surprise. I wasn't there, so I don't rightly know, but I hear tell that a bad time was had by all."

She bent over, slapping her knees, and let out a screech of laughter as she straightened up.

"What happened to Mrs. Quackenbush?" Fortune asked with a chuckle.

"Land! As quick as she'd sold them all she traveled out of there like all get out."

"Two-fifty," Solomon bid dryly.

The fat woman picked up her cards.

"Four hundred," she said. "Any dispute?"

The playing went on until about ten o'clock, when the fat woman got up to go.

"When are you traveling to Rome?" she asked Dan.

"To-morrow morning."

"So're we. The Berrys'll be coming through from Port Leyden. We might as well all go together. It'll be a regular party."

"Sure," said Dan. . . .

Next morning the three boats started down, the Sarsey

Sal, the Nancy, Berry's boat, at the head of a line of nine.
On deck Dan stood with Molly close beside him.

"You ain't afeard, Dan?"

He did not answer. It was early morning; there was no
up traffic yet. Behind him the boats wound silently under
the sunrise; a sweet, cool day, with dew on the meadows,
and the bells of cows sweet in the night pastures. Ahead of
him, somewhere, Jotham Klore was coming up with his
boat.

They wound down along the valley until the roar of the
falls sounded ahead and the upper gate beams of the Five
Combines stood out white against the trees. Dan sounded his
horn, and the gorge took the echoes back and forth, down,
down, below the line of sky.

Then, at the foot of the flight of locks, another horn
broke out in three sharp blasts.

Molly's head sprang up, and she looked square at Dan.

"It's Jotham Klore."

Dan nodded. . . .

The Fight at the Five Combines

It was a morning of bright sunshine and swift white
clouds. They scudded over the gorge on the breast of the
wind. But in the meadows there was no feel of the wind,
which passed high up, stroking the leaves of only the top-
most trees.

The Lansing Kill and the overflow from the canal fell
into the gorge within sixty feet of each other; and between
them a diamond-shaped patch of grass made even footing for
the fight. The crowd had taken up their places on two sides, so
that the space of short grass resembled a square — on two
sides people, on two sides the open gorge and the falling
water, and the Kill seething into foam eighty feet below.
The roar of it rose up, passing the ears of the crowd, until
it seemed a wall against the open sky.

As their boats stopped at the lock, both Dan and Klore

had gone to the lock-tender's shanty to wake the old man. The other boaters were too far back to hear what they said, and Ben was too deaf; but they stood opposite each other by the door until the old man came out, his trousers in his hand. Then, as they stepped together, he poked his staff between them.

"No one ain't going to fight in front of my house," he said. "There's a good patch of grass up by the Kill. If you're so all-fired eager, get up there."

"It don't matter to me," Klore said. "One place is as good as the next."

"I'm agreeable," said Dan.

"Then come along with me," said the old man.

He walked with a long stride, his red underwear bright against the grass, his bare feet gripping the earth, his staff swinging, his white head bent, like one of the prophets. Dan and Klore walked behind him, a little apart; and after them the boaters came sprinting from their boats as the word spread that Dan Harrow was to fight Jotham Klore. As they ran they made bets.

The fat woman came running down the towpath, one hand holding her bonnet down, the other holding up her skirts; but before she reached the locks she turned, sent Solomon scurrying back for a vinegar bottle and a sponge, and then came on more slowly. Hector Berry, hanging back among the others to put money on Klore, found himself suddenly face to face with Solomon, who was returning with the vinegar. The little man's thin nostrils were white with scorn.

"You're betting against Dan?"

Berry flushed and screwed a new cigar into his mouth and put his hands in his pockets and crossed one foot before the other, and managed to appear even more embarrassed.

"Why," he said. "I was asking how the odds was."

"What was they?"

"Two to one on Klore most people're giving."

Solomon set down his sponge and bottle carefully and yanked his wallet out.

"I was n't going to lay no money against him," Hector said uneasily.

"Did n't I hear you ask for money on Dan?"

"Well . . ."

"How much?"

Berry hesitated. "Ten dollars," he said at length.

"All right," said Solomon.

He fished out five dollars, and they looked round for a stakeholder. Fortune Friendly was going by. He affably consented to hold the money.

"Sol!" cried Mrs. Gurget.

The little man snatched up the vinegar and ran across the meadow. The fat woman was standing close beside Molly in the front of the crowd, her face flushed, her eyes dancing.

"Take off your shirt," she said to Dan. "Here, put down your head."

She stripped the shirt over his head and then the undershirt and laid them across Molly's arm. Klore had taken off his shirt and waited in his undershirt. He stood now with his heavy legs spraddled, his thumbs hooked in his belt, and looked the crowd over. When his pale eyes came to Molly, he grinned slowly. She saw his teeth white through his beard.

She met his eyes squarely, and for a moment Mrs. Gurget's quick glance caught a faint flush in her pale cheeks. She rumbled faintly some remark to herself, then smiled as Molly, without changing her expression, turned to Dan. The girl's lips moved stiffly when she spoke; her voice was strained.

"Lick him, Dan. You 've got to lick him."

Solomon bustled through the crowd behind them.

"Shucks," he exclaimed. "Dan 'll lick the poison right out of his hide."

He reached up to rub Dan's shoulders, found the muscles loose and easy, and grinned.

"Watch him, Dan. Watch his right. Watch it all the time. Don't never let it get out of your sight."

Old Ben was putting on his trousers. Years ago he had fought in a ring.

"No gouging by Ben's lock," he said. "No tripping nor sabutting."

As he buttoned up his trousers, he pointed one hand to his stick.

"I'll lay out the first one that does. I'll douse him back of the ear."

Jotham Klore grinned.

"No bother. I can lick him without that."

"You'd better," said the old man. "I'll give the word, and then you can commence. Now I'll announce you and make it a regular occasion."

"Make it quick," said Klore, clenching his heavy hands and turning his pale eyes to Dan's.

Suddenly Dan's eyes lighted. He had caught sight of a white head over the crowd. Julius Wilson and Ben Rae came up to him, and shook his hand.

"We're with you, Dan," said Julius. The Jew nodded. They stepped back.

"Say, what're you doing up this way?" a voice asked.

Fortune stepped up to them, shook hands, introduced them to Mrs. Gurget and Sol and Molly, and they all shook hands.

"We're taking a minister up to Lyons Falls. Reverend Williams — him and his family." Wilson chuckled. "'What's the delay?' he says to Ben. And then he locks his family into the cabin and comes along to see."

He pointed to a black-clad dignified figure on the edge of the crowd, a man with a pale face, watching the proceedings out of timid eyes. The fat woman was impatient. Her whole soul was shining in her eyes, and her eyes were on Dan. "I could dang near say a prayer, dearie," she said to Molly.

Molly gave her a small smile. She stood stiff, trembling slightly, pale.

Mrs. Gurget patted her shoulder.

"Cheer up, dearie. He'll win with half a chance."

Molly did not answer, and again Mrs. Gurget saw her eyes meet Klore's and a smile in the man's, confident, not only of Dan but of the girl. The fat woman read it as plain as print.

"Snake's eyes," she said to herself — it felt like a shriek inside of her. She grabbed Molly's arm and squeezed with all her might. "Look at Dan — he's looking at you. He's got to lick him, you hear me? That's what you took up with him for, ain't it? To make him lick Klore. You told me that yourself. Don't tell him in that measly voice. Look like you meant it."

She felt Molly wince.

"Remember how Klore licked you?"

She felt Molly's arm stiffen, and saw the hot flush come for a moment into her cheeks.

"Give him a smile," she said grimly.

She was watching Dan, now, and the fat woman thought she had never seen anything handsomer than when he grinned.

"If he's scared," she said to herself, "and I'll bet he is scared hollow, he don't show it."

She waved her arm and shouted to him.

"Watch his right! Watch his right and break his eyes. Blind him."

There was a little bitterness in her as she saw his eyes on Molly's. For a moment her hand caught at her fat breast. Then she threw up her head, took a deep breath through her nose, and roared, "We're all with you, Dan! Take off his pants and hang him over the edge for the flies to bite. Blind his eyes, Dan, blind his eyes."

Dan heard her and gave her part of his smile. Then his glance went to Klore and fixed in an unmoved stare. It had come at last and it was to be. He heard dimly, through the roar of water, the crowd's murmur still, and Ben's voice, "Dan Harrow versye Jotham Klore, unbeat Bully of the Big Ditch."

Ben's staff fell forward to meet its shadow on the grass; the old man's resonant voice lifted in a shout: —

"Fight!"

They met in the middle of the open square of grass, neither giving an inch, striking for the middle, landing. Then came the Jew's voice: "Block with your elbows, Dan."

But Dan knew no more of the science than did Klore. It became a question of which man could wear the other down. The fists of Jotham Klore came in against his belly, and he felt his own fists sink into Klore's undershirt, felt the leap of muscles under his knuckles.

Then the fat woman: "Blind his eyes!"

He raised his hands, felt a stunning smash on his ribs, and, as he slipped a little to the left, brought his right forward to Klore's eye. Klore snarled, shook his head, and the blood came down from the cut.

As they drew apart for an instant, measuring each other, the complete stillness of the crowd was broken by a rising mutter of voices.

"Did ye see thim belaboring?" exclaimed a red-headed driver. "Did ye ever see the loike?"

"It's a fight," said his captain, driving his wooden leg into the grass for a firmer stance. "The lad can stand up to him."

"What 're they fighting for?" a man asked. He worked on a farm whose buildings stood scarce a hundred yards above the locks.

The Irishman whistled a bar of a jig.

"Phwat would they be fighting for? Sure for a girl, and there she is herself, her with the brown hair that's holding the young feller's shirt on her arm."

"I wonder how our passenger's doing?" Julius Wilson asked the Jew.

The Jew grinned, and pointed.

The Reverend Mr. Williams was shinnying up the side of a boulder, a few yards back of the crowd. His black coat tails fluttered over his thin hams in an agony of excited haste.

But Mrs. Gurget and Molly and Solomon never for a moment took their eyes from the two men before them.

Solomon was down on one knee, leaning his forearms on the other out in front of him, and he kept saying, over and over, like a prayer, "Watch his right, Dan. Watch his right."

The fat woman stood with one hand on his shoulder and one on Molly's arm. She breathed as heavily as the two men, and her eyes glared at Klore's as if she would blister him. At every blow a little grunt escaped her, as if she had hit or been hit herself. As for Molly, the fat woman could make nothing of her, and once the fight began she tried to make nothing of her. She stood, as white as before, but a feverish shine was in her eyes and she clutched Dan's shirt in her arm.

The two were circling warily now, taking time between their blows.

"Keep him away, Dan, keep him away!" the Jew cried suddenly. "You've got the reach. Don't let him get close."

Jotham Klore came in slowly on Dan, his arms half raised. He stamped slightly as he put down his feet, digging his toes into the sod, as a bull steps to settle himself before a rush. His pale eyes, generally on Dan's, darted now and then to one part or another of him, as if he were selecting his point of attack. His grey undershirt clung to his back and wrinkled from one side to the other between his shoulder blades as he moved his arms. It was sweat-soaked in a darker stain round his neck, but the half-length sleeves left his massive forearms free, yellow-skinned and furred with close-curled black hair. As he moved his head, the hairs of his black beard caught on the undershirt and jumped free, like small released springs. Once in a while he snatched the blood from his right eye with the back of his hand.

Dan moved backward before him, with a lightness of tread that was almost delicate. Sweat glistened on his shoulders. His hard flat stomach was reddened, but he breathed easily. There was no readable expression on his face; it was almost vacant; but his greenish eyes kept steadily on Klore.

Suddenly Klore led with his left, and, as Dan's hands dropped, he brought his right over in a heavy swing. Dan heard Solomon's voice shrill; he ducked, and the blow took him on the top of his head. His back bent under the shock, and the people in front could see his heels sink into the sod.

"Watch his right!" Solomon cried.

And then again there was silence, except for the roar of the falls.

Klore rushed suddenly, head down, both fists driving from the shoulders, and, instead of dodging, Dan stepped in; his back jumped straight as a whip, and his fists found Klore's eyes. The boater's head snapped back, and when they drew apart the people saw the blood blinding one eye completely and the other getting brown.

Then he came in again, more slowly, more steadily, his hands high to guard his face. The two came together and the blows sank in.

"Go after his belly!" shrieked Solomon.

Again they stood close, trading massive, slow blows. The fight became an impersonal thing to the onlookers. The roar of the waters in their ears grew small and far away. They held their breaths and watched and heard the grunt of the man hit, and the sigh of the man striking. There was a deliberateness in both of them.

They saw the slow rage climbing in Klore, but he did not shout and growl as they had heard him in other fights. He kept his head down and a little to one side, to see better. As if he knew that he must wear Dan down before he could beat him, he went slowly, getting in a heavy blow at times, and taking one with a short shaking of his head.

The knees of both men held; there was no sign of a knockdown. It came to the crowd that the first man down would be the man licked.

The fight went on. The hot sun shining under the high cloud made a bright carpet of the square of grass on which the shadows of the men fought as they did, following each other here and there and hitting heavily. As the warmth increased, the people caught the hot smell of sweat when the fighters came in close to them; and a pair of bluebottle flies flew round their heads investigating.

The whole of Dan's chest and belly began to darken; but there was no mark to see on the bully, beyond his swollen eyes. He guarded them now like precious things. Dan's breathing had shortened. His hands were slower to meet a blow. Both men used their fists as though there were weights tied to them. . . .

The morning pared their shadows on the grass to little men. But the slow fight went on, the harsh breathing, the long thud of blows.

Even Solomon had fallen silent.

The roar of the water was forgotten; the passing of the day; the sun and the clouds. All the world came in upon the little square of bright green grass, on two sides the small figures of the boaters, on the others the forgotten chaos of the water.

The men fought with the persistence of the two flies buzzing.

All the world came in upon them in the hush, on the fighters, on the crowd, on the straight brown-haired figure of Molly Larkins.

More boats tied up, a long line either way, and the canawlers crossed the meadow to look on; but the silence remained, and the harsh breathing of the two men marked the time. . . .

"God!" cried Solomon. "It can't last no longer."

The two stood still again, facing each other, their hands hanging like lead balls.

Painfully they raised them. Old Ben, clutching his staff, his chin resting on his wrists, watched them with sombre eyes. The fat woman let the tears run into the corners of her mouth. There was a misery in the eyes of many people.

The bearded man's face was a mass of blood and raw flesh from which his beard grew. It had no shape, it flecked drops when he shook it. The nose was a lump over the hair raised on his swollen mouth, and one eye showed as a slit. He kept spitting, trying to stir the hair that cut into his mouth, and he made a blubbering sound when he did so that suggested the color of his face to the people on the outskirts of the crowd. Yet he came on, peering out of the corner of his partly open eye.

The younger man could scarcely lift his hands; his body was livid, in places the skin had broken; and his chest heaved and heaved, and yet he seemed to get no air. But his face had almost no mark, and his blue eyes were as calm as those of a farmer who harrows his meadow.

"It can't last no longer," said Solomon, and he found the fat woman's hand awkwardly trying to get into his.

Without a sound Klore rushed, his head down.

"He's going to butt!" someone shouted. "He can butt in a door."

Dan tried to dodge, was slow, turned his body slightly and took the glancing blow of Klore's head on one hip. They both went down. They struggled up together, and the movement seemed quick and light to the stiff watchers.

Dan had his back to the lip of the falls. He backed away slowly. All sense of direction had gone from both men. There was only one space in the world, and that lay between them.

Shrill cries rose warning Dan; but it was too late. He could not dodge to either side. And with a harsh, half-swallowed roar Klore rushed again, butting with his head. His short legs bowed; he leaped with a fumbling ungainliness; his hands swung.

The crowd saw Dan rigid, outlined against the sky, with the roar of water behind him. They saw his hand come up, gnarl to a fist, come down on the back of the black head — a heavy blow.

They heard no sound. They saw Dan standing with his hands at his sides. They saw Klore lying on the ground, his legs twitching, his shoulders still. They said nothing. It was the end.

Dan stood looking at the black head at his feet, the raw face hidden on the grass, looking down. He wavered a little on his feet, but he stood looking down. Then he felt someone beside him. Molly, slipping his shirt round his shoulders. She lifted his arm over her shoulder; and she looked down at Klore. Then he heard the fat woman sobbing and saying, "Dan, Dan, Dan," over and over. And Solomon had his hand. Then the Jew. But the others, like Dan, still stood looking down at Klore.

Then, all at once they heard a voice over their heads, and glancing up they saw the minister on the boulder, hands stretched upward, his timid eyes lost in the sky: —

"Praised be the Lord!"

A murmur grew among them; it swelled and swelled; it ended in a shout.

They went back to their boats slowly, by twos and threes, and Ben began locking them through.

Gentleman Joe Calash

Brown and squat upon the water, the old Sarsey Sal worked down through the locks of the gorge. The other downstream boats had gone ahead, the Nancy last of all, the fat woman waving her arm to Molly from the stern.

They had put Dan to bed in the cabin; he was sleeping there now; and Fortune walked behind the team. Solomon had relieved him of the stakes he had held on the fight — at the last minute, for Fortune had made himself as inconspicuous as possible.

Molly steered. Where they had a mile stretch ahead of them, she called Fortune on board, for the big team could be trusted to hold their steady pace. He sat down on the cabin, folding his hands round his knees, and looked at her with his keen black eyes.

"It was a great fight," he said after a while.

"Yeanh," but a shiver passed up her back and she set her teeth.

The ripple cuddled on the old bow and ran along the

sides gently, and the team went steadily, faithfully on the towpath.

"I did n't think Jotham Klore had that much grit," Fortune said after a while.

"He 's got a lot," Molly said quickly. "I 'd thought Dan would do a quicker job."

The shiver ran up her back again. Both she and the ex-preacher saw the battered face in their mind's eye, and the squat legs bent, and the heavy hands raised as Klore kept heading in.

She brushed the hair back from her forehead and let her hand rest there. The same tired, white look that had been on her face all the while Dan was fighting still lay in her eyes.

Far ahead a horn wailed for a lock.

"Did Dan tell you he 'd got a job offered him on a farm at Lyons Falls?"

"No," said Fortune.

"It 's a fine job," she went on; "only they want a single man."

"What did he say?"

"He said he 'd take it double. Mr. Butterfield 's going to let him know about it when he gets to Rome."

"It 's the kind of a job he wants. It 's what he wants to do."

"That 's right."

Her voice was tired.

"He ain't no boater. He won't stay long on the canal, no matter what."

The ex-preacher glanced at her with a worried, affectionate look.

"No," he said, in a little while.

"All he wants to do is farm — clean out a stable — watch his wife do chores."

"Maybe he don't look at it that way, Molly."

The sudden flush went down again.

"I know, Fortune. I had n't ought to 've said it. And he ought to take it."

"It would be a good thing," Fortune agreed. "Suppose you did marry him, Molly?"

"Suppose I did marry him," she repeated, turning her fine frank eyes to his. "Suppose I did. Supposing I could love him like I did. Would I help him any? Wouldn't it come around how I'd lived? Them are fine folk he's going to — they'd be notional having a canal cook living on their place, whatever she was then."

"They wouldn't have to find out," he suggested.

"There's people would know inside of a week. A man can keep secrets about himself and nobody mind particular. But a woman hasn't any show in a small town."

He nodded angrily.

"It wouldn't be right by Dan," she said. "And I can't love him like I did. I'd get tired and I wouldn't be happy. Then he wouldn't either. Even if he got his own farm, people would talk about me. It ain't as if I was even middling old."

"No," he said. "You're too pretty."

"He's a good boy. He's close with money. That ain't his fault — it's into him to be. But I couldn't stand it. I've got my wages now, so I don't mind. Alone on a farm, all the year . . ."

Fortune stared at her sympathetically.

"He's a good boy. He's done a great thing," she said proudly.

"Yeanh. He's licked Klore."

"Yeanh. He was afraid of him, and he licked him." Then she said, with almost a wail in her voice, "If he'd been licked, maybe it would've been easier for me."

The old man clucked his tongue on his teeth. For all she looked so pretty, she could not live with a strong man unless he made a slave of her. While she had thought of Dan as weak, and seen him afraid, she could love him. She must rule or be ruled.

"Molly," he said suddenly, "you ain't going back to Klore?"

She caught her lower lip with her teeth.

"No. I can't now, after being with Dan. I did love Dan, Fortune. I loved him hard. I could n't go back."

He understood. She could not let a beaten man override her.

"What 'll you do, then?"

"I don't know, yet. I 'll go back to Lucy Cashdollar's a while, maybe. I don't want a job, but I could stay with her. Maybe if I could get a boat I 'd go boating for myself. Mrs. Quackenbush does that."

He grinned suddenly.

"Want a driver?"

She smiled.

"Shucks. You? You 'd be running off all the while to play pinochle." Her face sobered. "Anyway, it ain't possible."

"When 'll you quit?" he asked.

"I don't know. Dan ought to have a free hand when he gets into Rome. He had n't ought to stay on the canal."

"How is he?"

"Sleeping," she said. "It don't seem possible. But there ain't a single mark onto his face. You 'd hardly know . . ."

She shivered, as poplar leaves shiver, at a touch.

On the next bend, Fortune jumped ashore. The black turned his bald nose round and gave the old man a glance.

"It don't seem right," Fortune said to the rumps of the horses. "Each one thought he was fighting for her. And neither one won."

Down the old Sarsey Sal sank in the walls of the locks. It grew colder. An old man sat on the dock at Han Yerry's fishing for sunfish.

"Frost to-night," he prophesied to Fortune.

Dan came stiffly on deck. His eyes fell first on the plank road where it ran into the gorge. There was a rope stretched across it, and two men sat under a tree, holding shotguns over their knees.

"What 's up?" he asked the old man.

Without removing his eyes from his float, the fisherman gummed snuff.

"They swore in twelve men here in this town," he said.

"They 've closed all the roads. It 's said Calash is headed this way. All them that hain't swore in is out watching for him. There 's a reward onto him — two thousand dollars, dead or alive." He rolled the sum over his tongue.

The Sarsey Sal pushed on into a green twilight. The cold bit sharper. Twice they saw men posted near the towpath, their eyes roaming, as men watch for a fox.

Dan said little, standing beside Molly. Once again the chase for Calash was coming toward him on the edge of night.

"I wonder if they 'll get him," Molly said.

He did not answer. Perhaps this time they would; but he did not think so. Always he had seen the man come, and go again; and he had never seen his face. Men were out after him, but they had never seen him. None of them had any record of the man's past; but they feared him and discussed him angrily among themselves and waited by the roads to kill him.

"I 'd like to see him," Dan said.

He had a superstitious foreboding. The man had come into his sight always at the moment of some happening to Dan — when he first came on the canal; when he first saw Molly; when Samson Weaver died, to leave him the boat; and again before his fight with Jotham Klore.

"I 'd like to look at him," he said again.

Under the flap of his shirt pocket, he carried the little diamond horse, and now he felt of it with his hand.

In a wide piece of water they tied up the old boat and brought the team aboard. Dan put light blankets on them. Fortune lit the night lantern and hung it out.

Their supper was very quiet. Dan moved awkwardly, his muscles aching. But his eyes, as he followed Molly's movements between the table and the stove, were steadily calm. Now and then a smile played over his mouth.

After supper Fortune went out. He said that he would walk on to the Delta House — it was but a mile down — and find a pinochle game. "My luck ought to be smart after to-day," he said. "I'll strip Davis dry. You can pick me off the towpath in the morning." He smiled at them, sitting at the table, with the lamplight on them. His face looked older and friendly to both of them. "So long," he said.

Dan dozed in his chair, his weariness still on him, while Molly cleared the supper things. She glanced at him from time to time and gave him a tender smile. Then she interrupted her work to get him his pipe, filling and lighting it for him. He puffed at the tight-wadded load for a while; but his lungs were still sore, and the effort of making the pipe draw was too hard on them. So he grinned and put it down. . . .

The striking of the clock made him open his eyes at the little prancing horse. "When it strikes I think he's crossed a bridge maybe." That was what Samson Weaver had said.

Molly was standing at his side. She stood very straight.

"Don't you think you'd ought to go to bed, Dan?"

He smiled at her.

"I guess that's right."

Then they both started. A horse was trotting swiftly along the towpath. They glanced at each other, seeing the same thing in each other's eyes.

She put her hand under his arm, helping him to get up.

"I'm going up, Molly."

She brought him his hat and sweater without speaking.

On deck they found a white moon shining. The smell of frost was on the air. It was very still. The light of the night lantern made a faint light on the old boards of the deck.

On the towpath stood a grey horse, dark with sweat, breathing in deep steady pants. But his head was up. The rider dismounted slowly.

"Henderson's pretty close after me," he said in a dry voice. "Can you put up this horse and hide us till he goes by?"

Dan felt Molly take his arm.

"No," she whispered.

He thought of the roads and the men watching.

"Yeanh."

The gang was still out. He saw Gentleman Joe stagger when he tried to walk.

"I 'll take the brown horse out," he said. "You can take him into the pasture back of them bushes. I 'll blanket your horse alongside of my black."

Calash tried to take down the bars of the pasture.

"I can't do it," he said. "One of them got my arm."

They noticed then that his left arm was tied up with two handkerchiefs.

"You do it," Dan said to Molly.

He took the grey in and put the blanket on over his saddle. In the far corner a man would have to look twice to see it. The horse was as tall as the brown and his grey legs might be mistaken for white stockings. The brown came out good-humoredly and went into the pasture with the fugitive.

It was still in the cabin again. Dan and Molly sat opposite each other before the stove without speaking. The clock ticked quickly.

After a minute or two their ears caught the murmur of running horses on the towpath. It grew swiftly, and beats made out a rhythm. Then the jingle of bits, the scrape of shoes, and the long hard breathing. Men spoke.

"Sarsey Sal," one read.

"Harrow's boat. Jeepers! He 's the man beat Klore. I 'd like to look at him."

Feet pounded on the deck. Henderson came in, fat, puffing slightly, a dead cigar tilted in the corner of his mouth. His red cheeks were smooth as ever, but there was a hot light in his brown eyes. As he pushed the pot hat back on his head, they could see that his mind was only on business.

"Seen Calash come this way?"

"Yeanh," said Dan. "He come on the towpath five minutes ago."

"That right?" Henderson jerked his question at Molly. She nodded.

"Did he come aboard?"

"No," said Dan.

"Better look," Henderson grunted to the men peering
curiously through the door. Dan saw the long pale moustaches
of one of the deputies, and a stir of air brought him a smell
of violets.

"How many horses?"

"Four," said Dan. "One a heavy team."

"Take the lantern," said Henderson.

The deputy was gone a minute.

"All right," he said when he came back.

"Come on," said Henderson. In a minute they were gone.
When Molly and Dan came out on deck again, Gentle-
man Joe was leading the brown horse out of the pasture.
Dan brought the grey off the boat and took his own horse
aboard. By the time he had the stable hatch closed down,
Gentleman Joe was mounted.

"Thanks," he said. "I owe you a lot."

He sat staring up the towpath, a tired man. His coat hung
limp against his horse's flanks, the brim of his hat slouched,
and the words came past his lips with a drag, as if each
one hurt him.

"Where 're you going now?" Dan asked him.

"I guess I 'll keep on back of them and try to slip through
when they turn back at the Kill."

"Everybody 's turned out there. I seen 'em when we come
down."

"Maybe I can break through."

"There 's a couple of men along the towpath waiting with
shotguns."

The man sighed.

"I ought to have got out last winter. Damn Henderson.
Who 'd 've thought a little fat man like him?"

"Why n't you cut back?"

"No use. A water rat could n't get by them."

"They 'll be coming back this way," Dan said.

The man sighed again. Then he drew up his shoulders.
The horse, feeling the movement, lifted his head and tested
the ground under his hoofs.

"I tell you. I 'll cut across to the Watertown road. The

guard won't be so heavy. It's only a couple of miles cross-lots. The horse can jump."

"Yeanh."

"So long."

"Good-bye." And again Dan had not seen his face.

Calash turned his horse at the bars, and he cleared them from a standing jump. The tall figure atop him seemed to have lost its weariness. It sat straight as the horse went away at an easy lope.

Dan went back to the boat, but on deck he turned to look west to the Watertown road. Against the sky he could see the low hill it passed before taking the climb up Tug Hill. There was the place to watch. He sat down with his back to the cabin. Molly came out with a blanket and sat down beside him and spread it over both of them.

"I hope he gets away," Dan said.

"He's got a chance."

He felt drowsy in spite of the cold air, and a great content settled over him. At last the canal and Molly belonged to him. The tired figure of the highwayman hung in his mind; the same tired-looking body that he had himself. But he had seen the horse clear the fence, and Gentleman Joe headed for freedom. Only the man had had to go alone.

Affectionately he put his arm over Molly's shoulders and felt her draw in to him. They listened to the ripple against the boat and the small sounds of water washing the bank-side grass.

"Dan."

The light of the night lantern came to them feebly, barely tracing her profile. Her eyes were dark to the moonlight.

"Yeanh, Molly."

He felt her straighten up under his arm. For a bit she was silent.

"We'll get into Rome to-morrow," he said. "You and me both, and then . . ."

He felt her hard warm palm in his.

"Dan, if Mr. Butterfield gets word you can take that job double, will you take it?"

He paused, feeling his way.

"No," he said. "No, I'm going to stay on the canal. You and me are going to stay together, now, ain't we?"

"It's a good job, Dan, is n't it?"

He drew a deep breath.

"Yes. It is a good job. Mr. Wilder has one of the best dairies in the county. Blooded cattle."

She caught the thrill in his voice; his hand moved in hers.

"I'm going to stay here," he said. "Boating's the thing for me, with you along. You ain't changed your mind? You would n't come with me?" he asked suddenly.

"No, Dan. I've not changed my mind. I'd hinder you to come. I would n't have no heart in it; and then, after a while, you'd lose yours."

"It's best staying here," he said gloomily.

"Sometimes it's best for two people to hurt each other, Dan."

"What do you mean? It don't mean us. We're going in to Rome to-morrow. It ain't like him — " he pointed to the low hill by the Watertown road. "I wonder will he get through."

"Sometimes it's best, Dan."

He scarcely heard her.

"You love me, Dan?"

"Yeanh," he said, turning to grin at her.

Her face lay in shadow against his shoulder.

"You won't forget it, Dan?"

Her low voice was husky.

"Forget it? Say, to-morrow I'm going to ask you again."

She seemed to draw comfort from that and pressed closer to him. . . .

Far away, against the low hill, points of light flashed. They heard the raps of rifle shots.

Neither spoke, but Dan felt suddenly tired as he went below. He could not sleep. For hours he heard the water by his head, running in a ripple on the planks. A rat splashed in the mud. . . .

Slow hoofs on the towpath; men's voices; a snatch of
laughter; a voice hailing him — so they came back. They
had come across lots, three of them on their horses, leading
a horse, not a grey horse, but one which carried Gentleman
Joe.

They laid him on the cabin roof and spread a blanket over
him.

"We 're tuckered out," they said. "Can we sleep in your
cabin?"

"Yeanh," Dan said.

They threw themselves like logs on the floor — men he
had never seen.

"Special depities," they introduced themselves. "Just farmers," they said proudly.

"Where 'd you get him?" Dan asked.

"He come through the Watertown road. Henderson took
us over there. He 's gone to bring in his men now. He told
us to take him into Rome. George, here, shot him."

"Yeanh," said an old man, with lean strong hands and
bright eyes. "It was a running shot. He came right across
from me in the shadow, and I feared I 'd miss him. But
I always was good with a rifle. Shot a running fox when I
was eight."

"What was he wanted for?"

"How do we know?" the spokesman said. "Two thousand dollars — that 's what for. George got him — it 's
his'n."

"Well, I won't forget the man that stood with me," said
the old fellow. "I 'm no undertaker."

"Something he did out West. One of them states. Train
or something." The man yawned. "Me, I 'm right tuckered."

Very weary, Dan went back to his bunk. . . .

He woke in the breath of dawn. He was still tired. Beyond the curtain, the men snored heavily. Now and then a
boot scraped on the floor as one of them turned in his sleep.
Molly had got up, but Dan saw his clothes neatly spread on
the foot of the bunk ready for him. He heard a fire snapping

in the stove. She must have been quiet not to wake the men.

He got up and dressed and went into the cabin. She was not there; but the room was warm with the fire, and the coffee kettle was beginning to boil. Dan went on deck to find her.

As he turned round at the head of the stairs, his eyes fell on a stiff, blanketed figure stretched out on the cabin roof. The dim light of daybreak washed it with a pale light, bringing out a shadow between the rigid legs and under the left arm. The blanket had settled during the night, till now it shaped him.

For a long time Dan stared at it, not moving. He thought of how he had seen him, in action, riding his grey horse. Whenever Dan felt the canal come close to him, he had seen this man. He had had grace, beside which the determination of the fat marshal was turned into something drab. Now he lay here on Dan's boat in the early morning. . . . Perhaps, after all, he had escaped . . .

Always Dan had seen him at night, with his face in darkness. Something to draw him on, it had been; something to know, like his first embarrassed interest in the canal folk themselves. At last he had only to lift the blanket from it.

Very slowly Dan reached forward and drew the blanket from the face. For a minute he looked down at it in the morning light as it grew stronger, little by little, as if it were afraid to come — and as he looked he felt the lean dawn wind on his cheeks.

It was dead grey. The skin was stretched on the cheeks and down each side of the broad nose. The bitter thin lips drew back from snuff-stained teeth. The eyes were open, rolled upward, but Dan caught an edge of the cold grey. It was ugly, cruel, mean.

Dan let the blanket fall back and stood looking over the meadows where the grey light followed the shadows.

He had seen Gentleman Joe. He had looked for him wherever he went, like the canal folk and the farmers who shot him for the reward he represented, without knowing really why. He had felt a secret kinship for him, and built it up.

Only the fat marshal, who went round about his business with the methodicalness of a grocer weighing sugar, had known. Molly had once seen him. . . .

There was a dull ache in Dan's heart, and he looked round for Molly, wondering why she had not greeted him. But the boat was bare. He went to the stable, where the black horse scrambled to his feet, nickering gently. But the stable held only the two teams. He came on deck again and looked across the meadows. But the only things alive were the shadows. He went down the towpath, and there he found her narrow tracks.

He followed them down until he came to the landing before the Delta House. It stood gaunt and bare in the grey light, its windows curtained, a trace of smoke climbing its chimneys from the dying fires. The tracks ended on the wharf, but away ahead he heard the clink of trace chains. And then in the shadow of the steps he saw Fortune Friendly sitting, silent, his black eyes watching him, and he knew. . . .

"Set down, Dan," said the ex-preacher, quietly.

Dan sat down.

"She's gone."

"Yeanh," said Fortune. "She come down with her bag and went aboard the Nancy. I heard her waking Mrs. Gurget and pretty soon they put out."

"Did she tell you where she was going?"

"No. I was setting here. I'd never held such cards. I missed a thousand aces by one on the last hand; I could n't sleep. So I was setting here. She just went aboard."

"I wonder where she'll go."

"Maybe back to Lucy Cashdollar's for a spell."

"Yeanh."

They sat side by side, hearing the water wash the dock.

"Where'll you go?"

"Why, I don't know for sure," Fortune said. "There was a Brandreth man and a peddler and old Davis, and I cleaned them out. Just now I'd be rich if I had n't give Tinkle all of it."

"You done that?"

The old man grinned shamefacedly.

"It's time maybe I invested some. I thought I'd buy a boat, maybe. He's going to get me one in Rome if he can. Boats 'll be cheap in fall."

"That's right, I guess."

Dan got slowly to his feet.

"Maybe we'd better get back," he said dully.

Fortune coughed.

"Them horses could get you into Rome without no driving, couldn't they?"

"I guess so."

"I thought maybe I ought to stay here and give those rascals another chance at their money, while my luck's in."

"All right."

"If you could let me have my wages."

"All right."

Dan paid him.

"Good-bye."

"Good luck," said the ex-preacher, shaking hands.

Dan walked back till he came to the old Sarsey Sal, rubbing heavily against the bank. He gazed at it, half seeing, and then he turned to look toward Rome. His lean brown face did not change. He was very still, and a muskrat slipped into the water and swam just to his feet before it saw him. It looked at him out of its sharp eyes for an instant, saw that it was not observed, and dove without a sound.

A little way off, cows in their pasture lifted their hind legs and got up with a jangle of a bell or two. Dan went aboard to find that the coffee had boiled over.

Rome Haul

The men caught their horses in a group of trees a hundred yards from the towpath and tied the body to the spare one. It was an awkward job, but at last it held.

They came aboard to thank Dan and shake his hand.

"I shot him," said George, "but you licked Jotham Klore. You don't get no reward. It's tough."

"Yeanh," said the spokesman. "That's how it is."

Dan harnessed the big team and took them to the towpath. The black looked round till he had heaved the gang aboard and taken the sweep in his hands. Then, perhaps, he said something, for they both started together.

It was a silent trip. They passed the Delta House, blind and asleep. Dan was glad Fortune was out of sight. Going alone, the heart seemed out of the boat. He kept his eyes on the team, once in a while meeting the glance of the black as he turned his head.

They slipped into the morning mist. All round Dan the sound of cows broke out, the distant song of their bells. The mist was cold and wet on his face; there was nothing left to see but the dip of the towline and occasionally the rumps of his big team pulling faithfully.

He heard the water life awakening — the splash of a rat, the dive of a frog; the sounds slipped quickly to his ears and were gone.

So they went on — the Sarsey Sal, the two horses, and Dan. When the sun rose, flooding the sky above the mist with color, they were close to Rome.

They came into the bustle of the great basin in the clear day, and the team took him to Butterfield's wharf. There they stopped, both waiting for him to take them aboard.

When they had been unharnessed, he went to Butterfield's office. Men about him were talking excitedly at the double news, the death of Calash and the defeat of Klore. Some looked at Dan as he went past, and some pointed him out, proud of knowing who he was.

Mr. Butterfield shook his hand.

"I heard about the fight," he said. "It must have been a great one. I'll get you to tell me about it later."

"There ain't much to tell," Dan said heavily.

Mr. Butterfield looked at him keenly. Then he came swiftly to business. It was soon settled.

"About that farm proposition, Harrow. I'm sorry to say

Mr. Wilder writes that he can only take you on single."

"I'll take it."

Mr. Butterfield said nothing for a moment, but there was understanding kindness in his eyes that embarrassed Dan.

"I'm glad. It's a good job for you. You'll do well. You ought to go at once, if you can."

"I'd like to start to-day."

"What will you do with the boat?"

"I think I know a man that will buy it and the light team," Dan said. "They won't fetch much of a price."

"No, not now. But how about your fine team?"

"I was wondering about them," Dan said shyly. "I was wondering would you keep them for me awhile? They could earn their keep."

"Certainly. But I'd be glad to pay you a full price for them."

"I wouldn't want to sell them."

"I see."

They shook hands, and Dan went out.

VIII

THE ROAD AND THE PEDDLER

HE was walking along the Watertown road. A man driving a buggy had given him a lift as far as Ava. Now he was climbing the long slope of Tug Hill from the south.

As he went on, the stiffness began to run out of him; his back limbered and his breathing eased. He stopped to eat a sandwich under a tree beside a small spring. Close to him a pair of cows looked on affably. It had come out hot after the cold night; there was a dry dusty August gleam on everything.

The little cool pocket off the road, where the cows discussed the world together over their cuds, invited him. A little way off wasps whined about their nest; but they had no quarrel with the three at the spring.

The cows were thin, scrawny creatures, with matted coats and little pinched bags.

"Dinkeys," Dan said to himself; and he thought of the fine cattle he was to work among. Already he was looking forward.

It was only when he came to the great hill, where the road was no better than a track, that he stopped to look back toward the wide Mohawk Valley. He could see the thread of the canal and the white lines of bridges; and to his left, five miles away, he caught a glimpse of the Black River Canal, and a small boat on it. The boat was the merest speck of white in the rolling land of green. But it seemed to him that he could hear its horn, echo after echo, in the Lansing Kill. . . .

The imagined sound brought back to him a picture of the fat woman; she had come down to the Sarsey Sal that

morning and had taken him into her arms. For some reason
he had not been embarrassed, even when Solomon poked
his bald head through the door and, after looking at them
asked, "Can I come in?" The three had sat together without a word for several minutes.

Then Solomon had cleared his throat nervously and
asked him what he would sell the boat for. "I'm not buying it for us, Dan." "You'd understand that," the fat
woman had said. "It's Fortune" — and Dan told them
how he had talked to Fortune at the Delta House. "He
would n't buy a boat for himself," the fat woman said, and
Solomon nodded — and then they had all three looked at
each other, guessing whom he wished to buy it for. "How
much did he give you?" Solomon had told him, "A hundred
and fifty dollars." And Dan had given him the boat and the
bays for that. "My land, it's giving it away!" said the fat
woman; and she and Solomon had looked at each other.

Then Dan had told them his plans. Mr. Butterfield had
offered to invest his money for him and had promised to keep
the big team; but they, if Dan could have use for them,
would be sent on in the late fall — "in time for fall plowing," Dan said, and Solomon had nodded. For a young man,
he was well off.

"I should think you'd farm it your own self," said the
fat woman.

"I got to learn more about dairying," Dan said. "I did n't
have only a few dinkeys on Pa's place. There's a lot of
things to learn handling good land."

"I guess that's right," she said.

"Plain horse sense," said Solomon.

"Later I'll maybe get me my own farm," Dan said.

He got up and went forward to the stable. Solomon made
a move with his feet; but Mrs. Gurget said, "Leave him be
alone." And he went in by himself to thump the ribs of the
brown and stroke the bald white nose of the black. The
brown stared stolidly at the wall and rested his nigh hip; but
the black nuzzled him for sugar and blew gentle breaths into
the palm of his hand. They were a good team.

When he returned to the cabin, Mrs. Gurget and Solomon had helped him to pack his bag.

Then he gave her the clock — and the tears had jumped out on her cheeks. "My, my, I always did like that little pony, prancing and raring like he 'd just been stung! Ain't he pretty, Sol?"

Dan had put an envelope in Solomon's hand. The couple could not say very much. The fat woman kissed him good-bye and Solomon wrung his hand, muttering something about stopping off at Lyons Falls to see how he was. "If anything comes wrong, just write and we 'll turn the old boat and come galloping," he promised. "Shucks," said Mrs. Gurget, "gallop them mules?" "I 'll leave you on shore, then they can," he said. The fat woman kissed Dan again and whispered in his ear, "Don't remember her too hard, Dan."

They had waved to him till he turned the corner. He had had a last glimpse of the little bowlegged man and the great woman, with her high bonnet, her red hair, her scarlet petticoat, and the boats going by behind them.

Of all the people on the canal, they were his best friends. . . .

Then he turned himself.

For a minute he saw Molly before his eyes, as she had come aboard that night, flushed cheeks and blowzy hair, and he felt heavy and sad.

But the road led downward under his feet and he stepped ahead. The road would take him down past the barren farms to rich meadowland where fine cows grazed. He would feel them with his hands and milk them in the dusk of the great new barn.

As the shadows came in on the track, he made out the marks of wagon wheels, fresh in the dry road. From the first they seemed familiar. Then he remembered. They went from side to side of the road and stopped where the grass had been lush. There a horse had cropped it up.

Farther on, where the road ran up a short ridge, he saw where the old horse had lengthened his stride; and now he was certain that the old peddler was ahead of him, riding

his wagon, wondering where the road would bring him out.
He would be reading a book.

Dan changed his bag to his left hand. Perhaps he would
get a lift.